FORTY PACES EAST

SHEILA M BEARMAN

Matador
9 Priory Business Park,
Wistow Road, Kibworth Beauchamp,
Leicestershire. LE8 0RX
Tel: 0116 279 2299
Email: books@troubador.co.uk
Web: www.troubador.co.uk/matador
Twitter: @matadorbooks

ISBN 978 1800460 942

British Library Cataloguing in Publication Data.
A catalogue record for this book is available from the British Library.

Printed on FSC accredited paper
Printed and bound in Great Britain by 4edge Limited
Typeset in 12pt Adobe Garamond Pro by Troubador Publishing Ltd, Leicester, UK

Matador is an imprint of Troubador Publishing Ltd

CHAPTER
ONE

•

AT FIRST SIGHT, the group of young Turkish Cypriots had appeared to have been caught up in an argument, but Daisy, having watched them for the last fifteen minutes or so, realised it was merely a heated debate. Most of these were smoking, and small cups of strong black coffee were set before them. None wore jackets, just shirt sleeves, even though a fresh breeze ruffled the waters along the harbour wall.

Daisy, sitting alone, shrugged into the light jacket she'd brought along, then gazed across to the old sandstone castle which she'd recently visited. This stood to the right of the harbour, and its honey-toned walls looked ethereal at night when lit up. Inside the castle walls was an ancient wreck, and included in its cargo were a couple of amphora, still holding almonds and wine. She could hardly believe this wreckage was over two thousand years old. Daisy knew this area as the pearl of all Mediterranean islands, but, as beautiful as it was here in north Cyprus, she wasn't here for a holiday; she was here to work on her new book. She hoped to find out as much as possible concerning the fighting that took place between north and south of the island.

At the moment, golden sunlight shimmered across the water, and a couple of small boats could be seen far out to sea. Still, although very pleasant, it was too chilly to sit around the harbour for too long. But when Daisy had come out here, booking an air ticket a month or so ago, she knew that January and February would be the coldest months, even though temperatures could fluctuate daily. Only yesterday, huge hailstones had clattered noisily against Daisy's bedroom window, while today, as she had eaten her breakfast, she had felt the warmth of the sun as it bathed the room with bright yellow sunlight.

Daisy sipped her coffee, then, shading her eyes, looked up at an azure-blue sky, before turning her attention back to the harbour. This wasn't her first visit to the island, and in the summer months many boats would be moored along the waterfront, but there were just a few now. And, since she'd been sitting here, about half a dozen weather-faced men had been working aboard their crafts, while now and then the throbbing of an engine could be heard.

Turning her attention back to the group of young men at the table, she saw they were laughing at something. She recognised one of them, had seen him often in and round the harbour. He was of medium height and well built and had thick dark curling hair. He was also quite attractive, and she could see now that it was this one that had caused the humour. She cast her eyes elsewhere, and mused on the fact that, up until eight years ago, in 1974, the people here had known nothing but trouble. Before then, this place had been a fighting ground, with much bloodshed and the most appalling atrocities carried out. But now, since the north and south divide, only Turkish Cypriots lived here. The division, or buffer zone, was just a zigzag line of green oil drums which separated the two sides, therefore housing the Greek Cypriots in the south. This could be seen and looked rather odd from one rooftop restaurant in Nicosia.

But Daisy loved it here in Kyrenia. She liked the cafés and bars that looked onto the harbour, even though the façades of many looked rather jaded. Most of these did a good trade, especially during the finer weather, when you could sit outside. And expats would frequent the bars and restaurants throughout the year. Daisy recognised a few of these about to sit at one of the tables, sitting well back from the harbour wall.

There was of course plenty to do and see while here. 'The Museum of Barbarism' was of much importance. This 'tourist' attraction stood just outside Nicosia, in the village of Kumsal, and she would certainly need to visit this. She wasn't looking forward to the experience, but a writer couldn't dismiss such things. In fact, anything relating to the conflict between the two warring sides would be most beneficial to the story she wished to tell.

A voice broke into Daisy's reverie, and she turned to find a portly built man at the next table. He was well dressed, carried a cane, and gave Daisy a slight nod of the head. 'Are you on holiday? Come here for a winter break?' He was smoking a fat cigar which caused puffy little clouds of smoke to hover over nearby tables.

A sudden chill breeze made Daisy shrug deeper into her jacket and she wondered why he had sought her out for conversation, but she smiled back at him. 'Not a holiday exactly,' she said at last. 'I'm here to do some research, for a book I'm writing.'

His skin was darker than the more sallow-faced Turk, and deep furrows creased his brow as he gave Daisy his full attention. 'And are you here for long, seeking out your research?'

'Well, a couple of months at least,' she answered. 'Though we'll see what happens.'

The big man, looking to be in his sixties, smiled, showing long, yellowing teeth. 'So, why here? You like this part of the country so much that you decided it was worth coming all the way out here to write about it?' His words were not without humour.

Daisy didn't know what to make of the man, but he seemed to be taking a genuine interest in her. She knew, too, that this race of people were often friendly towards the newcomer, having had dealings with them before. However, she took some moments before she spoke. 'I'm here to find out about the troubles between yourselves and the Greeks. I have one problem, though. Before I do anything else, I'll have to look for somewhere else to stay. The room I'm renting is far too cold.' Daisy shivered at the thought of returning to the modest little house in one of the back streets.

The cane which he carried beat monotonously at his feet. There was a long pause, but when he spoke his words startled Daisy. 'I have just had a thought. You could rent from me. I have a studio – a very comfortable one, I might add.'

'That's very kind,' she said. 'But I know nothing of you.'

He smiled. 'This is true, but this we can remedy. Miss, er...'

'Collins,' Daisy assisted, still taken aback.

'Well, Miss Collins, I am Osman Bilekler.' He fumbled inside his jacket. 'Here is my card. As you can see, I own some property.' He waved his arms to the left of the harbour. 'My home is in Bellapais.'

While sitting there, his dark eyes had missed nothing. Daisy's abundant chestnut hair and her general appearance enchanted him. But most importantly she was a British girl, which would prove most suitable should she accept his offer.

Daisy, completely thrown by all this, stood and gazed up to where Osman Bilekler had gestured. She shook her head. 'I'm still uncertain. I mean…' She broke off, not knowing what to say.

Bilekler also stood, stretching his large frame. 'Look,' he said, 'you have my card, my good name. What more? And, you would have the whole place to yourself. A garden, such beautiful views, perfect!'

He looked like a man highly regarded in the local community, and with many influential friends, but did he have some hidden agenda, thought Daisy? No, surely not. Why read anything into it? The man was naturally friendly. She watched him now, as he too looked over at the group of young men seated around the table. 'Well,' she told him, 'Bellapais is lovely. I've often walked up there. But I'll need to give it some thought.'

'Well, we are in a good spot. And, if I might add, it should be peaceful for your work.'

Having taken his business card, Daisy inclined her head, thanked him for his offer of a studio in which to work, then started to walk away.

'By the way,' he called, 'do not think too long about it. I will await your answer.' He paused, then added, 'A writer, eh?'

As he watched her walk away, Osman's thoughts were of his son, Hasan. He puffed hard on his cigar. His aim was to keep his son happy, something he felt that was missing from his life. Picking up his cane, Bilekler walked in the opposite direction to Daisy. He smiled, thinking her a pleasant young lady. Had he done the right thing? Anyway, he hoped the woman didn't turn down his offer. Though he would be very much surprised if she did!

Daisy had given a lot of thought about her meeting with Osman Bilekler. In fact, she had hardly slept that night, looking for reasons why she shouldn't move into the studio, though in truth she couldn't find any. But what finally made up her mind was that the rented room where she was staying was lacking any sort of comforts, and most of all had a noisy leaking gutter.

It hadn't taken Daisy long to pack, so after breakfast she rang to say she would look forward to staying in the studio, but wouldn't arrive until early afternoon.

The local taxi, winding its way through Bellapais, passed lush green land. It was strewn with tiny yellow flowers that many said had the scent of lemons. Clumps of small lilac cyclamen also thrived here. Careful of the stray sheep nibbling at the grass verges, the driver crawled slowly as the narrow road became a little steeper. To the left, the main herd of sheep grazed, and goats could be seen, their tinkling bells ringing across the upper slopes. A florid-faced shepherd hovered close by, stopping in his work to watch the taxi. In the centre of the village, under the 'Tree of Idleness' that Durrell wrote of in his *Bitter Lemons*, sat an old man. He was dressed in black, and his head and shoulders were draped in a traditional white scarf.

Sitting on a rickety stool, his once-handsome face deeply

lined by the weather, he peered into the windows as the taxi passed by. Beside him, a young boy, oblivious to all, used a stick to mark patterns in the dusty ground.

Further on, the road became steeper and more winding until at last, away from the odd cottage or two, the driver pulled up. Daisy had never seen anything so grand. She was looking at a large house which was painted white, and at each window there were pale green shutters. In the same grounds, a smaller one-storey building looked to be the studio, its shutters matching the larger house.

Although still winter, cascades of scarlet geraniums tumbled from window boxes, and purple shrubs, unknown to Daisy, filled big stone urns.

Daisy must have been seen from the main house, because a woman, in her middle years, came down the gravel drive. Behind her a teenage boy hurried hastily forward. He spoke to the woman before picking up Daisy's two cases, then took them across to the studio.

Dressed in sombre black and grey, the woman's keen eye surveyed Daisy from head to foot. 'You are the lady to stay in the studio, yes?' she said at last.

Daisy extended her hand, but the woman ignored this, though she hadn't taken her eyes off the newcomer. 'Come,' she said, leading the way towards the main house.

Following behind, Daisy thought the woman to be older than her first impression. Her black hair was flecked with white and was pulled back into a soft coil. She also walked with a heavy gait.

Once inside, Daisy found herself walking on elaborate patterned tiles. The walls were painted spotless white. She was led into a huge reception room, and then the woman indicated Daisy to a comfortable chair.

'I am the housekeeper,' the woman told her. 'You call me Fatma.'

There was no time to reply to this, because, as soon as Fatma had spoken, she disappeared from the room.

There were three ornate sofas in this room, each a deep red edged with gilt. Large terracotta pots on plinths stood at various positions, while handwoven rugs in rich hues hung on whitewashed walls. There were three tall windows: one to the side, and two at the front of the house. Beyond these two, a wide area of paving was shaded with a vine, which covered a pergola.

Footsteps along the tiled corridor told Daisy that Osman Bilekler had arrived, but on hearing the voice, in conversation with Fatma, she realised it wasn't him but someone younger. He appeared then, tall, lean and of the same dusky complexion as the older man.

He stood in the arched doorway, looking straight at Daisy, and she was instantly arrested by his striking good looks. She guessed him to be somewhere in his mid-thirties. 'Pleased to meet with you, Miss Collins,' he said huskily. 'My father is out now, but I am Hasan.' He extended his hand.

His hands were soft, and his long sensitive fingers gripped Daisy's for longer than was necessary. On his small finger he wore a silver and turquoise ring.

Embarrassed, she slipped her hand from his, and then said, 'By the way, I'm Daisy. And I've seen the studio; it looks really nice. Of course, I haven't seen inside yet.'

Hasan spread his hands. 'My father thought it ideal for your work.'

Waving aside the cigarette he offered, Daisy watched as he lit his. 'So,' he continued, 'you have returned to Cyprus to do a book. Is this your first novel?'

'My third, though I started off writing short stories.'

'But surely,' he questioned, his green eyes never leaving her face, 'that could not make enough money?'

'Not at first,' Daisy answered, 'though many do. But you get there eventually.'

While they were talking, Fatma had brought in a tray, which she placed on a small side table. There was a pot of coffee, milk, plus a large and small cup. Hasan walked over to this. 'I took the liberty of having some milk brought in,' he said. 'Our way does not suit the English.'

He looked more relaxed when he smiled and this had Daisy feeling at ease. 'Have you met many?' she asked. 'British people?'

Handing her some coffee, he smiled again. 'With the expats over here, how can I help it? Anyway, have you seen the United Nations in our towns? There are plenty of British among them.'

'Yes, I've come across them. They can be most helpful.' She laughed. 'I particularly like those blue berets, too.'

Hasan looked thoughtful before replying. 'But remember, also, that your people helped in our war. Thirty thousand British troops were assigned, which did much to calm the situation.' He pulled a face. 'Mind you, when the battles ended, we had to go it on our own, with help from the Turkish mainland.'

'It's a pity, but...'

'I know,' he cut in. 'We couldn't wait, you see, thought we would finish it there and then. And, as you probably know, we landed ourselves in trouble with America as well as Britain. We are known to be rather hot-headed, us Turks.'

'It's understandable, I suppose. I mean, what you've been through,' she agreed.

Hasan shrugged. 'It is in the past. We try to forget, if not succeeding.'

A painting hung on the wall facing Daisy. She went over to it and looked with interest. Reminiscent of a Vincent Van Gogh, the oils were mainly orange and greens.

'What do you think?' Hasan asked, standing beside her. 'You like the arts?'

'Very much so.' Daisy thought the painting looked not only professional but very striking. 'I like it; it drew me in. I can't see a name, though. Do you know whose work this is?'

There was a long pause before Hasan answered. 'It was me. I painted it. A very long time ago.'

Daisy examined the painting more closely. 'Have you sold any?'

'There are many artists,' he replied abruptly. 'Anyway, who would be interested?'

Daisy didn't answer but continued to gaze at the picture, which was mainly of a floral nature. A small boy, peering through some colourful foliage, seemed to be at the heart of the picture, though it was his large, sorrowful eyes that gripped Daisy's attention. To the rear, a woman could be seen, though her face, unlike the child's, wasn't clear. It was as though the artist had deliberately camouflaged the features.

'You shouldn't hide your talent,' remarked Daisy, turning towards Hasan.

He grimaced. 'It does not matter. Anyway, I do not need the money.'

'Surely the recognition…'

'I said it does not matter,' he interrupted.

Daisy was puzzled by his change of attitude, and walked to the door. 'I'd better settle myself into the studio. I won't take up any more of your time. And thanks for the coffee.'

'I'm sorry, Miss, er, Daisy. Please, ignore my rudeness, but there are some things that bring back painful memories.'

Daisy turned to find Hasan close by. His incredible green eyes were thickly lashed. Then a moment later she left, unsure if she'd made the right choice in moving close to the Bileklers. She also wondered what went on inside Hasan's head.

This was soon forgotten because during the following week Daisy visited libraries, newspaper archives and anything else of interest relating to her work. While at the newspaper archives situated in Kyrenia, an attendant recommended that, apart from the newspapers, she speak to some local men who had fought during the troubles. Having read and noted many articles in the newspapers concerning the war, Daisy thanked the man then made her way into the nearby village of Ozankoy.

As was their usual habit, these ex-soldiers were gathered outside a café bar, albeit a make-do hut set up to provide a meeting place for locals. These men were a friendly lot, offering useful information about their personal experiences during the war. However, it was the younger men who had better command of the English language, and they too had been in combat.

At times they spoke with much bitterness, unable to forget the terrible atrocities against their people between the years of 1963 and the first few years of the 1970s. Daisy was to learn more when, later that day, in Bellapais, she spoke to Refet. He was the old man who had been sitting beneath the 'Tree of Idleness' when she had first arrived in this hilltop village.

Refet, the oldest man in the community, was sitting outside Mustafa's when Daisy found him. This was a much smaller but similar type café to that of Ozankoy. 'Yes,' he said, in answer to Daisy's question. 'I saw some things. I fought in another war, long before, but this…' He spread his gnarled hands. 'I live next door to a couple who have lost three sons. It was in the Tokhni-Zyyi massacre.' Refet closed his rheumy eyes. 'It was in 1974, and now these poor people have only one living son.'

Refet also knew of an old man, now crumpled with grief, who had lost four sons as well as a son-in-law. Like the previous boys, they each perished in the same massacre. Another villager in Tokhni lost a husband, four sons and a brother in that terrible plight.

Refet was about to speak of more atrocities but Daisy had already had this information from a centre in Nicosia. It was officially stated that a group of EOKA-B men, under the leadership of the ferocious 'Andriko', had entered the Turkish Cypriot quarter of the mixed village of Tokhni. There, sixty-nine men between the ages of thirteen and seventy-four were rounded up. The following day, 'Andriko' and his men brought in fifteen more Turkish Cypriot males. They had been picked up in Mari and Zyyi. Fifty of their captives were driven by bus in the vicinity of Limassol. There, a ditch had already been dug. They were shot, but one man, though severely injured, managed to crawl to safety. He lived to testify as to what happened.

Most of the population now living in Bellapais originally came from Mari. It was in 1976 when Turkish Cypriots moved to Bellapais. Before this, it was an entirely Greek Cypriot community. This followed the agreements of exchanging populations. This allowed thousands of Greek Cypriots to go south, while Turkish Cypriots came north.

The latter were then saved from their Turkish villages, which had previously had Greek control.

Many would tell you that, although this arrangement was far better as regards safety issues, they missed their former homes, and had found it difficult settling into pastures new.

CHAPTER

TWO

•

OUT OF SEASON, only a few cafés and bars were open in Kyrenia. Apart from expatriates, it would be young local men seen mostly around the bars. These would freely vent their feelings at government policies, or the fact that they were without jobs. Most were trained waiters, and, although the pay was low, it was better than the long, cheerless days of doing nothing. Moreover, they were a proud lot. Often, with only one job going, the owner of a restaurant, bar or café would have to turn as many as a dozen applicants away.

Looking over at a group of these men from a nearby table, Daisy's heart went out to them. It was evident by the raised voices that lack of job prospects had robbed them of self-respect, especially that of one speaker, who was obviously married with a family to support.

The sky was brightening now, almost cloudless, but earlier, up in Bellapais, dark storm clouds had brought heavy rain. Hearing voices beyond the harbour wall, Daisy saw that a few fishermen were working aboard their boats. She frowned. Hasan had just appeared from beneath deck. He was in deep conversation with a much younger man, but things took a sudden change when Hasan looked as if he might hit him. Then, soon after, the younger man disappeared below deck.

Hasan waited for a delivery van to pass before crossing the road, and, still looking angry, he made for one of the tables which had been set out. He looked up then, saw Daisy, then joined her. 'Hello,' he called, walking towards her. 'Enjoying the break?'

Daisy looked at the sky. 'I was, it was lovely just now, but the weather keeps changing. Look at those clouds bubbling up!'

'Well, you cannot sit here,' Hasan answered, his features having softened. 'I'll give you a lift back.'

Without replying, she walked with him to his car. He had just started up the engine when a loud rumble of thunder could be heard in the distance. 'Damn this bloody weather,' he groaned.

Driving through Ozankoy, there was a sudden downpour. So great was the deluge that even the windscreen wipers couldn't improve visibility. This had Hasan mumbling expletives, but, like the weather, his mood suddenly changed when slits of blue showed through broken cloud. The rain had eased too, and soon they were driving away from Ozankoy and heading in the direction of Bellapais.

'You had me worried back there,' said Daisy. 'These roads can be treacherous.'

Ignoring this, Hasan turned briefly. 'I know a nice fish restaurant in Catalkoy. You hungry?'

'I was planning to go back home,' stated Daisy, 'but I could manage a bite.'

'I do not know about a bite,' he said, 'but maybe, I think you should eat more!'

Daisy saw that he was smiling. 'So, you think I'm too thin?' she teased.

He cast a glance in her direction. 'Not really, just a bit.' He turned the car then, and drove back through Ozankoy and into Catalkoy.

All chairs outside Kemel's fish bar were upended against plastic tables, everything soaked and dripping wet. However, inside the airy diner, a steady hum of voices came from packed tables, while a couple of waiters darted to and fro among their customers. On seeing the young couple walk through the door, Kemel's chubby face was a mixture of expressions. At first he was hesitant, and then, bustling towards Hasan, he greeted him warmly. 'How very nice to see you, Mr Bilekler. A table by the window? Follow me.'

Steering Daisy towards the table, Hasan acknowledged the owner. 'And this is Daisy – Miss Collins,' he said. 'She is staying with us.'

A smile lit up Kemel's round face. 'Ah, a new visitor to my little place. I hope you enjoy our hospitality, Miss Collins.'

A pungent smell of garlic hung in the air, while the sound of shellfish clattered against plates. Laughter drifted from one table, and, gazing over, Daisy guessed that it may have been due to too much wine. During their meal, Daisy was to find that Hasan also liked his alcohol, too. But she wasn't much of a drinker. Having enjoyed a few of the chef's mezes, she had followed this with a beautifully cooked flatfish with preserved lemons. This was washed down with plain mineral water.

Now and then, she had caught Hasan snatching glances at her. He spoke now, his voice attractively husky. 'I hope that you like it here, Daisy. I did not know if you had been before.'

She liked the way he spoke her name, and was enjoying his company, too. 'No, I haven't been here before,' she answered. 'Anyway, you heard Kemel. He would have recognised me, surely?'

Hasan's deep green eyes sparkled. 'Do not take too much notice of Kemel. He likes to make much of the ladies.'

Looking across at Kemel fussing around a middle-aged Turkish woman, Daisy didn't doubt that. She smiled, amused at his gushing behaviour.

They drank coffee afterwards, chatting for a long while until Daisy said she had work to do.

As they were getting into the car, Hasan turned to her. 'Of course, I did not ask how your book is coming. Are you keeping busy? My father mentioned you'd been to the library, but did not go into great detail.'

It flattered Daisy that he should care about her work. 'Like I have said, I need to get first-hand knowledge. The way I see it, everything seems to be centred on the Greek side of things; you read about it a lot. But I want to tell it from your side. We know of course that it wasn't the ordinary man in the street. I have been to Greece and found the people very nice. But 'National Guard,' well, just look at the terrible things they did storming into your homes and such.'

For a while, Hasan looked thoughtful. 'It is good that you are putting our side of the story forward, and, yes, our people did suffer. They were shot in the street by that lot for going quietly about their business.'

They were sitting in the car and Daisy noted Hasan's glum expression, and thought that the drink he'd imbibed had a bearing on his mood. 'You must have feared for your own life and that of your family?' she told him.

Some youths were playing along the road. One was kicking a ball, while another, separating himself from the rest, came closer to the car. Hasan had just started up the engine, but ignored the lad when he scowled close to the windscreen while raising a clenched fist.

Daisy frowned. 'What was all that about?'

'You need not concern yourself with him, Daisy,' advised Hasan. 'In fact, be watchful of who you talk to. People have loose tongues.'

The Five Finger mountain range loomed darkly against a leaden sky, and among the lower slopes a row of cypress trees stood proudly erect. Further ahead, a faint arc of a rainbow was emerging. 'I don't understand,' said Daisy. 'Are you talking about anyone in particular?'

It seemed that the alcohol that Hasan had drunk hadn't affected his driving ability. He slowed at a sharp bend and managed to manoeuvre the car around a sizeable boulder which had tumbled from a steep cliff face.

'Certain people are not to be trusted,' Hasan warned. 'I mean, they will tell you lies.'

Trying to fathom the meaning behind all this, Daisy said no more, but now and then took a sidelong glimpse at Hasan. He was a complicated man, but a very handsome one indeed. She said no more, and Hasan drove the rest of the way in silence. But Daisy wanted to know more about the man at her side, for there must be something in what he'd said. At the same time, she didn't want to complicate things. Why though, did he speak about people lying? What would they lie about? And everyone seemed to know him, even that young boy. And it hadn't gone unnoticed how Kemel had looked at Hasan when they had first entered his restaurant. What was the meaning behind that? Yes, of course he knew Hasan: he was a regular visitor, maybe bringing good business to his premises, but there was more to it than that. The more Daisy thought about this, the more she wanted to know.

Of late, there had been far fewer arguments with his son, and Osman Bilekler had a fair idea why that was. From the covered terrace, he looked across at the studio, a smile playing at the corner of his mouth as he removed the fat cigar he'd been smoking.

Unlike his father, Hasan had never had to work, not real, hard graft. He was restless, discontented, and any amount of money had little effect. It had been different for Osman. As a young man, he and his two brothers had worked all hours in their father's small dairy business. They also tended sheep and a sizeable goat herd, working from dawn until dusk. They were in awe of their dominant father, and their mother was no different with her constant nagging. However, as soon as was possible, Osman broke away, promising himself that his life would change. It did, but this wasn't brought about by more physical labour. And, if asked, Osman Bilekler would not have admitted to dishonesty but more a case of survival. It was a tough world. People got hurt. Man had to take care of his own.

Sucking in more smoke from his cigar than was good for him, Osman hoped that his son, Hasan, was at least a little more content than he had been. Unlike the other vain creatures who hung around him, Daisy was proving to be a steady influence.

There had been little shift in attitudes here in Cyprus. A girl's father expected marriage if she formed a serious relationship. But Osman didn't want his son to make the same mistake as he did, when he was pushed into an early marriage, the result of which was that Osman had never grown to love his wife, Limone. Because of this, or not, she developed into a pathetic creature, seemingly fragile with imaginary or real ills. The family doctor would forever be at her beck and call.

Moreover, Limone seemed incapable of any show of affection towards her children. It affected Hasan, deeply, something Osman could never forgive. Nobody guessed that Limone's early death, due to heart failure, had had a helping hand. Now, since his daughter's absence there was only Hasan. Both men knew the reason why his youngest child, Aisha, had left home, and both knew she would never return.

It was late afternoon when Daisy opened the studio door. She was most surprised to see Fatma Bartu standing there. The woman smiled, holding out a spray of freshly cut flowers. Daisy took them and invited Fatma inside.

Instead of the severe hairstyle, the woman's hair hung casually loose. Her normally sallow skin had been touched with a hint of rouge. 'I hope you like the flowers,' said Fatma.

Daisy held the scented pink blossoms to her nose. 'Thank you; it was nice of you to think of me.'

'No, no, Mr Osman sent them,' replied Fatma. Her dark brown eyes sparkled. 'He asked if you come over for dinner.'

This was the first time Daisy had been asked over for a meal. She told Fatma she was looking forward to it. So it was that evening, when, having dressed carefully for the occasion, Daisy knocked on the door of the villa. She was feeling quite nervous as she followed Fatma through the hallway. A couple of lamps, on small tables, threw a rosy glow onto the pristine white walls, and the scent of lilies pervaded the air. She was somewhat taken aback when she entered the dining room. Two others, a man and a woman, were sitting in a curved area beneath the large window. They both held drinks, while Osman Bilekler stood a little further away. He was tossing back what looked like whisky, or brandy.

The male guest, silver-haired and much shorter than his host, stood when he saw Daisy, though the raven-haired woman, decidedly younger, paid scant attention to her.

'Miss Collins – I mean, Daisy.' Osman had stepped forward. 'Let me introduce you. My good friends, Richard Hampton and his charming wife, Melanie.'

Daisy wondered if the couple were English. She held out her hand to the man. 'Pleased to meet you,' she smiled.

Richard Hampton smiled back. 'I hope you're enjoying your stay, Daisy. Not working too hard?'

Daisy was right, and thought that the well-spoken man may have a military bearing. She accepted the white wine that Osman offered her, aware all the while of Melanie Hampton's eyes on her. However, it was some minutes before she joined the trio.

'So, when do you return to Britain, Miss Collins?' she drawled. 'I heard you were here for a short while.'

'Oh, not yet,' answered Daisy, unaware until then that the woman was an American. 'It depends on how things go.'

'Holidaymakers always enjoy the first few weeks away from home,' stated Melanie. 'You'll see, you'll probably become bored, unless you're one of the expats, of course. They're the ones that settle.'

'Ah, but I'm not on holiday,' answered Daisy, noting that those penetrating eyes were still scrutinising her. 'My work keeps me busy.'

They were interrupted when Hasan walked into the room. Following was a young female servant wheeling a food trolley. Melanie Hampton smiled at Hasan, tilting her head seductively, but he failed to notice.

Against the lamplight, his skin looked a deep bronze. He smiled at Daisy as he drew closer. 'Hello. I hope the flowers were to your taste?'

Daisy, wearing a knee length violet dress, and make-up carefully applied, glanced at Osman. 'But I thought...'

Helping himself to a drink, Hasan looked sideways at Daisy. She was the most desirable woman he'd ever known.

None of this was lost on Melanie Hampton. She seethed, gulping back yet another drink. This was the closest she'd been to loving a man. No other could take his place.

Osman had skimped on nothing. Smoked salmon, chicken, and local lamb which had been slowly cooked in a clay oven were among roasted peppers and other vegetables. The long table had been set with fine china and, in the centre, a tall dish over-spilled with fresh fruit. A large chandelier hung above the table, lending soft, sparkling light.

Daisy's attention had been drawn to a painting. Gilt-framed, it held pride of place above a marble fire surround. The more she looked, the more sure she was of the artist. She cast her eye towards Hasan. He looked thoughtful, and she wondered again what those thoughts were.

Osman raised his glass. 'Well, what more could a man ask? Cheers to all my good friends.'

'I second that,' said Richard, his glass also raised.

His wife scowled at Daisy. The younger woman was too pretty for her liking. Hasan had been paying her too much attention. Once, she had experienced the same from Hasan, but that had long cooled. Not that this had put her off. Any flattery, no matter how false, was a welcome relief from her husband's advances. Still, Hasan and she shared something that few knew about. It could be said she had a hold on him. Bleary-eyed, Melanie smiled at the thought.

Richard was laughing loudly at something his host had said, but Melanie inwardly sneered at her husband. She turned now, raising her glass. 'Here's to happy times,' she drawled, her eyes fixed firmly on Hasan. 'But then we share so much, don't we?' she added.

Richard smiled. 'We do indeed. In fact, you and Hasan go way back.' Reaching for a bottle of sweet, white wine, he added, 'See why I love my wife? She shows such warmth.'

Daisy wondered if the others had sensed the irony.

It was well into the night, but Daisy didn't feel it right to leave, especially as Hasan had put on some music. He'd chosen modern, instead of the traditional Turkish music, so often played, especially in the bars.

Osman, his eyes red-rimmed owing to an abundance of fine living, puffed on the fat cigar he was smoking. 'By the way,' he enquired, turning to Daisy, 'how is the book developing?'

'Very well. The newspaper archives are great. One man who works there has been kindness itself. I'm getting plenty of accounts from individuals, too.'

Osman nodded in answer.

'It's amazing how some of these people had managed to

escape from terrorists' hands!' added Daisy. She pondered for a moment. 'There is something that bothers me, though. It may have no significance, but I was amazed at one story I heard.'

As Osman loosened his collar, the flesh around his fat neck hung in flabby folds. 'Oh, and what might that be?'

'It was something I was told by an elderly man in Ozankoy. It seems that his soldier son was also killed during the fighting. Thing was, he was most certain it wasn't by "National Guard".'

The music had stopped. Everyone's eyes were on Daisy, while Osman used his napkin to mop the sweat that had trickled down his brow. 'Go on,' he urged.

Daisy couldn't understand why her words had caused so much tension, but felt she had to continue. 'The man did babble on; he was extremely agitated but said he knew the killers. Local men. Did any of you hear about it?'

Bilekler ignored the last question and looked at the others. 'You see, what do you expect? Anyway,' he grimaced, 'some of these locals often talk rubbish. Especially so if they have a good audience.'

Daisy too glanced at the others, recalling that Hasan had made a similar statement.

Osman turned to her. 'I'm still thinking about what you said, my dear. This man in question, who was he?'

All eyes were on Daisy except that of Richard.

'Ahmet,' she answered. 'A very nice man, I thought. And, losing a son, he'd naturally taken it badly.'

Osman Bilekler poured himself another drink. 'Pay no attention; the man was probably drunk. He sounds like an utter fool. Who around here would want to murder somebody's son? No, our community is tight-knit.'

Little was said after this, and soon Bilekler's guests took their leave, though on her way out, Melanie Hampton completely ignored Daisy, apart from a sidelong glance.

CHAPTER
THREE

•

WITH HER HEAD bent against the chill wind, Daisy was deep in thought as she made her way towards Ozankoy. In the short time she had known Hasan, her emotions had become quite mixed. She was well aware of the complexity of the man, and was loath to get involved with him. Nonetheless, she found herself drawn like a giant magnate. The other evening around the dinner table, she was surprised at the tinge of jealously she'd felt in Melanie Hampton's presence. Moreover, Hasan would surely have numerous female admirers.

A strong gust of wind tore through some nearby trees, scattering blossom from an almond, while, on the banks beside the narrow road, the little lemon-coloured flowers moved vigorously among the lush grass. A few scarlet anemones, dotted among the banks, appeared oblivious to the lower temperatures; this was the same with other wild flowers that thrived out here.

Daisy had almost reached the coffee shop when she recognised the elderly man. The tall wooden doors were open and he was sitting just inside along with some other local men. He waved when he saw Daisy, giving an almost toothless smile, but the others either carried on reading their newspapers, or simply stared.

'So, this is how you spend your day?' Daisy called, making towards him.

The dark-haired young man, who she recognised from around the harbour, came out from the rear of the shop. He was carrying a tray laden with small, steaming cups of coffee, along with glasses of water. He offered these among the men. Ahmet, the elderly man, spooned a good measure of sugar into his coffee. 'Daisy, he said, 'meet my son, Namik.'

The young man turned, his black curls tousled as if he'd not long arrived. 'You know my father, then?' he asked, a smile playing at the corner of his mouth.

Daisy said that she did, and then watched Namik disappear out the back. She had to screen her eyes against the dazzling sunlight as she sat beside Ahmet. Nothing, though, would entice her to remove her coat. Looking around, she noted that most men had done just that.

Namik returned with another coffee. He placed it on a scuffed chair, giving Daisy a quick glance. 'Are you on your own?' His tone was somewhat disapproving.

Daisy was surprised at his manner. 'Why, does it matter?' she scowled.

He shrugged. 'Not really, but you have to be careful. The women here do not mix with groups of men. You should take note.'

Daisy frowned. 'Why is that?'

'Well, people talk. It is not done around here.'

Having noted the café's run-down appearance, Daisy considered the possibility that Namik was only helping the owner. If he were a waiter, surely Kyrenia or another town would have been better suited. He was, after all, a presentable young man. She turned to him. 'I'm not sure I understand, but I'm my own person, and don't mean to offend.'

'Maybe.' He smiled now. 'But you need someone to show you around.'

'I'll think about it.' In spite of herself, she smiled back.

Studying him, Daisy saw no resemblance to his father. His shirt, open at the collar, revealed a thick neck. His dark hair gleamed like a raven's wing, suggesting good health. He spoke quickly, too, unlike Ahmet, who could just manage the basics of English.

'My father say you are welcome at our house. It is warmer,' Namik offered, as Daisy shivered.

She rubbed her hands. 'Another time, maybe, but don't you feel the cold?'

Ahmet overheard this and gestured towards the men who were still reading. 'Strong, we are. Look,' he said, spreading calloused hands.

Namik leaned closer to Daisy. 'My father herded goats. The cold does not bother him.'

Looking at the weather-beaten faces, Daisy felt that all these men were used to the outdoor life.

'You seem to have mixed a good deal with English people, and the like,' she questioned.

Namik's hazel eyes widened. 'I worked in England, six years. Oxford Street mostly, as a waiter.' He laughed. 'What else?'

Daisy noticed that Ahmet seemed lost in thought. She recalled the photo that he'd showed her, of his youngest son, creased and dog-eared. The lad was dark-haired like Namik. Aygun had been seventeen, and he'd been killed, murdered. Ahmet hadn't been too clear in his explanations, but he had been very distressed. 'Murderers!' he'd repeated. 'Murderers!'

'My uncle has a small boat in the harbour,' Namik said suddenly, breaking into Daisy's thoughts. 'You can see it if you like. Tomorrow, or today, maybe?'

Just then, Daisy thought she saw Hasan's silver Porsche pass the coffee bar. If it had been him, she didn't think he'd seen her. But why did she feel so uneasy? Was it because she had been talking to these men, the very people he'd accused of gossiping? For some strange reason she felt like a small child caught playing truant from school!

The following afternoon, Daisy followed Namik down the narrow steps to the cabin, which had been anchored in the harbour. It was quite compact, having only one small window with a grubby curtain sagging on a wire. A fly repellent hung there, covered in various insects. The air was rancid, and beneath a tiny sink, a plastic bucket over-spilled with empty beer cans and other debris.

Namik filled a small kettle and put it to boil over the gas ring. Then he pushed a brown glass plate towards Daisy, piled with cream biscuits. 'Here,' he offered, before grabbing two mugs, 'the kettle won't be long.' She wasn't hungry, but took one of the biscuits.

'By the way, did you know that man, the one in the fancy car?' enquired Namik, already on his third biscuit.

Daisy frowned. 'What, yesterday at the coffee shop? What makes you ask?'

'I noticed your reaction. You looked a bit wary.'

'I wasn't aware of it,' she lied. Daisy eyed him keenly. 'Do you know the Bileklers?'

'Yes. Yes, I do,' Namik snapped. He turned to fill the two mugs with coffee, but Daisy had already seen the change in him.

Neither spoke for a while, but Daisy watched as he moved around. She noted how his well-developed chest gave way to narrow hips. And, although casually dressed, his shirt sleeves rolled to the elbow and worn with dark trousers gave him a boyish quality.

'Your father seems nice,' said Daisy. 'He showed me a picture of your brother; did he tell you?'

A cigarette hung loosely from Namik's full mouth. 'Yes, and it upsets him. My mother, too, even though some time has passed.' He peered at Daisy through half-closed eyes. 'What did he tell you?'

'About your brother? Well, he told me about his death. Mentioned the fact that he'd been killed.' She hesitated before going on. 'Though not in combat.'

'That is right. We know it. But who'll believe us. We cannot prove it; that is the problem, always has been.'

'Has it something to do with the Bileklers?' asked Daisy. 'Only it seems that way.'

'Yes,' he answered swiftly, 'but, like I say, nothing can be proved.'

'Oh, that could be awkward. I'm renting their studio.'

Namik jumped down from a worktop he'd perched on. 'Let's not talk about it now,' he suggested. 'Anyway, I'm keeping you from your work.'

Daisy thought she shouldn't push the matter further, but as they were leaving she asked him about his uncle. 'Does he take his boat as far as Adana? Some small crafts seem to be heading there.'

'He has done, though mainly it's fishing. Usually at night like a lot of boats.'

Outside, Daisy pointed to a plaque on the side of the boat. '*Yaz Breeze*: what does it mean?'

'Yaz means summer. Summer Breeze.' Namik laughed. 'I don't know why; he uses it at all times.'

She had been thinking about something that he'd said yesterday. 'Why do you feel I should be chaperoned?'

'It is only some places. The women here do not go into bars alone, especially where there are lot of men. They lose face among their community. Clubs are the same. It is not done.'

Daisy thought about this. It was going to prove awkward, what with her research and so forth. Still, she'd try to respect their culture. She was, after all, only a visitor here.

It was dusk when Daisy arrived back. She had a lot to think about concerning the Bileklers. What grounds did Ahmet have for implying that his son was murdered? And what of Namik, he was saying the same thing. He certainly had a down on the Bileklers. The question was: why? Furthermore, the Bileklers sometimes appeared edgy, as if they really did have something to hide.

There was a tap at the door, and when Daisy opened it she saw Hasan standing there. He was holding a huge bunch of flowers. 'May I have a moment, Daisy?' He was smartly dressed, with a single white carnation claiming the top buttonhole of his dark suit.

'I'll be opening a florist's soon,' said Daisy, grinning at him. 'But thank you, anyway.'

'I,' he paused. 'I have to tell you something, but do not take offence, Daisy. Please stay away from Ahmet Guven. His family, and some of the people in their village, they are against us.'

Daisy stared at him. 'Have you been following me?'

He shook his head. 'Not following you, no, but I know you have spoken with them.'

'Are you saying you've had me followed?' Daisy found it incredible.

Hasan stepped forward and took hold of Daisy. 'You are new here; you don't know the way of things. Please, I beg of you, do not listen to anything they might say.'

She wanted to free herself from his embrace, but couldn't bring herself to do so. The truth was, and she had to admit it, that she found him too attractive. For a while now, she had wanted this to happen.

'Please, Daisy; you have to put your trust in me. I need you to believe in me, not anyone else.' His face was close to hers.

'But you have been watching me. How can I trust you?' She struggled in his hold.

'I should not have done, and I know that now. Please, let us forget it.'

He relaxed his hold and she pulled away. 'All right.' She tried to appease him. 'But could you leave now?'

Hasan stood looking down at her, then turned and walked up the path. After he'd gone, Daisy wondered again what this was all about. Hasan was an enigma, but his presence was also spellbinding. She could still smell the scent of him.

But the following day, while walking through the village of Bogaz, Daisy's thoughts were still centred on Hasan. She should move out, but what would she tell the Bileklers? They had been very good to her, so what excuse could she give? Could she, for example, say she had reason to believe they had something to do with Aygun's death? So far, there was no evidence, just hearsay. Anyway, in what way could they possibly be involved? Why murder a young, innocent soldier, a young man fighting for his country? Moreover, if truth be told, her feelings for Hasan were deeper than mere friendship. The other night, for example, she wanted to stay in his arms, feel his kisses.

Angry with herself for ever doubting the Bileklers, Daisy determined to put such thoughts from her mind as she remembered her reason for visiting this village. She had previously bumped into Namik at the harbour, and over coffee he'd told her his family had once lived here in Bogaz.

It seemed that during the crisis, between 1963 and 1964, his family had fled from Ozankoy, and after their hazardous journey, on an outmoded bus, they had arrived here. Other families, also present, each brought goods and chattel, as much as they could carry, and had no option but to settle here.

Looking around the village, Daisy saw that most of the houses seemed reasonably comfortable, but that hadn't always been the case. Like many other ordinary folk, those without means, the Guvens lived in huts. These Turkish enclaves were comparably safe, she was told, but nonetheless inhospitable.

A group of children in school uniform chatted excitedly as they passed by. Daisy had started to take photographs, and, seeing this, they mimicked her actions. They pointed to a man with a heavily laden donkey, and, seeing his cheery face, Daisy asked to take a snap of him. He obliged readily, and tried to get her to snap him in various poses.

It had become warmer, and, removing her jacket, Daisy took a deep breath of fresh air. She thought about sitting beneath the cedar tree which was in the village, to drink some coffee from her flask, but decided against this when her eye was caught by a door set in an old sandstone wall. There were two doors, in fact, and the planks of wood looked to be cobbled together in a roughshod fashion, fixed to the wall with heavy hinges. Close to this was a tall window with iron bars, while, along the base of the walls, clumps of straggly weeds grew out from cracks in the crumbling mortar.

Puzzled as to what it had been used for, Daisy pulled at one side of the door and walked in. She trod carefully over some animal droppings, which by the look of things had been here for years. She noted some unusual apparatus, and realised the place had once been used as a small factory.

Something like a large ceramic bowl had two stone crushers slightly above, and these seemed to be led by a rotating cog. Beneath was a deep trough, the glazed tiles badly chipped. Another door led off this room, and in here were similar machines. One was far bigger than the rest, circled with steel tubes that were almost ceiling height. This was worked by a much larger cogged wheel.

'It hasn't been used for years now.'

Startled, Daisy turned to find Richard Hampton.

He smiled. 'Sorry. I saw you come in.'

Stroking a finger over the contraption, Daisy cringed at the rancid grease. 'What is this place? An olive press?'

'Was,' he amended, bending down to inspect the machine. 'Now, we have modern factories, more sophisticated.' He looked up when Daisy clicked her camera. 'That interesting, eh?'

'All part of the job,' she told him, clicking away at other objects. 'You get a better idea from photos. If needed for any reason, you can refer to the snaps.'

This room led through to another, and in here a single contraption had a double-spoke wheel. A steel pole bore through it, which was held by concrete supports. Wooden rafters reinforced the ceiling, while beneath, giving extra support, sizeable tree trunks were evenly spaced.

Daisy didn't like the look of the huge pair of grinding stones. The shaft that had held them had broken loose, hanging perilously out from the vat beneath it.

Daisy shuddered. 'If a child were to play in here!'

'Yes, pretty deadly, that thing up there,' agreed Richard.

It was rather gloomy in here, and airless, so they both stepped outside. Richard slipped on his sunglasses. 'Well, at least you've got your pictures,' he laughed.

Daisy studied him. He seemed a nice man, easy to get along with. 'Have you lived in Cyprus long?' she asked, shielding her eyes from the bright sun.

'I was in the army, an officer.' He lifted the trouser of his right leg to reveal a large knotted scar. 'But, as you can see, I was pensioned off. Like it here, though, so stayed.'

She had noticed the slight limp, and saw, too, the built-up heel of Richard's shoe. 'Were you here in 1974?' she enquired.

He nodded, looking perturbed.

'Those villages where the massed graves were found, what actually happened?' asked Daisy.

Kicking the ground with his good foot, he shuffled uneasily. 'It would seem that you already know!'

'Only from newspapers, though I'd appreciate your account.'

'Well, I don't know if you are aware, but it was on the fourteenth of August that year that the National Guardsmen and EOKA-B terrorists entered the village of Aloa near Famagusta. They rounded up as many Turkish Cypriots they could find. Fifty-seven were actually taken.'

'Wasn't that the second peace operation?'

'Yes, but they were taken to a field and shot and buried there,' answered Richard. 'Bulldozers were used to earth them over.'

'They were found a few days later, according to reports,' said Daisy. 'Would that be true?'

Richard hung his head. 'That's right: limbs, heads torn off.' He shot Daisy a glance. 'Reduced to a heap, it was terrible. Only three survived that ordeal and were able to give an account as to what happened.'

'But what about the other massacres? Was it true that Maratha was one of them?'

Richard stepped back to allow a pregnant woman to pass. 'Yes, this time a group of Greek Cypriot armed men slaughtered the inhabitants. Then they took their revenge on the nearby village of Sandalaris.'

'I remember,' said Daisy, pulling a face. 'They took those to Maratha and executed them too, carrying out the same burial system.'

Richard looked a little tense, and Daisy thought she should make her excuses and leave him to go on his way, but he continued, as past memories flooded back. 'On the first of September, both Maratha and Sandalaris were investigated.' He cleared his throat, then, squaring his shoulders, 'Eighty-eight corpses were found in those common graves, mutilated beyond recognition!'

Because of his sunglasses, Daisy couldn't see his eyes, but, going by his demeanour, he was clearly overcome. 'I'm sorry,' she apologised. 'Here I am going on, and you, presumably, were out for a walk.'

'You're wrong,' he told her, making an unnecessary attempt to close the ill-fitting door. 'I was visiting an old army friend.' He brushed the dirt from his hands, and crooked his thumb towards the old olive factory. 'You see, you may be curious, but then sometimes I can be inquisitive.'

Going their different ways, Daisy couldn't help but think about what Richard had told her. Her mind was also on that dilapidated olive press. That loose shaft, which had once supported those huge grinding stones, looked awesome. She felt that both she and Richard had had a lucky escape!

CHAPTER

FOUR

•

KYRENIA IS ONE of the greenest islands in the Mediterranean. This is due to the high rainfall, which creates lush pastures and acres of citrus groves. The dry, warm weather that had been enjoyed of late had now reverted to the former. Daisy had just left Namik's home, and, although the rain had eased, she found herself treading carefully between numerous stones that had been washed from higher ground and found their way onto muddy track.

Namik's mother was a friendly woman, offering coffee from the little copper pot in which she brewed it. Her fruit bowl, too, piled high with oranges and lemons from her own garden, was forever being offered. Carob logs burnt in the kitchen grate, giving off a warm scent.

The woman spoke no English, but her gentleness touched Daisy, and she saw where Namik got his looks from. Both had the same aquiline nose and hazel eyes. Daisy found herself smiling as she thought of Namik. He always had that effect.

He was born here in Ozankoy, and Daisy wouldn't mind betting he'd been a bit on the wild side as a boy. But, together with his large family, and others, he had suffered the torments of the fighting here. He'd been ten or eleven in 1964, when the whole area was surrounded by Greek Cypriot soldiers. Outnumbering Turkish Cypriots, they had more ammunition. It took five days of fierce fighting before Turkish Cypriots took empty guns and retreated to the hills. Namik's father, Ahmet, told how the men in his village had walked all night to reach St Hilarion. Daisy had also read about this in all the newspapers, national and international.

There were some horrific incidents in those papers. Gruesome, bloodcurdling events, accompanied by equally sickening pictures.

Ahmet, and the rest of the men, had walked barefooted to those mountains that night so as not to create disturbance. They arrived at the fort at sunrise, blistered, bleeding and exhausted, some wounded on makeshift stretchers. Here they joined the rest of their force. However, it took a few months before the authorities were able to help families who'd been left behind. Namik's mother bundled her children, two boys and five girls, along with a few possessions, into a clapped-out bus which was bound for Bogaz.

During that evacuation, Namik, older than his brother, Aygun, volunteered for army service. He was now sixteen.

A sudden clap of thunder startled Daisy, and her shoes were squelching mud. The heavens had opened in force, and she stumbled several times on uneven track. She could just make out the faint outline of Bellapais's ruined abbey. Head down, and soaked through, she was totally oblivious to the black Mercedes as it approached. The passenger door opened and Hasan stuck his head out. 'You had better come inside,' he called, 'you are drowned.'

Osman was at the wheel, but he seemed to ignore Daisy as she got into the rear seat. Then, a little later, he peered through his mirror at her. 'What are you doing out on an afternoon like this?' he questioned.

'I was visiting the Guven family,' Daisy answered. She took out a tissue to blot her face, stiffening at the awkward silence that ensued. Wet and bedraggled, she fingered her hair, wondering what on earth she looked like! As for Hasan, why had he gone quiet?

A dog ran from the verge, and the car, swerving, splashed ochre-coloured mud onto the bonnet and windscreen. Osman shouted, and his tone suggested he'd sworn. 'My father loses his patience at times,' said Hasan, over his shoulder.

'Yes, but those dogs are a pest,' grumbled Osman. 'Anyway, I'm sorry. I'm an old man; I get tired.'

The car pulled up outside the studio, and as Daisy got out Osman wound down his window. 'I think it better if you stay away from the Guvens, Daisy. Why don't you listen?'

Daisy bent her head to his partly opened window. 'I've had no reasons to do that,' she snapped angrily. 'You don't explain yourself!'

'It is best like this,' Hasan coaxed, stretching across his father. 'But I would like to see you later. The "Abbey House", perhaps?' His smile was beguiling, and for an instant he looked like a small child begging forgiveness.

'Perhaps,' she repeated, before dashing to the studio out of the teeming rain.

A little later, having ran a hot bath, Daisy found her mind all over the place. She knew she shouldn't trust the Bileklers. There were some dark secrets lurking there. She didn't know what had really happened between the two families, but somehow she'd find out. It all seemed a complete mystery. And, yet, Namik and his father were making serious accusations against the Bileklers. A thought suddenly struck Daisy. Supposing Namik's young brother, Aygun, had been murdered. But why? What had the young man done to cause someone like the Bileklers to kill him?

Daisy knew one thing. As much as she liked Hasan, she would not be told what to do, not by them or anyone. Daisy wondered what would happen if she asked Hasan about all this. Get his side of the story. The thing was, would he be willing to give her the answers she wanted?

But Daisy didn't have to wait too long for some answers, even if they weren't the ones she expected, for a few hours later they were sitting in the warm and cosy Abbey House restaurant. This got its name from the ancient abbey, set in the same beautiful grounds in Bellapais.

Logs were crackling in the open fireplace, and, sipping a small glass of white wine, Daisy glanced across at Hasan, while trying to work out her feelings. She was wearing a grey silk dress, and her hair was held in place with a diamanté clip.

'You look nice, Daisy,' Hasan said softly. 'That colour suits you.'

She felt awkward sitting here with him, and would have loved to know his true feelings.

'Why do you look at me like that?' he asked suddenly. 'It is though you do not trust me. You do, don't you?'

Daisy shrugged. 'That is something I'll find out, surely, though I certainly wouldn't be here if I felt threatened by you.'

He studied her for a moment. 'Do I look dangerous, as though I could hurt you?'

'Who said anything about hurting me?'

'Ah, so you are suspicious of something, but you do not say what.' Hasan put down his glass and sighed deeply. 'Anyway, if that were the case, and there was something you wished to ask me, then go ahead. I promise not to bite.' There was a glint of mischief in his eyes as he spoke.

'Well, for a start, I've been thinking of moving on,' she said. 'I can't stay under the circumstances, not knowing if something did happen in the past. Something to do with the Guvens, Namik's family.'

'You are very persistent, Daisy, but you ought to get your facts right, if you are saying what I think you are.'

'Well, there must be something going on. The Guvens have a huge grudge against you. As you know, it concerns their son. Can you tell me, honestly, that his death had nothing to do with anyone in your family?'

Hasan leaned across the table. He spoke softly, but angrily. 'Some of these people are uneducated, Daisy. They will say anything, believing they may have a place in your book. Oh yes, does that surprise you?'

Daisy sat back as the food arrived. She couldn't believe the local people would be so shallow, telling her anything just to have a place in her novel. 'I'm told that the young soldier was most likely murdered. What earthly reason would that family have to suggest a link with your family?'

'Ah, you see, they only suggest. Just that: it means nothing.'

'It's an odd accusation, though, isn't it?' continued Daisy. 'And I've also heard that Aygun's death was planned.' She wanted to clear up this matter now, especially if there was a chance of anything developing between herself and Hasan.

Two middle-aged men sitting near their table looked blankly at Hasan, and then carried on with their meal.

'These rumours must stop!' Hasan hissed. 'My father and I stand accused of something we did not do. Look, Daisy, if you left I could not bear it. I have grown quite fond of you – no, more than that. My feelings are much stronger. Do you believe that?'

'Daisy shook her head. 'Frankly, I don't know what to believe, though in fairness I'm willing to give you a chance.' She smiled at him. 'Let's change the subject, shall we?'

'Yes, please do.' His voice was almost playful, and golden lights twinkled in his green eyes.

'I don't think your friend Melanie Hampton liked me much,' said Daisy, 'but her husband was friendly. In fact, I saw him only recently.

'She's like that, but, if she was rude to you, accept my apologies.'

'Apart from that, she comes across as a very hard woman, but then that's the writer in me, I suppose. We tend to see things that others may not. Now, Richard, he strikes me as a very gentle soul. Wouldn't offend anybody.'

Hasan blotted his mouth with his napkin. 'Like you say, they are different, but we cannot all be alike.' Hasan could never tell Daisy that, although he'd like to avoid Melanie, it wasn't to be. She knew how Aygun had died. She was there to witness everything.

Gulping back the rest of his wine, Hasan loosened his collar as perspiration glistened on his brow.

While Daisy had been watching him, she had been aware of the little knots of fear tugging at her stomach. She had begun to think that she loved Hasan, but did she? Was that just the allure of a good-looking man, and the attention he afforded her? And this country, it seemed to hold a spell on her. Still, if the Bileklers had committed murder, and she kept close company with them, wouldn't that make her guilty by association? Especially if she stayed on their premises, taking advantage of their generosity.

After that night out with Hasan, Daisy found herself still wrestling with her emotions. One's feelings weren't like a tap, to be turned on and off whenever it suited, and there were times, when lying awake at night, that Hasan's dark brooding looks had haunted her. His scent, and his masculinity, had turned her otherwise sensible head. Moreover, Hasan and his father had shown nothing but kindness. This didn't, though, make everything right, and, if the old saying was to be believed, there was no smoke without fire.

Beside her, on a small table, were the flowers that Hasan had given her, which had now wilted. She gazed at them sorrowfully, thinking that roses without perfume were like love without hope. Daisy wondered why that thought had popped into her head.

At the desk, she stared blankly at her notepad and pen. She got up then, not wanting to work but instead walked to the door. The air was very still, and carried on this was a faint tinkling of bells. Then, a little later, a few goats appeared from a narrow passage opposite the house. Daisy walked to the bottom of the garden and saw that the rest of the herd had followed, where they spilled into the road. Many leapt at a stone wall for succulent hanging vines, while the heat from their bodies sent up a haze of perspiration.

This calm was soon broken by a car's horn. The vehicle sped past the Bileklers' residence at a dangerous speed, the brakes screeching along the road. Daisy caught her breath now, as the car mounted a grass verge, hit a large shrub, then, after a difficult manoeuvre, sped away.

While that had been happening, she hadn't noticed the dead goat. The creature was lying in the road, a pool of blood oozing from its twisted body. She couldn't comprehend why the car failed to stop, but she had spotted the driver. It was Melanie Hampton!

Hasan appeared first, followed by his father. Osman was holding a stout cane and he used this to support his heavy frame when he stopped to speak to Daisy. 'That woman will never learn,' he grumbled, smoke billowing from the cigar.

Hasan was walking towards the dead animal. 'She was very lucky she didn't kill herself,' he called out, pointing to a trail of skid marks.

'My son is right: she was,' Bilekler agreed. 'Though I'm not sure if Richard was with her. Anybody know?'

'I never had time to notice,' said Daisy, 'although that woman shouldn't be driving.'

'There is another on the bank,' Hasan told them, walking towards the house.

The older man pulled at some jasmine, not yet in flower, which had caught at his shoulder. 'Melanie is not the best of drivers. I have told her often enough.'

'The one on the bank, is that dead too?' enquired Daisy.

Hasan touched her shoulder. 'Do not let it upset you. They are only goats. Fortunately, they are not mine. They are kept away from roads, with somebody looking after them. He is paid well, too, so he knows better than to do otherwise!'

The shepherd appeared then, and Daisy averted her head as the first mangled body was hoisted into a sack. After this she went inside the studio, wanting to erase the horrible images that she had just witnessed.

'I'll show you those Greek tanks,' said Namik. Both he and Daisy were returning by bus from Guzelyurt. Growing along this stretch were hectares of lush citrus groves.

'I'd love to be here when the trees are in blossom,' Daisy told him.

Namik wiped a sleeve over the dirty window and peered out. 'You would love it, because the whole area is heavily scented. It reaches as far as Lefka. Anyway, it is almost spring; you will not have to wait long.'

'Do you think those old men minded having their pictures taken?' asked Daisy.

'What, the ones in the café playing cribbage? No, they would have covered their faces otherwise.'

'Well, those children outside the patisserie didn't. They even offered us a pastry!' laughed Daisy.

At Alsanak, the old bus, which had rattled and bumped on its journey, hissed fumes from the exhaust as it slowed at the kerb. Only Daisy and Namik alighted, then the bus trundled on its way.

A glum-faced Turkish soldier stood guard at the entrance to the tank museum. Daisy, ready with her camera, made to take his photo, but Namik's arm shot out. 'No, they do not like it,' he said, hurrying her forward.

'You're a strange lot,' said Daisy, wrinkling her brow.

'Maybe, but if you lived here you would understand more about our country.' Namik brightened. 'Anyway, what do you think of the tanks?'

'I'm impressed,' said Daisy, looking at the orderly rows of well-kept vehicles. Close by, as though surveying all this, stood a statue of the unknown soldier.

'Why don't you climb up there and I take your picture?' Namik suggested.

'On one of those tanks?' answered Daisy. 'I can't anyway: I'm wearing the wrong shoes.'

'All right, take my picture then, but you should not have worn high heels!' He ran to one of the tanks and climbed up.

Daisy laughed at his boyish behaviour, snapping Namik a couple of times.

'Oh, come on up,' he called. 'Your heels are not too high.'

Daisy did as he suggested, and he helped her climb up, laughing when she lost her footing a couple of times. 'It feels strange looking down from here,' she said, 'and I never thought I'd be standing in one of these big hulks.'

Namik seemed to be lost in thought. As always, he had dressed casually, and it was clear he had no money for new clothes. Though, when his restaurant reopened, he would at least have a regular wage, a few lire in his pocket to make him feel good. But none of this took anything away from his good looks.

At the turn of his head, Daisy noted the full curve of his mouth, wondering once again why she hadn't realised his appeal.

Perhaps he'd known Daisy had been watching him, perhaps not, but suddenly he pulled her into his arms. His kiss was warm, sensual and full of longing. However, as suddenly as it had happened, he pulled away. 'I have been longing to do that for a while,' he admitted.

'I had no idea,' said Daisy, breathless. 'But why did you stop?'

'That guard had walked away, but he has just returned. Like you say, we are a funny lot. We do not parade our feelings in public.'

Daisy's mind was in turmoil. Sometimes, Namik infuriated her, and then there were times when he made her laugh. He could be preoccupied, moody, and full of self-doubt. His sense of fun, though, would always win through, and all this made him the man he was.

Snapping out of her reverie, Daisy smiled at Namik. 'I find you difficult to understand at times. Just now, for instance. Why exactly did you kiss me?'

He shrugged, and then looked into her eyes. 'I have strong feelings for you, Daisy.'

'You don't give much away, do you?'

'Perhaps, but it is something. Something I just feel.'

Moments later, leaving her to ponder on his words, Namik jumped down from the tank, and then helped Daisy down. 'By the way,' Namik pointed out, 'you will not get your photos developed here, in the north. They will not touch them.'

'Why is that?'

Namik laughed. 'These are Greek vehicles, remember? They will have nothing to do with them. I know they are here, all nicely laid out and that, but that is different. A reminder to let others know something of our history.'

Daisy took more photos, including another huge tank, a field gun and, lastly, an armoured contraption.

'I know an English man who works in the south,' said Namik. 'I will get him to take them there. They will develop your photos, no problem.'

'So they allow him to work there?'

'A few English people who live here work in the south. They have special passes. Anyway, when you get them back, you should show them to Ibrahim. He's my friend. He was a commander, working with the British during the war against EOKA.'

'Does he speak English too?' asked Daisy.

'Not as well as me, but good,' he laughed. Namik gazed at the armoured vehicle. 'I think it was about 1954 when EOKA was founded, but there had been trouble before. George Grivas was very bad man. He obtained Makarios's support at this time.'

Daisy propped herself against the field gun. She then produced some bread, cheese and olives, offering some to Namik. 'It was Grivas who formed the clandestine revolutionary army, wasn't it?'

Namik broke off some bread. 'Yes, and in case you do not know what EOKA means, I will tell you. Ethniki Organosis Kypriakon Agoniston.'

'Quite a mouthful,' said Daisy. 'And the English translation?'

'National Organization of Cypriot Fighters.'

Daisy had to smile. 'You missed your vocation,' she teased. 'You should have been a war journalist or something.'

'Instead, I became a waiter, as soon as I finished in the army.'

'But you were telling me about Ibrahim,' she reminded him.

'Just before 1970, he finished fighting, bought a lorry and worked for himself, odd jobs, that sort of thing. Then, soon after that, he became the Turkish Underground National Liberation leader of Ozankoy area.'

Daisy chewed on an olive. 'He sounds interesting. But what does he do now? Returned to odd-jobbing?'

'He has a bar in Ozankoy, also, he is muhtak. It means mayor. Looks after the area, and collects post for our village. You must have seen him.'

'I can't recall this Ibrahim, but you'll have to point him out,' she told Namik.

They had finished their lunch and were strolling among the military vehicles. 'Look over there,' said Namik. 'That is Pentamili beach, where the Turkish army landed. It was 20 July 1974, about five thirty in the morning, I think. You see, I never forget, never!'

'I know the opposition were caught off guard,' said Daisy.

'Yes, that's right. Although this was the first peace operation. The second was 14 August. Turkish jets bombed and strafed Greek Cypriot strong points, in and around the seaport of Kyrenia, on Cyprus's north shore. Transport planes even dropped paratroopers in the vicinity of Nicosia International Airport. Then, early morning, three brigades of Turkish troops, consisting of around 6,000 men and forty tanks, landed over there on that beach.'

'I read much of this,' said Daisy, 'but as you yourself were involved with the fighting, you have it first hand.'

'Well, me and many others,' stated Namik. 'but during the landing, under naval and air cover, two Greek Cypriot torpedo boats were sunk. Meanwhile, heavy fighting was going on in Nicosia. As Turkish paratroopers closed in on the airport, machine gun mortar and rocket fire were exchanged between the Greek and Turkish quarters of the city.' He paused, then turned to Daisy. 'Are you taking this in? It may prove helpful when you are writing to know these facts.'

She nodded repeatedly, eager to know as much as possible.

'Well,' he continued, 'Turkish fighter bombers repeatedly bombed Greek Cypriot strongholds in Nicosia, while smashing two motorised columns of the Cypriot National Guard. They were trying to reinforce the Greek Cypriot garrison in Kyrenia.' Namik touched Daisy's arm. 'When you have fought in a war, it never leaves you. Never.'

Daisy felt very much affected by all this, and reaching out she squeezed his hand. However, as soon as they returned to Ozankoy, she would ask Namik to put everything down on paper, as it was impossible to take in all what he'd said.

There was a lengthy wait for the bus, and, as nothing much was in the vicinity, they bided their time by taking a quiet stroll. The sun had gathered strength, and had begun to sear into Daisy's back. 'I can't imagine this heat back in England,' she told Namik, producing a bottle of mineral water.

'Well, I suppose that is something,' he said. 'At least we have good weather.'

'Look at that mountain range.' Daisy pointed towards some high peaks. 'It's awesome.'

Namik, shading his eyes from the strong sunlight, was already looking, but he seemed troubled. Dotted amid scrub, cypress trees, of varying height, stood proud. And, while parts of the craggy peaks showed clearly against a blue sky, taller, distant ones were softened by grey cloud.

Daisy frowned, wondering why Namik had become subdued. 'What is it?'

Namik seemed to be mesmerised by the sweep of these mountains. He didn't speak for some moments, then said, 'I know I should try to forget, but I cannot. It will never go away, our problem.'

The scent of wild thyme wafted on the air, and Daisy saw she was treading on large clumps of the common herb. 'Well,' she prompted, 'what problem are we referring to?'

'You know,' answered Namik. 'My brother. He was supposed to have died up there.' He gestured towards the mountain range.

'And didn't he?'

'No!' Namik took a packet of cigarettes from his pocket. 'That is what we were told, but it was not true.'

'But...' Daisy was puzzled. 'But why do you doubt it? Why would the authorities tell you this?'

Namik hung his head. 'What else would they tell us? It was no use arguing, though, but they got it all wrong. When we saw my brother's body...'

'You don't have to tell me,' Daisy told him. 'It's too upsetting, I see that.'

'It was his injuries,' continued Namik, as though her words hadn't registered. 'I have seen many dead soldiers: disfigured, missing limbs, all kinds. It wasn't the same, Daisy, I can tell you. Aygun had none of these injuries, those found on the battle ground.

'What do you think happened?' she asked.

'I will tell you another time,' he said. 'But we had better catch our bus.'

They both gazed back at the unknown Turkish soldier, standing forlornly on his plinth, and at the tanks and various military machines which were now idle.

Daisy sighed, thinking of all the poor souls who'd lost their lives fighting for their beliefs. Namik, however, had left her wanting to know more. If Aygun hadn't died on those battlefields, how had he died? And was Namik suggesting his brother's body may have been taken there? All this was a complete mystery to her.

CHAPTER

FIVE

•

A RARE GRIN spread across Fatma's face. She was on the
bus heading for the Ozankoy area, and shifted nearer the
window, making room for Daisy. With the engine running,
the bus waited, allowing a steady flow of passengers to get
on.

Daisy smiled back at the housekeeper. 'I see you've been
to the shops.' A bag of fruit and vegetables were at the woman
feet, and she held on to the straps as the bus rattled its way
out of Kyrenia.

'Yes, I come here to buy a few things,' said Fatma, 'but I
have a sister that I often visit.' She had peeled an orange, and
offered half of this to Daisy. 'You have family?'

'Yes, my mother, and two sisters.'

Fatma used a large white hanky to wipe juice from her
chin. 'I never see you with friends. You have some, yes?'

The old Bedford bus churned up dust as it left the depot,

which was really some waste ground. 'Yes, I do have friends, though most are back in England.' Daisy smiled.

'Hasan, what about him, is he your friend?'

When Daisy hesitated, Fatma waved a hand. 'Sorry, I am too much gossip. Please, forget I ask.'

Most of the passengers got off the bus at Ozankoy, and the door was left open for a short while, allowing a thick cloud of cigarette smoke to escape. 'It's all right,' said Daisy at length. 'I don't think you're a gossip.'

Turning to her, Fatma's voice was guarded. 'I like you, Daisy; you are a good woman, but sometimes I worry.'

Daisy was puzzled. 'Not about me, surely?'

Peering around the almost empty bus, Fatma spread her careworn hands. 'I hear things about Mr Hasan, bad things.' She turned abruptly, looking out of the window as if she'd said too much.

Daisy wanted to know more, but respected Fatma's loyalties. Instead, she said, 'One more stop, then we have to tackle that hill.'

Throughout the short journey, Daisy had seen a lighter, friendlier side to Fatma, though it was most unlikely that anyone could really get close to her. It was clear she was afraid of something, always cautious, as though she nursed a terrible secret.

Namik's mother put another log on the fire. It was extremely hot in her kitchen, what with the warm sunshine flooding the room, but the fire was needed for the huge blackened pot that bubbled on the flames. This was full of washing, which by now would be ready to take out.

A scarf was tied around Mrs Guven's head, and her lined face showed long years of sorrow, but the woman never grumbled about anything much, and appeared to enjoy her duties.

Daisy liked this gentle woman, and guessed that she was a very proud person, never asking for anything or expecting help of any kind. Nonetheless, at the moment, Daisy was helping to lay the table. It was the least she could do, having been invited for a Sunday meal.

Namik had obviously noticed his mother's tired state and told her that she did too much, but she said it gave her much pleasure in doing her daughter's washing. As they were all married with children, they had enough to do.

Mrs Guven was about to lift the heavy pot from the fire when Namik rushed over. 'No,' he cried, taking two thick oven cloths from her. 'I will lift it.'

When he'd finished helping, Daisy took him aside. 'I have to speak to you,' she said. 'I'm thinking of leaving the Bileklers' place. I don't know where I'll be, but I'll look into that.'

Namik breathed a sigh of relief. 'You worried me there. I thought you were going back to England!'

'Are you saying you'd miss me?' she teased.

He looked across at his mother who was putting a dish of glistening stuffed peppers onto the table. 'Of course,' he replied, rather awkwardly. 'I never want you to go, never. You will keep in touch, won't you, Daisy?'

'I may need your help sometimes,' she answered. Some places perhaps, where I wouldn't venture alone.'

'This makes a lot of sense,' agreed Namik, 'as there are certain areas where I should be on hand. I do not mean dangerous – no, that is seldom the case – but, as I have mentioned before, it is best I go with you.'

His words touched Daisy, and attentively she held his

hand. Namik didn't object, and stood there looking at her, a touch of mischief in his eyes.

She read everything she wanted to know in that look. Moreover, she noticed the slight smile on Mrs Guven's face. Just the three of then sat around the table, as Namik's father, Ahmet, had gone to collect logs with his donkey. There wasn't much conversation during the meal, as Namik's mother spoke little English, but this didn't matter because Daisy enjoyed being in Namik's company.

It was the second time Daisy had heard the dogs baying. She had no idea where the din came from, but felt it couldn't be too far from the Bileklers' premises. Walking up the path to the big house, she also heard the plaintive chanting which came from Bellapais's mosque. This she had got used to, as the woeful sounds drifted over village rooftops, but, having not yet seen any dogs, Daisy had no idea to whom they belonged.

When she rang the doorbell, Fatma told her that Hasan was waiting outside on the veranda and would like to see her. She felt somewhat nervous when she walked out there, and more so when she found him pacing to and fro. 'Hello,' he started, but Daisy cut him short.

'I won't stay.' She blurted the words out quickly. 'I've something to tell you, and you may not like it, but I'll be leaving the studio.'

Hasan looked at Daisy in disbelief. 'I do not understand. You… you love it here.'

'I'm not leaving Cyprus,' said Daisy, hastily, feeling somewhat ungrateful for the generosity she'd been shown.

'Then why leave?' he said tersely. 'Why' – he waved his arms – 'this place is perfect; you must see that.'

Last night, Daisy had been unable to sleep, wondering how she'd explain her reasons for leaving. After all, they mustn't suspect anything. Not that she had proof of any wrongdoing.

'Yes, you're right, I do like it here, there's no question of that. Thing is, I've been offered accommodation on the outskirts of Ozankoy. An English woman whose husband works away.'

Hasan stepped forward. 'And what of my father?' he said, angrily. 'He will think I have not made you happy.'

'Why should it matter? In any case, I have been happy.' No sooner as she'd spoken those last words, she'd realised her mistake.

'Then why leave? Is it to get away from me, Daisy?'

'No, of course not. There are other reasons. I can't go into them, and I shouldn't have to explain myself, but I am thankful, for everything.'

Hasan moved like lightening, and before Daisy could protest he'd grabbed her, pulling her close. 'I love you,' he blurted out. 'I could not live my life without you, and that is what I wanted to tell you. Do you feel the same? Tell me, Daisy.'

'I… I don't know how I feel. Too much is happening lately. I came out here to work; you must know how strongly I feel about that.' Daisy managed to break free, but at the door he caught up with her, grasping her so tightly she could hardly breathe. 'Anyway,' he added, 'you belong to me. We are as one now, after that night.'

Daisy pummelled at his chest, and, pushing him with force, she freed herself once more. 'What on earth do you mean? What night? Nothing did happen!'

He sniggered. 'Oh, Daisy, you forget so quickly.'

Although nothing had happened between them, except when they'd kissed, the fact that he could say such a thing perturbed her. Her eyes blazed in disbelief. This wasn't the man she'd once known, an educated, almost perfect gentleman. Without another word, she fled from the house.

Daisy was halfway down the path when Hasan called after her. 'But who will you convince? Not that Namik; he'll not believe you!'

Back in the studio, Daisy watched from the window to see if she'd been followed. She had broken out into a sweat, her cotton dress clinging damp to her body. Why had Hasan said that, suggesting they had shared more than a few kisses? It was all a lie, even though at one time she would have welcomed him into her bed.

She stood with her back pressed against the door. What should she do? Supposing lies were spread about her? And if this got back to Namik, to his family even, what then? This wasn't like England. They had strict codes here and she didn't want to be known as someone who slept around.

Checking to see that nobody was in the grounds, Daisy started to pack her suitcase. She felt that the sooner she got away from here, the better. Still, while she was packing, nagging little pains shot through her insides, and it made her doubt if she would ever be free of the Bileklers, let alone feel safe. For why else did Hasan say what he did? Was he trying emotional blackmail? It would seem he'd try anything to prevent her leaving here. It came down to one thing. She already knew too much, and that is something Hasan hadn't reckoned with!

The woman was seated at the bar, the flirtatious air unmistakable. Every now and then, she leant closer to the barman, and giggled.

Daisy had popped into the bar for something to eat, and from her corner table she couldn't help but watch Melanie Hampton playing up to the young man. She swung round now when she sensed she was being watched.

'Why, fancy seeing you in a bar,' she called to Daisy. 'Anyway, I hear that you've moved on. Must say, I'm not at all surprised. A bit claustrophobic up at that hilltop village, was it? I just knew it would be. But where are you now? In some cheap digs, I suppose.'

Daisy had been eating some meze. Putting down her fork, she gazed up into a pair of steel-blue eyes. 'That's correct. I have moved out, but nothing like you call it. The new place suits me better. Closer to things, you know.' This was no lie: Daisy did find the move to her liking. The Bileklers weren't looking over her shoulder, meddling in life.

'I'm surprised a young woman like yourself is still around.' Melanie pulled a face while making a gesture with her hands. 'There's nothing much here, not at this time of year.'

'I told you once that I'm here to work.' Daisy tried to keep her voice steady. 'Anyway, why should it bother you? You seem to be taking an enormous interest in my life.'

Melanie Hampton's mouth twisted into an ugly line. 'Of course, you are in love with Hasan. I thought as much. Well, you'd best forget him. That man will never return your feelings. He's incapable of any deep affection, believe me, lady. Oh yeah, and another thing. I know it was old Osman who set you up. Remember, I've known that family for years.'

Her words cut deep. All this time Daisy had believed Hasan had really fallen for her. He'd seemed so nice, thoughtful, and all that time he'd been driven by his father.

Melanie Hampton narrowed her eyes. 'Did Hasan talk about us? How we had something special? No, I thought not. He'd rather keep that to himself. Mind, if anything had happened between you two, he wouldn't have been averse to letting that slip.

'Nothing did happen,' snapped Daisy. 'If he's said otherwise, then he's lying!'

'Well, if he did, it's over, so I'm not bothered. But you'll soon learn that word gets around quickly here, wherever you are staying. Some of the old women just love to gossip.'

Daisy didn't want to hear any more, and after paying her bill she brushed past Melanie Hampton and strolled along the harbour. What had Hasan been saying? Whatever it was, why was he being so spiteful? Then it came to her. He'd become quite nervous when she'd told him she was leaving his property. Her chance meetings with Namik and his family had not been reckoned with, and that's the last thing Hasan would want: Daisy learning more than she should.

Namik may not have much as regards riches but, from what Daisy knew of him, he was an honest, decent man, not somebody with a hidden past. Suddenly, Daisy felt a tremor of fear wash over her. Suppose Hasan spread rumours, telling lies about himself and Daisy. If this got back to Namik, what then? In his eyes she wouldn't be worthy of him, and Daisy had come to realise now that it was Namik who she was in love with.

Daisy rued the day she had met the Bileklers. Hasan could never be trusted again, especially if it were true he'd had a hand in Aygun's death. If so, he was plain evil.

Namik on the other hand was so different. He was not the kind to fall in love lightly. He was a one-woman man, and expected that woman to share his principles. They'd had this light-hearted conversation in Ibrahim's bar, but he was making a point, and the very idea that she had been with another man, having known him for such a short time, would shame him. His village, he'd said, did not take kindly to easy-going women. They were still very much steeped in tradition concerning anything of this nature. Yes, even Daisy thought this outmoded, but then she was a Western woman, not like most Muslims, who saved themselves for marriage.

Daisy looked out across the sea, mesmerised by the gentle lapping of water swishing against the harbour wall. She now knew why the Bileklers were fearful of Namik's family. It was because Namik had known from the start how his brother had died.

Namik had told Daisy that he would tell her more about Aygun's death, but it wasn't her place to question him. However, if she were being honest, she would dearly love to know how the young man had died, if not on the battlefield. But, just as important, why had the Bileklers murdered that young lad?

While Daisy had been pondering on all this, Melanie Hampton had taken herself off to another bar, where she had since imbibed a few strong spirits.

Nothing would please her more than to be shot of Daisy, as she knew Hasan had feelings for her. In fact, ever since he'd met her, he had become stupidly obsessed with the woman.

Recently, after a bout of heavy drinking, he'd confessed his feelings openly, speaking of his love for the English girl. He'd added that maybe it was a selfish love, but he needed her and no other woman could fill that need.

Melanie, heavy-eyed, looked into the half-empty glass and swirled the contents around. Since Daisy Collins had got to know some of the locals, the Bileklers and she had lived on tenterhooks. On its own, there wouldn't have been a problem, but that chance meeting with the Guven family, and researching her book, had caused more trouble than they could ever have imagined.

It was at times like these that her thoughts would dwell on that fateful night. Hasan had asked for her help, and because of her attraction for him she had complied with his wishes.

How Osman had despised the Guven family. Their son Aygun had been meeting up with Osman's daughter, but he wasn't going to allow it. Many a time he tried to put paid to the young couple's meetings, but it hadn't worked. The two families were living in Bogaz after EOKO had driven them from their homes, and very soon Osman hatched a plan to see the end of Aygun.

Even now, after all these years, she could clearly recall Hasan's voice: 'Melanie, listen to me,' he'd said. 'Tonight, I need your help. My sister is supposed to meet that boy, but she will not be there. You will take her place. My father wishes to be present, to make sure his plan is carried out.'

Osman's daughter, Aisha, had been kept at home on the pretext that Aygun was unable to escape his duties, as were pre-arranged. She was told that his officer in command had orders to hold a roll call, before leading them to the mountainous area which overlooked the region. Under nightfall, their task was to keep a watchful eye on any activity involving the opposition.

All this was supposed to have come from a chance meeting with an old and valued friend whose son was with the same unit as Aygun.

Sixteen-year-old Aisha had had no idea that her family had known the whereabouts of her secret trysts with Aygun. And so, reconciled to the fact that her beloved young soldier had been unable to meet up with her, she had done as bid and stayed at home.

Melanie, still sitting in the bar and having drunk more than her usual daytime quota, could barely stand when she'd tried. Also, she'd had no idea that she was the only remaining customer. Instead, during her melancholy, she had drifted into a soporific kind of dream. In that dream, she saw Osman, his large presence looming over her. As usual, he was puffing on his cigar, the smoke thick, suffocating.

'Yes,' he mocked, 'that boy Aygun will wonder what is happening. Hasan, he knows what to do. And you, my dear, will beckon the boy. Don't worry: it will be dark in that old olive press; he'll not know the difference!'

Melanie Hampton didn't really want the remains of her drink, but knocked it back anyway. She noticed now that most of the lights had been switched off. There was only one barman now, who was busily wiping tables. Wearily, she got up, teetering unsteadily to the door. She would look for a taxi and ask to be taken home. Melanie sneered at that particular thought. As always, Richard was the last person she wanted to see.

His face set like stone, Namik turned to the sports section in the newspaper. Unlike Daisy, he lacked any kind of enthusiasm. He already knew about breathtaking views, sweeping hills and ochre-coloured landscapes.

'It was nice of your friend to drive us up to Karaman,' said Daisy. They were sitting on a café terrace, and she was filling their cups with tea. 'Anyway, where is he?'

'Inside the restaurant, suppose.' Namik's head was still bent over his newspaper. 'Anyway, what does it matter?'

Daisy scowled at him, but was determined not to let his bad mood affect her. 'Perhaps Mehmet will join us in a moment.'

'I doubt it; he is probably talking to somebody. I'm not bothered, anyway.'

Daisy's insides jumped. Had those nasty rumours got back to Namik? He'd been grumpy all afternoon. Up until then, they'd been getting on fine, planning all kinds of trips. Then, on the other hand, it could be something quite different. Perhaps it was the lack of work. With no money to contribute towards his keep, or pay his way, it would be more than a man could bear. Daisy decided that this was more likely to be the answer to Namik's bad moods. Even so, he'd accept nothing from her, as she had offered him money before.

Nothing much had been said at the table, and the little that was spoken had come mostly from Daisy. As though in deep thought, Namik folded his newspaper and strolled aimlessly to the edge of the terrace, and as Daisy gazed after him her heart was filled with compassion.

She noted that his trousers had seen better days, and his shirt, supposedly white, had taken on a dull tinge. And, although his dark curling hair gleamed with good health, it was in need of a good trim. She saw, too, that his shoes were a little run-down, and this also saddened her. But what could she do to help him? He was far too proud to accept anything from her.

He let out a huge sigh when she walked over and joined him. 'I don't know, Daisy, I'm fed up! There is nothing this side of Cyprus. No money, nothing. You can see that for yourself.'

'No matter: your restaurant will be opening soon; at least that's something.' Daisy didn't quite know what to say.

From the terrace, which was high in the hills of Karaman, Namik gazed down to a plethora of various scrub, including fig, which, once in fruit, would then eventually rot. 'Yes,' he finally answered. 'Now the weather is better, there will be more tourists and restaurants will open.' While he'd been speaking, he'd been groping in his trouser pocket. He now pulled out a crumpled note. 'Look!' He brightened, showing Daisy the Turkish lire. 'Maybe I am lucky after all. Anyway, would you like anything?' He made an attempt to laugh at his words. 'Anything within reason, of course.'

Daisy smiled at him. 'You won't get far with that!' she joked, glancing down at the crumpled note he'd shown her. 'But no, you spend it on yourself. You look as though you need a drink.'

'You are right, Daisy. I do, I need something.'

Mehmet had left Namik at the bar, having put a little towards his beer, because the Turkish note he'd found in his pocket was too small a denomination. He grinned when he spoke to Daisy. 'How is it that Namik is only happy when he has a drink in front of him?'

'So you've noticed too?' replied Daisy. 'But, in fairness, he isn't always like that. I think that everything has got on top of him. Some bad memories have...' She broke off, feeling that what Namik had told her about his brother was in confidence.

Like his friend, Mehmet also had a thick mop of dark curly hair, which he wore a little shorter. He also favoured a bushy moustache, which he'd grown over the last couple of years. 'I know, you are right there.' He laughed. 'I have known Namik for, well, for many years, and he has many sides, most of which are good.' He took a packet of cigarettes from his pocket. 'Anyway, what do you think of Karaman?'

Daisy found it difficult to tear her eyes away from the sweeping, panoramic landscape. 'What can I say? Look, see that!' A bird of prey swooped, then ascended high above, its wings spread gracefully against the clear blue sky.

'That was a vulture,' Mehmet informed her. 'All of this is the Kyrenia range,' he added, seeing how far he could throw some small stones. 'And that high one, on the right, is St Hilarion. You have visited the ruined castle up there?'

Daisy shook her head, and then moved away from the parapet, with Mehmet close on her heel. As they walked, a sharp, aromatic smell of pine wafted around them, together with sage and rosemary. On one side of the wall of the café, which was run by an English couple, an unruly vine scrambled, its leafy buds looking ready to shoot.

Looking sideways at Mehmet, Daisy said, 'I've seen Namik in one of his dark moods before. It won't last. He'll be fine when he's back at work.'

Mehmet ushered Daisy to the side of the road as a car came towards them. 'Namik is a good friend, has a good heart.' As they moved on, he crooked his thumb towards the craggy peaks. 'We were both up there on Saint Hilarion fighting those bloody Greeks. Did he tell you?'

'Yes, but he hasn't spoken much about it. He did, however, tell me he'd been made a commander. I gather, though, that those years with all the fighting going on, both sides lost out.'

'Yes, that would have been the case.' He gave a small laugh as he turned to look at her. 'Since our army days, Namik always seems, well, you know.'

'Did you evacuate to Bogaz, too?' she asked, noticing how the bright sun caught the gold medallion at his neck.

'We all did. But, apart from everything else, Namik was a good soldier. Did you see his arm, where the bullet hit?'

'He hasn't mentioned it, but I thought it was something like that.'

They had walked well away from the café, and now stood outside some derelict houses, which had been peppered with ammo. Daisy went towards one of these and peered through the opened door, which had been jammed back on its rusty hinges. She stepped inside and was met by a rank smell of dirt and debris. 'I hope the family got out well before this happened,' she commented, turning to Mehmet. 'If they didn't, God help them.'

'If they were anti-war, I hope so too. But not if they were fighting for EOKA. Look what they did to us!'

'Of course, this was a Greek community, wasn't it?'

Mehmet nodded. 'That is why Turkish Cypriots will not live here now. Did you not guess?

'No, I hadn't thought. But what about the children? Supposing they were hurt, or killed...'

'Look.' He shook his head. 'You cannot go round picking one by one. We were at war. It was them or us,' he stated, with a fierce edge to his voice.

She tried seeing it from his point of view, that in war it was a matter of survival.

There were similar houses like the one next door. Inside one of these, all manner of debris littered the floor, including an upended table, a man's shoe and an old blanket that had been thrown across a badly damaged armchair. In the small kitchen, a large plastic bottle of cooking oil had been left to spill across the stone floor.

It was too distressing to stay any longer. Daisy's eye caught sight of a child's cot, the bedding still inside but covered in a thick layer of grime.

Outside, Mehmet brushed dirt from his hands. 'Look what they did to our Turkish communities in the south! Paphos, Larnaca, Limassol and Famagusta. There was no discrimination between the military or civilian targets. In both towns and villages, the National Guard and EOKA indulged in the most terrible evils.'

Here in Karaman, quite a few houses remained unscathed. One pretty stone dwelling, with jasmine climbing its wall, had a plaque on the door which read: 'Honeysuckle Cottage'.

'I suppose you have guessed that these are owned by English people,' he said. 'Dutch as well, but mostly English.'

'I can't help thinking about those other poor houses,' said Daisy. 'I've never seen anything as bad as that.'

Mehmet looked at her gravely. 'Here is something people ought to know. When the Greek National Guard entered Turkish homes in Famagusta, they not only shot women and children but cut their throats. After that, they rounded up all the rest of the women they could find, and raped them. And if that wasn't enough, they burnt out the Turkish quarters of Limassol.'

Daisy shuddered. 'Sheltered as we are in England, we have no idea what you suffered.'

'The rest of us survived; we were lucky, including your Namik.' He turned to Daisy. 'By the way, do you suppose he is waiting for us?'

'Maybe,' she answered. 'But I hope his mood has improved.'

'So do I, Daisy. So do I.'

CHAPTER
SIX

•

A FEW DAYS later, a bitingly cold wind tore across the wasteland on the east side of Ozankoy. Even the many birds that hunted in this area had seemingly disappeared. Daisy shivered. 'This must be the coldest spot,' she told Namik.

'You are lucky we are not getting snow,' he answered. 'Turkey has. I saw it on television.'

A few gnarled, old olive trees grew here, and their silvery-grey leaves blustered so violently it looked as though at any moment these trees would be wrenched from their moorings. This time it was Namik who shivered, shrugging further into his jacket. 'You are right, though. It is bloody cold!'

'Well, I can't find any more asparagus,' shouted Daisy, her voice catching on the wind.

'This will do,' he said, handing her a small bag for the wild vegetables.

All manner of flora grew in this hardy area, including sage, rosemary and common thyme. Daisy had been crouching among some of these herbs, as well as the stubborn sword grass that grew throughout. When she stood to take the bag from Namik she gasped as he grabbed hold of her.

'Daisy, I am sorry. Why did I do it? Why did I go off like that up in Karaman? It is wrong, and I should not behave like that but sometimes, oh, I do not know what is wrong with me.'

She gazed up at him, and realised that, if that was his only failing, she could hardly grumble.

He kissed her lightly on the lips, and then her throat. 'I don't deserve you. Do I?'

'It isn't your best quality,' she told him, 'but no one is perfect.'

'Are you liking your new place?' he asked, changing the subject.

'Yes, the woman's British and very friendly, but her husband's Cypriot. He travels back and forth to England, on business.'

'You could, if you wanted come to live with us, but…'

'I understand,' said Daisy. 'Your poor mother has enough to do. No, this place is good enough.'

'Well, we cannot stand here,' said Namik, as the branches from a nearby tree cracked and creaked with another strong gust.

As they walked towards his house, with the intention of cooking the asparagus with their evening meal, Namik squeezed Daisy tightly. 'I don't want to lose you, ever.'

She frowned. 'Why do you say that?'

'I'm not sure. It is something I just feel. Something that might happen.'

'Is it anything to do with the Bileklers? Hasan, for instance?' Daisy felt quite concerned at the tone in his voice.

Namik chuckled. 'I'm not afraid of them, Daisy. At least, not like that. But they have a lot of power around here. Wealth. It always comes to that. When you have that kind of influence, those sort of people get away with, well anything.'

Daisy considered his words. In fact, she had long wondered if Melanie Hampton was tied up with any wrongdoing concerning the Bileklers. She glanced at Namik. She wished he'd confide in her. Tell her everything he knows. At least she may be able to make some sense of things.

As they stepped into Namik's kitchen, they found his mother crying, curled up on the daybed. Ahmet was home, and his donkey was tethered outside feeding from a bag of oats. He turned when he'd heard the back door, but carried on with the job of brewing some coffee. Daisy noticed the table had been laid, but was concerned at Mrs Guven's obvious distress.

Namik pulled Daisy aside. He spoke softly. 'I know why my mother is crying. It is my brother, Aygun. She cry all the time; she will never get over it.'

There was nothing Daisy could say. On the wall, above an ornate but ancient sideboard, were some family photos. Among these, there was an imprint where one had been removed. Gazing over at Mrs Guven, she saw her clutching the photo to her bosom. Daisy didn't have to be told it was her dead son in that picture.

'Here, let me help, there must be something I can do,' suggested Daisy.

'No, you sit and have some coffee first,' Namik told her. 'Maybe you can help later.'

He was concerned for his mother, but knew her melancholy would soon pass. He went over to her. 'We have some asparagus, Mama. Perhaps you can help us pick more tomorrow, or sometime soon. But remember' – he laughed – 'if others get there first, there will be none to pick.'

At her son's words, Mrs Guven struggled up against the cushions and she showed a trace of a smile. Then, reaching out, she took hold of his hand. 'Look.' He turned to both his father and Daisy. 'My mother knows what those locals are like. They know the best places to find the asparagus.'

Daisy and Ahmet laughed too, and, soon after, Mrs Guven was bustling around her kitchen.

'Well, I see you have sorted yourself out.' It was Namik's first visit to the house on the outskirts of Ozankoy. It was a large property, classed out here as a villa, having two balconies, one facing south, the other west. Daisy had the use of a sizeable room, and, if she wished to do so, was welcome to sit outside in the garden, which was mostly laid with patterned tiles.

Daisy held up a cushion. 'I bought these myself,' she told Namik. 'Everything else belongs to the owners.' The silk cushions, in jewelled colours, were edged in metallic braiding, and were piled on an Ottoman which was against one wall.

'It all looks very nice, but listen: I have good news!'

It pleased Daisy to see a smile lighting up his face, but before she could say anything Namik had crossed the room and swept her off her feet. 'It's my uncle, the one who has small boat. He also has restaurant, but has never really made anything of it. He wants me to look after it when he goes to England!'

'Oh, I am so happy for you, Namik, but when do you start?'

'As soon as his arrangements are settled. But, like I say, it has not done very well; it needs something. I don't know what, but I will make it nice. Better music, definitely. I would have had to sign a new contract anyway, when my old job opens next week.'

Daisy laughed at his exuberance. 'Everywhere we go, you have uncles!'

'Everyone here is my uncle or cousin. Didn't you know?' His tone suggested he was joking, but then a lot of people here were somehow connected.

They were about to leave the house when Namik noticed Daisy's large notepad, left open on a small table. He was always interested in what she was writing and kept abreast with most of what she did. 'You have not written for days,' he questioned. 'Why? Are you having problems?'

'It's nice that you're taking so much interest,' she said, 'but I had to stop at that point. There is something I have to do first.'

'You are writing about my country; of course I am interested. But what is it you have to do?'

'Before I go any further, I want to visit that museum, the one near Nicosia.'

'Of course,' he answered, flatly. He had said he'd take Daisy, but secretly he was off the idea. Still, he would keep his word, even if the whole thing appalled him.

Namik had been looking out of the window of their local bus. He'd been in a reflective mood for the last part of their journey.

'What's up?' asked Daisy. 'You've been very quiet.'

'Sorry.' He turned away from the window. 'I did not realise, but I was thinking how dreadful that museum will be.'

Daisy grimaced. 'Yes, I know, but I have to go. As I've said before, getting the true facts, no matter how awful, is paramount to everything I do. Anyway, how far is Kumsal?'

He frowned. 'From Nicosia, you mean? I'm not sure, but then I have never actually been to the museum, only heard about it.'

'But you were telling me the other day you have relations there.'

'Had, but not any more. They were killed. It was on my mother's side. Entire family, wiped out.' He thought for a moment. 'Ortakoy, that was it, not far from Kumsal, I think.'

Daisy felt a cold shiver down her spine. It was almost unbelievable what these people suffered. 'I don't know much about those areas,' she told him, 'hardly anything. I know only of that poor family, relating to the museum.'

'So you know that what is now a museum used to be their home?'

'What exactly happened there?' she enquired. 'I have heard conflicting stories; that's why I must visit this place.'

The bus pulled up at a stop, and two people got off. When the bus resumed its journey, Namik explained. 'Well, two RAF officers witnessed the event. Thing is, they were powerless to intervene when the family were slaughtered. There was a landlady, or neighbour, who locked herself in the toilet, but she was also shot. The bullets were fired through the door and she would not have stood a chance.'

He went on to tell her about other houses, and how their doors were smashed down, how occupants were clubbed and beaten. He likened it to the Nazis, when they persecuted Jews.

'This must have taken a huge toll on the population around those parts,' said Daisy.

'I think about 160 were taken hostage that night,' he answered. 'All from Kumsal.'

'My God, were they ever found?'

'Oh, no; they must have died.' He remained quiet for some moments, before adding, 'Terrible things happened, Daisy. They were screaming in the streets, with children crying and men thrown to the ground. As for Greek Cypriot-controlled radio in Nicosia, they told many lies. Turkish troops, they said, had embarked on wholesale slaughter of Greek population. This not only encouraged Greek Cypriot militancy, but misinformed people like you.'

Daisy raised a finely arched brow.

'Well, not you exactly, but people in general. They issued statements, saying that, for fourth day running, Turkish fanatics attacked security forces, and Greek civilians!'

'But why do this?' she asked.

He spread his hands. 'To give us bad name, so we lose support from other countries. At the same time, making Greek blood hot about us. Know what I am saying?'

About half an hour later, Daisy walked into the 'Museum of Barbarism' alone, and the first thing to meet her eye were the photographs. Gruesome and appalling, the stark monochrome enlargements formed neat rows along every wall. Some prints were of Turkish Cypriots, shot in their homes, here in Kumsal and in the surrounding areas. Others were of people who'd been clubbed to death in the streets. One was of a soldier, his limbs missing, and captured on his face was the agony in which he'd died. In the blood-soaked earth where his body lay, one solitary boot brought home the hideous reality of it all.

Namik had stayed outside, not wanting to witness such things, and Daisy understood this after everything that had happened to his country.

All the same, at one point, Daisy had two minds whether to join Namik outside because she found one of these photographs the most disturbing of all. This was of a nine-year-old boy whose internal organs bulged from his wounds.

The inscription below the photograph, read: 'Shot with dumdum bullets while playing near the Greek sector in Nicosia.'

Slowly, she moved on, torn between getting her facts first hand and fleeing from what was once described as a house of horrors. Then, struggling with her emotions, she took a deep breath and decided she must stay.

About eight or nine people shuffled into a nearby room, and when Daisy followed she saw that they'd formed a semi-circle. She had thought that this was the bathroom, where most of the slaughter had taken place, but she was mistaken.

The reason why these people had formed a semi-circle was to view a glass showcase. Inside were household items which had belonged to the family. Among the items were faded pink towels, badly stained with blood, an assortment of shoes, including a few small ones, which had probably belonged to the couple's children. And, along with these, a blood-spattered robe.

A door had been left slightly open, and when Daisy tentatively pushed it further she found herself alone in the family bathroom. What she saw horrified her. The blood-spattered bathtub was so badly grazed by bullets that not much remained of the enamel surface. Though worse was the full-blown photo above the bath. This showed a mother and her three young sons, just as they were found. Their bodies had been piled into the bath; all had been shot. One child, whose face couldn't be seen, had an arm hanging pitifully over the side. The rest of the corpses stared up, their blood having splashed the tiled wall behind them.

A plaque beneath told Daisy that the children were aged between six months and seven years. These scenes were far worse that Daisy could have bargained for so she left the room and moved along the corridor. Here, there were many family snaps. They were taken just a few days before the massacre. Some of these photos were of the seven-year-old at his birthday party. There was a cake and colourful balloons. Another showed the children's father, who, the inscription read, was a Turkish major.

As Daisy was looking at these photos, Namik had decided to join her. He read the inscription himself. Afterwards, he said, 'That is the reason for all this. Him being a Turkish major. They were determined to take their revenge.'

All the walls were covered in small craters where the soldiers had opened fire, but Daisy tried not to look at the horrid mass on the ceiling, which, according to a printed card, were the remains of brain fragments.

The door next to the bathroom had been left open, and this too was punctured with shells, as was the toilet. On a shelf was a small denture, fallen from the mouth of the woman who'd sheltered here. There were also a pair of slippers and a bunch of keys, all a vivid reminder of what had taken place here.

'That poor lady did not stand a chance, did she?' Namik pointed out.

'It looks as if nobody did,' answered Daisy. Then, noting his glum face, she suggested they leave the museum to get some much-needed fresh air.

Namik readily agreed to this, and as he ushered Daisy from the premises a small group of people walked through the door.

Outside, Namik pulled out his cigarettes and lit one up. 'I tell you, Daisy, that place in there is terrible. They have to keep that museum anyway. It is our history; we must never forget it.'

I think we all agree with that,' said Daisy. 'And I have to remember to make notes, as it's the reason I came here.'

After, they made their way into Nicosia and looked for a café. It was a fine day and a few tables had been placed outside, and around these were the usual 'Van Gogh'-style chairs. After Namik had ordered some coffee, he returned to sit with Daisy.

Apart from locals, busy doing their daily shop, here and there, a group of soldiers strolled casually along, stopping now and then to check out the town's offerings. Also spotted were a couple of Asian men who were riding bicycles.

Daisy shuffled her chair closer to Namik. There was something she wanted to ask him, but until now had been reluctant to do so.

'What is it?' Namik enquired. 'You seem bothered about something.'

Daisy made sure nobody could hear them before she spoke. 'I suppose I am, but there are things I need to know, like the Bileklers and why they are so against your family.'

'You can ask me about anything, and I will tell you what I know.' He brushed her hand with his own.

Daisy didn't know how to start and she swallowed, ill at ease, as though Namik was suddenly a stranger, but she needn't have worried, because he guessed her thoughts. 'It is about my brother, isn't it?' he asked.

'Yes.' She looked at him squarely. 'But I was afraid of upsetting you.'

One corner of Namik's mouth turned up as he gave a brittle laugh. 'Upset me?' He shook his head, looking into the depths of his cup of black coffee. 'You could not upset me, Daisy. It wasn't you who killed my brother.'

She reached out for his hand. 'You mentioned once about Aygun's connection with Bilekler's daughter. It's about that.'

'Yes, her father was opposed from the start, but she disobeyed him. She knew Aygun would not be with his unit, so they met in secret.'

'A case of rich man, poor man?' said Daisy, 'I mean, Osman thinking he wasn't good enough.'

'Mostly, yes, but remember when I said it isn't easy courting a girl if your intentions are not honourable? Well, Aygun was too young at seventeen to think about marriage anyway, even if they had agreed. Still, he did love her, oh yes.' He gave a deep sigh. 'This is a funny country,' he admitted, 'and this goes for similar places. People are not free, especially young Muslim girls. No, our ways are not like it is in England. I know, because I have been there.' Namik turned to her. 'I like your way of life, Daisy.'

'I understand, but tell me more about that family.'

He lit another cigarette. 'Well, Aygun definitely planned to see Aisha that night, although he was due on duty, but I have already told you that, haven't I?' Namik let out a small laugh. 'My father said he used my aftershave, wanting to smell nice.'

Daisy gave some thought to this. 'So would you have both been on duty that night? Is that how it works?'

Namik shook his head. 'A few of us soldiers were sent elsewhere. But he definitely met that girl, because who would bother with the aftershave if they were off with their unit?' His face clouded briefly, before adding, 'Officially, Aygun should have been scattered along those mountain slopes I told you about. But we know different, have for a long time. It was all very strange, because his body was nowhere near there when he was found.'

'What do you mean?' asked Daisy. 'You mentioned something before, but nothing more was said about it, and I didn't like to ask too many questions. But, to be honest, I'd like to know more about the Bileklers. They were always guarded; something's not right there.'

'Well, whoever did that to Aygun, or wherever that took place, they must have taken his body to another area on that hillside. Yes, the soldiers would have been scattered around, but nothing like where Aygun was found. I mean, more remote, like.'

Daisy felt a shiver creep up her spine, and with trembling fingers dropped her cup noisily onto its saucer, which caused some of the coffee to splash onto the table.

'There were two others killed that night,' Namik went on. 'But they had been shot, and very close to where they were supposed to be. Anyway, apart from anything else, when my brother was found, his skull had been fractured, his face smashed in. And' – he paused briefly – 'there were other signs that did not add up.' Namik's hazel eyes narrowed, as he drew smoke deeper into his lungs from the stub of his cigarette.

She saw now why he felt this way. 'So you think that the Bileklers had a hand in this?'

'Well, what do you make of it?' he replied, bitterly.

Daisy shook her head. 'I don't really know. None of it makes sense, does it? No wonder you find it a mystery. Who wouldn't? Anyway.' She thought it wise to change the subject. 'Did you ever meet the girl? Aisha, wasn't it?'

'Yes, I did, and after my brother's death, she moved away as soon as she could. Ankara, yes, she moved there.'

'How did she manage that?' Wouldn't her parents have been protective, being a young girl?'

'One parent: her mother died when the children were quite young.'

A few moments passed while Daisy thought it through. 'So she ran away from an overpowering father?'

'When she was able, yes. She teaches now.'

Daisy remembered speaking with Fatma, on the bus that day, and she had wondered ever since why she had warned her against Hasan. All the same, it was out of character for the housekeeper to speak about her employees.

'When I lived with the Bileklers, I found Hasan troubled at times,' said Daisy. 'Perhaps losing his mother had some effect.'

'Maybe. I think he was about seven at the time. Some say she was not right here.' Namik tapped his temple. 'But my mother say different. I tell you sometime.'

'Wasn't your family living in Bogaz back then?' asked Daisy.

'Yes, and the Bileklers lived quite near. They had a proper house, not a makeshift hut like everyone else, you understand.'

For a while, they sat there, Namik in deep thought, Daisy wishing she could be of some help, but of course she couldn't.

CHAPTER

SEVEN

•

As THEY LEFT the café, they strolled along without talking. The town was quite busy, and especially now that many soldiers had found their way here. All were smartly attired in thick serge uniforms, which were ideal in the cooler months. But Daisy remembered last summer, when temperatures reached over a hundred degrees and they were still in the same outfits. She wondered at the time if those poor soldiers ever passed out in that heat. However, the weather hadn't reached those dizzy heights yet, although the troops still carried heavy holdalls and kitbags around the streets. The soldiers seemed to have swelled in numbers here in Nicosia, and for whatever reason were hanging around in small groups on street corners. Some of these lads looked barely old enough to be in military service.

Daisy had been looking at a bunch of young recruits, guessing rightly that they were Turkish soldiers. And, anyway, what else could they be with their pale olive skins, distinctive high cheek bones and shaven heads? These days, there were no Turkish Cypriot soldiers on the island. Instead, Northern Cyprus's president, Rauf Denktas, sent his army to help with the peacekeeping force.

Born in Paphos, and the son of a judge, Denktas had studied in England before finally settling in Turkey. Of strong character, and great charisma, he was well respected among Turkish Cypriot communities, and therefore known to be a good and trusted man.

There was no mistaking the younger soldiers' peers. Their set faces showed that they'd seen it all, their demeanour lacking the zeal and spirit of the new recruits.

As often happened, a Jeep would thunder through the busy streets, as one did now, and Daisy looked up to see it loaded with helmeted soldiers. 'I wonder where they're off to,' she enquired of Namik.

'I don't know, but sometimes they drop someone off to stand guard at sentry boxes.' He chuckled. 'What a boring job that is. I'm glad it's not me: they stand for hours! Anyway, come on, let us find that hotel. It has interesting views from the terrace!'

Ignoring the hotel lift, they walked in silence up to the top floor of the Merhaba hotel. During this time, Daisy took a sidelong glance at Namik, noting the set jaw. She thought it may be to do with the museum, bringing back all sorts of dark thoughts. If that were the case, she could well understand how he must have felt. Some of the things in that museum were enough to shock the boldest of men. As for herself, it was something she'd had to do. How else could she write with such honesty if she hadn't seen those awful photos for herself? As gruesome as they were, they bore proof of the evil events that had taken place in that village, as well as other such places.

On reaching the top floor, they found the lounge empty except for a young couple sitting in the restaurant area.

Namik walked over to the sliding glass doors, opened them and then stepped out onto the terrace. 'Do you see down there?' he said, some moments after Daisy had joined him. 'Cars everywhere, like little matchboxes.'

'Yes, I thought the same myself when I came last year.'

'I tell you what,' he said, his arms resting on the wall, which surrounded the terrace. 'This is the only place on the north side of Nicosia where you can relax in comfort.'

Taking in his attractive profile, Daisy felt a strong desire to be in his arms. 'You're right, and they have real leather seats in here. Did you notice?'

A soft warm breeze caught the voile curtains at the large glass doors, making them billow onto the terrace. Namik pulled himself free of one of these, and turned to look inside the restaurant. 'Yes,' he agreed, 'it is a nice place, and it gets very busy at certain times.'

Again Daisy wanted to reach out, pull him towards her, but guessed it would always be like this. Instead, she moved a fraction closer, wanting to show Namik that he'd always have her support.

Looking towards the hills, they saw the star and crescent, carved deeply and painted white. It was the work of the Turkish army, to cock a snook at the Greeks, supposedly. 'It looks impressive, doesn't it?' said Daisy. 'And how about the other side, beyond that cut-off line; see how affluent they are?'

Just visible were the green oil drums. Snaking across the border, they looked menacing.

Namik edged closer to Daisy. 'Like you say, the buildings are so different from our side, but they have the resources.'

Daisy looked first at him, then at the town below. Most shops here aimed at local residents. No hint of tourism. To say they were shabby was putting it mildly. Also, many were still boarded, owing to shell damage during the troubles. Previous owners of many lock-ups could no longer afford expensive goods. It was a vicious circle; trade was poor.

'The south gets plenty of help,' said Namik. 'If it was not for Turkey, we would have none at all.'

'I imagine that their own economy could suffer, if they continue helping you out,' put in Daisy. '

Surprisingly, Namik gave her hand a brief squeeze. 'Then who else will aid us? Many feel it was petty when other countries turned their back on us.'

'More tourism, that's what you need.'

Namik looked thoughtful, then said, 'I know, my darling, but what can we offer? Beautiful country, yes, but what else? Our government cannot build much, and there is plenty to do, I tell you. Financial difficulty, that is the problem.'

Walking to the corner of the terrace, he screwed up his eyes against the bright sunshine. 'Everyone goes to the south for their holidays, more commercialised, so I can see their point.'

'I know,' she agreed. 'America, other countries, including Britain, they all help them, and that is the big difference between the two sides. Well' – she sighed deeply – 'we can't stay here all day. There's a bus to catch, remember?'

Daisy's insides jerked. There was no mistaking the man walking towards her. Today, he was dressed in a silver-grey suit, although, because of the warmer weather, he carried his jacket. He was also wearing a homburg hat, different from Osman's usual style.

As he got closer, Daisy wondered if he'd put on more weight. She thought of ducking into a doorway, but Osman Bilekler had already seen them, his face having broken into a wide smile.

'Ah, Daisy, my good friend. We have not seen you for some time.' While he spoke, his arm came out as though barring her way. 'Where have you been hiding?'

Resentment built up in Daisy. Why should she tell him anything? However, sooner or later he'd find out. 'I'm staying in the village not far from you. But I'm surprised you haven't heard!'

Bilekler cleared his throat. 'I did,' he admitted, showing those long teeth. 'But you have not paid us a visit. Why is this? Have you grown tired of us?'

Feeling uneasy, Daisy swallowed, while the portly man used the silence to shift his gaze onto Namik, making it clear how he despised him.

But Namik did likewise, his eyes never leaving Bilekler's face as if daring the man to say something.

Daisy knew instinctively what Namik was thinking, because guilt was written all over the older man's face. And she'd seen that look in his eye before when he was hiding something. Namik had also told her that the Bileklers had never once shown any sympathy when his brother had died. After all, Aisha and Aygun had been close, even if their romantic association wasn't recognised by the girl's family. No, never, in all this time, had they expressed a word of condolence.

'We have been visiting the Museum of Barbarism.' Daisy said, breaking the silence.

Bilekler switched his gaze back to Daisy. 'And will all that barbarism be helpful to your writing?' he quipped.

'I am sure it will, and anything else she learns,' Namik taunted. Again they glared at each other, until, at last, Bilekler, who'd since lit up his cigar, blew a cloud of smoke into Namik's face.

Daisy and Namik were about to move on, but not before Bilekler threw his ace card. 'By the way, my dear, Hasan has been missing you. After all,' he paused briefly, 'you were quite close, weren't you? Anyway, a silly misunderstanding, and such a pity I think, seeing the way you felt about each other. But' – he looked up at the sky – 'I will take my leave. Such a fine day.'

They didn't see the smile playing at the corner of Bilekler's mouth as he moved away. And no time had been allowed for Daisy to hit back, contradict these allegations which Bilekler had vastly exaggerated.

Gathering herself together, Daisy cursed when Namik hurried ahead of her. She dashed after him, but a group of soldiers, spreading themselves across the pavement, slowed her pace. Trying to catch up, Daisy was filled with something she'd never felt before, and that was hatred. This wasn't just for the older man but for Hasan too. Both were as bad as the other, and that casual encounter had worked, because they would stop at nothing to keep her away from Namik.

Catching up once more with Namik, Daisy caught at his arm. 'If you believe what that man said, I'll have nothing to do with you. Anyway, you can see why he said those things. They hate us being together. They're afraid I'll learn too much!'

Namik stopped in his tracks. 'And why would they mind? That Hasan must be crazy about you, and why? Because he knows you return his feelings.'

Daisy saw the tear fall before he could brush it away. He carried on walking, and she, trying to match his stride, struggled to find the right words. 'Look, I was infatuated, but that was all.'

'You did not tell me.'

'There wasn't much to tell. When I told Hasan I was leaving Bellapais, we rowed.'

Namik glanced away. He couldn't bear to think of those two together.

'After that, Hasan became aggressive, begging me to stay.' Daisy had become breathless. 'But as you can see. I didn't want to, I just couldn't.'

Nothing seemed to persuade Namik otherwise, and shortly afterwards they were heading back to Kyrenia on the old dust-covered bus.

It was to be some days later that Namik had turned up. Contrite, he'd knocked at the door where Daisy was staying, asking to be forgiven. Of course he believed her; it was his own silly pride which had been hurt.

He was here now, asleep in her bed, and Daisy, having been awake for some time, looked across at him while he slept. He seemed relaxed now, with hardly a care in the world. She sighed. If only she could feel the same. She had tried not to show her true feelings but inwardly she felt tormented. This was the very reason she'd woken early, just like she did every morning. She had good cause too, to feel as she did. At any time they could encounter Hasan, or even Melanie Hampton. They could cause more trouble between herself and Namik. The woman was an ally of the Bileklers', and was so spiteful nothing would stop her trying to oust Daisy out of north Cyprus. She wanted her as far away from Hasan as possible. Apart from her jealousy over Hasan, there was surely something else bothering her. Daisy would dearly love to know what that was.

Now and then, Namik stirred, and, leaning across, Daisy brushed her lips against his. On a table close by were the remains of a bottle of white wine. Last night, Namik had slipped out while she'd been cooking, then returned half an hour later with the bottle wrapped in tissue paper. An Asian friend, already back in work, had given it, partly on loan, because Namik always repaid a favour.

Daisy had to smile. While Namik had opened the bottle, she'd wound up an old gramophone, belonging to the owners. On this, she'd put on an equally old record, one of a small collection found in a cupboard. It was the look on Namik's face when the needle kept jumping, admitting he'd never before seen such a contraption.

CHAPTER
EIGHT

•

With Namik looking after his uncle's restaurant, and therefore happy in himself, Daisy worked with more vigour. It helped too, that all was well between them. Apart from that incident with Bilekler, in Nicosia, no more ugly rumours as yet had reached Ozankoy, least of all to Namik. Maybe they wouldn't. Melanie Hampton and the Bileklers had most probably given up all that nonsense, and moved on to more interesting things.

The infatuation with Hasan had been real enough. Most women would have fallen for a man such as that; those melting green eyes, the attention, and that rare quality of not realising how handsome he is. But looks alone weren't enough. Beneath the surface lay a vicious streak and Daisy had not a shred of feeling for him now.

As for Melanie Hampton, how could she run down those poor animals then drive off like that? This proved she had no regard for living creatures, or anything if they weren't of any benefit to herself.

Daisy thought of everything Namik had told her concerning his brother's death; the way he'd explained it, his injuries and so forth were something of a mystery. Was it possible that Melanie Hampton knew anything about this? She could be as deeply involved as the Bileklers.

On another visit to Kyrenia newspaper archives, Daisy learnt more about the troubles between the two opposing sides.

On 26 May 1965, Archbishop Makarios made a public speech, one of many he made throughout Cyprus. Addressing a crowd at Rizokarpasso, he declared: 'Either the whole of Cyprus is to be united with Greece, or it will become a holocaust. The road to fulfilment of national aspirations may be full of difficulties, but we shall reach the goal which is enosis, alive or dead.'

But, soon after making these threats, he no longer believed that enosis could be achieved by force. He then devoted his energies to winning over the nations of the world to his point of view.

Makarios intended to make life as unpleasant as possible for Turkish Cypriots, hoping they would emigrate to another country or bow to his will.

Even the freely elected Turkish Cypriot representatives were ousted from office. And when in July 1965 they attempted to make their way into the House of Representatives they were informed that 'Unless the Turkish deputies agreed to the abrogation of the constitution, and endorsed the unconstitutional laws enacted in their absence by their Greek counterparts, their return would be prevented by force!'

However, because of this, Turkish Cypriots were not recorded in the State Register of Persons. This would blight their future in many ways, one being that they were unable to obtain passports.

There was something else in those notes that struck Daisy. The same newspaper stated that: 'No Greek Cypriot was prosecuted for crimes committed against Turkish Cypriots.'

When Daisy had read enough, she folded the broadsheet, thanked the man in charge of the archives, and left the building with plenty to think about.

When she arrived home, Daisy pondered on something else. Surely Turkish law was different. If someone took a person's life, wouldn't they be prosecuted? And what if someone had been brutally murdered, but as yet not found out? Would the law rest before the killer was caught?

But Namik stood by his word. He knew how his brother had died. Before burial, the whole family had seen Aygun's injuries, injuries that had nothing to do with a Greek bullet, or anything else of that nature. Except for a couple of others, who'd been shot, the rest of the soldiers in his unit had stayed safe on those hills that night. Poor Aygun, of course, had been found nowhere near the designated patrol area.

Lack of evidence was the reason why Namik's family had kept quiet. But once he had said bitterly, 'The Bileklers are too powerful, Daisy. Who is going to believe us if we accuse them?'

For the rest of that day, Daisy struggled to write up her notes, but visions of a young Aygun, remembered from a photo on his mother's wall, dominated her thoughts.

The girl looked up as the doorbell tinkled, then carried on typing until the carriage stopped. Smiling at Daisy, she asked her name before calling to a man in the back room of the car rental. An assortment of gold neck chains gleamed against the girl's olive skin, and her lacquered nails shimmered as she deftly touched the keys. Behind her, a man aged about forty made his way through a multi-coloured plastic curtain. He grinned at Daisy, showing good teeth, then spoke to the typist in Turkish. He waited while she typed an invoice.

When it was ready, he pushed this across the desk towards Daisy, then produced a set of keys from a row of hooks behind him. He gave just a brief glance at her driving licence, before saying, 'There is a little problem, Miss Collins. You follow, I show.'

Outside, a red Mini Cooper with white flashing along the side was parked at the kerb, gleaming like new in the morning sunshine. 'What is the problem?' queried Daisy.

The man opened the passenger door. 'Please,' he said, gesturing towards the seat.

Daisy frowned, ignored this, and then walked to the other side, sliding behind the wheel.

'Not there,' he said quickly, indicating the passenger seat once more. 'It will be easier if I drive.'

Reluctantly, Daisy shifted, and he hurriedly took her place. 'This is the problem,' he explained, his hands locked around the wheel. 'Not too bad, but not good. We change car, I am afraid. Is only mile along road, the garage.'

'Dangerous, you mean?' asked Daisy, eyeing him gravely.

'Perhaps, but you can never be sure,' he answered, giving her a sidelong glance. 'But better safe, eh? We do not want our customers having an accident, so better I drive as I know how to handle the car.'

At first, Daisy thought she'd been dreaming, but soon realised she wasn't. Clutching at the bed cover, it felt rough, unfamiliar. There was a strange smell, too, a mixture of fly repellent and lavender. The odour wafted strongly through her senses. The pains in her head were unbearable, and, lifting herself from the pillow, large objects appeared to spin in circles.

She tried moving her head from side to side, hoping to rid herself of the shooting pains which had caused her neck to go into spasm. Daisy felt quite dizzy as waves of nausea swept through her. Where was she? Whose place was it? And what was she doing here?

Her mouth was unbearably dry, but when she tried to swallow she found it impossible. Then, with much effort, Daisy stretched out an arm, and found that the bed had a brass headboard. She grabbed this, and, although her body felt leaden, she was at last able to pull herself up. It was some minutes before she was able to get her bearings, and was greatly relieved that the nausea was subsiding.

On the wall, ahead of her, was an unframed picture of two small children, a girl and boy. And directly below, on a tiny table, tall plastic bulrushes threatened to overbalance a small ceramic vase. Ahead of her was a small window, but this only let in a thin chink of daylight because of an ill-fitting curtain which had been stretched across.

Daisy thought she heard a cracking sound. This was followed by a sweet smell like pine or cedar. Yes, that was it. Someone had lit a fire in another room.

The door was being opened slowly, and now she smelt something else. This was more intense, spicy and very familiar. A moment later, Daisy, having kept her eye on the door, was startled to see Hasan standing there!

She was about to speak, but he disappeared, then shortly after he returned with a glass of water.

'Here,' he offered, 'or would you prefer coffee?'

Daisy's hand trembled as she reached out for the water, but was unsure if she'd grasped hold of the glass because her hands still felt numb. 'The last thing I remember was the road leading to Bellapais,' she uttered. 'But we're not there, are we?'

Hasan studied her. 'No, not Bellapais. And I am sorry, but I could not let you stay in Ozankoy, or anywhere near that family. It is better this way, safer.'

'Safer with you, you mean?'

'Resign yourself Daisy. I cannot let you go now, you must understand.'

Daisy recoiled when he sat on the bed. 'You have no right keeping me here. Anyway, where are we?'

'It belongs to me. Don't worry. The family are in Turkey for a while. We keep an eye on it for them.'

'And the prisoner in it too?' she chided.

'A prisoner?' He smiled. 'No, you are wrong. You must not think of yourself as a prisoner. I will look after you.'

Willing herself to get up, Daisy tried to swing her legs from the bed. 'Then why aren't we at your home instead of here? Who are you afraid of?'

Hasan walked to the window and lifted the curtain. 'Fatma,' he answered softly. 'She is not a bad woman, but even the best people are not to be trusted.' He turned to face her. 'Like your friends in that village. They are all the same, out to cause mischief.'

Daisy knew now that Hasan was afraid. He wasn't as popular as she'd first believed; he had many enemies. Well, if ever she got out of here, she would be hard put to hold her own tongue. Everyone would know what had happened to her, and that would make things even worse for the Bileklers.

She took a few gulps of the water. 'Anyway, why am I really here? Why this particular place?'

He turned to face her. 'I will tell you, but you have to be patient. There are some things that you would not understand.'

'I understand one thing,' she said, her eyes blazing. 'You had me drugged. How else do you explain how I got here?'

He looked at her for a few moments before he spoke, then said, 'Sometimes we do things for the best. For the right reasons. As for my driver, at the car rental, he knew what he must do.'

There couldn't be a right reason, not for Daisy, for she was beginning know how his mind worked. Everything Hasan did was for his own purpose. He would stop at nothing if he thought someone was on to him for all his misdeeds. She looked across at him as he made to leave the room. Who was he really afraid of? She doubted it was just Fatma. Then what about Namik? This must be the real reason Hasan had arranged for her to be brought here: he was nervous of what she might learn had she stayed in that village. But Daisy was worried, fearful for her well-being, for how long would she be kept here? She wondered also if anyone would learn of her whereabouts. Not Namik, surely. How would he ever guess she had been kidnapped?

Namik rapped loudly on the door where Daisy had been lodging. It had been a few days now since she'd been seen, and the woman who owned the house was unable to offer any help. Well, he hoped that, wherever Daisy had been, she was now back home. But during her absence he'd been extremely worried, his insides tied in knots, and because of this his new job at his uncle's restaurant had been neglected.

Standing back from the house, he looked up at the windows and called out. 'Daisy, it is me, Namik. Why don't you answer the door?'

Where was she? And why had she not been in touch? There were a couple of hours to spare before opening the restaurant, and he had hoped to see Daisy, find out if everything was all right between them.

Namik swore under his breath. 'Damn, where the hell was she?' Wherever she had taken herself off to, surely she would have been back by now. He looked around and found the area strangely deserted. Well, what did he expect? With a modern house surrounded by a couple of hectares of private land, it was bound to be quiet.

Irritated, he finally walked away, failing to understand why Daisy hadn't even called in at the restaurant. It was possible she had gone on somewhere to research her book, but that was no excuse, either.

But soon after, Namik made his way into Kyrenia, as he remembered Daisy saying she'd been thinking of hiring a car, but the man he spoke to wasn't much help. He said that a Miss Collins had hired one of their cars but had not yet returned the vehicle. It was for one day only, he told Namik, so everyone at the office had wondered what had gone wrong. They had considered an accident. Or that the car may have broken down. The man had then said how absurd that was, because they would have most definitely heard something.

Namik left the office and walked along by the harbour. He hadn't liked the man, thinking him a shifty character, and the man hadn't seemed put out by the fact that the car hadn't been returned. Yes, thought Namik, it was all very strange, especially as the man had added jokingly that they were not short of cars at that moment. As for a probable accident, how utterly ridiculous! The police would have been quick to inform the car rental of that without delay!

Namik was still mulling all this over while sitting in one of the bars in Kyrenia. There was still an hour to go before opening up his place, though he had to admit he didn't feel much like it.

Sitting there with a beer, he realised that the music being played on the sound system was a favourite of his and Daisy's. The door was open, and, looking out, he didn't see much going on; in fact, the harbour looked rather deserted. Suddenly, he felt very alone and a wretched emptiness swept over him, a feeling he'd never before experienced.

His mouth curled in a bitter smile. He had changed. Once thought of as tough, independent, never relying on anybody, he was now a different man, at least where his emotions were concerned. Daisy was partly the reason for this. Supposing something had happened to her. Something really terrible. She'd been gone but a few days, but no knowing where she was, it seemed like a lifetime. Namik was filled with sheer panic, and in those moments he knew that it could be a very long time before he saw Daisy again. No, worse than that, Daisy may never come back, most probably because she was no longer alive!

Now, feeling even more downhearted, Namik picked up his beer, gazing into the depths of its golden colour. Since leaving the army, he'd always worked hard, willing to do most things: farmhand, labourer, general lackey, waiter and now running his own business, in fact anything, which got him by.

But there were times when only one job had been going and he'd bluffed his way in, knowing others were in line, better qualified. Still, he'd never wronged anybody, or done them harm. As he'd once told Daisy, during the troubles, when Greek Cypriots invaded their villages, they had to do what they could as breadwinner. He'd reminded her that their fathers were not always at home, because either they were away fighting, or, as many had done, had taken themselves to a remote mountainside in the dead of night, in fear of their lives.

Swallowing the remains of his beer, the ache in Namik's heart was stronger than ever. So, Daisy had taken the car on Monday, with the intention of returning it that same day, but had not done so. Well, it was now Wednesday, and getting pretty late, and still there was no sign of her. None of this added up, and it was so unlike Daisy. There was no way she would have stayed away that long, not without word.

Crushing his cigarette stub into an ashtray, Namik glanced up at the clock. It was six twenty. In another ten minutes he'd be opening the restaurant.

The restaurant, named 'the Turtle's Rest', on behalf of the creatures found in those areas, was situated opposite the ruined castle. It was close by that Namik happened to bump into Mehmet. 'Ah, I do not suppose you have time for a drink,' said his friend.

'I haven't,' Namik answered despondently. He searched his pockets for another cigarette.

'You should not smoke too much,' Mehmet told him. 'You know it is not good. Remember what that doctor said? Anyway, what is with the glum face?'

'It is Daisy, that is what's wrong,' Namik snapped. 'And, if I want to smoke, I will.'

A frown creased Mehmet's brow. 'Daisy, you say. What is the problem?'

Namik looked away, his voice low. 'I don't know if there is a problem, but…'

'Are you saying you have not seen her? Though maybe you do not wish to say.'

'Sunday, I saw her then, but on Monday she seemed to have vanished. She told me she'd like to visit Famagusta sometime, and maybe she did, but, wherever it was, she has not returned.'

Mehmet looked thoughtful. 'Monday, you say? I saw her; they left early.'

Namik's features sprang to life. '"They"? Who's "they"?'

'I was buying a newspaper. It was early, around nine, I think.' Mehmet fingered his gold medallion. 'I saw a man at the wheel of the car, along by the Izmir hotel. Yes, I'm sure.'

'Did you notice the car?' Namik became alert.

'Oh yes. A red Mini Cooper. Almost new, I would say.'

'Anything else?'

It seemed an age before Mehmet answered, then suddenly he said, 'Yes, I remember. One side of the car had white markings. A chevron design.' His cheeks glowed imparting this knowledge.

For Namik there was a glimmer of hope, something to go on, for he couldn't rely on the man in the car rental. Something about him didn't ring true. He'd see if that man's story tallied with Mehmet's.

For the first time in days, there was a hint of a sparkle in Namik's eyes, and when he left his friend he felt a lot brighter than he did earlier.

Daisy had counted every minute of the four days she'd been cooped up with Hasan. He'd hardly left her side, and during that time she had often fought off his unwanted advances.

True, she had her own room, but there was no key. This meant that little privacy was afforded. Without warning, he would often enter her room.

With no change of clothes, Daisy felt unclean, and the need to bathe was even more crucial. Even this became a battle, seeing as the bathroom also had no lock.

Not that the immersion heater worked to order, so back and forth with boiling kettles was a daily grind. She had again questioned Hasan about the man in the car hire, and how he knew she'd be renting a car, but Hasan hadn't been forthcoming, except that the man there was an associate of his father's. After that, it wasn't hard to work out how she'd been taken off in that car. She had popped in there previously to make enquiries, and that man had obviously been given orders, on account of the odds of her eventually hiring a car.

There was a radio in the kitchen, and Daisy, having found World Service, was listening to this when Hasan made an appearance. For a few moments he stood watching her, then, stepping closer, he stroked her hair. 'Daisy, why are you so afraid of me?' he asked. 'I would do nothing to harm you, you know that.'

As always, she had flinched from his touch. 'Then why keep me here?'

He ignored this, and walked across to the dresser, where an assortment of crockery lined long shelves. He picked up a plate, grimaced on seeing the dust, and then returned it to its place.

'I know you are used to better things than this,' he said. 'Me too, but we have little choice.'

'You do,' she argued, getting to her feet. 'You could let me go, then you could return to your life of luxury.'

'No, no, I could not. I could never let you go,' he stated, shaking his head. 'And it is unwise to take you to my home.'

If she could choose, Daisy knew it would be the Bellapais residence. This small stone house where they were staying was a desolate abode. There was only a small area of concrete at the front. And, beyond this, all that could be seen was a rough terrain of scrubland.

'Someone will find out,' she said, defiantly. 'Namik, he will be looking for me.'

'And why should he do that?' he mocked, a wicked glint in his eye. 'He feels nothing for you. It is all a sham, hoping for information concerning that brother of his.'

Daisy stared at him. 'How do you know anything of his feelings, our feelings?'

Striding across the room, Hasan caught Daisy by the shoulders, his grip tightening. 'When I think of him holding you, I cannot sleep some nights. You have lain in his arms, haven't you?'

'Namik and I are in love,' said Daisy, battling to free herself. 'And he isn't using me as you seem to think.'

'I hate that man,' he snarled. 'Maybe I will have someone take care of him. It would give me great pleasure to see the last of him. That family have been a constant pain in my life.'

She at last freed herself from his grasp. 'Because you killed his brother!' she accused. There, she had said it. The words she thought she'd dare not say were out.

He stared at her, his jaw twitching, and Daisy felt her courage slipping. Had she gone too far? She hoped Hasan hadn't meant what he'd said about Namik.

'You know, Daisy, you could be right.' He began to laugh, a high-pitched sound bordering on hysteria. 'If it's the truth you want, you ask Hasan,' he added, crooking a thumb towards his chest.

Daisy didn't think he'd been drinking. She would have smelt alcohol when he'd breathed into her face a moment ago. Though why was he behaving like this? As she looked at him, she could hardly believe he was the same man she'd met the day she'd arrived at his villa.

She hadn't, of course, known him at the time, but now she was certain he was capable of anything. Apart from young Aygun, had he killed others he'd wanted to be rid of?

If she was afraid before, Daisy was more so now. Would Hasan carry out his threat, kill again? And what about his father, Osman Bilekler? How far would he go to rid someone from his life? It would appear that anything was possible with these two men, as it had become quite clear they were used to getting what they wanted.

She walked over to the window and looked out across the scrubland. How was anyone to find her here? Who knew of this isolated place? In that moment, Daisy believed she'd never get out of this place, and she was suddenly filled with utter terror.

CHAPTER
NINE

•

Fatma had been home some time now, having finished work at the Bileklers'. She'd eaten her evening meal, and gone about her own chores, but had to sit when the pain from her calloused feet caused her to wince. Being on her feet all day, then walking just under a mile, aggravated the condition.

Her old stone cottage, one of a few, was situated within walking distance from Bellapais Abbey, but her employer hadn't seen fit to improve any of these dwellings. The residents here thought it a great pity considering this area was one of outstanding beauty. However, Fatma, like the other residents, kept their interiors spotless.

Fatma walked painfully over to the radio, turning it low because she'd heard a noise outside. She listened, recognising the pop-pop of a motorcycle. Whoever it was had turned off the engine now, and she tried to think of anyone she knew who had a motorcycle.

It was six years since Fatma had become a widow, but, living on her own, she wasn't nervous. Such things as break-ins were unheard of. As for someone beating up middle-aged ladies, it wasn't known, at least not since all the troubles, when people were turned from their homes.

From the window she saw that the lights on the scooter had been switched off. Still, there was enough light from her kitchen window to fall across the dark clothed figure, but she didn't recognise the man.

The man, sitting astride the machine, was combing his fingers through a head of thick curls. He turned when the window creaked open. 'Who is it?' called Fatma, through the night air. 'What do you want?'

He swung from the scooter and called softly back. 'Are you Fatma Bartu?'

She nodded, and he edged forwards. 'It is about Daisy, Daisy Collins. I want to speak with you.'

Dropping the net curtain, Fatma walked slowly to the door. 'So why do you come to me? Who are you?' she asked abruptly.

'I'm a friend of Daisy's. My name is Namik, and I live in Ozankoy. Perhaps you know my family, the Guvens?'

Fatma's whole body tensed. Then, seeing Namik's obvious distress, she opened the door wider. 'Better come inside,' she told him. 'Cannot talk here.'

Namik looked towards the scooter, borrowed from a friend, and then followed Fatma inside. He was tired after his day at work, although he'd left earlier tonight. Still, what with busy lunchtimes, and evenings, the fatigue showed.

A chair was offered, but he declined this, saying he just wanted to get the matter dealt with. 'Anyway,' he went on, 'nobody seems to know of Daisy's whereabouts, so I wondered if you knew anything.'

Falling wearily into her only armchair, Fatma ignored this, and, looking across at him, narrowed her eyes. 'Ah, but I think I have seen you before. In Ozankoy, the local butcher's shop, that is it.'

'Yes, it is near my home. My mother buys our lamb there. It is the best.'

'Yes,' she answered, 'his own freshly slaughtered baby lamb.'

Namik didn't want small talk, just facts. 'You work for the Bileklers, don't you?' There was urgency in his voice.

A look of annoyance settled across Fatma's features. She didn't want to discuss her employers, but the man looked troubled. For a brief moment she pondered on the son she had lost. He was eighteen years old when her neighbour's house had been stormed during the troubles. The boy was with them, and killed along with the whole family.

Fatma dabbed at her eye. 'I have worked for the Bileklers for a long time; they have been most kind.'

Namik stepped closer. 'Some may not agree with you about that. What about Bilekler's son, can you say the same about him?'

She shifted uneasily. 'I do not always see Mr Hasan,' she said evasively. 'His business takes him away. Anyway,' she added sharply, 'how did you know where I live?'

'That does not matter, but has Daisy been back to see you these past days? Pay a visit?' Even as he spoke he doubted that was likely, owing to the reasons she left.

'No, she has not, but it is not my place to question why.' Fatma had risen from her chair. 'All I know is that Mr Hasan was very fond of Daisy. That I am sure of, so, please, I have nothing more I can tell you.'

Fatma's mind was on her good fortune. She relied on her job, and, there being few, was thankful. It brought her the little extras she would otherwise not have, especially when her poor late husband had been unable to work.

All this time Namik's mind had been working overtime. How many times was he going to hear that, about Hasan's fondness for Daisy? Perhaps there was more to it than Daisy had let on. Namik cursed himself for thinking along those lines, and wanted to believe the best in Daisy, but he wished she'd get in touch, put his mind at rest. Nevertheless, the thought of that man at the wheel of that car, with Daisy beside him, was difficult to erase, and he couldn't even guess where they had been going.

'I would like you to go now,' said a weary Fatma. 'You can see yourself out.'

'I hope you are not hiding anything from me, Mrs Bartu,' said Namik, pointing a finger.

Fatma turned away, unable to look at him, but was unaware how ashamed he'd felt for his rudeness.

He was at the door. 'I am sorry,' he stated humbly, 'but I will find her. Believe me I will.' As he left the house he struggled to convince himself of that.

In a small lock-up, in the village of Ozankoy, Namik peered down at the trestle table, worn smooth now after years of use. He was examining the post that Ibrahim, muhtak and general job man, had already bought back from Kyrenia post office. Ibrahim kept the letters in neat rows, fanned out so as to be easily identified. Eventually, three letters turned up for Daisy, and after a quick scan Namik put them in his pocket.

Ibrahim had been sorting through another bag, and,

tipping them out, began to do the same to these. He glanced round. 'You have found some then?' he said.

'Yes, and here's another.' Namik plucked this from the latest pile.

Ibrahim, his shock of white hair neatly groomed, looked sideways at his friend. 'No luck then? Still no trace of her?'

Without looking up, Namik shook his head.

'You tried her place again, in the village?'

'What do you think? Anyway, nobody has seen her, and somehow I don't think they will!'

'Nonsense! Anyway, how about some coffee?' suggested Ibrahim, chucking the canvas mailbag to one side.

Namik almost snatched the cigarette from the packet which was offered to him. 'How is the bar coming?' he enquired after lighting up. It wasn't the uppermost thought on his mind.

Ibrahim grimaced. 'So-so. It will pick up later, eh.'

The bar, situated in Ibrahim's ramshackle garden, had been running for a few years. In good weather locals gathered here, where a few high-backed chairs were placed around a curved bar which he'd built. Customers had the use of the outside toilet, which was the only one on the property. It was unclear if a licence had been granted for selling alcohol, or indeed if one had been applied for, but Ibrahim was on good terms with local authorities, and a blind eye may have been turned.

The small copper pot had boiled over, causing the thick, treacle-coloured liquid to spill onto the little stove. Grabbing an old rag, Ibrahim removed the pot. 'Anything on the car hire?' he asked.

Namik exhaled a lungful of smoke, tapping his cigarette against a tin ashtray. 'They say she still hasn't returned, and

I believe them. I tell you what. There is something they're not saying. I strongly believe that the man in there may be a friend of the Bileklers'. I don't trust him one bit.'

Sipping his hot coffee, Namik noticed the ever-increasing drink supply on the stone ledge above the long trestle. 'I'll tell you something else. The man she drove off with, I bet he's the same one I spoke to!' He paused, his brow furrowed in deep lines. 'To be truthful, I don't know what to think.'

Ibrahim's thick dark brows drew together. 'What about the Bileklers' house? Checked that yet?'

Namik shook his head. 'I could not get near. Bloody animals, four of them, maybe more. Barking, barking. Dobermanns, I think. But I have spoken to Fatma.' He sighed. 'I don't know, but I think she's afraid.'

'Why?'

'Don't you see?' Namik put in quickly. 'She has everything to be afraid of. The Bileklers own all those properties. Where would she go if they threw her out?'

There wasn't much Ibrahim could say, but, walking to the door soon after, Namik turned to him. 'If I see Melanie Hampton, I'll make her talk,' he warned.

An owl hooted from somewhere nearby, and, as Hasan let in the dark clad figure, he showed his wrath. 'Why are you here?' he hissed.

Melanie Hampton shed her jacket. 'It's Guven's son. He's looking for me.'

Hasan pushed her roughly into the room. 'Keep your voice down,' he hissed again. 'Anyway, you have no right here.'

'Where else should I go?' she exploded.

'What about Richard? Why aren't you at home with him?'

A look of sheer hatred showed on Melanie's features. 'You know how I feel about him.'

'Do calm yourself.' He took a deep breath. 'If anyone questions you, you know nothing about this place. Do you hear?'

He paced the room. Melanie's arrival had unnerved him. He knew from past experience how weak she was. Under pressure, she would cave in like a frightened rabbit. Not that he'd ever give her the chance, but who knew with her temperament?

Aware of her feelings for him, Hasan reluctantly made a move towards Melanie, but just in time stopped himself. He couldn't do it, force himself to show affection, not now after Daisy.

Melanie had watched him, waiting for his arms to enfold her, but his actions had deeply disappointed. 'You are silly, you know.' She tossed her head towards the small flight of stairs. 'Nobody could care for you the way I do.'

The thought of the two of them together made him squirm. 'That finished long ago. Though I am fond of you,' he lied.

She may have been most things, but never a fool. 'Fond, yes, I've settled for that, haven't I? Not any more, though; I have some pride left.'

'We cannot put back the clock, Melanie; it is too late,' he declared. 'Anyway, we have to be careful.'

'We!' she cried, her voice rising. 'If I remember, it was you who lashed out that night.'

'You remember too much,' he scorned. 'You were also there, and as much to blame.'

She changed the subject. 'Why don't you get rid of her?' she drawled.

'Get rid of Daisy? What do you mean?'

'Anything, surely you can think of something.'

'She would not leave Cyprus, if that is what you mean. She claims to be in love with that… that boy.'

'I've never seen you so obsessed about anything, or anybody.'

'I need her,' he said quietly, while averting his eyes.

'Well, she doesn't want you. It's best she's got out of the way.'

Hasan sprang at her, grabbing her wrists. 'Kill her, you mean?'

Her eyes narrowed. 'Why not? You've never hesitated before.'

'That was different, an accident. I set out to warn that Guven boy, frighten him into leaving my sister alone.'

'Are you sure? I'll always remember that look in your eyes. You were crazed, out of your mind that night.'

He slackened his grip. 'Leave this house at once. It was a risk coming here.'

She rubbed her wrists. 'But not before I say me piece. First, you knew I loved you, but you never really felt the same. I did as you asked that night, masquerading as your sister.' Her scarlet lips twisted. 'I did it because I loved you.'

A slight smile started at the corner of Melanie's mouth, followed by shrill laughter. 'That's a joke. I see it now.'

'Careful, you fool,' warned Hasan. 'She will hear you!'

'Do I care?' she asked mockingly. 'Melanie Howard-Coberg, the Cobergs of Georgia. Do you know, I was someone until I came here. Walking into a room, I could command attention; people would sit up.' She paused to light up a cigarette. 'Say what you want, but I think you meant to kill that boy.'

Daisy had heard most of what had been said. Hardly daring to breathe, she'd had her ear to a gap in the door. Slowly, she made her way to the bed. That was it then. It had come to her first hand. Hasan had killed Aygun. But where had that happened? It certainly hadn't been where his body had been found, Namik had been certain about that.

Somewhere close by, Daisy heard a car start up, then the swish of tyres. It must have been Melanie Hampton. She was a wicked-minded woman, but no worse than the man downstairs who was keeping her prisoner in this isolated cottage.

A door shut, close to her own. Hasan must have turned in. She felt desperately thirsty, but if she crept downstairs to the bathroom she was sure to be heard. The last thing she wanted was to disturb Hasan. His unwanted advances were wearing her down.

Outside, in the night sky, clouds scurried across an almost full moon. Watching this, Daisy's thoughts turned yet again to Namik. How long was he safe before someone was sent to get him? Had he been to her lodgings? And finding she wasn't there, gone on to the Bileklers' residence to ask if they'd seen her? He'd never find this place. It was too remote, and who would tell him she'd been taken away?

Daisy wondered how long she'd be here. The occupants wouldn't be away forever, so what was the plan?

Another thought struck Daisy. If Namik thought she'd gone off willingly, would he even bother to look for her?

Something bordering on a panic attack gripped Daisy. She could barely breathe, while her lungs seem to cave in at her efforts. Her emotions were spinning out of control, and it felt as though she'd never be able to function normally again. She didn't get to drink anything that night, but lay awake until at last, as dawn broke, she fell into an uneasy slumber.

The man at the car hire had made a fatal mistake. And, if Hasan had known, he would have dealt with him in no uncertain manner. For outside the office, parked at the kerb, the red Mini Cooper, with its white flash markings, had Namik burst through the office door with an angry scowl on his face.

There was only one person in here, the same man as before. He glanced up briefly when he heard the door, then pretended to busy himself. 'I haven't much at the moment,' he mumbled. 'March is the holiday season, you understand.'

'No?' answered Namik. 'What about the car outside?'

The man's brown eyes darted towards the door. 'That one?' He shook his head. 'I am sorry, but it isn't ours.'

'But you used it to take a customer for a ride,' said Namik, unable to keep his voice steady.

The man spread his hands. 'I don't understand. You say I took someone in that car?'

'You were seen,' Namik cut in. 'A British lady, Daisy Collins, came here to hire a car. She has not been seen since.'

Perspiration showed on the man's brow. He turned, flicked the switch on the cooling fan, then opened the drawer of a metal filing cabinet. He spent some moments shuffling among papers.

Namik's patience was running low. 'Perhaps you have no records of this.'

'We always keep records. But you are right. I cannot find this one.'

Namik held his gaze.

'Ah, yes,' the man edged. 'I remember, I have spoken to you before. She came in here like you said, a pretty young lady. Let me see, it was about…'

'I know when it was, but where did you take her?'

It was plain Namik was getting nowhere. He waited and waited, but all he could hear were the mournful sounds of a man's voice echoing loudly from the nearby mosque.

'You cannot fob me off,' he warned at last. 'You were seen, I have a witness. Anyway, why do you tremble? It is very warm in here.'

The man swallowed hard. 'A witness? Are you saying that somebody in this office knew the girl who came in here?'

'Exactly that.' Namik stood for some while staring at the man, who seemed to have suddenly been struck dumb. But he wasn't about to leave it at this. Now he had started his search for Daisy, he would not stop until he found her!

'You should eat something, Daisy. Otherwise you will lose that beautiful figure.' Hasan was sitting at the kitchen table reading a newspaper.

Daisy had just walked into the room, and noticed that Hasan had already eaten breakfast, but didn't think she could manage any. Still, she had lost a few pounds; the waistband on her jeans proved that. Her shirt, too, appeared ill-fitting.

On the table was the traditional flatbread, rose petal preserve, and a bowl of fresh fruit. Daisy wondered if somebody had brought the provisions here or if Hasan himself had been out.

He pushed a knife and plate towards her. 'Try to eat,' he told her. He glanced around at his surroundings, then let out huge sigh. 'I suppose, like myself, you are tired of this place. Personally, I need more space. How about you?'

Daisy stared at him. 'But I thought you said…'

'These people will be back soon,' he interrupted. 'It will be better, I think, if we moved back to my home.'

She had been pouring herself some coffee. 'You said you were afraid of Fatma, in case she talked.'

'Yes, I did say that. But I have nothing to be afraid of, have I, Daisy? And, anyway, I will not allow one of the servants to rule my life. What was I thinking of moving out of my own home? No.' He cast Daisy a sly look. 'Nobody gets the better of me. Any hint of trouble concerning my private affairs, and that person or persons will be dealt with.'

He was watching her closely. Did he think she may have overheard that conversation that night? It was a veiled warning, whichever way you looked at it.

If they did leave here, it would be better than this, thought Daisy. It was like being a caged animal, confined to the minimum of space, especially as she was unable to feel the fresh air. But, apart from this, she hadn't been able to get Namik from her thoughts. Was he still alive? She sniffed away the tears that had sprung up, but not before Hasan had seen them.

'It is Namik, isn't it?' he said angrily. 'Well, your tears are wasted. He will not be looking for you.'

'What have you done?' she demanded.

Hasan couldn't help himself. He sprang from the table in a jealous rage, although he ignored her question. 'Why are you so hung up on him? What can he possibly offer you?'

'Money isn't everything,' she told him. 'But since all this, everything you've done, I certainly don't trust you. Or Melanie Hampton for that matter.'

He grabbed her roughly. 'So, you did hear us! Listen, that woman is crazy. And she drinks too much.' He spoke softly now. 'She is jealous of my feelings for you. That is why she said those things.'

Daisy knew what she'd heard, though she'd best hold her tongue. Her life could well depend on it.

It was only the second week of March, and any cold weather had now become a distant memory. Namik was feeling the heat, and, dressed in a cotton shirt, he'd rolled the sleeves to the elbow. He had not long arrived in Famagusta, and, shading his eyes from the strong sunlight, he looked up at the walls of the old monument with more than a touch of bitterness running through him. For these were peppered with shell holes, so numerous it was amazing they were still standing. The fortifications, built to keep out marauding armies and part of Famagusta's proud heritage, had taken a thorough hammering.

There were many such as this. Ancient buildings, all built in the same rosy hues, and these too had fallen prey to invading armies, though their ramparts still remained.

A close friend was looking after the restaurant, but Namik had been there for the lunch period, and had planned to be back for the evening session. He'd borrowed the scooter again, and ridden that here, in the hope of finding anyone who may have seen Daisy. It was a slim chance, a very slim chance, but he had to try all avenues.

There weren't many people about, just a small group of Turkish soldiers walking ahead of him. Namik combed his fingers through his tousled curls, then bit at his lip. There were times when he wondered if he was chasing after the impossible. After all, was the car standing outside the rental office the same one as Mehmet had seen? The one Daisy had been driven off in? Or was there a similar car, left at the kerbside because the owner found it convenient to do so?

Whatever way Namik looked at it, he kept coming back to the same question. Who was the man at the wheel of that car? And, more importantly, where had he taken Daisy?

The temperatures seemed to be rising, with not a leaf stirring, and the only noise to break the silence was an overhead plane, the soft murmur of its engines droning across a cloudless sky. Namik dashed a hand over his mouth and licked his lips. He could do with a drink: anything, coffee, even a cold beer. Still, that could wait; he had to find Daisy. Seek out anyone who may have come into contact with her. Even as these thoughts ran around his brain, he was beginning to doubt that would happen. Still, he couldn't have sat at home regretting his attempts at finding her.

CHAPTER

TEN

•

NAMIK'S THOUGHTS TOOK another turn. Perhaps Daisy had been dropped off somewhere, left to her own devices? The more he thought about it, he felt it was something to hang on to, so with this he carried on as before.

Namik trawled bars, cafés and petrol stations, showing a photo of Daisy, but still had no luck. Salamis was his next stop, as he thought she may have gone there. This wasn't too far from Famagusta, and the ruins, amphitheatre, columns and statues would have been of interest to Daisy.

Namik first made enquiries at the tourist centre, then again at the site where he spoke to an attendant, but had no luck here either. It was useless, a complete waste of time, but in one way he was glad he'd come here. What was the use if he didn't cover every possibility? Eventually, he had no choice but to give up on this, so started up the scooter to make his way back to Kyrenia. During the journey, he felt as though his blood pressure had hit the roof.

Looking up at the clock, Namik hoped the few straggling customers would leave. He'd started the habit of biting his nails. It didn't look good, least of all in the catering business. He nibbled at them now, gazing again as the hands of the clock moved slowly on.

He had to leave soon: enough time had been wasted. He would also have to buy a drink for his friend Asil, sometime. If it hadn't been for him he'd never have known the whereabouts of the isolated house, the house where Asil's suspicions had been aroused. The man was quite certain it was Daisy he'd seen at the window. It had to be; he'd got to know her well enough, and nobody could be more reliable than Asil.

Asil was Namik's mute friend. The man had been on one of his expeditions up in the mountains that flanked the isolated cottage. His hobby wouldn't have been popular with animal lovers, or indeed animal welfare, but killing snakes for their skins was his way of earning a living, or just getting by. He would make belts from these snake skins, selling them on to any outlet that offered to take them. Not that Asil killed every living creature. He'd saved the lives of many animals, including birds of prey, nursing them back to health until they were ready to fly.

Namik breathed a sigh of relief as the last of the customers took their leave. It was eleven-twenty, and in a few moments he'd be heading in the direction of that house in which Asil had spotted Daisy.

The roads were almost deserted, except for the odd car or two, and Namik was able to keep a reasonable pace. He was now out of Kyrenia, and heading in the direction of Catalkoy. When possible, he accelerated, glad that certain parts of the road were straight. Namik silently thanked Asil for his wanderlust. Not much escaped his notice. Remarkable, too, that he'd taken the route he had on his recent exploits!

Now and then, a streetlamp helped him see the way, but otherwise all else was black. Earlier on, back in Kyrenia, there had been a short, but heavy shower and because of this, Namik had to slow down at times as he tried to avoid some large puddles which had spread across the road.

After another kilometre or so, he took a right turn, away from Catalkoy, and headed towards the peninsula. The road was unlit, but every so often the moon peeped from a silver-edged cloud.

This area was rural, a stark landscape broken only by the ridge of the Five Finger mountain range. Namik had left the road, and turned onto a rough narrow track. The track meandered, giving way to small craters, which because of the recent rain had filled and therefore became a handicap.

To his left, there were two houses on the scrubland. But another was some distance on. Namik could clearly see this from the scooter's headlights as they threw long shadows onto the stone walls.

He switched off the headlamps, but could see no light coming from the house. Looking around, he noticed a lone olive tree. He left the scooter here, half hidden by its thick knotty trunk.

As he walked towards the house, a couple of rats scuttled across his path, one in chase of the other. He was only aware of these because the moon had made another appearance. Namik breathed a sigh of relief as they disappeared into the darkness.

He knocked at the door now, waited a few moments, then, becoming impatient, knocked again, but much louder.

Namik's heart had been beating rapidly as he'd waited. What would he have done if someone had answered the door? Who was holding Daisy here? It may not be Hasan or even his father, but somebody else put in charge. He didn't know what to expect, or who he was up against.

Stepping back from the house, Namik looked up at the windows and called out. 'Daisy, it is me. Can you come to the door, or the window, perhaps? I just want to know you are safe.'

A light came on in one of the upper rooms. Then, soon after, the window opened and a woman appeared. 'Go away!' she called. 'There is no Daisy living here. You will wake the children.'

'Sorry, so sorry,' Namik called back. 'I meant no harm.'

Moments later, as he leaned heavily against the olive tree where he'd rested the scooter, Namik felt lost. What else should he do? Where would he look next?

He was running out of ideas. There was nowhere else he could look, unless of course he should get a good lead. Until then, he would just have to carry on without Daisy. Though he doubted if he could do that.

Fatma sat nervously, wondering why she'd been summoned to Bilekler's office. From across his desk, she could feel her employer's gaze upon her, even though her own eyes were averted.

Her attention was focused on him now when he cleared his throat, a deep, husky rattle as he removed the fat cigar from his mouth. 'You are happy working here, Fatma?' he questioned.

She wrung her hands. 'It is a privilege, Mr Osman. Happy to be of service to you.'

There was a long pause while he studied her. 'You have been with us for some time. You work hard, and we would like you to continue.' He sat back in his leather chair, puffing out great clouds of smoke.

This was only the second time Fatma had been summoned to this room. The first was when Osman had kindly given her a few household trinkets that would otherwise been thrown. She twisted in her chair, considering the possibility of her being sacked. After all, someone may have seen Namik pay her a visit the other night. She hadn't of course told him a thing, nothing that could cause trouble. Still, you never knew!

Osman's eyes were mere slits as he continued. 'You know, Fatma. It would never do for you to gossip about anything here. Personal, or otherwise.'

Fatma felt her cheeks growing hot under his scrutiny.

'After all,' he went on, 'you have a comfortable home at the moment – cosy, shall we say? And, apart from this, we would hate to lose you.'

That was a threat. Her employers needn't worry, though. She wasn't about to risk her job, let alone her home.

Osman Bilekler had little to say after this, but the look he had given her said everything. She would be watched very carefully. Leaving Osman's study, Fatma felt a sense of panic. Someone in this house must have seen her visitor that night, and, if that was so, she must, on no occasion, be drawn into anything that didn't concern her.

It was hoped that this time Namik, determined as ever, would find Daisy. He still believed Asil's sighting of her, but could only guess that Daisy had since been removed from that house on the scrubland. There was, he reckoned, another likely place, a more salubrious abode, where comfort was everything, especially if you were one of the Bileklers.

He could have kicked himself. Enough time had been wasted. Why hadn't he thought of the Bileklers' villa before? He had weighed everything up in the last couple of days, and decided that it was probably one of those who'd held Daisy prisoner, and not an associate of theirs after all. But what they had been doing in that old house where Asil had seen her was a complete mystery.

He still had use of the scooter, and, as before, he'd set out at nightfall. The thing was, Namik hadn't the heart to tell Mehmet that his scooter was faulty. Recently, the gears had started to stick, causing the engine to stall.

The gears were playing up now and, as Namik gently braked, he was suddenly thrust forward, throwing him clean off the scooter. He hadn't done much damage to himself, but the few grazes he did have would be quite sore later. Namik caught a whiff of burning rubber, but he could waste no more time.

Cursing, he hoped the scooter would hold out as he heaved the machine up, straddled it and then switched on the engine. Soon, he was making his way up the winding road to Bellapais. Ahead of him, dotted among the hills, little lights twinkled like distant stars.

As he got closer to the Bileklers' residence, he mused on the prospect that those dogs that they kept were shut away. Once before, when he got near to the place, and before Daisy's disappearance, they'd barked so loudly and for so long, he'd turned away, unable to go any further. Still, if they weren't shut away, Namik would knock up the Bileklers no matter what.

The raucous sound of the dogs cut through the darkness. A smell of damp pervaded the air, throwing up scents of plant life, both sweet and earthy. Namik had already knocked at the door, wondering if he could be heard above the din. He blasted those animals, hoping against hope that they were safely caged and he wouldn't be set upon. He skin prickled at that thought. Having once been badly bitten, he'd needed several stitches, and after that he tried to steer clear of dogs!

Chinks of light showed at the downstairs windows, where the curtains had not been pulled across properly. Namik heard footsteps pad to the door and suddenly he found himself face to face with Osman Bilekler. 'What is it at this late hour?' the man demanded angrily.

Namik squared up to him. 'Is Daisy here?' He did his best to sound confident.

'Why would she be here? Anyway, you have no right on my property, Guven.'

'Well, it is the only place she could be,' Namik answered back. 'I've looked everywhere else.'

Bilekler grimaced. 'Such a pity you should think you are worthy of her. Now, leave at once or I'll…'

'Set those dogs on me?' Namik finished.

The big man made to shut the door, but Namik's foot swung out stopping his action. 'If she is here, you might as well tell me, because I'll keep on until you do.' Namik hoped that his tone had an effect.

Osman's bloodshot eyes bulged, while his face turned almost puce. 'I'll call the police. That will stop your meddling, Guven. But better if you leave now.'

Lunging forward, Namik grabbed at the man's silk robe, almost throttling him. 'If Daisy is here, you had better let her go, or you will be in more trouble than you are now,' he warned. Now he'd started, any misgivings he'd had, dissolved. 'Oh yes,' he added, 'I know a lot of things!' Just then, the shrill sound of a dog could be heard, and the noise grew louder when another joined in.

Bilekler had been taken aback by Namik's words. He gulped, pushing his attacker's hands away. His own hands were trembling, but he did his best to hide them. Bilekler wasn't a well man, and the dizzy spells he'd been having of late had him worried. He'd seen his doctor three times recently, and each time had been strictly warned to stop smoking. In fact, the doctor in question had advised him to see a London specialist, owing to an irregular heartbeat, but he'd refused. He didn't want to travel overseas, not at his age. He was afraid, also, that something else may be found.

Having heard raised voices, Hasan appeared at the door. He looked furious when he saw Namik and gently moved his father aside. 'You were told to leave,' he raged. 'If you don't, there are always the dogs!'

They had long stopped howling, but at the very mention of them Namik felt the colour drain from his face. His eyes focused on the younger man's jaw. There was a red, slightly raised weal which seemed to be growing in intensity. Namik's pulse quickened as he shot a glance across both men's shoulders.

Then, in a split second, Hasan grabbed Namik roughly and pushed him onto the path. 'There is nothing here for you,' he told him. 'Get back to your own village, people of your own kind!'

'I'll go,' said Namik, smoothing his clothing, 'Though I might have a word with Melanie Hampton. Maybe she can help me.'

Hasan made to go after him, but Namik was already out of the gate, not because he was afraid of the Bileklers but because those dogs could be set on him at any moment.

Upstairs, in his own room, Hasan paced the floor. Sleep was evading him. All he could see was that red light on the rear of the motor scooter as it disappeared into the night. How he hated that family. Namik was so like his brother, and each time he saw him he wanted to... Yes, to kill him. If he were out of the way he couldn't ask any more questions, make any more threats. As for Melanie Hampton, he would think of something suitable.

There was no sleep for Hasan that night. Instead he continued to pace the floor.

Hasan touched his face. No bruise had appeared; the raised mark from last night had almost gone, but it remained tender. Daisy was standing by the bedroom window with her back to him. He wanted to go to her, apologise, but she wouldn't have accepted it, and may have hit out once again.

'Why do you hate me so?' he asked, and not for the first time. 'I give you everything, and still you reject me.'

She turned to him. 'Hate is a funny word, Hasan. They say it's a close relation of love, but you can forget that, too.'

He winced at that. 'Perhaps you would not say such things if you knew what my life has been.'

'Oh, stop whining. Do you think I care? At least you're alive. Many died in those battles so you've nothing to grumble about. And you have everything.'

'But what has that young man got to offer you? He has nothing, and never will have.'

'No, but he fought in that war. Where were you?'

'Do not question me,' he chided. 'You were not here; what do you know?'

Daisy turned back to the window, still hearing Namik's voice in her ears. At least he was still alive, and not buried in the hills or somewhere.

Anger festered inside Hasan. Why couldn't she love him? Of all the women he ever knew, none could come close to Daisy. She had become an obsession, and if his father hadn't brought her into his life he would just have carried on as before.

Yes, his father felt he was doing his best for him, and at the beginning it worked, until Namik Guven had become involved. What did the English call it? That was it: 'the fly in the ointment'.

Now and then, the scent from a potted gardenia filled the room, Daisy's favourite perfume. Hasan seethed, and, tortured with hate for the other man, he strode across to Daisy and grabbed hold of her. He wasn't letting her off lightly this time. She was his, and always would be.

A myriad of coloured lights, strung across the harbour, shimmered on the water's surface, while a soft shushing of waves lapped at the surrounding wall. Namik had come out onto the veranda, taking a break from the restaurant. It was a warm night, and, with the rest of the cafés and bars now open, the town buzzed with life.

Traditional music came from one of the bars, accompanied by the warbling voice of a male singer, but it wasn't to Namik's liking. Like most modern young men, he enjoyed Western music. The sort he played in his restaurant.

Because of this, and the food, both Turkish and French, his place, or rather his uncle's, brought in many customers.

Yes, he could say he'd made the place pay. Much improved since running it himself.

He had stood here now for about ten minutes, mesmerised by the lights as they quivered in a warm breeze. Having cooled down from the kitchen's heat, he went back inside.

In a small area, where customers waited to be shown a table, were a man and woman, she admiring a watercolour. She stepped back, viewing it from various angles. Namik approached the couple and asked if they were interested in the picture.

The woman turned round. 'No, not my husband,' she drawled, 'but I am.'

It was common to see Americans in northern Cyprus, so Namik wasn't surprised that one was here in his restaurant. 'Well, that picture was painted by a Scottish lady,' he told her. 'She is local, and has lived here for a while now.'

The pastels, in blues and sandy hues, depicted the ancient dwellings of a back street in Kyrenia. Richard Hampton took a closer look. 'That woman is a good artist,' he said. 'I don't know where my wife's going to put it, though. There's no room on the walls!' His voice was jocular.

Melanie Hampton, knowing full well who Namik was, gave her husband a darting look. 'He's exaggerating, of course. Anyway, if you see something you like, buy it. That's my motto.'

Long resigned to his wife's fancies, Richard excused himself. 'I'll be outside, my dear; need the air.' He gave Namik a friendly smile as he left.

After this a cheque was scribbled out and Namik got someone to wrap the painting up, though he was somewhat taken aback to see the name on the cheque.

While she had been admiring the artwork on the walls, Melanie had been taking a few sly looks at Namik. It was Hasan who'd pointed him out to her, and ever since she'd been determined to meet him. Her aim was to warn him off, stop him from probing into their affairs. It affected her, after all.

'Look, let me be honest with you.' Melanie eyed Namik from head to foot 'I know who you are; someone pointed you out to me. Personally, I don't want any trouble, but it would seem that you've been looking for some. Am I right, Mr Guven?'

'Trouble?' echoed Namik. 'What kind of trouble is that?'

'To put it bluntly, I'd say you were making a fool of yourself. That girl, the one you've been looking for. Best forget you ever knew her.'

'You mean Daisy? Why, where is she?' Namik felt prickles run up his back.

Her eyes flashed. 'If I knew, would I tell you?'

For a moment, Namik was lost for words. All this had caught him off guard. His mind did a quick shuffle. 'If you have nothing to hide, you would tell me.' He tried to keep his voice even.

'And if I don't, what then?'

'What do you think?' he said, inwardly seething with anger. 'And if you think I would let this go, then you and your friends have a surprise in store.'

She was already a decent height, but stretched her lean body, making her appear even taller. 'Is that a threat? Because I don't take too kindly to those.'

'Well, you can take it any way you like, Miss Hampton. Anyway, I was trying to look for you, actually. Not that I knew what to look for. But, now you are here, perhaps we can talk.' Namik looked over his shoulder, hoping nobody could hear this conversation.

She gave him a long, hard look. 'You are meddling with things you don't understand. Some have come to a bad end doing that.' She paused for moment before adding in a softer tone, 'I'm only telling you this for your own good, but keep your distance from the Bileklers. They are powerful people.'

'Thank you for your concern,' he said. 'But I do not know if I can do that.'

She reached for the picture but Namik grabbed her arm. 'If any harm comes to Daisy, the police will be onto the Bileklers faster than you can imagine. Oh, do not think I am that naïve. I know full well that one of those men have Daisy. It took a while, but there is no other explanation why she has gone missing.'

He wasn't feeling as confident as he'd sounded, and as he watched her walk away he wondered how it would all end. Let alone if he'd ever see Daisy again?

As for Melanie Hampton, the idea of the law poking their noses into things unnerved her. Not that the Bileklers and she were too afraid of them; they and the local police were on good terms. Still, too many questions regarding a missing British woman was something they could do without.

Melanie stroked her arm where Namik had grabbed her. She could still feel the warmth of his fingers. She liked those hands: masculine, strong but boyishly youthful. In spite of herself, she had to admit there was an attraction there. Her scarlet lips broke into a smile. She wasn't unduly concerned about the threats he'd made. Men such as Namik Guven should be easy enough to handle. He lacked sophistication, had never known wealth, so this could prove beneficial, if she could get him on side.

Joining Richard, with the picture clutched beneath her arm, she knew she'd be returning to the Turtle's Rest. As soon as was possible!

As they drove home, Richard glanced at her. 'It's a lovely night, my dear. Just look at that sky; it never ceases to amaze me.'

Melanie let out a long sigh. Moonlit skies held no fascination for her; in fact, she had little in common with Richard. He not only bored her; she was sick of his suffocating attention. He was always there, hovering in the background. It was a disastrous marriage. Had been from the start.

They were nearing their beautiful home, a sumptuous villa overlooking the spectacular Basparmak mountain range. Not that Melanie had been aware of her surroundings. Her eyes had been closed, her thoughts full of that young man who ran the restaurant.

CHAPTER
ELEVEN

•

For the last hour, Namik had been sitting in his back garden, a sprawling area that had been very neglected of late. A huge fig grew along one side, and off centre a lemon tree now in full blossom, filled the evening air with a delicious scent.

He'd come out here, hoping to shake off the morbid thoughts that had plagued him. It hadn't been much of a success, although there was one bright light on the horizon. He stubbed out his cigarette, then bounded into the house.

In the large kitchen, Namik found his mother on the narrow bed which was placed against the wall. Her back was turned, but he doubted she was asleep at this early hour. He watched her for a few brief moments, knowing too well what her thoughts were. Would there be a day when she didn't think of his dead brother? Believing this wasn't to be so, Namik went to his room.

There, he lit up another cigarette, then shuffled his plans into motion. Since Melanie Hampton had paid him a visit, he'd had time to examine the situation. What if he saw her again? Although she had warned him off, told him to keep his nose out of her affairs, he had a strong feeling that this wasn't the last he'd see of her. She'd want to keep an eye on him, track his whereabouts. Well, if this was the case, he'd change tack, flatter her ego. By seeing him as an admirer, and not an adversary, she may open up. Anyway, he had a fair idea what kind of woman she was. She most probably would enjoy the attention, as she obviously didn't think much of her husband, as he was quick to spot.

He would convince her that Daisy was something in the past. She wasn't coming back, had probably lost interest, and that was that.

But, standing in front of that full length mirror, Namik was beginning to doubt himself. What smart, sophisticated woman would look at someone like him? Jeans that had seen many washes, faded shirts owing to similar treatment, and shoes that had seen better days. Mind, he could give these a good brushing, or, better still, buy new ones. On reflection, perhaps a new shirt wouldn't go amiss.

Of course, when Melanie Hampton had seen him, he'd been in smarter garb: black trousers, white shirt and a red bow tie.

Namik reflected on what he'd learnt about the Hamptons. Rumour had it that it was she who held the purse strings. The daughter of a rich family, she had married beneath her, misguided or otherwise.

Namik took a closer look at his appearance, turning his head as he did so. Well, he may not be the best dressed of men, but he had youth on his side, and he supposed he wasn't that bad looking! So, was there a woman, a woman like Melanie Hampton, whose youth had long passed, that wouldn't be flattered by a young man taking an interest in her?

Still looking in the mirror, he smiled. He could be as devious as the next man. Or woman!

It was a few days later, almost closing time, when Melanie showed herself. The last two customers were just leaving the restaurant when she stepped through the door, at the top of a flight of steps.

When Namik spotted her, his lip turned up at the corner, a feeling of self-satisfaction sweeping over him. She was holding a package, and he guessed it to be the painting, but he couldn't think why she had changed her mind about it. He came towards her, trying his utmost to appear pleasant. 'I must say I did not expect you back,' he lied.

'I was hoping you might change this,' her tone sounded flirtatious as she offered him the picture. 'Not because I don't like it. It's lovely; they all are. But that's the problem.'

'So you would like to choose another?' Namik cast his eye to the wall.

'If you don't mind,' she answered huskily. 'But perhaps not now. I can always come back, have another look.'

As he took the picture, her hand brushed his, and he wondered how hard he would have to try winning her over. It was as if nothing had happened, but it didn't take a fool to know why she'd returned. If she felt she could soften him up, then she wouldn't have to try very hard.

'I can tell you, it's so good to be on my own for a while,' she lamented. 'Do you know, that man stifles me. It's true: everywhere I go, there's Richard.'

Namik hung up the painting. 'Perhaps he thinks other men will find you attractive.'

Melanie had been casting her eye over the other pictures hooked on the wall, but wasn't at all interested. She turned, arching her brow. 'Why ever should he? I'm nothing special.'

'That is your opinion,' Namik told her. 'But I am sure some men would disagree. Anyway,' he continued. 'We got off to a bad start the other night. Perhaps we could put it behind us. Believe me, I am not one to hold grudges, never have.'

She nodded towards the bar, walked over and perched on one of the stalls. While she was doing this, Namik locked up, then joined her.

'You know,' she said, a glint in her eye. 'I was thinking the same. I'm all hot air, but harmless really.' She laughed at that.

It hadn't gone unnoticed, the way she'd hitched her skirt. Furthermore, it would be daft not to admire the long, shapely legs, clad in a pair of sheer tights.

She asked for a glass of white wine, and after Namik brought it round to her he perched opposite. 'You do believe me when I said I never hold grudges, don't you?'

'Oh, life is far too short for those,' she said, 'so don't worry. Anyway, I'm sorry I arrived late, but I had the most awful job getting away.'

Namik grinned, showing long dimples. 'No problem. I have nothing else better to do when I leave here.'

Sipping her drink, Melanie eyed him over her glass. 'Nothing?'

He ignored this. 'You do not have to believe what I say, but maybe I had you wrong. You see, the army toughens you up, but it also teaches you not to trust strangers, so I hope you understand.'

'Perfectly.' She held his gaze.

Throwing back his head, Namik laughed. 'When I first saw you, I made you out to be a spy or something.'

She also laughed. 'Like the infamous Mata Hari, you mean?'

He frowned. 'I am sorry: who is this?'

She rather liked his naivety. She was also drawn to the fact that he was so different from the men she'd mixed with.

'It doesn't matter,' she said at last, 'but I can assure you I'm no spy!'

Namik topped up her glass. 'Not exactly a spy, perhaps. Still, I thought you were a terrible lady. All stuck up, and mysterious.' He laughed again and hoped he sounded genuine. He also felt ashamed of himself for playing up to her, now realising how difficult this charade was.

'What do you think now?' she teased.

Namik wished she would refrain from rubbing his leg with her foot. 'I do not think anything,' he edged. 'You just ordinary, now I talk with you.'

'Not too ordinary,' she challenged.

'Oh no,' he corrected, tossing a drink down his dry throat.

Watching him, Melanie felt her pulses raising. She was enjoying his company, and hoped to see much more of him.

A large butterfly, unlike any seen in England, settled on a purple scented shrub. Daisy had been watching this for what seemed an age, and now and then rubbed at her temples. Sitting in the shade hadn't lessened her headache; in fact, it had worsened.

She had been in Cyprus for some months now, but how she longed for those cooler days back in England, though most of all her freedom.

Daisy winced as a sharp pain tore through her skull, then winced again when another followed. She had had these headaches on and off since. If only she could erase it from her mind. She could hardly face Hasan since that ordeal. She had wondered how he'd kept control of his feelings before, considering how passionate he was. She amended this. Wild, that was more the mark. Still, he hadn't touched her since, and that was something. Well, how could he when her bedroom door was firmly locked?

'I have brought you out a drink.' Turning her head, Daisy saw Fatma. She hadn't heard her soft approach across the lawn.

When Daisy took the cloudy lemonade, she put it first to her brow before sipping it. She forced a smile. 'It's very considerate of you, Fatma. And much appreciated.'

'You should see a doctor; you have me worry,' said the housekeeper.

Daisy sipped her drink. 'I'm not used to this heat like you, that's all.'

'I understand this.' Fatma looked furtively towards the house, then spoke in a low voice. 'But always, you must be on your guard.'

Even the sunshine had no effect on Fatma's complexion. It remained as sallow as ever. It saddened Daisy. This kindly woman brought her tea first thing, ran her bath, and did her laundry. In fact, it was she who did everything. Osman Bilekler was loath to employ extra help. Even Oktay, their secretary, was given his marching orders. The fewer people who knew Daisy's whereabouts, the better; at least that was the way she saw it.

'I miss Namik,' declared Daisy. 'He'd have no idea where to find me either, so this worries me.'

'I know, my friend. If only I could…'

Fatma had spotted Osman. He was watching from an open window, although it wasn't known how long he'd been there.

Daisy said no more but closed her eyes, not wanting to cause trouble for the housekeeper. Her head was still hurting, but somehow she must have dropped off to sleep, unaware that Fatma had gone back into the house.

She had no idea how long she'd been sitting here, but Daisy's eyes flickered open when she heard a movement close by. 'Oh, it's you!' she breathed, shifting in her seat.

'I'm sorry to disappoint,' said Osman. 'Did you think it was Hasan?'

Daisy ignored this, though she hoped Fatma hadn't been overheard earlier.

Bilekler smiled. 'Very nice, the weather. Getting warmer each day. Anyway, how is the head?'

'A little better,' she answered, knowing her health was of no interest to him.

'Good, can I get you anything?'

'No, but you can let me go,' she sneered. 'What good am I to you?'

He sighed, the copious stomach distending. 'My dear, you are asking too much. Surely you know that is out of the question.' He paused, his eyes burning into her. 'So please do not ask again; you are trying my patience.'

For weeks now, Daisy had noticed the change in Osman. His jaw had slackened even more, his red-rimmed eyes heavily veined. Moreover, his drinking had increased, putting away vast quantities of spirits. She had often seen him clutching at his chest, and thought that maybe he had a stomach ulcer, and she could only guess at the state of his liver!

He said no more but looked up at a bird as it settled on a weeping birch. He sniffed disdainfully, then walked back inside.

But later, when Daisy left her room, she found Osman reading a newspaper. Beside him, on a small table, was a whisky decanter and a crystal glass half full of the stuff. He was wearing thick-rimmed spectacles, which he removed when Daisy came into the room. However, there was no sign of Hasan. In fact, she hadn't seen him all day.

At first, Osman looked at Daisy without speaking, then, leaving his chair, he picked up his drink and walked over to the window 'How well do you really know my son?' he asked, turning now to face her.

Daisy frowned. 'I don't understand.'

Osman Bilekler bit at his lip. 'I think I should enlighten you. You see, there are certain things he does not talk about,' he said, rather dramatically.

She shrugged. 'Such as?'

He studied her. 'You look drained, Daisy. Sit down; you will take tea with me, won't you?' He pressed a bell, then, with one hand in his pocket, moved about the room. 'Hasan was excused during the fighting. They would not take him; he was sick. Nervous breakdown, I think they called it.'

'And why was this?' she enquired flatly.

Bilekler withdrew his hand, waving it round the room. 'Some bearing on his childhood, I don't know. Anyway, he was ill for a long time. Not that he ever went without, I mean when he was growing up. No, he had everything, that boy.'

Casting his eye to the framed picture, the one Daisy had once remarked on, he beckoned her over. 'He never knew his mother, not in the direct sense.'

'Is that her?' Daisy asked, pointing at the faceless woman.

'Yes,' he breathed. 'But that is how he saw her: faceless, without a soul, you might say. As for the small boy, well, I expect you have guessed.'

'He told me he painted it,' said Daisy. Perhaps he felt rejected, unloved.'

'That is not true! I loved him, still do. I will do anything, give anything. His happiness is all I want.'

Daisy looked at the woman again, then at the child with the big doleful eyes. 'It's a strange picture. Beautiful, but strange. Did he ever get over it?' She was digging, but hoped she sounded genuine.

Bilekler turned away. 'Why should he not? All this was long ago. I just thought you might like to know something of Hasan's background.'

Just then, Fatma appeared with a tray. She looked uneasy, but seemed to relax when Daisy caught her eye, giving her a slight nod.

As for Daisy, she was still no wiser as to their plans. Her thoughts turned to Melanie Hampton. There were no signs of her recently. So where was she?

While she drank her tea, Osman told her a little more about his son, though Daisy guessed he'd chosen his words carefully, relaying only what he wanted her to know. During this time she'd sat there quietly, alert in case Osman should say more than he meant to. She'd nodded her head in sympathy for Hasan's somewhat unusual behaviour, and uttered 'I see' in the right places, but in truth felt not an ounce of sympathy at all for any of them. Then, excusing herself, she went back to her room, leaving Osman alone with his glass of whisky.

The long slim legs swung from the driver's seat most provocatively. Holding the door open, Namik thought they were definitely Melanie's best feature, if nothing else.

They had previously driven to Buffavento, but had been turned back because of army training. Namik had tried to jest with them, but they were having none of it, owing to strict measures concerning the danger involved. Moreover, Turkish soldiers, his own kin, had flashed crossed bayonets across their car, as was their usual habit when a vehicle turned up during army practice.

'Well, how do you like this place?' enquired Namik.

She breathed in the cool air. 'In all the time I've lived here, I've never been here. How come you know it?'

They were standing on a kind of plateau, having driven off the main route to Buffavento. The area was surrounded by craggy peaks, while closer proximity gave way to rough scrubland, a haven for wildlife, especially birds of prey.

'You forget that I'm native to this,' answered Namik. 'I know all around here.'

'It certainly takes your breath away,' said Melanie. Moving closer, she took his arm. 'Tell me, do many people come here? It looks rather desolate.'

'Locals do not bother, and most tourists do not know of it. Besides, you could consider it dangerous up here, though it has a rare beauty.'

Her blue eyes widened. 'Now that's something I appreciate even more. Beauty, but with a sense of danger.'

Namik gazed back at the murderous track from which they'd come. It was so narrow in places, where a car could easily topple into a steep gorge, he wondered why he'd chosen this place, although where else could he find such a solitary spot?

He smiled at her. 'Would you call yourself dangerous, somebody who likes to take chances?'

She shook her head. 'Not usually. Only if I'm crossed.'

'Then anyone would be wise not to fool with you,' he bantered.

'How right you are.'

Reaching into her car, Namik picked up a blanket and a cool bag. He then headed for a flat, grassy patch of ground.

Melanie dropped down onto the blanket. 'I hope you like champagne,' she said, unzipping the bag.

'Of course I like it, but I cannot afford the luxury.'

She leaned closer. 'Then why not live a life full of luxuries? Every day, with me.'

Inwardly, Namik felt annoyed with himself. Perhaps he shouldn't have started this farce, and her familiarity made him cringe. He'd try not to show his feelings though; he couldn't afford to, not if he wanted to find Daisy.

He sipped his drink, unaccustomed to the tickling bubbles. 'But it would not be a luxury then, would it? I mean, if you drank it every day. It is same with most things.'

She acknowledged this with a slight movement of her head. 'Anyway, you're not eating,' she scorned, nibbling on some of the smoked salmon she'd also packed.

He popped a few olives into his mouth. 'There's plenty of time. No hurry.'

Melanie giggled. 'Perhaps you think I'm trying to poison you. If so, you needn't worry.' Her eyes were a mere slit as she looked at him. 'Or perhaps you're thinking about that girl. Well, you're wasting your time there, as I've told you before.'

'Why do you say that? It is all in the past. I know Daisy has gone from me, I have to accept this, and I want to look to the future.'

He watched Melanie help herself to more wine. Seeing as he didn't drive, he hoped she wasn't exceeding the limit! Still, if he needed information, he felt it best to do this away from prying eyes. Anyway, causing trouble with her husband was the last thing he wanted, and it would complicate matters.

'Hasan hasn't bothered with me since that girl's been on the scene,' grumbled Melanie. She pouted. 'Do you think he's a fool?'

Namik was taken aback. It hadn't taken long for her tongue to loosen. 'Yes, he must be. A bloody fool at that. You are a very sophisticated woman. Clever, too, unlike some I know.'

'I'm not happy, you know.' She looked at him, her eyes heavy. 'Anyway, why are you sitting over there? Come here.' She patted the space beside her.

Reluctantly, he moved over. 'I have not heard good things about the Bileklers, but they cannot be all bad.' He watched her closely. 'What do you think?'

'It won't last, not when she finds out,' she said, ignoring his question. With this, she stretched out onto the blanket.

'Finds out?' Namik was alert.

'That he's a madman. Always has been.'

'You mean he's killed someone? That sort of thing? I don't quite understand.'

'That house where he'd taken her, I expect she complained, wanted the big house. Miss bloody almighty.'

Namik stared down at her, noting she'd closed her eyes. He felt a flutter of panic, and hoped she wouldn't fall asleep. 'You didn't answer. Has someone been killed? Is that what you meant?'

'Oh, ages ago,' she said impatiently. 'A barn, that's where it happened.'

His heartbeat quickened. 'Barn? What about it? What happened there?'

'An old olive press, then, I don't know. Anyway, it's all in the past.'

Namik stroked her hair, his face close to hers. 'Did you know the person?'

She suddenly sat up. 'What's with all these questions? I thought we'd come here to enjoy ourselves, to be alone together.' Melanie snuggled up to him. 'You do like me, don't you?'

'Yes, of course,' he answered hastily. 'Very much, now I get to know you.' Namik felt a moment of panic when she helped herself to more champagne. That track was steep. As for getting more answers, he didn't think that was likely. He'd have to try harder next time, but wondered how he'd possibly keep this up.

He glanced at the bottle, which was almost finished, then cast his eye towards the steep hill. Melanie could barely keep her eyes open, and he inwardly shuddered at the thought of getting into that car.

CHAPTER
TWELVE

•

A LETTER HAD arrived for Namik. After Ibrahim had sorted through the post, he'd delivered it personally, as a kind gesture.

To say Namik was shocked when he'd opened it was putting it mildly. In fact, Aisha was the last person he expected to hear from!

He said nothing to his parents, not wanting to drag up bad memories. All the same, she wished to meet with him, and was hoping he'd be at the arranged spot.

Namik shook his head. What was Aisha doing here in north Cyprus? Surely it wasn't just to meet up with him. He felt a flutter of excitement. After all, she had a connection with his brother, a close one at that. Anything that may throw light on that mystery was worth chasing up. Anyway, she'd always been a pleasant girl and his brother had been very fond of her.

Namik scanned the letter again before slipping it into his pocket, but while he was doing this he turned his thoughts back to Melanie Hampton, and the accusation that the Bileklers had killed someone. Who was that person? Might he have known them? And, for that matter, where was that barn, or olive press as she had called it? It was an odd place to kill somebody.

Back in his room, Namik sat on his bed and chewed at his lip. Suddenly, everything seemed to be happening at once, but first he must meet up with Melanie Hampton.

'You fool! You should have kept Melanie sweet.' Osman found it difficult to keep his temper. 'Look what's happened now.'

Hasan stopped pacing the floor and glared at his father. 'I am sick of that woman. Don't you know how hard it is, keeping her sweet, as you say?'

Osman tapped the ash from his cigar. 'I know how hard it is, but she was seen with him, and her tongue runs away with her, especially after a few drinks!'

'So, your man has been at it again,' Hasan retorted. 'Can you trust him? You haven't always.'

The older man ignored that last remark. 'Of course I can,' he snapped. 'I've known the man forever, and, anyway, he's paid too well to cross me. Found that out long ago.'

'Yes, I expect he did, but watch him all the same,' suggested Hasan. 'Anyway, I can't stand too much of this.' He let out a huge sigh. 'As you say, that woman talks too much.'

'Yes, she does.' Now Osman paced the room, puffing out curls of smoke as he did so. 'Of course, we could put a stop to this. But leave it with me.'

Hasan threw a look at him. 'What do you mean?'

'Everything would have been all right if that Guven fellow hadn't stuck his nose in,' Osman hissed angrily. 'Him and that father of his. And, if that wasn't enough, Melanie Hampton makes matters worse. Well, I'll sort things out. You'll see.'

They looked at each other, as if reading the other's thoughts.

A few meetings had taken place since the picnic near Buffavento. It was against Namik's nature to be something he wasn't, but he'd do all it took to win Melanie Hampton over; he had to. The place he'd chosen this time was closer to home, but enough distance to warrant privacy.

It was a lovely morning, and they had left the car and were strolling along a craggy ridge, above a little hamlet a mile or so inland from Acapulco beach.

'I was surprised you wanted to see me again,' said Melanie, rather coyly.

He chuckled. 'Why wouldn't I? You know how I feel.'

She was surprised at her own feelings. It wasn't how it was meant to be, and she had fought against it. Someone from the local village, a lowly person at that; she'd never have believed it of herself. Well, she was quickly falling for this man, regardless of how little he had to offer her. And, if she wasn't wrong, she was almost certain that her feelings were returned, for Namik had changed since their first meeting.

'You did not answer me,' said Namik, cutting into her thoughts.

'I was thinking, that's all,' she edged. 'Remember when we first met?'

Again he laughed. 'Of course. And you were horrible. What was it you called me? Mata Hari?'

'A spy, actually. As you hadn't heard of the woman.' She laughed, a high-pitched sound, and it somehow grated on Namik.

'Well, we know you are nothing of the kind. It was stupid of me, and I am sorry. I did not know you then, but now…' Namik forced himself to smile at her, while hating every minute.

As her feelings had become stronger, Melanie had grown ever fearful. Namik was no fool, and this had become more apparent of late. A poor villager, maybe, but he wasn't as ignorant as Hasan had made out.

'I don't see them now,' she drawled. 'The Bileklers, I mean.'

'That is even better,' Namik enthused. 'It means we do not have to hide anything, no secrets, you know. Unless, of course, it's your husband!'

Melanie wasn't much concerned about Richard, but looked at Namik from beneath her lashes. 'You sure you're over that girl? Only I don't like being made a fool of.'

'Namik feigned a look of surprise. 'Now I'm with you?' Of course I am. And do not worry; she will have forgotten me.'

This seemed to have pleased her, as a big smile spread across her face. 'I don't know why we can't be alone somewhere,' she paused. 'Somewhere where we can be together, you know.'

'Well, we cannot go to your home, never. You have a husband, remember.' His heart had missed a beat when she'd made that suggestion.

'Yeah, but he's an ass; forget him.'

'No matter, we are here now.' So many thoughts were going around in Namik's head, one of which he acted on suddenly by pulling Melanie close, kissing her hard on the lips. He only hoped his actions were convincing.

'My, aren't you the dark one?' she breathed, her pulses quickening.

He stroked her hair. 'Not only that, but someone you can trust.' He swallowed hard, hating himself for his dishonesty. 'There is nobody more true, believe me.'

Melanie studied him. She wanted to unburden herself. All these secrets, the lies. How long could she live with this hanging over her?

'I never thought I'd meet anyone like you,' she declared. 'OK, so you haven't the big house, like... well, like the rest of us, but who cares! You're who you are, and a nice guy. I can see any woman appreciating that. Still, I do know you were looking for me once. Wanted to question me. Do you still?'

Namik decided to put his skills into practice, the ones he'd learnt to survive on when every man, and boy, were up against their adversaries. 'No,' he said, shaking his head. 'I no need to question anyone. Not now. Anyway, I cannot get enough of you. Come here.'

It had been a long time since Melanie had been held in a man's arms. She positively glowed.

As for Namik, he would have to keep up the charade. How long for, he didn't know, but with every kiss he languished on this woman it was giving him sheer hell.

With not a soul around, Namik relaxed, as much as was possible, and played his card to the best of his ability, albeit no further than custom dictated. However, this didn't bode too well with Melanie Hampton, but when the situation was explained she reluctantly let it go.

Then later, on the way back, with Namik feeling his efforts had been wasted, Melanie at last confided in him. They were on a straight stretch of road when she suddenly pulled over. 'Are you wondering why I did that?' she asked.

He shrugged, fearful that she may want to continue where they'd left off.

'Perhaps it shouldn't be you who I'm telling,' she explained nervously. 'After all, you may want to finish with me when you've heard what I have to say.'

Namik pulled a face. 'I wouldn't, whatever it was. So, if it makes you feel better, then go ahead.'

'It's about your brother,' she gulped. 'I was there.' Melanie hesitated, clasping her hands together to stop them trembling.

'You?' Namik had turned a deathly colour as he struggled with his feelings.

'I was used,' she put in quickly. 'Hasan was the one. It was him.'

For years he'd carried this around, guessing but having no proof, and here sitting beside him was someone who'd actually witnessed the killing. It was some minutes before Namik could answer, though his heart felt like a ton weight. 'Who else was involved? You might as well tell me everything.'

She gripped hold of the steering wheel. 'His father, and he was the clever one. It was him who planned it.'

It felt as though someone had fired a shotgun through Namik's stomach. 'Why are you telling me this now?' he asked, unable to look at her.

She licked her lips, then swallowed hard. 'Because of us. I thought you had the right to know how your brother died that night. And, anyway, it hasn't been easy. These past years have haunted me.'

Namik sucked in a lungful of air. 'Where?' he questioned. 'Where did this happen?'

'Bogaz, where you were living at the time.'

'I said where?'

'The old olive press. But I didn't kill your brother. You understand that, don't you?'

Everything about the woman nauseated him, angered him, making him want to lash out. 'Not really,' he answered bitterly. 'But tell me something, and I want the truth. Did my poor brother suffer, or did he die instantly? I have to know; it's been torturing me all these years. My parents, especially.' He made to grip her arm, but stopped himself in case it frightened her off.

Melanie hung her head, and for the first time since he'd known her Namik thought that she felt some remorse. 'I don't think so,' she said at last, 'It happened so quickly.'

Why he'd asked that question he didn't know, but hoped that she was telling the truth. Better to believe this than think that Aygun had suffered a lingering death. As for how he had died, well, this was enough for now. There was only so much he could take at the moment. He turned to look at her. 'I cannot forgive – that could never happen – but it is better I know, and I thank you for telling me this.'

Starting up the engine, Melanie continued the journey in silence. Had she done right? More importantly, would he want to see her again? If what he'd said was true, had really fallen for her, perhaps he would. She lived in hope.

Back in his village, Namik found himself wandering around the riverbank, rich with flora and a habitat for birds. The local abattoir was here, his sheep, grazing close by. Namik didn't want to go home, much preferring the solitude instead.

Covering his face with both hands, he wrestled with his jumbled thoughts. Among these were images of his beloved brother. He could still see those injuries, terrible ones, as he had lain there in his coffin. They weren't caused by someone's fists, either. Maybe an instrument of some sort was used. But, whatever it was, it had caused instant death. If of course that was to be believed. And what of the barn the woman spoke of? What was it, an old olive press? Well, he only knew of the one in his village, not Bogaz, where he'd once lived.

When Melanie Hampton had told him this, he certainly hadn't expected that sort of information. Hoping for some answers, yes, but her confession at having been present: that had come as a bombshell!

Namik could have kicked himself. He should have asked a lot more questions; she was there, in the palm of his hand. What a fool he'd been, a bloody idiot. The woman may have told him more. He wanted to know, needed to… or did he? The fact was, he'd been knocked sideways, could hardly take in the reality of it all.

The thought of seeing that woman again, get her to talk, filled Namik with utter dread. Earlier, on the clifftop, she'd tried to coerce him into spending a night in one of the hotels. He shuddered. The very thought made his skin crawl.

As for Daisy, with these latest developments, he'd even forgotten to enquire about her, ask if she knew anything. Still, he had a pretty shrewd idea where she was now. It was definitely the Bileklers' villa. When he'd gone there to enquire about Daisy, they couldn't see him off the premises soon enough. But if they'd thought he was ready to give up on her, then they had better think again.

Later that week, while on her way to Nicosia, Melanie peered through her wing mirror yet again. She'd been doing this on and off for the last fifteen minutes, and was curious as to why she was being followed. This must have been the case, because, whether she slowed down or picked up speed, the driver behind did likewise.

She'd left Richard at home, his injured leg evidently playing him up. Anyway, she liked it this way. But, with no sign of Namik, she wondered if he'd lost interest, especially after her confession. It was a pity. She'd got to like the man, had become smitten. Still, if the truth be told, the real reason for coming clean about his brother was more to allay her own conscience than anything else. A few more days, perhaps, then she'd seek him out.

She slowed down on reaching a sharp bend, then once round gathered speed. A kilometre or two on, and, checking the mirror, she saw no sign of the car that had been trailing her. She could have been mistaken, thinking she was being chased, and the driver of the car had simply turned off somewhere.

Shortly afterwards, Melanie sat up with a bolt, afraid for her life, because, directly behind, the same car she'd seen earlier was side by side with a large truck. The driver of the car was having difficulty overtaking, and, when nuzzled out, it nosed behind the truck, intent on trying his luck again.

It was, as usual, a warm day, so warm that Melanie wished she hadn't worn the silk scarf which was draped about her neck. She tugged at this without success, if anything pulling it tighter.

Another glance in the mirror showed that the car behind wasn't afraid of danger, as it forced its way alongside the truck's cabin, on a narrow stretch of road. The truck driver beeped his horn several times, but it didn't stop the car from trying to overtake him.

Rivulets of sweat trickled down Melanie's back when the car came close to her bumper. Panic-stricken, she pressed her foot on the accelerator, acutely aware of the danger on these roads. There was no knowing who the driver was, but she knew without doubt that someone wanted her out of the way, but for what reason she didn't know.

As was the terrain here, this road was quite winding, flanked on one side by towering craggy peaks, which demanded utmost respect for safe driving, though Melanie had enough to think about keeping her eyes glued on the car behind her.

However, there was no sign of the truck now, the driver perhaps having turned off somewhere, but oddly enough, not being able to see it, Melanie felt even more vulnerable.

But this was the last time she would check her mirror. With her heart thumping, and her eyes widening in absolute terror, she hardly felt the force of the other vehicle as her own veered across the road, hit a safety barrier and hurtled several feet into a deep ravine.

Melanie's car had upturned, its wheels still spinning, when moments later, a dark clad figure watched impassively from the broken safety barrier, as if making sure that Melanie Hampton was dead.

Returning to the bar, having left the kitchen, Mustafa looked across at the young man sitting at a table. 'Still waiting?' he called.

'Yes,' answered Namik, 'still waiting.'

Mustafa drew on his cigarette. 'Um, well, I hope she turns up.' He smiled knowingly, then returned to the kitchen.

Namik was sitting in the Five Finger. This restaurant took its name from the group of mountains which were close by, which looked very much like giant fingers. He hadn't mentioned anything about meeting a woman; Mustafa had just assumed this was the case. Though, as it happened, he was, and trusted that Aisha would make an appearance. It was relatively safe here. The Bileklers never patronised this place, according to Mustafa.

Namik checked the time on the cheap watch that he wore. She had to come; she must. His head shot up when the door opened, but he was disappointed to find one of the old farming labourers shuffling in.

Mustafa's son, who was the main cook these days, passed by with a plate of lamb cutlets. Cooked in a clay oven, having been ordered well in advance, it was the restaurant's speciality. Namik, watching this being placed on a customer's table, was unaware of the woman who'd just entered the bar. He turned now and saw the lone figure.

Could it be? Was that really Aisha? He half smiled, uncertain, then the woman smiled back. Coming to his feet, he went to her. 'Aisha?'

She nodded in reply. 'I didn't know what to expect,' she answered, 'but then I recognised you.'

Namik ushered her to the table. 'Same here, but let me get you something to drink.'

A few minutes later, sipping his beer, Namik noticed how much Aisha had changed. She was no longer the slim young girl that he remembered, but slightly plumper, and with a few lines etched across her brow. But her dark almond-shaped eyes were how he remembered, and they lit up now as she spoke. 'I was worried about coming, but I'm glad that I did.'

'How long has it been now? Eight, nine years? I lose count.'

'Enough,' smiled Aisha. 'But you: how are you?'

'As expected,' Namik laughed, trying to sound upbeat, but seeing Aisha stirred up so many memories. 'Anyway, you said in your letter you had an interview, I was not sure what you meant. Are you still teaching?'

Aisha nodded. 'But the school governors want us to send our top students to England, for further education.'

While it was nice talking to Aisha, Namik wanted to tell her all he knew about Aygun, what he'd recently learnt. 'You wanted to meet up, though, didn't you? Was there a special reason?'

She cast her eyes around the bar before she spoke. 'My family: do you see them?'

For a brief moment Namik turned away, then looking at her said; 'I wouldn't usually, but of late there have been some dealings.'

'Oh?' Her eyes opened wide at that.

He decided to come straight to the point. 'Melanie Hampton, a friend of your family, she told me stuff.' He paused, finding this extremely difficult. 'It seems Aygun met his death in a disused olive press.' Namik faltered yet again. 'I am sorry, but it was Hasan, he killed him.'

'If I do not appear shocked, it's because I'm not,' said Aisha. 'That is why I went away, remember?' She stared into her drink. 'That was our meeting place, you know, but my father made excuses. Told me Aygun could not get out of his duties that night after all. This had supposedly come from good authority.'

'So you suspected Hasan, or your father, all along?'

'Who else? Though I had no proof, and that was one of the reasons for seeing you. In case there had been any developments.'

Namik bit at his lip, hesitant about his next words. 'Did you guess your father might have been involved? That both had a hand in this?'

She shook her head. 'If he was, I'm not at all surprised. No disrespect, but my family look down on the lower classes; that is why, well, you probably know.'

'Do not blame yourself. Not everyone is the same. Though I was surprised when I got your letter. Never thought I'd hear from you again.'

'While I was over here I thought it a good idea. A chance to…' She searched for the right words.

'To lay the ghost, so to speak,' said Namik, cutting in.

'Something like that, seeing as you were Aygun's brother. I hope that makes sense.'

'Yes, it's the same for me. A connection, perhaps.'

She sat up straight, pulling her shoulders back. 'I never married. I couldn't, not after Aygun. Yes, I know I was very young back then, but feelings can run quite deep no matter your age.'

Namik smiled at her. 'Maybe one day, eh? You are still young, so who knows?'

Aisha didn't answer but looked pensive.

'They will not get away with it, you know. Anyway,' Namik added, a glint of malice in his eyes. 'I have other unfinished business.'

Her brow creased, but she didn't ask what he meant by that remark, if he had something going on between himself and her family.

Like most Muslims, especially women, Aisha never drank alcohol, so sat there with a soft drink. They stayed talking for a good hour and a half, with Namik telling her about his own restaurant and how nice it was to be in regular work.

When they were ready to leave, Namik glanced over at the customer who'd ordered the lamb. He didn't much like the look of him, and could swear he'd seen him before, but where? He wasn't quite sure.

With less help, now that Osman had sacked another member of his staff, Fatma looked more drained than ever. Not that she ever complained, but this was clearly evident to Daisy. Another observation was the fact that there was still no sign of Melanie Hampton. Daisy thought this strange since the Bileklers were supposed to be on good terms with the woman and her husband.

Richard had visited the house on a couple of occasions, but, apart from that, there had been no more dinner parties. Daisy was sure she'd have known.

There was, of course, the time she'd overheard Hasan and Melanie arguing, though that in itself surely wouldn't have explained her absence.

Apart from the garden, Daisy spent a good deal of her time up in her room. To fill in the hours, she would do some writing, though this seemed futile. What was the use if she never got out of this place?

However, she had given this a lot of thought. There must be a way of getting out of here. There had to be. She had been afraid to chance her luck before, as there was always someone about. Apart from Fatma, the rest of the staff couldn't be trusted, and she most probably wouldn't make it to the end of the drive. Still, it was always worth trying. In the meantime, she would bide her time for the right moment!

Daisy had come into the library, and was looking at a book concerning the recent fighting among Turkish and

Greek Cypriots. She turned when she heard soft footsteps approach. 'Oh,' she uttered, 'it's you.'

'Yes, it is me, I'm afraid,' answered Hasan. 'How very disappointed you must be.'

'I suppose you have every right to come in here,' Daisy gave him a withering look. 'I don't have a lot of choice myself, though I know where I'd rather be.'

'Of course, you would rather be with him, wouldn't you?' Hasan replaced a book he'd taken from the bookshelf. 'But forget him, Daisy. He'll not come back; the man is weak. No backbone.'

Daisy made to slap his face, but Hasan caught hold of her wrist, his eyes full of fire. 'And why did you think he was suitable? You are worth so much more. No, he will not show his face here.' He was watching her closely, as if looking for her reaction.

'Yes,' said Daisy, 'as you keep telling me, but what makes you so certain?' She felt a little dizzy, and put her hand on the bookshelf for support. 'What have you done?'

Hasan walked to the door, an air of defiance about him. 'Please do not question me, Daisy. It does not help.'

Somehow, Daisy found her strength and dashed across the room. 'Namik's done no harm to you,' she said. 'You'd be in too much trouble if you've harmed him. Have you?'

Hasan arched a brow. 'Not me, no, but there are people out there who have little thought for a person's life. If someone happens to get in their way, well, so be it. The thing is, Daisy, you seem to have scant knowledge about human nature, believing everyone's perfect, but it isn't true.'

After Hasan left, Daisy, her hands trembling, pulled a chair from beneath the table and sat down. She may never again see Namik. Like his younger brother, he too may have been killed.

CHAPTER

THIRTEEN

•

HAVING JUST BOUGHT a newspaper, together with a packet of cigarettes, Namik shot forward when he saw the woman approaching. 'Fatma!' he said, barring her way. 'I wish to talk.'

She gave a slight shake of the head, then turned, avoiding his gaze.

'Why do you not want to speak with me?' questioned Namik. 'I am not your enemy.'

'I know, but I must get along. I am a busy woman and I have jobs to do.'

'I am aware of this,' he said, 'but, look, have some coffee with me. I won't keep you, I promise.'

Fatma made to push past. 'No, I mustn't. Somebody might see us,' she retorted rather brusquely.

'Why are you afraid?' Namik looked about him. 'Everyone is going about their own business, not looking at us.'

Much to his surprise, Fatma gripped his arm. 'Daisy is good. We talk and she seems in good spirits. But you, you must be careful, it is best you stay away from the house.'

Without another word, Fatma hurried off, weaving her way among a crowd of jubilant young men. Namik hurried after her, hoping to hear more regarding Daisy, but in the end he had little choice but to let her go. She hadn't said, but her words had much the same meaning. He'd been right all along. Daisy was back at the big house, and the Bileklers' attack on him had said as much.

With the knowledge that he now had, it made things a little easier. At least Daisy was somewhere relatively safe. Not what Namik wished for, but it was far better than the little stone cottage out in the sticks. All the same, he would love to get inside that house up in Bellapais, find out what he was up against. Namik started to give serious thought to this, but at every turn he came up with nothing. How on earth would that come about, with him checking out all those rooms? For there would be lots: the property was vast!

It wasn't in Namik's nature to give up that easily; he had tackled bigger tasks, hadn't he? So the Bileklers' property did pose problems, what with the house full of staff, and he guessed there would always be more than a few present at any one time, so this could be a drawback. No matter: he could work something out, and, if not alone, then a little help may be available.

With all this in mind, Namik's spirits rose a tiny fraction. It wasn't much, but it was all he had. Just a small chance of finding Daisy, and setting her free, away from the Bileklers' clutches.

There had been a phone call from Richard Hampton. Hasan had taken this and wondered why the man wished to speak with him. The voice at the other end had sounded urgent, unlike the usual calm man that he was. Hasan thought it might be about Melanie, though her name hadn't been mentioned. Still, Richard was coming over later. He'd know then.

Standing by the window, looking out onto the garden, Hasan's thoughts turned to his sister. It wasn't as though he hadn't loved her, but that was then, before she'd met that boy. He hadn't liked that village where they had been forced to flee. And when his sister, Aisha, had fallen for someone like Aygun Guven, something had to be done about it. The young soldier was a mere nobody.

So, Aisha was now back in north Cyprus. But what was she doing with Namik, the young lad's brother? His father would have to know. He couldn't keep it from him. Hasan wondered if she was returning for good. Though, whatever she had in mind, her movements were being well monitored.

Hasan's feelings were mixed. A family member who brought disgrace on his family wouldn't be tolerated. And, as for his father, he would be hell bent on keeping his daughter and someone of a lower class apart. Hasan felt pure hatred running through his veins when he thought of the Guven family, especially that troublemaker who'd recently called at the house. Hasan thought of Daisy. Well, she would never see Namik again; he'd make sure of it.

Feeling quite agitated and therefore unable to settle, he paced from room to room, awaiting Richard's arrival, though it was some time later that Melanie's husband showed up. The ex-serviceman sat facing him now, and it was clear the man was quite troubled. Osman had also joined them.

'The last time I saw her?' Richard paused, as if trying to remember. 'She'd driven out somewhere, hadn't told me where. Took no notice at first: you both know what she's like.'

'Well,' said Osman, shaking his head. 'It may not be for me to say, but another man, do you think?'

They were sitting in the drawing room, and, while Osman toyed with a glass of Scotch, Richard sipped tea. The latter put down his cup. 'It's possible, I suppose. If I'm being truthful, I know she never cared much. Yes, maybe at first she did, but after a while I came to accept it was a one-way street.'

'Although you didn't mention any of this when you called earlier, you sounded rather anxious,' said Hasan. 'I mean, what are your thoughts on her disappearance?' He was watching Richard closely.

Richard shrugged. 'I don't know what to think. Melanie has just gone off somewhere, but it's most unusual, and I'm worried about her safety. Anyway, if in a day or so she still hasn't surfaced, I'm sure the local police will be on to me. Being her husband, I'd be their first suspect, wouldn't I?'

Osman looked across at Richard. 'You mean, you have not rung them yet?'

'No.' The ex-soldier shook his head. 'The police wouldn't have thought it odd, but if anything has happened I'll hear soon enough.'

Hasan felt his father's eyes on him, and, glancing up, he couldn't make out if he were angry at Richard for coming here.

'What are you going to do now?' questioned Osman.

'What can I do? Nothing, I suppose, until I hear from her, though I don't know when that will be, or if I ever will.'

Hasan was beset by waves of nausea, and he put a hand to his stomach. He waited until it passed, then said, 'I'm sorry but we cannot help you. We haven't heard a thing.'

Richard nodded, but on his way out, he turned to Hasan. 'Of course, if you do hear anything, you'll let me know?'

'Most definitely.' Osman touched his arm. 'But don't worry, my friend, she's bound to turn up. As you rightly say. Melanie is unpredictable.'

When Richard left, Osman poured himself another Scotch, his bloodshot eyes hardly straying from Hasan, who was watching Richard from the window.

There had been no word from Aisha, not even a phone call to Namik's restaurant. This bothered him seeing as she'd promised to stay in touch. Her appointment at the college must have taken place, so why would she return to Turkey without a word? He sighed, twisted the sign to 'open', then went into the kitchen to have a word with his chef.

Though there was more on his mind than Aisha. A couple of days ago, his poor mother had been taken into hospital. It transpired, that after many tests, the doctors had confirmed she'd suffered an angina attack. His father, Ahmet, had been very concerned, and had sat with her for most of the day, while Namik took his turn, as only one person was allowed by the bedside. He asked the hospital staff if he could stay the night with his mother, but was told it wasn't necessary. She was out of danger, and they'd call if there was any change.

Right into the following day, Namik had been worried in case she took a turn for the worse. If this should happen, he wouldn't know what he'd do.

Still, she'd be home tomorrow, he'd been told. And, with the medication they were giving her, all should be well.

If all this wasn't enough, Namik had been trying to work out a plan. This concerned Daisy, and to carry this plan through he needed to think straight. All sorts of ideas buzzed around his mind, until, at last, he came up with a solution. The thing was, could he carry this off? Of course, his plan would need a small army of helpers. It was the only way, seeing as the Bileklers' property was so heavily guarded.

All this thinking had Namik doubting himself at times. In theory, it seemed fine, but would his idea work? Moreover, would he manage to get the manpower? And, if he did, not only would his plan need to go smoothly, without a false move. Any man willing to undertake this job, would have to be one hundred per cent reliable.

Namik did a lot more thinking. The men's safety, as well as Daisy's, would be his responsibility if it all went wrong.

But Namik wasn't the only one with problems, as up in the village of Bellapais the Bileklers had a few of their own.

'Why have you only just told me?' Osman stomped to and fro, the veins in his neck bulging as if ready to burst. 'It will have to be stopped. That girl will not disgrace me.'

Hasan had flinched at that. 'I wasn't sure whether to tell you. I thought, perhaps…'

'That I wouldn't find out?' finished Osman. 'Oh, believe me, sooner or later it would have reached my ears.'

'So, what do we do?' enquired Hasan, keen to please his father.

Clipping the end off one of his cigars, Osman peered across at his son. 'What we will not do is to allow your sister to see that man again. Who knows what passed between them. Anyway' – he lit the cigar – 'she might consider coming here. I'm not prepared for her questions. There will be some. Mark my words.'

'What, then, do you propose to do?'

Osman smiled thinly. 'That I will leave to you. First you must trace her, but I want an end to her, for good. Do you understand?'

Hasan stood motionless. He'd guessed it would come to this, though how he would do as his father had asked he didn't as yet know.

An independent woman, Mrs Guven hated being fussed. Two of her daughters had come over, and Namik had done what was necessary to make things comfortable for her. His father, Ahmet, had also done his bit.

'Are you OK, Mama?' asked Fetine, her eldest daughter.

'Tut-tut.' The woman eased herself onto her daybed. 'All this kindness and flapping around. You'll make me feeble.'

Namik forced himself to chuckle. 'If that was a joke, Mama, it was very funny.' Secretly, he was rather concerned at her lack of colour. Her hands also had a slight tremor, something he'd never seen before.

Ahmet plumped up his wife's cushions, but when she gave him one of her looks he backed away. 'I'm trying to help,' he told her, 'but if you want I'll leave you be.'

An arm reached out and clutched his. 'What would I do without you, Ahmet? Ignore my grumbling.' She gave a wan smile. 'I am no longer a baby. That was a lifetime ago, but lately I suppose I have been feeling like one.'

As they talked, with Ahmet adding some light-hearted banter and both daughters doing their best not to fuss, Namik noticed how his mother kept gazing at him. If he could read her thoughts, it was likely she was worried about him. In fact, he was certain that was the case. He only hoped she wouldn't ask him any awkward questions, as he hated to lie to her.

At one point, Namik had to turn away quickly when he caught his mother's eyes on him. If she knew the latest happenings, that it was the Bileklers who killed her son, the news would do her untold harm. She would need to know sometime, in due course, but not yet. Not when she'd just left hospital.

The lone figure, sitting outside one of the bars, looked out over Kyrenia's harbour. Richard wasn't a huge drinker, but he was now on his third brandy, and had been here most of the afternoon. He'd been watching a hoard of people disembark from a craft, and make their way to the nearby customs office.

The visitors from the mainland were not only Turks but Israelis, all toting large bundles and other miscellany. Most would have come to visit relatives, and when returning would inevitably take home items which may not be available back home.

That morning, Richard, sleeping badly of late, had been out driving, although he'd no idea where he was going, as long as he got out of the house.

During these restless hours, he had naturally given a great deal of thought to Melanie's absence. He'd got to think that she'd never return, that he'd never see her again. This frightened Richard, as he did care for her, but couldn't begin to guess her reason for leaving him. Not another man, surely. Wouldn't he have known? And, if there had been an accident, the police would have been around by now.

As regards his home, he wished he'd never moved there, no matter that it afforded everything a person could desire. What was the use of comforts if his wife treated him with disrespect? It had been different in the earlier years, but things had changed and when alone she could hardly give him the time of day. However, it seemed strange at the house with only himself rattling about the rooms.

Richard picked up his drink, sipped it and then looked around at the influx of tourists now gathering. Some of these seemed in high spirits, stopping to look at café menus, while looking as if they enjoyed life. In general, the place was beginning to come alive, and, together with the fine weather, people were spending most of their time outdoors. Not that all this exuberance cheered him. The way he felt, nothing could.

And if only people would stop asking after Melanie. He had no answers, and it looked as if he didn't care. Had Osman been right, implying she may have gone off with another man? Richard sighed. Melanie had always been very fond of Hasan. Maybe no one else had noticed, but she was always playing up to him, so that said something.

Richard didn't like being taken for a fool, though he'd carried on, considering the circumstances. His army pension was a good one. But not enough to live the life that he and Melanie had enjoyed throughout their marriage, and most of that money came from her.

Money wasn't everything, though, he'd come to realise. It was having peace of mind, and that was all he craved these days.

Daisy knew for a fact that Osman wasn't going to be home. Directly after breakfast, she'd watched him leave the house, having overheard him telling Hasan he'd be away until the following day.

That was a few hours ago, and since then there had been no sign of Hasan, either. If he had been home, surely she'd have heard or seen him, for, although the property had many rooms, most were hardly used.

In one of the top cupboards in her bedroom was a small soft bag, enough to hold all her work relating to her writing. Excitedly, she stretched up and pulled this down. Then, looking swiftly around, in case she had overlooked something of importance, she crept from the room, making her way quietly down the stairs.

With a couple of the staff no longer working here, since Osman had seen fit to get rid of them, the place seemed morbidly quiet. So, with each carefully trodden step, she hoped that those who were around wouldn't suspect anything. Most of the staff were keen to keep their jobs, and would be very quick to run to one of the Bileklers telling tales.

But, luckily, the hall was clear, and, with her heart pounding in her chest, Daisy quickly fled from the house.

At first, not wanting to create suspicion, should anyone see her, she moved slowly, then once away from the house she hastened along the narrow road without looking back. Her heart was still beating rapidly, but Daisy's elation was so great she could hardly believe she'd finally escaped.

Only a few residents were about, and this included two elderly men, one of whom was digging his front garden while the other looked on.

Neither looked up as she passed them, so, feeling more confident, she moved at a faster pace. She hadn't got far, though, before she felt someone following her. Instinct told her to move even faster, but, when she did, so too did the echoing footsteps.

Daisy was tempted to see who it was, but decided against this. Her throat felt incredibly dry, and gasping for breath it crossed her mind that running away might not have been the best move.

Very soon, Bellapais Abbey came into view. The once-beautiful sandstone building, with tapering needle trees growing within its walls, seemed to beckon Daisy. She wanted to run, lose herself inside the darkened archways, but this was futile seeing as the walls were not entirely intact and she could be easily seen.

By now, she felt ready to collapse, the sweat pouring from her, but she was still gaining on her assailant.

With a snap decision, she ran for all she was worth, but, instead of choosing an entry point, she headed into the abbey grounds. Once here, a quick glance showed her a small flight of steps. She ran down these, almost losing her footing halfway down. Then, stooping low so as not to be seen, she retrieved the shoe which had fallen off, her fearful eyes darting this way and that.

As she waited, hardly daring to breathe, Daisy heard the shuffle of footsteps. She ducked back, but, when all was silent, she mounted a few steps, only to find a grizzled-haired man with a yard broom sweeping a path.

In the hushed atmosphere, she heard the echoing mantra coming from the nearby mosque, calling worshippers to prayers. Because of this, Daisy couldn't hear if the person who had been following her was still around. She realised that this wasn't as easy as she'd first thought.

After a while, Daisy started to think that whoever it was that had been chasing her may possibly have taken a wrong turn and lost sight of her.

She mused on this. Who on earth could it have been? Ruling out Osman, she thought of Hasan. But then he hadn't been in the house. Or had he?

The young Turkish soldier, sent here on guard, supposedly to keep an eye on the abbey grounds, halted in his duties to take refuge from the heat. He found this in the shade of some thick greenery. Removing his soft peaked cap, he brushed the back of his hand across his brow to wipe away the perspiration which had started to trickle down his face. He caught sight of Daisy then, and gave her a friendly grin. Apart from the grizzled-haired gardener, nobody else was about.

Daisy smiled back at the soldier. She too had sheltered among the dense shrubbery, having felt it safe to find a better place to conceal herself.

The soldier, lean in his khaki uniform, stared at Daisy through narrow slanting eyes. Then, moving towards her, he attempted to speak, but none of it seemed to make sense. She couldn't help but look over her shoulder, suspecting some hidden agenda. The soldier may have been asked to keep her there. But Daisy soon ruled this out.

The young man tried again, his gibberish tongue getting him nowhere, at which he shook his head.

'I don't understand,' Daisy finally told him. 'I'm English.'

Pulling Turkish lire from his trouser pocket, he thrust it at her. 'Chahy?' he said, and pointed to his right.

She shrugged, tucking herself back into the shrubbery. Why was he pestering her? She was afraid he would attract attention, too, had someone been following her. All she wanted was to hide away, until it was deemed safe to get out of Bellapais altogether.

'Chahy?' he reiterated, again gesturing to his right.

Of course, thought Daisy, he was asking if she'd like some tea. Somewhere hereabouts was a kiosk, and the Turks pronounced the beverage as *chahy*, not *cay*, how it was spelt.

He tried again. 'Bira.'

'No! No beer.' Daisy's heart was thumping, she wished he would go away. She wanted to run, but where? She guessed he was bored, wanting nothing but company, but she had little choice but to give him a gentle nudge. 'You leave now,' she said, while keeping her voice steady.

As the soldier left, heading for the kiosk, he gave a backward glance at Daisy, while she breathed a sigh of relief.

Some yards ahead was the Greek Orthodox church. A man had just locked the door and was walking away with a bunch of keys. Taking her chance, Daisy ran over, asking politely if she could see inside.

He was a burly-looking man, with rough features, which softened when Daisy explained why she was here in Cyprus. 'Ah,' he said, noting the small case she carried. 'You wish to make notes, to write!' He shook his head, his features returning to their set look. 'But no photos. No allowed.'

Unlocking the church door, the man ushered Daisy inside, then followed on behind.

This sanctuary, because that's how Daisy saw it, felt safe, and was the real reason for wanting to shelter here. Still, she wasn't sure about her escort, who kept a close eye on her.

As expected, it was very quiet, eerily so, on account of the church being kept locked and not used owing to the previous troubles. Nobody could deny, though, how beautiful it was, with its stained-glass windows and original artefacts still intact. And the Greeks were certainly masters at this.

Daisy had sat in one of the pews, making to take everything in, and in normal circumstances she would have, but she was still badly shaken at what had happened. She didn't know how long she could sit here, but hoped against hope that whoever was chasing her had given up, thinking she was no longer here.

'So, you like?' The man, or janitor, had slumped next to her, waving a burly arm at the interior.

A quick glance round told Daisy the door was shut, perhaps locked. Was she safe with this man? Who could she trust? She panicked. Perhaps no one could get in here, but could she, if wished, get out?

A rank body odour wafted from the man, and his breath smelt sour. She felt sick, and, getting to her feet, she moved towards the door. 'Thank you,' she said. 'It was very kind of you to show me the church. Though I'd better be off.'

It seemed Daisy had the man wrong; he was quite harmless, and, although his lack of hygiene was offensive, he opened the door and showed her out into the dazzling sunlight.

Thanking him again, she hurried across the sub-tropical gardens, where palms, oleander and frangipani grew, the latter already in flower and emitting a lovely almond scent. However, thinking about her next course of action, which was to get moving along to Ozankoy, the next village, she literally jumped when a pair of strong hands grabbed her.

'You!' she gasped, her eyes widening in horror. 'But I thought you were out.'

Hasan shook his head. 'Out?' he said, his eyes heavy. 'I was dozing, until I heard the door.'

'The door?' Daisy had been most careful. She could have sworn she had left it ajar.

He gave a short laugh. 'I have excellent hearing. Even if I have been drinking.'

It was like a long-drawn-out dream to Daisy. To get that far, then be practically marched back was the stuff of nightmares. She could still see Hasan's face when he'd grabbed her. He'd looked pleased with himself, like he was enjoying the chase, but then his eyes had glinted maliciously, as if her fate was already being considered!

Here in Bellapais, Daisy had seen and been inside another old olive press, similar to the one in Bogaz. She thought of this now, and prayed that her fate wouldn't be that of Aygun's.

Sitting on the bed, back in her bedroom, she closed her eyes. How could they do that to that young man? She'd overheard the Hampton woman loud and clear, at how Hasan had clubbed Aygun to death with some sort of object. Would this happen to her? She started to shake, while her eyes constantly darted towards the door.

CHAPTER
FOURTEEN

•

ALL SORTS OF names kept going around in Namik's head: men who lived not only in his village but on the outer fringes too. Mehmet was one of these, and it was most certain he'd be willing to help with Daisy's rescue. Some had served in the military with Namik, but those that hadn't were still worthy, and as far as he knew were of a reliable source.

The idea here was that they, if up for it, could band together. Of course, a plan, a thorough one, would have to be carefully thought out. Namik had thought of this before, but his mother had been taken ill so he had put it on hold. And, besides that, he hadn't been certain about Daisy's whereabouts. Though now, thanks to Fatma, he knew she was back at the Bileklers' residence.

At the bus depot in Kyrenia, a dusty wasteland where they picked up and dropped off passengers, Namik kicked his heels while waiting for his bus.

A couple of small trucks, also on the site, were selling fruit, bread and fish. A small queue formed at the fish van, but the other vendor looked ready to move on. Namik now recognised this man. He lived in his village, but he didn't know his name.

Namik continued to kick his heels. If the bus didn't come soon, well, he'd cadge a lift, if that lift happened to be going his way, of course. Anyway, it wasn't unusual with locals to give someone a lift.

The man looked across, waving a meaty hand while displaying a toothy grin. Doing likewise, Namik walked over. 'On your way back?' he enquired of the man.

The driver was of a good stature, with a thatch of dark wavy hair. 'Yes, I have these to deliver in the village,' he explained, pointing to boxes of vegetables and huge green melons. 'And the loaves. Must not forget them!'

The flat round loaves looked good and fresh, and Namik's mother always bought them. 'I'd appreciate a lift, if that is no bother.'

'Then jump in,' the man said cheerily, opening the passenger door.

Now on their way, the man indicated to the back of his truck. 'I think I'll charge service for home delivery,' he laughed, 'and then I might be able to retire early.'

Namik glanced at him. 'It's a good job you do. Some of the old ladies find it a struggle to get into Kyrenia.'

'Well, I help if I can; one of those old ladies is my mother. Have you seen her?' he asked dryly.

A grin softened Namik's face. Yes, he had seen the old woman. Hadn't everyone? She was an odd character, often talking to herself and shouting at children as they passed. Practically bald, the wisps of hair she did have were often held with a scrap of ribbon.

'Cigarette?' Namik offered the packet.

'No thanks. Doctor's orders. My cough is too bad.'

Namik lit one himself. 'Anyway, how is everything?'

'OK. My children are very well, all grown up. My eldest is expecting another little one. But what about yourself? You getting married?'

Namik shook his head, though it was doubtful if his companion noticed.

In the centre of the road, waiting to turn right, the man glanced sideways at Namik. 'Perhaps I shouldn't ask; it is none of my business.'

'Sorry,' came the reply, 'but there's plenty of time.'

The van moved on now, rumbling along towards Ozankoy. 'That nice girl I saw you with, still see her?'

'No,' answered Namik, hoping he didn't sound waspish. 'But it's a little difficult to explain.'

'Oh, well, I'm listening.' A chuckle. 'In fact, I'm good at that: years of experience.'

'The last time I saw Daisy, there was snow up there.' He inclined his head towards the Five Finger mountain range. 'Now look at it. So, you see, it was a long time ago.'

Namik's somewhat casual air didn't fool the big man. 'So where is she now, this Daisy?'

Namik paused, not sure how much to tell this man. 'Heard of the Bileklers?'

'Hasn't everyone? But what have they got to do with it?'

'A lot; it is their house where she is staying.'

The man frowned. 'But if she is staying...'

'Sorry,' Namik cut in. 'Being kept would be more accurate.'

A short coughing fit left the driver breathless. 'I see.' He took another breath. 'But they are very strong words, my friend. Are you sure about this?'

'Positive.' Namik turned to the man, 'But I need some help!'

'Look, we steer clear of that family, if we can.'

A long silence followed, and Namik wished he hadn't spoken out. His pride felt dented; it galled him to ask favours. It wasn't as though he knew the man. He had only seen him around his village.

How he loathed those Bileklers and Melanie Hampton. They, who not only held Daisy capture but had killed his beloved brother. They had even got him sinking to an all-time low, asking strangers for help!

During the journey, the driver had been thinking. He remembered his mother, who'd once pointed out this young man. Like himself, his passenger was ex-army, and had risen up to commander, so surely that stood for something. And what of his family? Like numerous others, they had lost their youngest son in that war.

Glancing at his companion, the man was surprised to find his head bent forward, and his eyes closed, as if very troubled.

They had reached Ozankoy now, and when the driver spoke his voice fell hard on Namik's ears. 'If it's help that you need, then we will do all we can, my friend.'

'We?' Namik's head shot up.

'Yes, there must be another willing to help a neighbour. And' – he paused, as if mulling something over – 'I have a score to settle. Something I'll explain another time. Of course,' he added quickly, 'I still wish to help in any way I can.'

Namik let out a long breath, his relief showing only too clearly. 'I'd been thinking along those lines myself,' he told the man. 'It's doubtful the police would be of much help. I have the feeling they see only good in those Bileklers. So we'd need a few strong men. As many as possible, if anything. By the way, did you know they kept dogs?'

The man shook his head. 'No, but dogs I am not afraid of.'

This man was certainly well built, and with his shirt sleeves rolled to the elbow his muscular arms looked as though he could tackle anything. Taking this all in, Namik's senses were stimulated. 'If we did this, I'd never know how to thank you.' A tear had sprung to his eye and he quickly dashed it away.

'Of course,' said the man, 'but we must be very careful, cautious to the extreme.'

'Very,' agreed Namik. 'The very thing we must do.'

A large, rough hand fell on Namik's shoulder. 'Say when, and we'll make our plans. And, by the way, my name is Kazim.'

Arif Camal nodded his dark head knowingly. Even after all these years he'd known it was the same girl, the instant she'd walked into the Five Finger bar. Now, having searched high and low, here she was in Nicosia.

Of course, much of this had to do with his cunning, asking many questions, and sometimes paying for information.

He checked the grin that had begun to spread across his face. The girl, or young woman that she now was, had been on friendly terms at school with his own daughter. He'd been struggling back then, with barely enough money to feed his family on, but not so now. His bank balance had become healthier since working for the Bileklers. Pretty healthy indeed. But Arif would need even more, if he was going to buy a better house, a house more suited to the needs of his mother, who'd be moving in with them.

Arif Camal was greedy, and, although working at the car hire, this still wasn't enough for his needs, so anything coming his way was an advantage.

Standing about twenty yards away, and out of sight, Arif Camal saw that a man had joined Aisha. Like her, he'd just come out of the College of Education. They stood for what seemed like an age, talking, the man appearing quite chummy.

A few others came out, and they too joined Aisha.

It proved to be a long wait for Arif, but when at last the gathering broke up he kept his eye firmly on Aisha Bilekler. He wouldn't lose her now; he couldn't. He had too much to lose.

'Well, what is it, son?'

'Nothing,' answered Namik. 'Nothing at all.'

His mother was still pallid, and even simple tasks made her breathless.

Mrs Guven studied her son through dark tinted glasses, which had Namik turning away. 'It is something, I know. A mother always knows.'

'You have enough to fret about,' Namik scorned. 'Anyway' – he gestured to a basket of clean sheets – 'you should not be doing your daughter's washing. They are more than capable themselves.'

'It is nothing. It keeps me from mischief, and I don't do so much these days.' The chest heaved, like someone fighting for breath.

Namik flinched at this. 'You look tired, Mama. A rest, that's what you need.'

'How can I rest when my boy looks so worried?'

'But I'm not. Look, I'm smiling!' A huge grin spread across his face.

Mrs Guven eased herself onto her daybed. A scarf was wound around her head, her grey hair peeping from the edges. 'I hope you are not worrying on my account,' she said. 'The doctor calls in when he can.'

'No, of course not,' hastened Namik. 'Concerned, yes, but that is it. But look.' He tried to sound cheerful. 'The restaurant is busy, though, and, as well as the locals, there are lots of tourists.'

She laughed at this. 'Of course, I might have guessed. You were always a hard worker.'

It was on the tip of Namik's tongue to tell her about Aisha, and how he hadn't heard from her, but thought it wiser to leave well alone. Reminding her of the past was not what she needed.

Shortly after, he left for work, wanting to be there when the chef arrived that evening. He was unaware of the dubious look his mother was giving him. But, on his way into Kyrenia, he remembered Kazim's kind words. The man was going to help get Daisy out of that house. And he said he wasn't afraid of dogs. Well, that was something, because he himself was absolutely terrified of the beasts. There must be more than a couple, and that would have been enough, but he'd heard them. The noise from that garden enclosure sounded like a pack of wolves when anybody came near. When one started up, the rest quickly followed. Like other times when he thought of those dogs, Namik felt his spine go all prickly, and this had him doubting his part in the break-in.

Of course, when that time came, Namik would make himself do it. He owed Daisy that much, and, equally important, he wouldn't allow himself to become a total weakling.

Hasan found his father in the garden. Osman rarely sat outside, hardly paid heed to the well laid out planting, but here he was looking up at a wall which was being taken over by a rapidly growing jasmine, whose heady scent filled the air.

'The matter is in hand,' said Hasan. 'Arif Camal is on the job.'

A nerve twitched in Osman's jaw. 'If that is the case, then we need not worry. Let us hope he will not let us down.'

'Has he ever?' asked Hasan.

'I hope not, but wait and see. He has his eye on a charming property. Small, you understand, but nonetheless charming. Enough for his needs, anyway.'

'Yes, no doubt.' Hasan was a mixture of emotions. It was years since he had seen his sister, and if she had been tracked down, what then? For his part, everything had been thought out most carefully. Though things didn't always go to plan; he was well aware of this. Hasan cursed silently. Why had Aisha returned to north Cyprus? Had this not been the case, and she had stayed in Turkey, it would have saved him from having to carry out such a harrowing task.

With his sister utmost on his mind, Hasan left the house and drove out to one of his favourite bars. He couldn't let his father down, and would have to do what was expected of a dutiful son. Osman was counting on his help, and would rather die than have a daughter bring disgrace on the family by hanging out with yet another common village boy.

While all that was happening, Richard Hampton had opened the dark panelled door at his home to find two uniformed police officers facing him. They had left their car the end of the curved drive, which was just visible from the arched door. Richard knew at once it was bad news, and, swallowing hard, he felt the colour drain from his face.

'Mr Hampton?'

'Yes.' Richard stood motionless.

'May we come inside? We have some news.'

A slightly shaken Richard let the two officers into the house.

'We have found a body. We believe it to be your wife, Mrs Hampton.' It was the same officer who had spoken earlier.

Richard walked to a chair, hesitated, then decided to retrace his steps. 'Where was this?' He still hadn't reported her absence, thinking it possible she may return, though he somehow knew this to be unlikely.

The officers exchanged a fleeting glance. 'The car, and the driver had plunged into a ravine. It was on a very sharp bend on the road leading into Nicosia.'

This time, Richard did sit down. A look of bewilderment was etched on his face. 'Nicosia?'

'Yes,' answered the second officer, 'but she may have been heading for another destination, who knows?' He'd forgot to remove his cap when he'd entered the house, but he did this now. 'How long has your wife, if it is your wife, been missing?'

Richard shrugged. 'A few weeks, maybe more.'

'And you did not report it?'

'No, I thought she'd come home, eventually.'

The second officer, whose hair appeared to be grafted to his head, cast an eye around the large, expensively furnished room. 'Is the house in your name, sir?'

'My wife put down the money. But it isn't a problem. Never has been. But why do you ask?'

The same officer, considerably younger than his colleague, raised a finely drawn brow. 'How come?'

'What's unusual about that?' Richard had come to his feet. 'My wife's from a rich family, but our finances are our own business, surely.'

There followed a long silence until the older officer spoke. 'Anyway, you will have to come with us. The body will have to be identified, too, though this will not be easy!'

Richard said nothing after this, and still hadn't regained his colour when he walked from the house.

Then, some time later, down at the station, Richard was given a glass of water, which he accepted gratefully. He had just returned from the morgue, having identified his wife's remains. He wanted to gulp back the full glass of water, his throat being so dry, but with each sip he felt ready to throw up.

There were two officers present: the older one, who'd escorted Richard from the house, and another who was new to him.

'We appreciate how shocked you must be, Mr Hampton, but we have to know everything, anything you can throw light on.' The older officer spoke decent English, though at times he struggled slightly with certain words.

'There's nothing much I can tell you,' answered Richard, his head cast down.

'Nothing? Are you sure?' A pair of eyes, having witnessed the most appalling tragedies, bore into him.

'Certain,' replied Richard. 'As I said, my wife just went off in her car. She was like that, had a mind of her own, so to speak.'

A window had been left open, but the heat was oppressive, which had Richard loosening his shirt collar. A door opened then, letting a bright beam of sunlight fall across the officer's desk. Richard looked up to find that the younger officer, who he'd seen earlier, had entered the room. He gestured with his head for the older officer to step outside.

It was eerily quiet in the interview room, but after about five minutes the senior officer returned. Standing behind the desk, arms folded, he scrutinised Richard before speaking. 'We have reason to hold you for a little longer, Mr Hampton. Something else has come to our notice.'

Richard frowned. 'Longer? How long?'

'That depends. We have many more questions, and we need you to answer them truthfully.' The officer's face was granite hard, while behind him someone brought in a mug of strong coffee. He placed this on the desk in front of Richard. Then, when the door closed behind him, more questions were fired at Richard, questions he didn't always know how to answer.

It was so hot that Kazim's shirt was opened almost to the waist. He took out his handkerchief, mopped his face and grinned at the group of women who'd formed an untidy queue at his truck in Ozankoy. The young woman at the front pointed at the tray of loaves. 'Ekmek.'

Kazim wrapped one up for her, and, just as he was doing so, Namik walked by, tapping him lightly on the shoulder.

Kazim greeted him with a thumbs up gesture and spoke in a low register. 'I have spread the word. Good men, too.'

This seemed to please Namik, and he carried on in the direction of his house. Once inside, he scooped some coffee into a small copper pot, then lit the gas beneath it. His father, Ahmet, was out working, his mother having been taken out by her youngest daughter.

Things for Namik, appeared to be looking up. The restaurant was doing nicely, he'd been able to buy himself some much-needed clothing, and his mother's health had improved, now that her medication had stabilised.

Of course, Daisy was always on his mind, and he'd never stopped fretting about her since she'd disappeared.

While the coffee bubbled, Namik opened the back door, lit a cigarette and then watched as he blew smoke rings into the windless air. He hadn't known Kazim long, but he was proving to be a most helpful friend.

Namik couldn't believe he'd soon see Daisy – well, he hoped and prayed this would happen. Daisy! His heart leapt at the thought of her.

'If you cannot do anything right, do nothing at all!' These words snapped out of Osman Bilekler's mouth in a fury of insults. 'And another thing. I asked you not to cut that cherry tree down!'

The gardener, having worked for the Bileklers for the past five years, cowered meekly. 'The tree was dying. It was big and dangerous.'

Sweat dripped from Osman's jowls, and he mopped this with a crisp white handkerchief. 'As if I care. I rarely sit outside, man.' The previous gardener had planted the cherry tree, and it was his son's favourite fruit.

Picking up a few of his tools, the middle-aged man skulked off.

Osman, his red eyes bulging, called after him. 'You'd better watch yourself. There are plenty more looking for work!'

As Osman walked into the house, he saw Richard Hampton walking along the path. He sighed, his mouth tightening. Visitors were the last thing he wanted.

'Dead? Melanie?' Osman moved to the cabinet and poured himself a Scotch. 'When? When did this happen?' he asked, flatly. His back was turned on Richard.

'The day she left for Nicosia, well, I don't know where she was actually heading for. But there was a nasty accident. Her car was found in a ravine. It plunged through the barrier.'

Gulping back about half of his Scotch, Osman didn't sit, neither did he offer Richard a drink.

'The police have been on my back,' explained Richard. Dark shadows beneath his eyes showed he wasn't sleeping, and his face had a greyish tinge. 'It's pretty well assumed it was me, that I had something to do with her accident.'

'But you never really cared for her, did you?' accused Osman. 'Although I am not blaming you for her death, you understand.'

Richard gave him a hard look.

'Anyway, if that is how it is,' shrugged Osman. He refilled his glass. 'It is well known that members of the family get blamed.'

Sinking into a chair, Richard covered his face with both hands. He was silent for a moment, then said, 'It's a mess, the whole thing. I don't know what will happen now.'

'If you've come here for sympathy, forget it,' said Osman, irritably. 'I have more pressing problems.' He seemed to have forgotten the deep friendship he'd once shared with the Englishman.

'But you're wrong about Melanie,' answered Richard. 'I did love her, very much. But things changed, or she had. Nothing I did satisfied her. Couldn't do a thing right. I suppose I was kidding myself in the end.'

Osman sat down now, but still appeared unconcerned. 'Well, what now?'

Richard threw up his arms. 'I have to sit and wait.'

More Scotch was poured, though this time a glass was handed to Richard, which he greatly appreciated, though his was well diluted with soda.

A young waiter at the Turtle's Rest handed the phone to Namik. 'It's for you, a woman.'

Namik frowned and put the phone to his ear. 'Hello, who is it?'

A pause, then: 'It is me, Aisha. I am being followed.'

'Aisha! Where are you?'

The voice at the other end was breathless. 'I was waiting for the bus, not knowing where I was going, but I had to get away.'

'And now?' Namik looked to see he wasn't overheard.

'At Guzelyurt. I'm at that little tamirhane. They let me use their phone.'

Namik knew this garage. 'You say "followed". Who is it, do you know?'

'No, but it has to do with my father, who else?'

Namik's mind worked overtime. He wasn't sure he could get hold of Mehmet, or if he was using his scooter. If he wasn't at home he may even have taken the car. 'Aisha, look, I will try to get to you. I'll have a word with one of the waiters; they can manage here.'

There was another pause, longer this time.

'Aisha! Are you still there?'

'Sorry, I had to duck out of sight. But hurry: the tamirhane closes soon.'

'I don't know how long it will take,' answered Namik. 'Ask that shop next door if you can shelter there. Explain to them.'

'Hurry, please hurry.' The voice faltered.

Still clutching the phone, Namik seemed to be rooted to the spot.

At last, he found his voice. 'Huseyin!' He called twice before the young waiter came, and Namik told him he had urgent business to attend to, and to tell his chef to lock up at closing time.

Mehmet lived on the outskirts of Ozankoy, not far from the road leading to Kyrenia. It was early evening and not too hot, which was a good thing as Namik had a fair walk.

On arrival at his friend's house, he noticed how quiet it was, as normally Mehmet's two younger brothers played outside. Puzzled, Namik wrapped at the door of the neat, stone cottage. Then, getting no answer, he tried again, but still no reply. He thought maybe that the family were out at the back, eating. He walked round to the side gate, about ten yards along a narrow walkway.

There was nobody in the garden, but a small cycle was propped against the shed, and a red football was close by, both belonging to the younger boys.

Next door, a woman of about thirty was taking her washing in from the line. 'Who are you?' she called.

'A friend of Mehmet's,' Namik called back. 'I need to see him, but it looks like he's not at home.'

'Ah, well, he is with his family. They are at a wedding, a relative,' she told him.

'I wouldn't ask normally, but where is this? It is very urgent, believe me,' explained Namik.

The woman folded the last of her washing, dropping it into a plastic basket. 'It isn't my place to say,' she said, shaking her head. 'They may not like it.'

'Please,' begged Namik. 'Mehmet is my best friend; I only want to borrow his scooter. It is, as I say, most urgent!'

The dark-haired woman, wearing a scarf which was wound around her head and tied at the back, carried her basket over to Namik. 'It is along there, two streets.' She pointed to her left. 'His mother's sister's girl.'

'I know it,' exclaimed Namik, somewhat mollified. 'Thank you.' He was already on his way.

It was another fifteen minutes before Namik returned to the cottage. Having explained to Mehmet his reasons for wanting the scooter, his friend had given him the key to the garden shed and wished him the best of luck. Namik took the scooter through the side gate, started the engine, then roared in the direction of Guzelyurt. His only hope was that Aisha had taken refuge in the little shop he'd suggested, and that she was still there when he arrived.

When Namik finally pulled up at the garage, he saw it had already closed. The shop, too, had also shut its doors. He cursed at this, left the scooter outside the shop and rapped hard at the double doors.

Very soon, a bolt slid back and a man of about forty appeared. 'Yes, what is it?' he asked. 'We are about to eat.'

'I am looking for a young woman. Was she here?' enquired Namik. 'I told her to take refuge in your shop. That's if you didn't mind.'

The man stepped outside, glancing up and down the road. 'She seemed agitated, especially when she saw this man. She ran soon after.'

'The fool!' Namik's mouth had formed a thin line.

'Pardon?'

'No matter. Thank you.' Namik set off on the scooter, one eye on the lookout for Aisha, while watching the way ahead.

CHAPTER
FIFTEEN

•

NOT KNOWING WHICH direction Aisha had taken made matters even worse. In fact, there was the possibility she may have left the area and headed for Kyrenia. Namik pondered on this, and it seemed most unlikely, seeing as he was expected to meet her here in Guzelyurt. Still, where was Aisha now, and was she safe? Namik hoped she was still in the area, because, if not, he hadn't a hope in hell of finding her.

Ahead of him, a young woman, fitting Aisha's description, was stooped over and talking to a small child. Namik hurried on, parked the scooter at the kerb, and jumped off. He ran the last couple of yards. 'Aisha!' he called.

The woman turned, then straight away looked back at the child.

'Sorry, mistook you for somebody else.' Namik's embarrassment showed.

'That is all right,' said the girl. 'I was telling this child to go inside. He must have run out of the house here. The road gets busy.'

The boy was no more than eighteen months old, and, without any more fuss, he trotted through an open gate and along the path leading to the house.

Namik gave the girl a nod, then ran back to the scooter.

A good hour had passed, and after a worrying search, on foot, as well as the scooter, Namik was ready to call it a day. But, just before he did that, he rode around for a few more minutes, all the time wondering who it might be who was after Aisha.

He was now on foot, a final check before heading back to Kyrenia. Suddenly, Namik pulled up sharp when he saw the man. At first, he couldn't believe it, but then it hit him. This was the man he'd seen at the Five Finger bar where he'd arranged to meet Aisha! Indeed, it was the same man he'd spoken to at the car hire!

The oily-faced man, with the bushy moustache, hadn't seen him. He was on the opposite side of the road, hovering, as though uncertain of which direction he should take. Namik had ducked inside a shop doorway, which looked like it had long ceased trading. Looking at the man, he wondered if he had been the one chasing Aisha, or if he were here in Guzelyurt for another reason. But the more he thought about it, the more reluctant he was to believe this. It was all too much of a coincidence.

The man took something from the inside of his jacket, glanced up and down the street, then started to walk briskly in the direction of which Namik had just come. Luckily, he kept to the same side of the road, so hadn't known he was being watched. But, just in case, Namik turned towards the shop window, making to peer inside. The window was quite grubby, but was still able to show a decent reflection, and through it Namik kept his eye on the man as he continued to carry on along the street.

When he felt it safe to do so, Namik followed. It didn't take long before he saw where the man was heading. A satisfied smirk settled across Namik's face. He'd guessed correctly. The little grocery store where Aisha had hoped to take refuge was about to be visited again.

Namik had kept well back but he was still able to keep a close eye on the man whose name he still didn't know.

Namik watched as the man rapped at the door, but moments later the proprietor, furious at being disturbed yet again, sent his visitor off with a flea in his ear.

There was nothing Namik could do now, and it would be useless checking out the whole area without a clue to where Aisha may have gone. Still, for the moment she'd escaped that man's clutches. She was probably miles away. But where was anybody's guess.

The man from the car hire firm was nowhere to be seen. He seemed to have disappeared somewhere. Namik walked slowly back to where he'd left the scooter.

As it happened, the restaurant was still open on his return, and had a fair number of customers, so he stayed until closing time. There was one thing that bothered him. What was it that the man had taken from his inside pocket earlier? Namik really hoped it hadn't been a gun, for, if he had got hold of Aisha, her life would have most definitely been in danger!

When Namik walked through his door that night, he felt ready to fall into his bed, but he knew he wouldn't sleep. How could he when so much was going on? Aisha was out there somewhere, but, with somebody out to get her, how safe was she? For all Namik knew, she may already be dead.

His thoughts then turned to Daisy. How was she faring? Did she miss him as he missed her? And, more importantly, would they really be able to get her away from that house? The more Namik thought about this, the more he doubted himself, because the Bileklers weren't the only problem. There were other risk factors. What about visitors? They would hinder things, surely. Namik's heart raced. The dogs had to be the biggest concern. The beasts were all over the place!

If Namik hadn't been sleeping well of late, he was to get none that night. None at all.

Standing by her bedroom window, Daisy seethed with hatred for the man sitting beneath the jacaranda tree. Hasan was reading a newspaper, his dark head bent forward, fully engrossed.

Was he even aware what he'd done to her? How he'd stolen her life, and made her a virtual prisoner? And had he no idea he may have made her pregnant! Daisy was sure of it, had been for some time.

Where was she to turn? Who would care? Even if it pleased Hasan that she was to have his child, it certainly didn't please her. Just looking at him made Daisy's skin crawl.

Apart from anything else, she hadn't been feeling too well, having had a few dizzy spells, so what was that all about? Of course, she could have asked for a doctor, but would that have helped? Foolish, perhaps, but she decided to wait. Truth was, the longer she kept Hasan in the dark, the better. The last thing she wanted was for him to fuss around her.

Daisy was about to move away from the window when she saw Fatma. The housekeeper had brought out a jug of iced lemon. She placed this on a small table, pushing back a large cluster of blue, bell-shaped flowers of the jacaranda which hung heavily from the tree. She spoke to Hasan for a minute or so, then, on returning to the house, glanced up at Daisy's window. She gave a tentative wave before hurrying on.

Hasan never looked up, unaware, it seemed, of Daisy being there. If he had been, she doubted he'd be at all interested. His ardour had waned, no doubt about that, for why else had he not been near her?

Daisy hoped that this wouldn't change. Her door was kept locked, but she still had to leave her room at times.

She had got back into her writing, something she'd neglected of late, but soon realised it was best to keep her mind occupied. Sitting at the table, she picked up her pen, then glanced at the rapidly growing manuscript. She already knew the title. It was to be called *Forty Paces East*. This was, after all, one of the eastern Mediterranean resorts. Daisy had often pondered on the first two words of the title, though she had an uncanny feeling this was meant to be.

Nevertheless, every so often, her mind drifted from the matter in hand and went back to her predicament. What the hell was she to do? She had tried to get away, but, just as she thought that might happen, Hasan had found her and brought her back here. He said he'd seen her slip out of the house. Though how he'd managed that after imbibing a few drinks, then having fallen asleep was quite puzzling. He couldn't have heard her, as she'd been extra careful, moving about without a single sound.

But someone must have seen her, even though she'd checked out everyone's whereabouts that day. So who was it? Who would be so cruel to want her caught, and therefore curtail her freedom? It wouldn't have been Fatma; she hadn't even been in the house at that time. Daisy was never too sure of the other staff. They hardly spoke to her, maybe because they preferred not to become involved with what went on, but, all the same, someone couldn't be trusted.

Namik was hoping to hear from Kazim any day now. Apart from his usual few hours off, when the restaurant was closed, he was spending more time away, leaving someone else in charge. For the last hour or so, he'd been working in his front garden. If Kazim should pass the house, he'd be able to spot him easily, and could keep him informed as to what was happening.

Now and then, Namik would stroll around the village, chatting to friends. He was careful to be on his guard, watching what he said but listening for anything that may harm his plans. Of course, most of these men could be trusted, though it didn't do to mouth off. Namik was shrewd enough to know not everybody was honourable, especially if a few words from them in the right direction earned them a wad of cash.

When a team of men had been carefully chosen, a meeting would be set up in Ibrahim's mail sorting office. Namik could hardly wait for that day.

As he hoed the many weeds, Mrs Guven bustled out. She placed a cup of coffee on a plastic table, then mopped her brow with the hem of her apron. Some years before, her husband, Ahmet, had constructed a pergola in which to grow a vine; now it was festooned with an abundance of purple grapes.

Looking up at his mother, Namik wondered, as he often did, how much she knew. She had, at times, asked after Daisy, but Namik always ducked out of an answer.

The sick woman sat down heavily on one of the chairs, the dappled shade from the vine giving welcome relief from the late morning sun. 'I am concerned about you,' she told Namik. 'You hate it when I fuss, but I do worry. It is only natural.'

Namik stood up from his task, stretching himself. 'You are the same as Mehmet's mother. She thinks he's still her baby!' He laughed as he said this.

'Oh!' Mrs Guven threw up her hands. 'To us, you are still our babies. You don't like it, but there you go!' She reached forward, touching his cheek. 'No colour here, and thin.'

Namik felt the gentle touch of her fingers, and, taking her hand, he squeezed it before letting it go. He'd finished his coffee, and followed this now with the water that was on the tray. Looking up at the pergola, he said cheerfully, 'Look, the grapes; they will be ready soon. Maybe my brother-in-law, Mustafa, will make more wine!'

They both laughed, remembering how dreadful the last lot was and how, behind Mustafa's back, they had had to tip the half dozen bottles away.

Mrs Guven picked up her glass of water, and, as she put it to her lips, Namik noticed how her hand trembled. How unselfish his mother was, never once moaning about her own health and never happy unless she was helping others. Namik felt a great tenderness towards her. He wanted to hug her, show how much he loved her, but being a man he refrained from that, feeling it to be a bit soppy.

Lighting up a cigarette, he knocked the earth from his shoes. 'I tell you what,' he said, perkily. 'I don't know when, but something could happen, something good. I'm just waiting for results.'

'Whatever are you talking about?' Mrs Guven shifted in her chair.

'Just wait.' Namik smiled knowingly. 'You'll see; Daisy may soon be sharing coffee with us.'

'You want to let her go? Are you mad?'

'That is not what I mean,' replied Hasan. 'Daisy almost got away from here, but luckily I caught up with her. I meant that something could be arranged. Perhaps, I don't know, but this might happen again. We cannot take that chance.'

'She is not a plaything,' Osman spat out. 'Anyway, I thought you were in love with her.'

They were having their evening meal, just the two of them. 'I was, but I'm not sure anymore,' answered Hasan, wiping his mouth on a white cotton napkin.

'You know what would happen, don't you?' said Osman, eyes blazing. 'As soon as she left here she'd go straight to the police. You've been foolhardy; the woman knows too much.' He sniffed. 'Still, at least we don't have to worry about Melanie now. You know what she was like when she opened her mouth. Especially when drink had loosened her tongue!'

Hasan ignored this, as his mind was on Daisy. 'I did not mean for her to stay in this country,' he explained. 'As I said, there would have to be some sort of arrangement, make a deal with her. It would mean putting many miles between her and us. If of course, she decided to fool us, then her life wouldn't be worth living. In any case,' he added, 'I've been thinking. If she did go to the police, would they believe her? Daisy doesn't know the law of the land; she's not one of us. No, I think they would ignore her story. I cannot see they would take her seriously. Do you?'

Osman got up from the table, and walking to the ornate cabinet, poured himself a Scotch. 'You talk as if she's a half wit, has no brain. If the police do take her seriously, and they may well do, they would be round here so fast—'

'You forget,' Hasan cut in, 'we are on good terms with the authorities. You, especially.'

'Nonsense! They still abide by the law,' snapped Osman. 'Have you forgotten Melanie Hampton, the way they went after Richard?'

Hasan wasn't looking at his father. He preferred not to think of Melanie.

'Anyway.' Osman Bilekler waved a hand towards his son. 'You've always been the same. Wanting something, then growing tired of it.' He swung round. 'Have you not thought of the other thing, that Guven fellow? No, I thought not. Together, those two would ruin us!'

'Perhaps you are right. But she serves no purpose here, except putting a huge strain on me. She has to be watched at all times.'

'That's as maybe, but Daisy stays.' Osman glared at his son.

Hasan didn't move from the table. He sat there brooding, his eyes downcast.

'Well, what now?' Osman was all too familiar with that look.

It was some moments before Hasan answered, and, when he did, his voice was solemn. 'Nothing, nothing for you to worry about.'

'By the way, have you heard anything from Richard?' asked Osman.

'No,' Hasan shook his head.

'You do not seem much concerned.'

Hasan looked up at his father. 'Perhaps it is best he stays away. But what about you? Are you worried about Richard?'

Osman looked out onto the garden. 'Not really,' he said, thoughtfully, lighting up a cigar.

Two heads were bent silently over the grave, a short prayer whispered by both men. Namik and his father had travelled by bus to the churchyard, which was not far from Bogaz, where they'd once lived. Mrs Guven was once a frequent visitor, but cried so much it left her ill for days, and now she rarely took the journey.

Namik focused on the spot at which his brother was laid. After all this time he still found it hard to come to terms with his death. And, with his father standing quietly beside him, he knew he wasn't the only one who felt that way. Ahmet, looking bent and very grey-haired these days, hardly ever spoke a word about his younger son, but his pain was obvious.

Aygun lay in a simple plot, marked only by a wooden cross. An inscription of a favourite poet, Thomas Gray, read:

Now fades the glimmering landscape on the sight,
And all the air a solemn stillness holds,
Save where the beetle wheels his droning flight,
And drowsy tinkling's lull the distant folds.

Like many times before, Namik dashed away the tears which had trickled from his eyes. He couldn't look at his father, but instead gazed back at the ancient church, its Gothic façade bringing a touch of comfort, as if to say, 'The Almighty is with you.'

When Namik looked back, he saw that his father had started to walk away. He caught up with him. 'There is something I have to say to you,' he faltered. 'I should have done so a while now, but...'

Ahmet halted, and blew hard into his handkerchief. 'Then why do you have to say it here?'

Namik shrugged. Because of the lovely weather, he didn't need his jacket, but did so today, out of respect. 'It is difficult at home.'

They had left the churchyard, and a little way along, Ahmet pointed to a low wall. 'Sit here; I feel I'm not going to like what you have to say.'

They sat, Namik hesitant.

'Well, whatever it is I don't suppose it'll kill me.' There was an irritable edge to his father's voice, and it flustered Namik even more.

'Perhaps we'll forget it.' Namik started to get up.

'No.' Ahmet's arm shot out. 'We'll talk now. I've long known something was amiss. Something that has had you in a state for too long.'

The low wall they sat on fronted someone's garden. It wasn't the tidiest of places, but a sprawling jasmine, growing close to the two men, filled the air with its heavy scent. 'You are right about that,' answered Namik, 'but I think maybe that things are about to turn.'

Ahmet dabbed his eyes, which were watery with the bright sun. 'Is this to do with those Bileklers?'

'You know about them?'

His father nodded. He had taken his cap off at the churchyard, but now replaced it. 'I'm not sure about your mother. She doesn't talk about the past; it upsets her.'

'We are talking of the same thing? My brother?' Namik trod carefully, not sure if he was doing the right thing.

'Of course. I've long suspected that family, though without proof…'

'I have something,' Namik cut in. 'A woman, you do not

know her, I got her to tell me everything – well, she told me some things. She told me about an old olive press, here in Bogaz.'

A frown appeared on Ahmet's weathered face. 'That old press? What about it?'

'Mind you, she was drunk. Said she was there when it happened.' Namik took hold of his father's arm. 'I never told you before, I felt it too painful, but that is where it supposed to have happened.'

The elderly man stood up, dabbing again at his eyes, but this time for a different reason. 'Don't tell me more; I could not take it.' He turned to his son. 'But those Bileklers will die in hell!'

'Papa.' Namik jumped up from the coping. 'There is something else I was going to tell you. They also have Daisy, and some of the men in our village are going to help me get her out of that place. If we succeed, it could be proof of their wrongdoings. Daisy has been in their house long enough to back my story. She will have learnt a lot about them.'

Ahmet nodded his approval. 'Take great care. To lose one son is bad enough, but another…' He broke off.

For the moment, there was nothing more Namik wanted to say, and as they waited for their bus to take them home they stood in complete silence.

CHAPTER
SIXTEEN

•

DAISY HAD BEEN feeling a lot better, and when Fatma came into her room she had been quick to notice this. 'Ah, a little colour in your face.' Fatma glanced towards the table where a writing pad and pen were laid out. 'You are keeping yourself busy now?'

'Yes, it's the best way,' said Daisy. She wasn't pregnant after all; it must have been a virus. The relief had been so great; it was one thing less to worry about.

At the moment, Fatma was clearing away a few items of crockery. Daisy often had her breakfast in her room these days. 'Yes, I always say it is the best remedy. To keep the mind occupied is good.'

Having Fatma to talk to was the highlight of Daisy's day. It broke the humdrum of the constant monotony, being cut off from normal activity. 'I've often wondered about your name,' she told the housekeeper. 'Does it have a meaning?'

The woman perched on the bottom of Daisy's bed. 'Ah, it isn't a name, not really. But I've always been called Fatma. It means maid, or girl.' She gave a little chuckle. 'When I was small, I could not sit still, always doing, always helping. Then my mother would call me her maid.' She turned to Daisy. 'You see?'

'And your sister? Has she a nickname?'

Fatma raised a thick dark brow. 'What is this?'

'It's what we say in England,' laughed Daisy. 'Like you, some parents call their children by a different name, such as Curly, or whatever. It sticks, but they don't always like it.'

'No,' Fatma shook her head. 'My sister has always been Kara. She is beautiful, but her legs…' She bent forward, stroking her own. 'They were wrong from birth, and she wears the braces.'

'I had no idea,' said Daisy. 'Does she get out?'

'Oh yes, we take her along the beach, she likes that. Deniz Kizi, do you know?'

'Yes, I have been there often.' Daisy refrained from mentioning Namik, but thought of the times they had enjoyed walking along the beach. Like most beaches in northern Cyprus, Deniz Kizi was well-kept, its stretch of golden sands a paradise for locals and tourists alike. There was always a queue on the top terrace for the hot tasty chips; crisp, and freshly cooked owing to popular demand. And there were tables here where you could sit and gaze out to sea, while watching small crafts taking people on short trips.

It had often crossed Daisy's mind to write to Namik; how good that would feel, but to do that she'd have to ask Fatma to post it. The housekeeper might be willing, but could she chance it? Suppose, somehow, that Hasan or his father found out. Fatma would no doubt be fired. After all, the woman was here only to work, and imposing this on her would put her in an awkward position.

When Fatma left, having made sure nothing was needed, Daisy sighed deeply, the tedium already returning.

Not long after, she sat down to continue her novel. All her notes had been carefully collated, so she might as well do this, as there was not much else to do. But, as always, Daisy wondered if it was all worthwhile.

'Where have you been hiding?' Ibrahim greeted Namik with a hefty pat on the back. Ibrahim's garden took on a complete change when darkness fell. The tangled weeds and unkempt borders seemed to have escaped the eye of any customer that had come for a friendly drink. This was due to the colourful paper lanterns, and fairy lights, that were strung overhead.

'Hiding? Not me.' Namik gave a low laugh. He was sitting at the little bar that Ibrahim had cobbled together. Made from timber, and a panel of Formica to form a counter, it served its purpose.

Ibrahim had just returned to the bar with empty glasses. He swished these around in a large bowl of clean soapy water, watching his friend through narrowed eyes. 'Er, well, I haven't seen you.'

'Well, I have not been hiding,' explained Namik. 'Busy, though, I must say that.'

The bar, constructed against a sturdy fence, catered for all tastes, including some soft drinks for the many who abstained from alcohol. Ibrahim poured one of these into a tumbler, then handed it to middle-aged man with a short whiskery beard. Another man, looking worse for wear, reeled his way over, flopping heavily against the counter.

Ibrahim winked at Namik, before attending this man. 'What is it now, more brandy?' he asked, good-humouredly.

Wearing a dark grey suit, in need of a good press, the customer, known to all as Doctor Yusuf on account of his own made remedies, held up his grubby glass. 'Put one in there, my friend. Make it a large one.'

Taking the brandy from a shelf, Ibrahim poured one measure into Yusuf's glass, then pushed it towards him. 'I think perhaps you'd better go home after this,' he said. 'Your wife will be worried.'

Yusuf looked ready to fall asleep. 'My wife!' he chuckled. 'No, she will worry if I do go home. And...' His eyes were heavy behind thick-rimmed spectacles, and it looked as though he was about to collapse at any moment. 'And...'

'Yusuf, are you all right?' Ibrahim had come from behind the bar to support him, while pushing a stool beneath his large frame.

There was no answer to Ibrahim's question, but the drunken man appeared to have heard by a slight nod of his head.

Namik glanced at Ibrahim. 'What do you think?'

'I don't know, though I'm still waiting to be paid. He owes me from last time, too.'

Ibrahim knew that when Doctor Yusuf was sober he'd readily pay for any drinks he'd had. This would amount to a fair sum, but the man never seemed to be short of money. Both he and Namik also knew that Doctor Yusuf was joking about his wife not wanting him home because he was drunk. How many times had she ran down her path when she'd spotted a couple of men escorting her husband home from a nearby bar? She had been so relieved that he'd been looked after.

At the moment, Doctor Yusuf was slumped at the bar, oblivious to everything. His eyes were firmly closed, though he still held his empty glass. While close by, three men occupied a small table, smoke from their cigarettes rising in the still night air.

'By the way, did you see the newspaper?' enquired Ibrahim.

Namik had been miles away. 'Sorry, what did you say?'

'The newspaper. It was that woman, I think you mentioned her. Well, she's dead!'

Namik's insides jolted, and he stared at Ibrahim open-mouthed, as he waited to hear more.

'Yes, a car crash, evidently,' continued Ibrahim. 'But you didn't see the papers?'

'No, I haven't had time to read. I have been busy, like I said.' Namik's face had drained of colour, but Ibrahim hadn't noticed.

'Of course, they have questioned the husband; don't they always?' Ibrahim pulled a face. 'The body was that bad, been left for too long.'

'You say husband? Who is this, anyone local?' Namik swallowed hard.

'A Richard Hampton, but didn't you know his wife? I am sure you mentioned her.'

On hearing it was Melanie Hampton in the accident, Namik felt a great sense of relief washing over him. It was Aisha that had first come to mind. 'So, when did this happen?'

Ibrahim shrugged. 'It wasn't clear. I think the papers were holding the story until they had the facts. That is what I thought, anyway.'

'It is hard to take in.' Namik drank the last of his rum and Coke. 'I hadn't seen Melanie Hampton for a while. I had wondered why.'

While Ibrahim collected up the glasses, and Yusuf still slept, Namik tried to digest this news. Had it been an accident, or had someone had a hand in this? If so, why would they want her out of the way? And, if it was murder, could it have been her husband, Richard? He may have known how his wife felt about him, but to go that far… no, who'd go to that trouble? The woman had been very thick with the Bileklers, and, going by what he'd been told, how human life didn't seem to hold much value to them, he wouldn't put anything past either of those two.

Namik's thoughts ran riot. Was Daisy to be their next victim? And Aisha? What about her? She had been running from the man he'd seen in Bogaz, and Namik had a strong feeling he was linked to the Bileklers. As if glued to his seat, his mind ceased racing, becoming numb as he stared into space. All around, the noisy chafing of the cicadas was not easily ignored, but Namik's ears were closed to these.

'Hello!' Namik had spotted Kazim. 'I was wondering why everything is taking so long: things we have spoken about.' His tone suggested he was impatient, and it seemed to have annoyed Kazim. It had just turned ten-thirty, and Kazim was sitting outside a café bar in Ozankoy, drinking his morning coffee. The usual locals were there, some reading their newspapers, others in light or earnest conversations.

Kazim had put down his coffee cup and was frowning at Namik. 'What is the matter with you?' he enquired. 'Are you in a bad mood today?'

His mood was worse than bad. Black would be a better description, but Namik couldn't bring himself to admit that. Instead, he forced himself to smile, and walked closer to Kazim. He spoke softly now, mindful of others who might hear. 'I'm sorry I addressed you like that, but…' He shrugged. 'I'd been waiting you see. Hoping to speak with you.'

Picking up his glass of water, Kazim nodded, a smile lurking at the corner of his mouth. 'You young men are all the same. Impatient, the lot of you. But, look, I can only do my best.' His eyes darted back and forth, and he said quietly, 'We can count on a couple of the men, but, well, the others are uncertain. Afraid to take that chance.'

Namik wrinkled his brow. 'But, in that case, what is the problem? I already have two lined up. They are very reliable.'

Both had kept their voices to a whisper, and now Kazim stood up, ushering Namik away from the rest of the men. 'I know it is hard. But you have my absolute word, my friend. These two men, they want to help, have real understanding of the matter, but they have families and have to weigh up the risks.'

'It is just taking too long,' explained Namik. 'Already one woman…'

'You say "one woman". What is this?' Kazim had become alert.

'A woman? Oh, it is nothing,' replied Namik. 'I was just thinking of something, that is all.'

Soon after, with a final promise from Kazim that all should work out well, Namik made his way back home. In future, he'd have to keep a tight rein on his feelings. He didn't want to upset Kazim. Or his son, who worked for the local abattoir, along with another man from the village. Namik had often seen his son; he was a big giant of a man, with arms the size of Samson's!

One of the waiters came looking for Namik. If not in the restaurant, looking after his customers, Namik was usually found in the kitchen, which tonight he was. 'Excuse, but somebody wishes to see you.' The waiter made a hasty retreat back to the tables where he'd been busy.

'Ah, Mehmet!' Namik's face lit up when he saw his friend. 'You don't usually come here during the week. A Friday, sometimes, but never on a Tuesday.'

Sitting alone, Mehmet toyed with the fruit juice which had been served a few minutes ago. 'Well, you know me, I don't always stick to the rules.' Both men laughed at this, reminded of certain escapades they used to get caught up in when younger.

Namik looked around, found they weren't very busy, and then pulled out a chair. 'You are here now, so perhaps it is a special occasion?'

Mehmet's features clouded. 'You could say that, but it depends. I'm leaving Cyprus, you see. I have met a nice girl; her home is in Izmir.'

Suddenly, Namik was filled with a great sadness. No longer would he be able to call on his friend, a friend he'd known since boyhood. Even when they'd been forced out of their villages and fled to Bogaz, Mehmet's family had shared the same rickety bus. They, like others, had taken as much belongings as they could gather. They'd fought in the army together, too, and been through all sorts of scrapes.

'When do you go?' Namik tried to look pleased for his pal but failed miserably.

'We are to be married, not yet but soon. I don't know where I'll be working, but I'll find something, anyway.'

'And do you love this girl?' enquired Namik, thinking that the marriage may have been arranged by the girl's father.

'Of course, she's very special. Works in a bank, too, so she has good brain.' Mehmet touched his head.

Namik put out an arm, tapping his friend on the shoulder. 'I'll miss you, but I wish you well. Izmir! I am trying to see you in that city. I hope you're not near that noisy airport?'

'Thank goodness, no,' laughed Mehmet. He picked up the menu. 'Now that I'm here I'll choose something to eat. Now let me see...'

'I recommend the shish kebab. The lamb is excellent, and from our village,' suggested Namik. 'My chef uses lots of wild herbs, too, and fresh lemons, of course.'

'With a glass of house red, perhaps?' added Mehmet. 'But make it a small one, eh.'

'You know what! I think I'll join you. It is never the same, eating alone.' Namik became serious. 'And, listen, this is my treat, and we will have a bottle of wine, the finest. Who knows when I'll see you again.'

While waiting for their order, Mehmet fished into his pocket and brought out a bunch of keys. 'These are for you. I'd like to pass on my scooter. I could not wish for a better friend.'

It was moments before Namik took the keys. He'd had to turn away so Mehmet couldn't see how emotional he'd become.

'My family will want to see me,' said Mehmet. 'I will not be able to visit too often, but I will visit when I can. Maybe we can meet up. Talk about old times.'

Namik let out a little laugh. 'You make us sound like old fogies.'

'Well, neither of us are getting any younger.' Mehmet chuckled. 'And the wine, just the small glass for me. I'll never manage more than that.'

Over their meal, they chatted about all manner of things, including Namik's plans to break into the Bileklers' property to rescue Daisy.

Mehmet showed his concern over this. 'I do not envy you. But if, like you say, these men from the village are helping, then I wish you luck.' He raised his glass. 'Let us drink to our future. For I'm sure that it will be a good one. For you, as well as myself.'

'Yes, I am sure it will,' said Namik. 'I hope everything goes smoothly for you.'

As for his own future, Namik wasn't so sure. But he didn't want to spoil the evening, cast a black cloud over Mehmet's happiness. He only hoped he was doing a good job.

On her way upstairs, after lounging in the garden, Daisy paused, her head turned to one side. Had she heard correctly? Had Aisha's name been mentioned?

From a room off the hall, a conversation was taking place, at times becoming heated. She was well used to raised voices in the house, but Osman in particular sounded even more angry than at other times.

'If that man expects any money, he can forget it!' he snapped. 'And why couldn't he keep his eye on her? Tell me that.'

The door was slightly open, Daisy could see this when she retraced her footsteps. Of course, she couldn't see who was in the room, but, apart from Osman, she guessed that the other man was most likely to be Hasan. Listening carefully, she found this to be the case; it was Hasan.

'I've already told him this, about not getting paid until he carried out your orders,' he answered. 'Camal looked abashed, couldn't look me in the eye.'

'Did he keep trying? Was she so difficult to track down?' Osman could hardly contain himself.

There was silence in the room for a few moments, before Osman started up again. 'Aisha has brought deep shame on our family. First that young soldier, and now his brother. She must pay for her stupidity. Whatever it takes.'

'Why do you look at me like that?' Hasan's voice didn't match that of his father.

'Because that man is a blundering idiot. I'll go to that car hire personally. Tell him what I think. And you, my son, will carry out the business that was arranged in the first place.'

A look of disbelief showed on Hasan's face. 'You want me to kill my own sister, is that it?'

Osman gave a kind of snort. 'Not only that, but... that damn man who started it all. The one who's running that restaurant. He'll have to pay too, for what he's done.'

Gripping the ornate balustrade, Daisy felt slightly giddy. So, Namik was still alive, for now anyway. But what about Aisha? Hasan had killed before, but his own sister? How could anyone do something so evil as to carry out a task like that? Outside, the dogs had started their baying. She could swear it was noisier than usual, and wondered if Osman had bought another couple of guard dogs.

Up in her room, the noise continued. She kept peering out of her window but failed to see any of the animals. Then, after what seemed to be a lengthy session, the barking ceased, perhaps because they'd been fed, but Daisy hated the sound of those dogs; they gave her the jitters.

But, when she went to bed that night, she was kept awake by Osman's threat to have Namik killed. It was during these hours that she made up her mind what she must do.

CHAPTER
SEVENTEEN

•

HAVING LOOKED FOR the housekeeper, Daisy had found her in the small laundry room along a narrow passage. 'You want me to give this to that young man?' Fatma stared down at the sealed letter which Daisy had just given her.

'It's the last thing I'd have done,' explained Daisy, 'but Namik's life is in danger.'

Fatma's fingers had started to tremble, and it looked as if the letter would slip from her hand. 'In danger? Why so?'

'I can't talk here, but please, he must get this.' Daisy's eyes flicked along the corridor. 'I know you are nervous, your job and so forth. Namik, though: how can we allow this to happen? He would be unaware his life was at risk so he'd be off guard.'

The housekeeper's sallow complexion became even paler. 'But if somebody sees me talking to him. They could, you know. What then?'

A door shut somewhere, causing both women to jump slightly.

'Please.' Daisy's face was drawn, and deep shadows circled her large eyes.

Fatma stuffed the letter down her bosom, making sure it was secure. She didn't answer Daisy but instead got on with sorting the linen.

Things weren't the same for Aisha, and if the situation had been different she would have loved to have spent more time in Cyprus, her motherland. However, she would soon be flying back to Turkey, her new home. Schools and colleges had broken up for the long summer holidays, so there wouldn't have been a rush to get back. Also, the meetings she'd attended at one of the colleges over here had had a good outcome. This concerned a few clever pupils from her own college, wanting to further their education in Britain.

As it was, the time spent here in her birthplace had been very stressful. There had hardly been a day when she hadn't had to look over her shoulder, watching for anyone who looked suspicious. Being chased several times had been terrifying, and only with luck was she able to outwit her assailant. But why had her father wanted her caught? She could only come up with one explanation, and that was to have her killed. If this was true, it must be because she had met up with Namik. Though, up until now, she'd only met him once, so what harm had been done? Furthermore, who was the man who'd been hounding her?

Aisha suspected it may have been someone at the Five Finger restaurant. A lot of locals frequented that bar, with its friendly staff and good food. Still, the idea of her being recognised that night wouldn't have crossed her mind.

Especially by anyone who knew her father. The chances of that were very slim. All the same, somebody wished her harm!

Of course, Aisha's family didn't think they would see her again, and if she'd never returned her life wouldn't have been at risk. Moreover, she wouldn't have known that Arif Camal, a man who'd do anything at the right price, had happened to be sitting in the bar that night. Her father may have remained ignorant of that fact, had the artful Camal not run to them with this bit of news, having remembered her and knowing the full story.

Well, whoever had chased her, she was safe at this moment, and the sooner she stepped on that plane the better. It was a pity about Namik, though. Meeting up with him after all those years, she had found a true connection. Since his brother, she'd been surprised at her feelings for him, albeit a warm sense of belonging.

'Namik!' a gruff voice called.

Turning round, Namik's heart leapt at the sight of Kazim at his garden gate. He dropped the spade he'd been working with, then hurried up to join him. 'You have some good news for me?'

Kazim fumbled with a packet of cigarettes he'd taken from his trouser pocket. He'd given them up but had recently succumbed to his lifelong habit. 'Not exactly,' he answered, 'but we have been talking. Not the meeting we were going to have, in the mail sorting office, but among ourselves. And, well, you know how it is…' Kazim made a gesture with his hands.

'Not really,' replied Namik, 'but you say you have been talking. What about?'

'We think the police should be informed. Not me, you understand, but one or two others think it best.'

Namik's expression looked pained. 'No, if I thought the police should be involved, I would have gone there in the first place. The Bileklers are hand in glove with them; they'll not believe any of it!'

'As I said, it isn't me, just a couple of the men thinking it through.' Kazim shifted on the spot, looking uncomfortable. 'Anyway, they have to take it up, check things out. We owe them that for their protection.'

'But if we did that, and nothing was proved, the Bileklers would know I had something to do with this,' argued Namik. 'Yes, I've threatened them with the law, but I would not have carried it out. For that very reason.'

'It's the only way,' explained Kazim. 'If they failed in their duty, then we would carry out what was intended. Our help is still there.'

When Kazim reached out to shake his hand, Namik appeared reluctant, though he did so in the end, if rather begrudgingly.

It was two days since Namik had spoken with Kazim, and even now, after much thought and many sleepless nights, he was still unsure what to do. For the last few hours Namik had even been wondering if he had been right to consider Kazim to help him out, but had finally decided he'd make up a good team. This was to be kept the same: a small band of trustworthy men, who were strong, muscular and, most importantly, athletic, because the rear walls surrounding the great house were quite lofty.

However, with his thoughts all over the place, Namik hadn't paid much heed to where he was going now, but, standing outside the building, he saw the word POLIS mounted on the stone wall.

He asked himself what had brought him here. Was it Kazim's insistence about informing the law that had decided it? No, he told himself, it wasn't just that. His own stubborn streak wouldn't have allowed it, not if he'd really been against it. So what was it? Still looking at those bold letters above the door of the building, Namik came to the conclusion that, subconsciously, he'd known all along it was the right thing to do. Kazim's idea that the law should be involved had only brought it home to him.

At the sound of the door being pushed opened, the grey-haired officer looked up from the desk. 'Yes?' he said, rather abruptly.

Uncertain of what to say, Namik wasn't in any hurry as he made his way over. And all he could think of was the possible outcome of all this, because, most certainly, having the law intervene must surely put his life in danger if the police did pay the Bileklers a visit.

'I have asked what the problem is,' said the officer, 'but you did not answer.' His tone was still tetchy.

'Oh, I have come to see you about… about something quite serious,' stammered Namik. 'You see, these people, the ones who are holding this girl, they refuse to let her see me. She is there against her will. I swear!'

'Now, where is this, please?' While he spoke, the officer glanced down at the paperwork he'd been working on. 'As you see, I am busy, but I need the name of the person you've accused of abduction.'

'It's the Bileklers, Osman and his son,' Namik gushed. 'There is a lot I could say, but, first, you must help. It has gone on too long.'

A frown creased the officer's brow. 'You mean the Bileklers up in Bellapais?'

'The very people. They'll take no notice of me. I have tried.'

It looked as though the officer was about to laugh, but instead picked up his pen. 'And your name?'

'Guven. I'm Namik Guven, but you will investigate, and soon?'

The officer spread his hands. 'Maybe, though I am filled with a certain doubt about all this. The Bileklers!' he shook his head. 'It seems…'

'Unlikely?' stormed Namik. 'Because I assure you it isn't.'

'Your manner implies that we do not take matters seriously. Our force has the best regard for public safety, Mr Guven.'

'I'm sorry, but the girl, Daisy Collins, she is being kept locked up. I have nothing more to add at the moment.'

Watching as the officer made a few notes, Namik wondered just how seriously his accusations would be taken. Somehow he couldn't visualise a police officer knocking on the Bileklers' door.

When he left for home, on foot since that was the way he'd arrived, Namik's mood still wasn't lifted. This didn't surprise him at all.

'I don't understand, I mean.' Bilekler threw back his head and laughed. 'What a silly accusation. To kidnap some woman! Why on earth would I want to do that?'

Sitting in Bilekler's study was the same officer that Namik had spoken to. The temperature outside was over forty Celsius, but in here a large ceiling fan kept the air reasonably cool. Shutters at the two windows kept out the blazing sun, while still allowing enough light to filter through.

'You see why I had to come, Osman,' explained the officer, holding a glass of Fatma's iced lemon, which she'd just brought in. 'I have to follow up these things.' Although appearing at ease, his sturdy frame stretched out casually, the officer felt awkward in Osman's company. If possible, he and his colleagues avoided any confrontation with both the Bileklers.

'No need to explain,' answered Bilekler, dismissively. 'I have nothing to hide, so no problem.' When Fatma had tapped on the study door earlier to tell him there was a police officer asking for him, Osman had broken out into a right sweat. Even the huge fan above his desk hadn't helped matters. Still, the house, as yet, hadn't been searched.

The officer remained quiet for a moment. There had been much talk at their branch concerning the death of Melanie Hampton. They had interviewed Richard Hampton many times now, but had got nowhere. Rumours were rife, with one story circulating that the married couple led separate lives, while another indicating that Mrs Hampton had been linked to Hasan Bilekler, possibly involving an affair. By rights, their top man, who'd recently retired from the force, should have looked into this, had every right to do so, but he'd dismissed this as nonsense. This was most unusual since he was a stickler for keeping this area's crime rate low. Expats and tourists alike would spread the word to all who visited this isle, saying how safe it was: virtually crime free. As for discos and nightclubs, no females were allowed in their establishments unless escorted by a male, so this kept any trouble at bay.

'By the way.' Bilekler snipped the tip of his cigar, before lighting it. 'I have opened up an account for the local fisherman's association. A sorry business, when those two men drowned. Something like that would affect their wives and families. Terrible,' he added, shaking his head.

'Yes, it is,' commiserated the officer. 'And most generous of you.'

'The least we can do. Help when needed, eh?'

The officer looked ready to leave, then hesitated. 'But you did know this Collins woman, this English lady?'

'As I have said, she stayed here in our studio. A nice woman, very nice. And clever! Oh yes, writing a book about our country. The troubles and so on.'

'And then she left?'

'One day out of the blue. Though she had said previously she'd be moving on. Wanted to finish her novel in England, I think. Already had the necessaries, notes etc. Anyway, I wasn't here. Gone when I arrived back.'

'Well, nothing to add, then.' Putting his empty glass on the desk, the officer bid him farewell, left the study and went out by the front door. He was unaware that Bilekler was close behind.

Standing outside the door, in the sweltering heat, cigar clamped firmly between his teeth, Osman puffed out clouds of smoke. His eyes never left his visitor until the police vehicle he was driving disappeared from sight.

Osman screwed up his eyes. It could only have been one person who'd caused all this: Namik Guven. And he wouldn't be hard to find, either!

At such short notice, Ercan airport could only offer an early evening flight. Not that this mattered, it being summer, with lighter nights, but, had it been otherwise, Aisha wouldn't have accepted it. How she hated flying through darkness. Once was enough, and looking down on all those twinkling lights, as the plane made ready to land, filled her with alarm.

On her way to the airport now, Aisha sat in the back of the taxi, her thoughts full of the things that had happened here. She'd met a man at one of the meetings. Turkish Cypriot by birth, and still living in north Cyprus, he'd turned out to be one of the school's governors. A nice enough man, early thirties and still single. Good-looking, too, though by no means handsome. She had felt at ease with him, as he had a wicked sense of humour.

He'd asked her out, had taken her for a meal, and a couple of times had insisted she have coffee with him. Aisha enjoyed his company, though she wasn't attracted to him, not in the least.

However, it was different with Namik. Over the weeks, she had thought a great deal about him, but had wondered if being Aygun's brother had anything to do with her feelings. Anyway, he hadn't felt the same way; he'd made that obvious.

As the taxi headed for the airport, skirting hectares of open, dusty plains, Aisha's thoughts turned to something quite different. What if the person who'd chased her in Guzelyurt had caught up with her? Was it the same man who'd terrorised her in Nicosia? She may never know, but now, hopefully, she was safe. The home she'd made for herself in Turkey was also a safe haven, and just a short flight away, with the wide expanse of the Mediterranean Sea dividing her father's home from hers.

As to be expected, the hot weather hadn't lessened, and even with her window wound down it was still quite clammy in the taxi. Aisha sipped readily at a bottle of mineral water, hopeful that the cooling liquid would lessen her thirst. But, with her head thrown back, she was unaware of the car that had crept up close behind. She saw it now, with hardly space between that and the taxi. Automatically, she grabbed at the seat in front, turning round for a better view. When she saw who it was her entire body froze, the bottle of water slipping from her hand. 'No…' The gasp she let out was low, barely audible, but to her it rang in her ears like a rumble of thunder. Hasan's face at the wheel was unmistakable, and Aisha knew then, without a doubt, that her father had been at the bottom of this all along!

The taxi driver, also aware of his passenger's safety, hooted his horn, and at the same time making a fist through his open window. He too gave a grunt, followed by a few expletives, apologising to his passenger for his bad language.

The car behind slowed, allowing more space between the two vehicles, but Aisha had already noted that her brother was the only occupant in the car. It was obvious what he was doing here, out to harm her. She was to be another of his victims.

'Everyone is in a hurry to catch their flight,' the taxi driver complained. 'Leave early, and there would be no problem.' He looked at Aisha in his mirror. 'I hope you weren't too shaken. I make it my policy to drive safely.'

'No.' Aisha swallowed nervously. For some unknown reason, she couldn't bring herself to tell him it was her brother behind the wheel, or that her life was probably in danger.

'Anyway, I'll fetch a trolley and bring your bags inside.'

They were at the entrance now. It took no time at all for the driver to grab a trolley, load on Aisha's two holdalls, then wheel it inside. As he did so, she glanced around apprehensively. There was no sign of Hasan, or the car, though he had to be somewhere close by.

Shortly after, Aisha made her way to the check-in, feeling slightly sick. She was about to join the queue when she felt a large presence beside her. At this, she spun round, her hands let go of the trolley, and, grabbing his chance, Hasan clutched at her clothing. He said nothing but forced her and the trolley away from the queue, his knuckles biting into her flesh.

Aisha wanted to scream out but all she could manage was a few intakes of breath, while her heart pumped furiously.

As Hasan marched his sister away, nobody in the queue paid much heed, except to give a desultory glance.

They were outside, and, although Aisha had begun to struggle, digging in her elbows and catching Hasan on the jaw, her efforts at making herself heard seemed to have little effect.

Hasan had parked his car along with many others, just a short walk away. Aisha was still held close, and before the trolley rolled away he threw her and her luggage inside, turned on the ignition and sped off, his tyres screeching, while leaving behind a trail of dust.

After about ten miles, the car looked to be heading back towards Ozankoy, or Bellapais, but Hasan took a left turn and carried on for another few miles; then, to Aisha's dismay, she found they were about to drive towards a wooded area. This sat atop a narrow earth track, the dark, dense scrub mostly conifer and myrtle. A short way in, Hasan stopped the car at a clearing.

Aisha's long dark hair clung damply to her face and neck. Her body felt limp, as if no life was there. 'I've asked you why you've brought me here.' Her dark eyes looked twice their size in her waxen face.

'You know the answer to that, Aisha,' said Hasan, sullenly. 'I cannot let you go, you know that.'

'I do not understand any of this,' she said, hoping she could talk him out of whatever he had in mind. 'What have I done? Nothing, that is what.'

Hasan had found a sheltered spot, with very little light filtering through. 'You have brought shame on our family by seeing that man from the village. It is against my father's principles.' His own face was perspiring now.

'But I had meetings here. Today, I'm going home. You must believe me!'

'We thought you'd never return, but you did, and you shamed us. You may do so again, Aisha, and I will have to stop you.' Hasan walked slowly towards her, his heart thumping wildly.

'But I will not do so,' she pleaded. 'There is nothing here for me.' Aisha's mouth dropped open as his hand slipped into a pocket, and, mesmerised, she watched as he produced a thin length of cord. Speechless, she stepped back into a dense clump of shrubbery and lofty pines.

Birds trilled through the thicket, but otherwise all else was deathly quiet as her brother's eyes bore into her own. Then the cord he'd been flexing came swiftly over her head, and slowly tightened. Aisha thought he'd spoken, but wasn't certain, though just before she lost consciousness she could just make out his tears.

CHAPTER
EIGHTEEN

•

HASAN FOUND HIS father in the library. He'd been home five minutes, poured himself a glass of white wine, and now slumped heavily into a leather chair.

'Well, what is it with your face?' enquired Osman, looking up from a large tome on his desk. His lifelong interest were butterflies, and he'd been reading about the adonis, the British blue which was prevalent in the Kent and Sussex hills.

It took Hasan some moments to answer, as he was gulping back the rest of his wine. 'I prefer not to talk about it, if it's all right with you.'

Osman grunted. He left his desk and stood facing his son. 'If that were the case, you wouldn't have sought me out. So what is your problem?'

'I feel sick, ill,' said Hasan, his hands gripped tightly around his empty glass.

'Sick, and yet you drink the wine. How so?'

'It was terrible, Aisha standing there like that. Her eyes, the way she looked at me.'

'Aisha!' Osman pulled himself up straight. 'It is done then, over.'

Hasan shook his head. 'My own sister! Her face, I can still see her.'

If Osman were affected, even though he'd wanted his daughter out of the way, he showed no signs of this. 'You did what had to be done. Nothing to be gained by false sentiments.'

'You think it was easy, that I did not care?' Hasan paced the floor. 'As always, you leave it to me.'

'You forget,' Osman touched his heart. 'My health, the strain, it isn't good.'

'You are unwell?' Hasan stared at his father.

'Nothing serious,' Osman gave a dismissive gesture with his hand, having remembered he'd never mentioned his ill health. 'I'm getting old. Happens to all of us.'

'Yes, but if you have problems, hadn't you better see a doctor?'

Osman shrugged. 'You leave those things to me. But in the meantime, we have sorted our other problem, that of your sister.'

'I owe you no more favours, so don't ask,' replied Hasan, stubbornly.

'Favours! You think that a favour? You don't mind that your sister was fraternising with that riff-raff?'

'Well, it will not happen again, will it?'

Hasan left the library, while his father watched silently. Then moments later Osman clutched at his chest as a darting pain tore through him.

Earlier, Daisy had been about to return a book to the library when she'd heard a snippet of the conversation. She'd reeled back. Aisha dead! Killed by her own brother! Daisy had overheard them discussing this once before, but now, it seemed, the deed had already taken place. Although she'd never met her, Daisy felt she already knew Aisha. Namik had often spoken of her; he'd had painted a picture of his brother and Aisha so vividly.

Up in her room, Daisy sat on her bed, the events of everything she'd learnt since coming to Cyprus, churning around in her head. If only she knew what was going on out there, and if Namik had received her note. Fatma had said nothing, and Daisy was loath to ask, for fear she was pressurising the woman.

Trying to console herself, Daisy decided that Fatma had passed on the note; it was just that Namik was unable to do likewise. He could, though, she thought. She may soon hear something, given time.

It struck Daisy that he may never know about Aisha, unless of course her body was found. Found and identified! Though why was she killed in the first place? Only part of the conversation was heard outside the library. If she had been found eavesdropping, there was no knowing what would have happened.

As it turned out, Fatma had been unable to give Namik the note until that morning. Before that, each time she'd tried to catch him at the restaurant, he hadn't been there. His face had lit up when he'd opened the envelope and recognised Daisy's writing. He was filled with even more joy when he read that she still loved him.

But all this couldn't compare with the knowledge that Daisy was still alive. Not that he thought she wouldn't be, but now he had the proof! Fatma had delivered the note personally, passed to him as he was about to mount the restaurant steps. She did speak, barely smiled, but had made certain it was only himself she saw.

It was eleven-thirty, almost time to close the restaurant, and having just re-read the note, like many times that day, Namik slipped the envelope into his trouser pocket.

He hadn't heard anything about the outcome concerning his visit to the police station, and therefore was left in the dark as to whether the Bileklers had been questioned. Not knowing bothered him, and each time he gave it any thought it made him quite jittery. Still, in his pocket was a firm reminder that Daisy was alive and well.

'Today! I mean, tonight!' Namik's jumbled words tumbled from his mouth in a flurry of confusion. He wasn't expecting to see Kazim when he opened his front door. Since he hadn't been troubled by the Bileklers, he'd assumed that the local police had not called on them, and that they weren't going to. Kazim had been informed of this, and as far as he was concerned Namik had at least tried. Nonetheless, it was still a surprise to find Kazim on his doorstep.

'That's right, we will be meeting in Ibrahim's sorting office,' confirmed Kazim. 'About seven, this evening.'

'I cannot believe it is happening,' said Namik, shaking his head.

'We have some good friends, and they'll not let us down. Besides, one or two tell me that they too have a score to settle with that evil family. One of the men's elderly father was evicted from his cottage. The stress killed him. I cannot believe that the police haven't been up there to see them. It was a wicked thing to do.' Now Kazim shook his head. 'You were right in the first place. The Bileklers have too much weight around here.'

'Well, we tried and failed,' Namik told him. 'Because I'm sure I would have known one way or another.'

'Well, I am glad to hear it wasn't the other!' answered Kazim, understanding the meaning behind Namik's words.

The two men looked at each other, as if reading the other's thoughts. Then, with a polite nod of the head, Kazim took his leave.

Ahmet had been reading the previous day's newspaper. He'd heard the mumbled voices at the door, looked out of the window to see who it was, and had now returned to his comfortable chair. Every now and then, he peered over the newspaper at his son.

'You saw him, didn't you, at the door?' Namik kept his voice low.

'All right, I did, but it was well that your mother was in the kitchen. What would she do if she knew what you were up to?'

'I have to do this, Papa. Daisy is in that house and we have to get her out. It is the only way to prove ourselves. Daisy will tell them everything, and, by doing that, the police will have no option but to see those Bileklers go on trial. They have, after all, a duty to serve the public.'

'It would kill your mother if she found out.' Ahmet's weathered face was looking far older than his sixty-five years.

Namik went to the window, gazing out at nothing in particular. 'This I have a problem with, Papa. Those Bileklers have to pay for their crime. My brother, your son, he's dead, slaughtered by that evil pair. The outcome I don't wish to think about, though my mother would find out eventually.'

Hearing about his dead son, that he'd been murdered, still cut like a knife through Ahmet's heart. When his wife learnt of this, that her younger son hadn't been killed by a

Greek Cypriot while keeping watch with his unit, would her poor health stand up to it?

'Anyway,' Namik turned away from the window, 'it is tonight. The meeting takes place tonight.'

Ahmet went to his son and hugged him, then, hearing the kitchen door open, he turned to see his wife. She looked from one to the other. 'What have you two been up to?' she enquired.

There was a lot of mutterings in Ibrahim's sorting office, bodies twitching in anticipation, and the odd chuckle of noisy laughter. Namik had been giving the men a rough outline of the events which had prompted this meeting.

Observing the small gathering, he held up his hands. 'Don't worry about the dogs. Ibrahim, as you know, was in the underground, among other things, during the conflict. He knows some tricks.' Mentioning the dogs had Namik break out into a sweat, but, hoping nobody had noticed, he dashed a hand across his face as the sweat began to drip from his jaw.

Ibrahim, too, was facing the men. He spoke for the first time. 'Of course, if anyone wishes to back out now, then do so. But this will be a challenge, probably the most you've faced since the troubles. Remember, that house up in Bellapais will not be easy to enter. The walls, for instance, are mighty high.'

'Yes,' cut in Namik, 'and we don't know what's on the other side. The dogs, where are they kept?' His shirt, which had previously clung damply to his body, was on the point of saturation now. 'Anyway,' he continued, 'Ibrahim here, he will watch the house, get an idea of the occupants' movements. We know, for instance, that Hasan pays regular visits to his properties, and his father often leaves the house on personal business.'

'What about staff?' one man called out, having propped himself against Ibrahim's sorting bench.

'Only a few are employed now,' answered Namik. 'We know some of those who were laid off, and they are angry about it.'

'Well, we are not happy that they keep the girl,' ranted another man. 'It is criminal!'

The rest of the men seemed to be unanimous on this, with one or two becoming quite vociferous on the subject of kidnapping a young British woman.

'Still, those dogs, what sort are they, and how many?' The question came from a young man about the same age as Namik. He was of medium height, lithe, but well toned, suggesting he used the local gym.

'The dogs?' Namik swallowed. 'Mostly Dobermanns, I believe, though how many... I couldn't say. They make a lot of noise, so who knows?'

The man didn't seem too fazed by this, and shrugged, as though just wanting an answer.

Namik exchanged glances with Ibrahim, then, looking around at the men, he summed them up. Among these were three ex-army comrades of his, who like himself had lived in Bogaz. All were extremely tough, courageous and trustworthy, and, although one of these had at least eight years on the other two, he was bigger in size and could outrun most younger men.

The young man with the well-toned body who'd enquired about the dogs was also a good catch, as was Doctor Yusuf's son, Ramsay, slightly older but with a good head on his shoulders, owing to a top education.

Standing next to Ramsay was Kazim. True, he was a straight-talking man, never one to hold back, even though it may offend, but he had kept his word, been nothing but helpful.

Namik's eyes now rested on Kazim's son, whose muscle-bound body looked strong enough to tackle a whole army. This, of course, wouldn't be a requirement, but, knowing the Bileklers, who knew what obstructions were likely to be put in place in the event of a break-in?

Ibrahim was standing close by, and Namik was startled to find him swigging something from a small bottle. It wasn't water, either, but something looking suspiciously like Scotch. Of course, he couldn't say anything, wasn't his place, but he hoped Ibrahim's taste for alcohol wouldn't interfere with any of their plans. Moreover, he hoped that his friend would refrain from imbibing anything alcoholic on the given day!

Namik glanced up at Ibrahim's shelf, the one above the sorting bench, which held a various array of different coloured bottles, some full, others already opened.

He broke out into another sweat.

Having slipped the bottle into his pocket, Ibrahim wiped his mouth with the back of his hand, then gave a rough outline of what he was proposing to do beforehand. He quietened the men before speaking, gesturing with both hands above their heads.

'Of course, a lot depends on the planning of all this. Those Bileklers lead busy lives: entertaining is one point in mind. We could, for example, settle on a date, only to discover, too late, that the house is full of visitors. It is my job to cover every eventuality, in other words take no chances. Remember, though, nothing – and I mean nothing – is fail-proof.' He scrutinised the men's faces. 'You all fought in the war, in some capacity or another; some of you in the toughest and most trying conditions. Every one of you, myself included, managed to come through it.' Ibrahim chuckled. 'What we propose to do doesn't compare, but our wits will be challenged nonetheless.'

The meeting continued for another twenty minutes, with one or two men putting their ideas forward, one of which everyone agreed was a valid point. Then, with nothing more to add at this stage, the gathering dispersed, leaving Ibrahim to lock up his sorting office. Namik and he thought that the meeting had gone well, with nobody looking to back out.

Osman Bilekler clutched his chest. The temperatures were higher today than it had ever been, or so it seemed, but, even before leaving home this morning, he'd felt the heat, regardless of the air-conditioning having been installed.

For the last few minutes, the tightening feeling he'd been having in his chest had become a vice-like grip. Waves of nausea had also been plaguing him too. Bilekler had left home without a jacket, his fawn linen one he usually wore in the summer months. He always felt he wasn't properly dressed without it, but not today: he had found it all too much.

He paused in his tracks to take a breather. Then, moments later, he stepped among the shade of the vines in one of his vineyards and mopped his brow.

Crows wheeled overhead, and voices from workers at the far end of the terraces could be heard, their machinery clacking in regular unison with each other.

'Why, Mr Bilekler! What is wrong?' The man in charge of this large operation had just emerged from another row of vines. On foot, he'd been checking for leaf-rust, not wishing to trust completely in the roses planted at each end of the vines. Luckily, there were no sign of disease on these, but the man was a stickler for a personal inspection.

Osman Bilekler acknowledged his man with a flourish of his handkerchief. 'I... I do not feel good. A little breathless.'

'But why are you here? Do you want me to call an ambulance? I can call from my house, no problem.'

'Yes,' Osman was close to collapsing, and his complexion had an unhealthy tinge to it.

Without another word, the man scurried off, racing to his truck, which was parked a short distance away. His home was within easy reach, too: a small vine-clad abode featuring a raised terrace, set amid the rolling hills.

It was later that day that Hasan rushed to his father's bedside. Seeing him lying there, gaunt and lifeless, had been a great shock, and he'd had to choke back the tears that had threatened. But, after a few minutes, he'd left the private room at the hospital as soon as decency allowed. In any case, a nurse had popped her head through the door soon after he'd arrived, and had issued an order of no longer than fifteen minutes.

Now, having driven back in the knowledge that his father's heart attack had been successfully treated and was being constantly monitored, Hasan could breathe a huge sigh of relief.

It was now late afternoon. He had dropped off at his home and checked Daisy's room was still safely locked, and at this moment was in earnest discussion with the man who'd rung for the ambulance.

The vineyards were a few kilometres from Kyrenia, in the direction of the Karpas Peninsula, and their tiered terraces, on the lower foothills of a sweeping mountain range, thrived well owing to enough rain during the winter months. 'So, your father is good now?' The man ran a hand over his whiskery jaw.

'As can be expected, yes, but has a way to go,' answered Hasan, still a little troubled by all the drama.

The man shook his head. 'Very unfortunate, that business.' He made a clicking sound with his tongue. 'Still, we have to forge ahead, I suppose.'

'It is why I am here.' Hasan didn't really feel up to it, but had decided that keeping busy was by far the best option. 'We thought, before my father was taken bad, that is, that we'd like to grow some different vines. Lebanon can do it, and so could we. Tastes change, people travel, and our exports are suffering.'

The man's weather-beaten face puckered into deeper lines. 'Different vines? But these work well, almost no decease, and they have been grown for centuries.'

'Most can stay. The sweet Muscat ones have their market, but we want to try blending a few, Cabernet Sauvignon, Syrah. The outcome should be similar to a Bordeaux, or Rhone.' Hasan shaded his eyes, looking up towards the top slopes. 'There,' he pointed. 'We will grow them high; conditions there will suit them.'

'I remember now, your father did mention something earlier in the year, said he'd think about it. That is it: he said a Xynisteri grape would improve the whites.'

Hasan nodded. 'Like I say, we are hoping to steer away from too many sweet, sticky wines.'

They spoke some more about the planting of new stock, and, satisfied that the foreman had understood his requirements, Hasan left him to it.

Before leaving the vineyard, Hasan cast his eye over the hectares of gently sloping hills, with their neat rows of vines stretching further than his eye could see. Above the majestic sweep of the mountains, its scrub bleached and burnt from the fierce heat, was an azure sky, flawless except for the odd cotton-wool cloud.

He turned, hurrying back towards his car, hoping that his father would live to see the planting of the new grapes.

But, as he drove, his mind wasn't on the planting of new vines, or how extra investment could triple their income. His father had a serious condition, and this latest episode could have cost him his life. Hasan was shrewd enough to know that his heart attack may have had no bearing on anything in particular, but nonetheless felt that blame should lie at someone's door. And that door wasn't too many kilometres from here!

Two days later, Namik, having locked up the restaurant around eleven-fifty, was walking to where his scooter was parked at the side of the building, when a blunt object cracked against his skull.

The night was pitch black, except for the illuminations of a few bars along the waterfront, and the twinkling lights strung around the harbour, but all Namik saw were a million stars, erupting in his mind's eye, before hitting the ground.

Unfortunately, nobody had the mind to pass this way during these hours, and throughout the night Namik would have been unaware of the stray cats, out on the prowl and in search of titbits. Or indeed the odd rat, kept fat on any garbage dropped by a careless lout.

Then, early next morning, an old man, on his way along the harbour for his regular constitution, stared in horror when he saw Namik. The old man's spine, hunched badly owing to osteoporosis, edged closer. 'Doctor? I call a doctor?'

Namik shifted, wincing with pain, though managed to open one eye. 'Who are you? Go away.' He spoke huskily, and in his delirium was telling the man to leave him alone, although this was ignored as the old man looked to seek help.

Along the front, everything was quiet, with no sign of a fisherman among the boats. But, moments later, as the man returned, the unmistakable sound of water slapped softly against a craft, together with the purr of an engine. The old man waved with his stick. 'Help, over here,' he croaked.

The fisherman looked up, dropped the coiled rope he was holding, and hurried across. 'Why, what is the matter? Are you hurt?'

The elderly man shook his head. 'Not me, no, but this person needs assistance.'

Looking to where the man was pointing, the fisherman rushed ahead, mortified at the prostate form of Namik, who was splattered with blood. Then, very carefully, he tried to roll Namik over, find the source of the injury, but was met with a few mournful groans.

With much effort, Namik reached up, groping at the rear of his head. His thick, curly hair was matted, sticking fast to his scalp, and as his fingers slipped away they too were covered in blood. His white shirt was also bloodstained, but, having spent all night on his back, it had dried to a sticky mass, where, unknown to him, he'd also received another blow.

The fisherman recognised Namik now, and was even more horrified. He scampered off in search of a phone, but as he did so a few more anglers appeared, ready to take to their boats. Apart from a cursory look, they paid little heed to the man running past them, and to what might be happening. But it took some time before an ambulance finally arrived.

Namik had been in hospital for two days, though Mrs Guven had been unable to visit her son. Now, looking down at him, she held up her hands in desperation. 'And what did the police do? Nothing, it seems. What good is the law if nothing is done?' She had just cleansed Namik's head, and applied a fresh dressing left by their doctor. When Namik had been taken to hospital, many stitches were needed to seal the gash, but it had since become infected.

'He is a fool that he doesn't want to go back to the hospital,' grumbled Ahmet. He was sitting at the table reading his newspaper, and knew why his son was reluctant to keep his appointment. He also knew that Namik's injuries weren't caused by a stand-up fight between him and a troublemaker. He could say none of these things, not in front of his wife. He was extremely worried nonetheless.

Namik was half propped up on the old daybed, the pillows having slipped from their comfy hold by his restlessness. 'No need for that.' He grimaced as a sharp pain shot through his head. 'The doctor here is fine. Look, he has left us the dressings.'

Three packs of lint, cotton wool and bandages were on the small table beside the daybed, all sealed in cellophane. Mrs Guven looked at them grimly. 'Yes, but you now have an infection. What if it worsens? What then?'

Namik had thought about that, all through the wakeful nights, while pain and nausea had stolen over him. He'd also thought about Daisy, further meetings with the men, and the raid itself. It was the latter that won. Hospitals were fine, but how often had he heard that someone was kept in because their temperature had risen? Or because some overzealous doctor wanted to play it safe. No: staying here, he could perhaps attend that meeting, keep up with the latest events.

Ibrahim was sure to have made some progress in his research on the Bileklers' movements.

Out at the sink, Mrs Guven filled the copper pot ready for coffee. There was a lot she wanted to say, but nobody seemed to be very forthright with the answers. In the meantime, all she could do was to be there to nurse her son.

Ahmet, on the other hand, thought he already knew what had happened, but for the moment would have to let things rest. Namik, still far from well, had enough to cope with.

But this coping mechanism didn't seem to be working very well for Namik. This was most unusual, and it greatly surprised him. This setback had knocked him sideways. It was completely different from the fighting during the conflict. At least then he was in a flight or fight situation, but this... He turned now, towards the wall, like he'd seen his mother do so often, when maudlin thoughts of her dead son had troubled her. What was the bloody matter with him? Where was his fighting spirit? Lying there, it slowly dawned on him that he could be on the verge of a mental breakdown. Never having had one, he wasn't sure, but then he'd never experienced these feelings. Truth was, part of him felt numb, especially his thought process, which, no matter how he tried, seemed to spiral into a cavern of nothingness.

If anything, his head felt worse, as did the injury to his back, which nobody seemed to be particularly concerned about, even though the bruises had begun to show. His ribcage was definitely giving him hell, though X-rays had proved nothing here was broken.

Namik's breathing became laboured, and it was a good job he wasn't in the hospital, because the gash in his head seemed to have triggered a soaring temperature!

Namik awoke to find his mother applying a damp flannel to his brow. He must have fallen into a deep sleep, or else had lost consciousness. He groaned, his whole body drenched in perspiration.

'The doctor has been, and will call back later, but he is not happy.' Mrs Guven reapplied the wet flannel. 'He cannot understand your refusal to go back to hospital.'

Mrs Guven's words echoed faintly in the background. Other sounds, too, seemed unreal, like music from the radio, which may have been in the room, next door, or perhaps this was imagined. A door shut somewhere, or maybe not. And was it Daisy's voice that Namik could hear, ripples of laughter carried on a windless air? He groaned again, this time flaying his arms about.

'You have to take this.' A glass of water was held to Namik's lips, and in her hand Mrs Guven offered the antibiotic left by the doctor.

Peering at his mother, under long dark lashes, Namik tried to focus on the medication. 'Take that,' he rasped, 'too big to swallow.'

'No.' She shook her head. 'You must try, see, not too big.'

Regardless, the capsule was pushed firmly towards Namik's mouth, followed by the water. 'There, but you'd be better off in the hospital.'

Namik was still on the old daybed, it being deemed the best place to leave him, and now he fell back onto two fat pillows, that smallest of exertions leaving him drained.

The back door opened, though Namik didn't bother to look round to see his father enter. As Ahmet stood there, a bunch of carrots in one hand, a fist full of parsley in the other, gathered from their garden, he looked towards the bed, then at his wife.

They didn't speak, but both knew what the other was thinking. If Namik failed to improve, then his request not to go to hospital would be ignored. Mrs Guven wasn't about to lose another son.

About a week later, Osman Bilekler was sent home to rest from that same hospital. Hasan had collected him, and now his father lay comfortably in the beautiful conservatory facing the rear garden. Around him, potted palms and other exotica made for a most relaxing environment, while eau-de-Nil shutters kept the place cool. He wasn't, though, on his own, as a male nurse had been employed to nurse the sick man.

Rauf, a rather tall man with dark brooding eyes framed by bushy brows, was a man of few words, but nevertheless an excellent carer. He was strong, too, and needed to be, with Osman's heavy frame to help lift. Rauf wasn't a sociable man, and the main reason he'd left his last employ was that the elderly woman, who was housebound and such a chatterbox, required her carer to be as talkative, and in the event had got shot of him.

'For heaven's sake, man, stop fussing!' Osman's snappy moods had been plenty of late, and it was wondered if the nurse would tire of this, or so Hasan felt.

'I fixed your pillows, that's all,' explained Rauf. He went to the shutters and adjusted them. 'A little sleep, perhaps.'

Osman's face fused a slight pink. 'Sleep! I have done nothing but.' He made a gesture with his hand. 'Now, leave me in peace. I am wanting to be left.'

After Rauf closed the door, having refilled a glass of water, Osman did close his eyes, but not to sleep. He wasn't at all tired, and wanted to sort out his thoughts, mainly that of his son, Hasan. For without him, their many business ventures wouldn't survive. The vineyards, for instance, were thriving nicely, and very soon the harvest would begin. There had been no damage to crops this year, so the rewards should be high, especially as any outlay would be kept to a minimum, with many peasants only too willing to toil for a small wage. Students, too, looked for outdoor work, many travelling from mainland Turkey, or Syria, and looking on it as part holiday.

Osman made a mental note to remind Hasan about the old barrels and concrete tanks. The wine in these had been left too long, and should therefore be checked. Dilapidated barrels, if there were any, would cause oxidation, as well as bacteria.

As it happened, Osman did feel drowsy now, but fought to shake this off, as something else played on his mind, something more pressing. Since the nurse had to be in attendance, what of Daisy? She only had to start chatting to him; then what? Osman's thoughts gathered momentum. She mustn't be allowed to, or, better still, his nurse would be cautioned against speaking with her, except to be civilised.

Musing on this, and the possibilities it would cause, Osman drifted into a troubled sleep. He stirred once or twice, thinking the worse had happened and that Daisy had spilled out everything and the fact she was held against her will. In the end, he drifted off again, this time into a much deeper slumber. When at last he awoke, it was to find Rauf hovering close by, a serious look on his dark features that was difficult to fathom.

Richard Hampton hadn't seen the Bileklers for some time. Once a frequent visitor to their home, he now kept away, partly because he felt nobody paid much heed to him and, anyway, he was no longer invited. As far as Richard knew, there was no reason for this, or perhaps there was, but nobody had told him. Anyway, it wasn't that he lacked friends; there were many, especially the expats who gathered at one of the bars, all too ready to meet another Englishman. Some of course could be stand-offish, only mixing with those who shared the same interests. Others, though, were very friendly, like Richard's old ex-army pals who'd settled in north Cyprus owing to the long hot summers and short winters.

Of late, there had been no more questioning by the police. There had been no fresh evidence on his wife, so for the moment it seemed they were letting things ride. As for Richard himself, he was getting used to being on his own, so didn't particularly miss Melanie. They hadn't much in common, but he couldn't tell any of this to the police. Knowing the law, they'd make all sorts out of it, and may decide he'd killed her after all. And, even if they had no proof, which they hadn't, the least they would do was to come knocking at his door regardless, and he'd had enough of that.

On the basis of all this, Richard kept his head down, went about his business and met up with old friends. Still, one thing sometimes bothered him. Last time he'd spoken to Osman Bilekler, he'd said that Daisy may have gone back to England. If she had, it was a pity. But funny she hadn't bid him goodbye, seeing as they'd got on so well. She was nice, too, and quite attractive.

There were times when Doctor Yusuf refrained from the strong stuff, times when he was happy to sit quietly sipping a coffee at the local café. However, there had been a heated discussion on the merits of Field Marshal John Harding, a tough, battle-hardened military man. In September 1955, Prime Minister Anthony Eden had appointed him governor of Cyprus. Between October 1955 and January 1956, Harding failed to negotiate a settlement of the conflict with Archbishop Makarios. He then launched a major offensive against EOKA strongholds. The following March, Makarios and three other high-ranking Greek Orthodox churchmen were deported to the Seychelles islands in the Indian Ocean.

'Yes,' said another old soldier, 'but Harding was dismissed in 1957. He lasted no time!'

Doctor Yusuf's jaw wagged. 'So you are saying he did not try? What about Grivas's guerrillas? Several of those were executed; don't forget those.'

'You seem to forget the bungled Anglo-French invasion of the Suez Canal,' added the old soldier. 'Harding tried to wipe out EOKA and failed. After that fiasco, there were no longer any British interests in the canal area to protect.'

Struggling for an answer to this, Doctor Yusuf had to concede that this was true. Still, he wasn't about to lose the argument, regardless. 'Anyway,' he said grudgingly, 'I suppose Harold Macmillan ran things better, when he took over from Anthony Eden. And at least Makarios wasn't allowed to return to Cyprus.'

This debate, over another few coffees, continued for the rest of the morning, with other interested parties joining in. They spoke for all Turkish Cypriots in the way they viewed these events, like becoming very much committed to the British cause, more so because of Harding's security forces. In truth, back then, they had come to rely on that protection.

In 1956, Alan Lennox-Boyd, the British colonial secretary, offered some hope when he spoke in the House of Commons. He stated that they might survive a British withdrawal from the island. Lennox-Boyd argued that, if the Greek Cypriots had the right of self-determination, then so did the Turkish Cypriots.

'Well, we all agree on the good sense of Lennox-Boyd,' said Doctor Yusuf. 'Proposing that Cyprus be partitioned between Greece and Turkey gave us freedom to live safely. "Partition or death", they called it, and no truer word spoken.'

There followed a chorus of voices, all in agreement of Doctor Yusuf's words.

In the event, musing on the morning's discussions, the latter felt fit to order a tot of his favourite whisky. After the coffee, he knew what he enjoyed most!

God, what had he done to deserve this? If there was an Allah, and he'd always believed there was, then why would someone be plagued with such terrible bad luck? Namik eased himself off his bed, the pain in his back making it difficult to breathe. Nothing was broken, but it made no difference, every bone felt as if it had been crushed. At the hospital, after yet another X-ray, nothing was found untoward, though severe bruising was blamed for the discomfort.

Namik's lips curled at the corners. Discomfort! What a stupid thing to call it. His body felt as though a steamroller had ran amok over him. He touched his head, which was healing nicely, but was quite tender to the touch. Since the assault, he'd often wondered what else his assailant had done to him. How about a good kicking? Being out of it, a boot may have been brought into play.

He reached out for his packet of cigarettes, lit one, then, about to inhale, he gasped, unable to use his lungs to their full capacity. In fact, he almost fell back onto the bed, only saving himself by clutching at the bedside table. This was the first cigarette he'd lit up since his injuries, and at the present it would appear to be his last. Reluctantly, Namik stubbed the cigarette out, while the dark moods he'd been having tended to multiply, filling his being with the most morbid of thoughts.

What the hell was happening? These feelings were alien. This couldn't happen to him; it mustn't, not now. Everything was spiralling out of control, and he couldn't even get his bearings! Was it his bedroom, or was he still at the hospital? He wasn't sure. Hunched over, his head about a foot from the floor, his lungs seemed to have packed up altogether.

Ahmet showed a look of surprise when he opened the door to find Kazim standing there. 'Yes,' he said, 'what is it?' Mrs Guven always went to Kazim's van to buy her bread and other requisites, so this was unusual.

'Namik: is he in?' answered Kazim. 'I have not seen him.'

Ahmet looked troubled, in his stance as well as his face, while his eyes were darkly shadowed. 'Namik is ill,' he finally said. 'He has not been out; that is all I can say.' Explaining that his son may be having a mental breakdown was the last thing he wanted.

'But is he at home?' Kazim had become anxious. 'Can I see him?'

'That is unlikely,' replied Ahmet. 'The doctor has given him something.'

Kazim shuffled uneasily. 'It was kind of urgent. Still, if he is ill…'

'Yes, that is it.' Ahmet, normally a genteel, courteous man, made to close the door, but Kazim stopped him.

'Please, I hear what you say, but I have to speak soon – we, that is, Ibrahim and others, are greatly concerned.'

Ahmet nodded. 'I am sorry, but…' He forced his mouth into a slight smile, then quietly closed the door.

As he walked away, Kazim looked back at the house, bewildered as to why Namik hadn't been seen for some time. Well, he would have to show himself soon. All this was his idea, anyway.

As a lad, on entering puberty, young Osman had experienced the most vivid dreams, and in the coming years he'd witnessed their actual reality. Shortly after the first dream, about an outbreak of smallpox, the newspaper carried that same story, stating that many lives had been taken by this disease. He'd even lost a distant family member, seen through yet another such dream.

Like most, Osman Bilekler couldn't recall everything he'd dreamt, or if he had it was such a fleeting reverie he'd paid no heed to it, but recently he'd had a recurring dream.

Sitting on the edge of his bed now, having not long woken, he looked around the large room. Two windows overlooked the rear garden, and at the front there were three, all with shutters. Keeping these windows open at night had never been a problem, but now he wondered if it was safe to do so. If someone were hell bent in breaking in, a ladder could be used. Of course, there were the dogs, but supposing they failed to catch an intruder, especially if the burglar had weapons!

In this latest dream, however, it was no ordinary burglar who'd broken in, someone out to grab a few items, but someone far more threatening. This person had a knife, a sinister-looking blade that flashed like an electric bolt. The man, dressed in black, had stood there staring down at him, his eyes like the Devil, full of malice.

From the pocket of his silk robe, Osman took a handkerchief and mopped his brow. There was no denying he had enemies. He guessed there were plenty, and if given the chance a few of these would set out to get him. Not that he'd ever given this much thought, at least not until he'd had this dream.

While awaiting Rauf, to help him into his shower, Osman Bilekler's mind went into overdrive. He'd do his best to stop anybody entering his premises. Whatever it took!

While Osman mulled all this over, down in the village of Ozankoy Ibrahim also had much to think about. Sorting out the mail, laying everything in alphabetical order, he paused to stroke his chin. Apart from Kazim, he too was unable to see Namik. They had both been told that their friend was unwell, though in what way they had no idea.

Ibrahim had visited Namik a few days after leaving hospital, but that was when he seemed to be making progress, so what had happened since then? Well, nobody had seen him, and it was unusual for him not to have turned up for his job at the restaurant.

Ibrahim had also seen Namik's father along the road, but he'd only shaken his head when asked about his son. This was strange, seeing as Ahmet had always been so amiable.

The thing was that, without Namik, nobody was willing to go through with breaking into the Bileklers' property to try to rescue Daisy. After all, seeing how it was his idea in the first place, why would others risk life and limb on his behalf if he'd decided to skip his part in all this?

As for himself, Ibrahim had done much of his homework, sometimes being out at all hours. For the last two nights he'd watched the Bileklers' residence, but had been more than surprised to find they'd had no visitors. Just why, he wouldn't know, but, before, there had always been vehicles pulling into their drive.

Reaching into another sack, Ibrahim scooped out an armful of post, and then dropped it onto the bench. He was about to continue, but instead eyed the bottles of alcohol on the shelf above. Then, scratching his unshaven jaw, he reached up and grabbed hold of a half bottle of vodka.

A short while later, a gusty breeze rattled the old wooden doors, the mark of the storm which was forecast, though, after a few glasses of vodka, drunk greedily, Ibrahim failed to notice what the weather was doing outside.

And later that evening, when the effects of the alcohol had worn off, he began to wonder if his time was being wasted helping out Namik. He would do so gladly if his friend were still up for the challenge. But, as things looked, it didn't seem likely.

Ibrahim strolled to the end of his garden path. He glanced along the road to where Namik lived. What was going on in that house? Nobody wanted to talk. Least of all Namik, who had been his closest ally.

All the usual housewives were lined up at the van, gossiping among themselves while casting a keen eye over Kazim's produce. Mrs Guven was in the queue, but she wasn't at all talkative and her face was grimly set. Kazim had noted this, just like he had on a couple of previous occasions.

When the two women in front of her left the queue, he waited while she chose a loaf of bread. 'Is that all, Mrs Guven?' he asked, politely.

'Yes, that is all for today,' she answered, still unsmiling.

'And your son, is he well?'

Mrs Guven hesitated. 'I am sorry, but I don't wish to talk now.' Putting the loaf into her shopping bag, she kept her head down, plainly indicating that was the case.

Never having been a nosy man, wanting to pry into people's business, Kazim couldn't pretend his curiosity wasn't aroused now. If only he could see Namik, speak to him, but he guessed this may not happen. Not at the moment, anyway.

Before serving the next customer, Kazim watched Mrs Guven as she walked back to her house. She hadn't looked at all well, and he wondered if some virus had affected her family. It could also be that some bad news had reached them, concerning a close relative. If that were the case, then why all the secrecy?

Well, one thing was certain. Until Namik came out of hiding, nobody was prepared to do his dirty work! Not even Ramsay, the big muscle-bound man who worked at the local abattoir.

Up in her room, at her window, Daisy watched the men at work. At first, she had wondered what on earth was happening, with all the comings and goings on the premises. Now, as things were getting under way, it was plain to see what was taking shape, for along one high wall a couple of men had fixed a tangle of barbed wire. To Daisy, it looked rather menacing, and, if someone were to chance their luck, she would hate to see the consequences! Additional security lights had also been added, two at least, seen from her window.

Daisy frowned. What on earth was all that about? Weren't the dogs enough? Anyway, who were the Bileklers expecting? While she'd been here, there had never been a hint of a break-in. She guessed they must have enemies, people who mistrusted them, but so far everything appeared as normal.

There had been a few times now that she'd seen the male nurse. He hadn't spoken, smiled or tried to be friendly, but avoided close contact, whenever possible. By now, she was well aware of Osman's declining health, but had the nurse been warned to stay away from her?

Of course, that was it. The man, whom she now knew as Rauf, had been issued with strict orders about gossiping.

Last night, she had heard someone outside her bedroom door, around ten o'clock, then again during the small hours. Her door had been locked, but it had still been unsettling. She had thought of Hasan, but that would have been odd seeing as he hadn't bothered her of late. Well, if it hadn't been him, who was it?

A thought suddenly struck, and again her eye took in that tangle of barbed wire fixed along the high walls. Was this just to keep out a would-be trespasser? Or did the Bileklers have anyone special in mind? A chill ran the length of her spine; her insides gripped with a new fear. Leaving the window, Daisy sank into a velvet cushioned armchair, picked up the book she was reading, and tried to concentrate on the words in front of her. But her thoughts were elsewhere and she put the book down. Still, it wouldn't be too long before Fatma appeared. The loyal housekeeper would befriend her, chat to Daisy in her badly pronounced English. She wouldn't stay long, wouldn't dare, but Fatma was wise enough to know that she was Daisy's only source of comfort.

CHAPTER

NINETEEN

•

THE WOODED AREA, set above a busy road, was humming with chainsaws and other sorts of forest machinery. Two trucks stood on the upper slope, which led to the woods, and both were filled to capacity with a myriad of sawn branches, their foliage now half dead. The forestry had commissioned that all wooded areas were kept in good order, a preservation system which only allowed certain species of healthy trees to flourish, therefore ridding unwanted invaders.

For a whole week the men had been working here, and during that time they had cleared vast spaces. Although they worked well, making sure only the wanted trees survived, nobody was bothered about wildlife or, if given orders on this, no one paid any heed. Instead, working so as to get the job done, and on to the next project, diggers and so forth cut through dense undergrowth with abandon.

'Danger!' shouted one man, as a tall, dead pine cracked cleanly away from its stump and thudded softly to the ground. 'Careful,' called another, while watching others working nearby.

Beneath this particular tree, and a host of bramble and other unwanted shrubs, nobody noticed the odd bone or two. Even when the tree was moved and placed onto a pile of others, there was still no recognition of anything untoward. All too often, skeletal remains of wild creatures were found in dense woodlands. Although close by, one worker did pick up a house key, along with a dirty lace-edged handkerchief, but made some lewd suggestion about a lovers' courting place.

They were still making coarse remarks about this when, a short time later, they left the woodland, agreeing that not many would think of using this off-beaten track to satisfy their lust. Not many, perhaps, and not always for the same reason. But Hasan had found his way here. This was the same woodland where he'd brought his sister, Aisha.

Osman, however, knew nothing of this, and he hadn't asked too many questions concerning his daughter. He may have wanted her out of the way, but how that was handled was left entirely to his son, as he preferred it that way. He also wished for some peace and quiet, and that his nurse would stop fussing around him.

'Anyway, how are you today?' he enquired now. 'Feeling better?'

Twisting in his chair, Osman peered at the nurse. 'Of course I am!' he snapped. 'Why shouldn't I? I'm not that much of a weakling!'

Rauf opened the French windows. 'Well, it is best you get some air.' With this he wheeled Osman outside in his newly acquired chair, while his patient grunted irritably.

'If my son were here, he would have stopped you doing that. I never sit in the garden, never have!' raved Osman, after Rauf placed the chair beneath a large parasol.

Having settled his patient, Rauf went back into the house, leaving a very disgruntled Osman to put up with his 'unfair' treatment at being taken into the garden in the first place. When birds twittered, Osman glanced up at them in distaste, and when a breeze caught at a nearby branch, making it rustle while shaking its leaves loose, Osman grimaced all the more.

While sitting there, with nothing much to do, the weary man gazed up at the garden walls, and at the work recently undertaken. He nodded, a self-satisfying feeling that nobody could possibly break in now. How on earth could anyone climb those walls! Why, it would take a superhuman being to manage such a feat. As for the extra security lights, well, surely nobody would chance their luck breaking in.

Osman sniffed, clicked his fat cheeks, and then felt inside the pockets of his light cotton jacket. He had a strong fancy for one of his cigars, but there wasn't one on his person. In the wake of things, he knew he shouldn't, but long years of smoking made it difficult to break the habit. Anyway, on reflection, he remembered that there weren't any cigars in the house, either. Hasan had been given strict orders by the family doctor on that score.

A movement at the top window made him aware that he was being watched. It was Daisy's room. With his eye cast on her window he waited for her to appear, but she didn't. Anyway, where was Rauf? Shouldn't he be out here, see what might be needed?

His eyes started to close, and, although fighting against it, very soon he drifted into a relaxing snooze. However, this solitude didn't last long, as Osman was suddenly woken by the shrill sounds of one of the dogs. He blinked his eyes several times before he was fully awake.

Osman's patience was wearing thin and he looked towards the house, muttering as other dogs joined in the hubbub. Why wasn't someone feeding them? Where the hell was everyone? Turning away, he closed his eyes again. Sometimes he wondered if getting more dogs was a good thing. But, there again, the more security he had the better protection. It was common sense.

His quivering legs almost buckled beneath him. Supporting himself with the help of the kitchen table, Namik finally made it to the rear window. During his illness, he lacked any desire to get out of bed, and without exercise his body was depleted of strength. Somehow, in the last couple of days, his thoughts had taken a different turn, and a more determined will seemed to have prevailed. Not that he had much energy, for his limbs felt numb, unable to carry his body weight.

With his father out working, and his mother over at Fetine's, her daughter's house, Namik had the place to himself, and therefore plenty of time to think. He wished his parents didn't fuss so much, especially his mother. It was wearing, extremely so. He sighed heavily, then gazed out at the garden. It looked strange, more spacious, as if he was seeing it for the first time, though perhaps that was to be expected after long days spent flat on his back. It didn't help, too, that he'd slept a lot, not necessary through choice but because of the drugs he'd been prescribed. Namik screwed up his eyes, opened them, then shook his head. It had begun to feel like cotton wool, light and fuzzy, and he still couldn't get his bearings.

Namik blamed all this on those blasted drugs! Apart from anything else, they stopped you thinking straight. No sooner did you start to think in straight lines and sort yourself out than you were back to zero, the mind a blank space.

Sometimes, when his thoughts cleared, Namik felt alive. All manner of ideas formed in his head, like getting outside, seeing his friends, finding out the latest events. Yes, what was the latest? Had – what was his name? That's right, Ibrahim. Had he sorted things? How far had he got looking into the Bileklers' lifestyle? In their comings and goings?

As he stood there, gripping hold of one of the chairs, he realised he hadn't seen anybody of late. Not Ibrahim, Kazim or even his mute friend, Asil. It was unusual for Asil not to call. Apart from Mehmet, who no longer lived in Cyprus, the deaf and dumb man, whom he'd known since boyhood, never failed to keep in touch.

Fighting against his lack of strength, as well as the inability to think clearly, Namik finally came to a decision. Somehow, no matter what it took, he'd pull himself together and get back out there. Things had slipped; nothing was being done. Daisy: what about her? Still, first and foremost, he had to knock off those drugs. It wasn't as though they'd made him better – worse, if anything, unable to function. Well, this would change. As from now, he'd stop taking the things, and that was a certainty.

Earlier that morning, Hasan had driven over to the vineyards. He wanted their manager to see a drawn-up plan on the new plantings of vines. After this, he aimed to see an elderly couple about the house they were renting. This nestled among some low-growing evergreens, and was surrounded by a few hectares of farmland in which goats roamed.

For many weeks now, the ageing gent, bent and worn by arthritis, had been unable to tend the herd, they being the major source of the Bileklers' cheese and yoghurt produce.

Surveying the gently sloping hillsides, Hasan watched the goats as they munched on the grassland. It was sparser than the last time he'd seen it, having had no reprieve because the goats hadn't been moved on to new pastures. Moving closer, he also noted the animal's lack of flesh, which wasn't good news for the purpose of milking. He swore, letting out expletives that only himself could hear. The man that usually attended the herd was again unavailable, as was the boy, employed to help out.

The rented cottage, where the elderly couple lived, could be seen from here, and Hasan guessed they might be home by the thin plume of smoke wafting from the squat chimney. Well, whether the man was attending the herd or not, Hasan had come on a mission, and he was determined to see it through.

It was the herdsman's wife who answered Hasan's knock. She was about to say something, but, before she could, Hasan stepped inside the small dwelling and into a well-kept room. The man he had come to see was sitting around the hearth, drinking something that resembled lemonade. A glass jug of the same was on a lace-covered circular table, with four chairs placed around it.

'Oh, Mr Bilekler!' The elderly man made to rise from his chair, but, stiffened by rheumatics, didn't quite make it, so sat back rather heavily. 'We weren't expecting you.'

Hasan glanced around his surroundings. All these homes were the same: mismatched furniture, an array of family pictures, and always a wooden crucifix hanging on one of the walls. He gave a soft grunt. He certainly couldn't live like this, in such a small confined place. Nobody could fault the cleanliness of most of these abodes, but himself, well, he was used to grandness, never having known anything else.

'Well, that does not matter,' Hasan said at length. 'But why are you not out there with those goats? It is what we pay you for.'

The man shifted uneasily, his weathered features showing pain as he did so. 'I have been, haven't I?' He looked at his wife for her support.

She caught the plea in her husband's eyes, and then turned to Hasan. 'Oh yes, he has. He is good, too, with the animals, sees they are cared for, Mr Bilekler.'

Hasan made a dismissive gesture. 'I am not talking about caring, or anything else you like to call it. I have seen those creatures. They are too thin, underfed, no flesh on the bone. Tell me, when was the last time you moved them? By the looks of that grass, beyond where the goats are, it would appear it hasn't been used. You can't expect them to move up by themselves, with the area fenced in!'

Mr Hamid, who'd worked for the Bileklers for the last five years, ran a rough hand through his short, greying beard. He tried to avoid the eyes which bore into him. At last he said, 'I have not been too well, Mr Bilekler. My back, knees too, have plagued me. I will do it, though. I promise.'

'Excuses, Mr Hamid. Every time excuses!' Hasan's anger was rising. 'Anyway, it cannot be tolerated. Bad management in animal husbandry loses money. We cannot afford to carry you; it's as simple as that!'

Just then, Mrs Hamid, a short, stout woman who'd been pottering close by, invited Hasan to take some coffee with them, although inwardly hoped there'd be a refusal, seeing as his presence was unsettling.

'I will decline, thank you,' answered Hasan, 'as I have further business to attend to.'

At the door, he hesitated, turning back to the herdsman. 'By the way, you must know, of course, that you cannot possibly remain here in the house if you are incapable of doing your job. I have spoken to you before and had offered you another chance. From what I've seen, you have not taken it.'

This time, though with much effort, Mr Hamid came to his feet. 'But, sir, look, you can see I'm in bad health. It is not always the same. It gets better, I promise.'

'No use, Mr Hamid. I need a strong, healthy man out there. Someone with stamina to see that the herd moves to fresh pastures. Someone reliable!'

The man looked aghast. 'You mean, we have to…'

'That is right, Mr Hamid,' Hasan cut in. 'New tenants will be moving into this place shortly.'

Outside the vine-clad cottage, Hasan cast his eyes on the vast herd of goats nibbling on the hillside. As they moved, trying to derive what little they could from the sparse grassland, their lean flanks spoke of much neglect. Well, they couldn't be left like this for much longer, and the sooner a replacement was found for the animal's welfare the better.

Hasan had no one particular in mind, though with his varying workforce, there was sure to be someone suitable.

Starting up the car, Hasan set out for the coastal road, a spot close to Deniz Kizi, where another tenant lived. There wasn't a problem here, but the young farmer had taken over another few hectares and it was always wise to keep an eye on things. As he drove, Hasan was fired up with anger, anger at people such as the Hamids. Did they think the Bileklers were a charity? His father had worked his way up to get where he was today. To keep all that, they weren't about to see idlers abusing their trust.

However, back at the cottage, the Hamids were left badly disturbed. Where on earth were they to go? Their son lived in Catalkoy, not too far out, but with four children, two of them teenagers, no extra room would be available in their two-bedroomed house. The sitting room already doubled as sleeping quarters. Besides, Mr Hamid would hate to impose on the family. As for their shrew-faced daughter-in-law, although they had tried, they had found it difficult to get along with her. The children's visits, when small, had been kept to a minimum, unless the Hamids' son brought them over.

Osman awoke with a start. His upper torso was bathed in sweat, and, looking about him in the dark, he was totally confused as to whether it was all a dream? Anxiously, he tried to focus on the windows, but the room was in complete darkness owing to lack of moonlight.

From somewhere outside, an owl hooted, followed shortly by a twit-a-woo. On this, Osman breathed a sigh of relief, though he was unable to suck much air into his lungs. Feeling for his handkerchief on the bedside table, he wiped the sweat from his face before doing likewise to his upper regions. He sighed again, this time fully aware that he really was awake.

The dream was the same as before: someone quite threatening had climbed through one of the windows, stood over him and held a gun to his head. His assailant's head and face were covered in a black shroud, allowing just a narrow gap to show his eyes. Then, nudged brutally with the butt of the rifle, the gunman fired a barrage of shots, the outcome forcing Osman into a rude awakening.

Lying back onto his pillows, thankful that it was just a bad dream, his eyes had now adjusted to the darkness. Still, it was some time before sleep returned, because Osman's brain went into overdrive. Was the latest security he'd installed enough? Apart from the extra dogs, was all that barbed wire fixed along the walls adequate?

All this, and more, crowded Osman's troubled thoughts, but to think clearly he would have to wait until morning.

But, throughout that morning, nothing of this was mentioned to Hasan, or indeed for the rest of that day, as Osman preferred to keep his fears to himself. So, early that evening, Hasan set out for the short drive into Kyrenia with a few troubles of his own.

Every so often, an unwelcome smell of sewage hung in the air on the terrace restaurant. It seemed to stem from a drain, situated at the bottom of the steps which led up to an otherwise pretty area. During the day it didn't seem that remarkable, but, as soon as dusk fell, coloured lights and paper lanterns festooned among trees gave an almost fairy-tale setting.

Customers rarely complained about the unpleasant smell, which wasn't always present, as it was unusual to find a pizzeria in these parts. Moreover, the owner had learnt his skill in Naples, home of this famous dish. Cooked in a stone oven, they were wafer thin and topped with the classic combo of mozzarella, basil, and ripe tomatoes. Pasta dishes were also available, and side dishes included garlic bread and fresh salads. The menu also boasted some a good red and white wines.

Standing on the top step, his eyes searching the tables, Hasan screwed up his face as a nasty smell made its presence once again. He saw who he was looking for and hurried over. 'I've found you at last,' he hissed.

Arif Camal was about to put his fork to his mouth; he stopped, dropped the food back onto his plate, then looked up at the angry face boring into him.

'I've been unable to find you at the car hire,' Hasan accused. 'Where the devil have you been?'

'Mr Bilekler, I… I was away, visiting my brother.'

Hasan pulled out a chair, sat down and glared at the man. 'That Guven is out and about! How did that happen?'

Two enormous pizzas were brought to the next table, and the shifty-eyed man waited until the waiter had gone. 'I did as ordered, Mr Bilekler,' he edged. 'He went down hard when I hit him.'

'Well, it didn't work.' Although seething, Hasan kept his voice low.

Arif Camal gulped back some beer. 'He must be strong, that man, I went for his head. And, anyway, you said not to kill.'

'Keep your tone down,' Hasan hissed again. 'But, no, not kill; to see that Guven is out of action, I mean, for a very long time. He needs to learn we are on to him. His meddling is something that will not be tolerated. Do you hear what I am saying?'

Satisfied that Camal had got his message, Hasan couldn't wait to take his leave. As he did so, he grimaced once more as the acrid smell wafted in the warm night air. Halfway down the steps, clinging to a wall, the heady scent of jasmine fought a battle with the ill-fitting drain as it emitted another rotten stench. The combination of both made Hasan want to retch.

'So, when will you be back at work?' An elderly man put this question to Namik in the local café in Ozankoy.

'I returned yesterday,' Namik answered brightly. He was pleased with his progress and matched this with a beaming smile.

'I saw your father recently, but…' The man shrugged.

'He wouldn't say how poorly I was, I know,' finished Namik. 'But I feel well now.'

Sitting outside in the sunshine, Namik sipped his coffee, his thoughts on his recent illness. In the last eight or so days, he'd felt his strength return. But it was true: Ahmet had kept quiet about his son's poor health, not wishing to speak of such things. It was something Namik expected.

He was relieved, though, to see his mother looking happier. Gone was that doleful expression she had carried around. Namik smiled to himself. Wasn't it the case with all mothers, in constant worry over their children when anything was amiss?

Since he'd been up and around, Namik had been eager to seek out his friends, especially Ibrahim. This he had done a few days ago, hoping to hear some news about Daisy's rescue bid. His friend, naturally, was more than pleased to see him; it was evident in both his hearty welcome and his general manner. Even so, nothing was said of the plans made before Namik was so viciously attacked, and the setback which followed after. Ibrahim did mention one or two of the others that had been chosen to help, but these aspects of the conversation had no bearing on what Namik wished to hear.

When he left his friend, he'd learnt nothing about what had taken place among the men since his absence. But why had Ibrahim kept quiet on the subject? Had most of these men lost interest? Was that the truth of it?

It was the same with Kazim. Yesterday, when his small truck was in the village, selling fruit and bread to the housewives, the man had acknowledged him, a big beam on his face, but no hint of anything else. This had left Namik very troubled indeed, and, turning away from that truck, he hoped against hope that all this upset wouldn't send his mind into those spiralling crazy thoughts again.

A soft breeze brought down a shower of leaves from a tree opposite the café, which rustled around Namik's feet. However, the weather was still warm, but this didn't stop the cold shiver that ran the length of his spine. Draining his coffee cup, he waved a farewell to the man who'd spoken to him, then turned and walked towards home.

During breakfast, a few days after Osman's last recurring dream, he gazed across the table at his son, his brow creased in thought. Of late, health-wise, he had started to feel his old self, though Rauf was still in attendance as the doctor felt it best in the circumstances. On the strength of this, Osman, always one to take chances, absolutely itched to light up one of his cigars, but always remembered at the last moment that none remained in the house. He'd asked Rauf to get him some, but the man always gave a polite but firm refusal. Thinking about this now, he wondered how many more pleasures would be taken from him.

'Oh well, I must leave,' said Hasan, breaking the silence while laying down his newspaper. 'I have some important business to attend to.'

'Wait!' Osman's voice came out louder than was necessary. 'There is something I'd like to discuss with you.'

Hasan glanced at his wristwatch. 'Can't it wait?'

'No, not really,' replied Osman, a grave expression on his clean-shaven face. 'It is something I wish to sort out now.'

'Well?'

'It is about security.' Osman cleared his throat, which had started to sound husky. 'You see, I do not think it is enough, what we have now.'

'Not enough!' Hasan swept his arms high towards the windows, indicating the outside walls. 'We have just installed all that wire. And what about those dogs? Their constant baying is enough, surely!'

'No, it isn't,' cut in Osman. 'We need more. Much more.'

'What?' Hasan was incredulous. 'What else could we possibly want?'

'Security guards. We would be much safer. Just think about it.' Osman was loath to tell of his dreams he'd had.

Hasan threw back his head and laughed. 'You are rather funny at times, father. Who are you afraid of?'

Osman started. 'Afraid? Why should I be afraid? I fear no one!'

'Then why all this security?'

Osman no longer used his smart cane, but, getting up unsteadily, he grabbed at a stout walking stick which he'd propped at the table. 'Why all these questions? Don't I settle the cost of everything here?'

'You talk as if I never lift a finger.' Colour stained Hasan's olive complexion. 'I am off this morning to see the new tenants for that cottage. I told you, the previous herdsman was not doing his job.'

'And you are well paid for your troubles.' He gave his son a sidelong glance. 'And more!'

'Anyway,' Hasan's tone was calmer. 'These security guards, have you looked into it?'

'Not yet, though we have to decide the hours. What is suitable, do you think?'

Hasan frowned. 'Has something happened? You appear to be troubled.'

'Take no notice of an old man.' All Osman wanted was for his son to be in agreement with his plans. 'Be off with you.' He waved his hand dismissively.

Before Hasan left, he watched his father's slow gait as he made his way out of the dining room. He had no idea what that was all about but was determined to find out.

Once outside, he glanced up at the barbed wire which had recently been installed. Secretly, he wondered if his father was beginning to lose his mind.

CHAPTER
TWENTY

•

THE DOOR OF the car hire firm cracked against the wall as it was flung open, causing Arif Camal's head to shoot up from the pile of papers in front of him. He was more than alarmed to see Namik standing in the doorway, and this showed in the wide-eyed look he gave him. His jaw, too, was gaping, giving him the appearance of a man just told he hadn't long to live. He'd faced Hasan many times, but, although always wary in his presence, knew that the Bileklers usually relied on him to carry out an order, so therefore needed him in their payroll. Seeing Namik Guven standing there, he knew by the hate written on his angry features that this was different, and he was all out for revenge.

Nobody else was in the office, and this was why Namik had chosen this moment. Without taking his eyes off Camal, he turned the key in the door, and then pulled down the sun blind. 'Well,' he said, 'are you surprised to see me? No, don't answer that, because I can see that you are.' Namik felt ready to spring at the man there and then.

Arif Camal fussed with his paperwork, hardly daring to meet the hostile eyes boring into him. 'What do you want?' he enquired timidly.

Namik stepped forward. 'It took me a while, you know, but I've had these flashbacks.' He waved a hand. 'Images of a face. Yes, Camal, your face!' Namik's mouth curled into an ugly snarl. 'Did you think I didn't see you? You came from behind, but this didn't stop this vision. It was fleeting I know, but it was just as you left the scene.'

'You would not have known it was me.' Camal's faltering tone was evident of how nervous he was. 'You cannot prove a thing.'

'I have more than one sense, you know. Your aftershave gives it away. Smells fake, cheap and nasty. Of anyone out to get me, it had to be you. Not Hasan himself; he usually gets others to do his dirty work. He would, wouldn't he?'

'So, you have come here, but to do what?' Arif Camal took on an aggressive tone, though Namik was quick to see through this.

'Not me, exactly, but do you know Asil? He's deaf and dumb, but is very astute. Doesn't miss much.'

'I…' A shrug of the shoulders, followed by a shake of the head. 'I don't think I know this man. I've never met anyone like that.'

'You were seen in the Five Finger bar, plying a man with drinks. You were after anything he could tell you about the Bileklers, as he'd only just left his job as their gardener. You could then relay all this back to them, as, going by the sound of it, was some pretty personal stuff. They wouldn't have been pleased that this man was spreading gossip, but for this information you were probably hoping to fleece more money from them.'

Namik came closer. 'Asil, my mute friend, has extra perceptions. No fool, you see. In fact, apart from his very good lip reading, he knew you were setting this man up. You were then hoping to lure him out to that ravine, never to be seen again. That way, you'll have done a good job.'

'I may have said,' he hesitated, 'I don't know, but I never mentioned a ravine.' Camal's face became ashen.

'You didn't have to. As I have said, Asil, who was sitting close by, is far clever than both of us. His instincts are second to none.'

'So, what do you gain from this?'

'I knew you were a fool, but not an absolute idiot! Surely you must know that Asil was – is – a very good friend of mine. Still, I suppose, like a lot of people, you think the deaf and dumb are less intelligent. So you see what I am getting at, don't you?'

Camal's mouth twitched. He stood there, lost for words.

'That is right. We have something on you. If Bilekler hears of this, how you tricked that man into telling tales, he would not think twice about someone like you. And, if you think of coming after me again, forget it. I am not on my own, you understand. All eyes will be watching! And that man you were talking to in that bar. Your plan to have him dead is already scuppered.'

When Namik left the car hire office, he knew his words had shaken Camal. The man would think twice about seeking him out after dark, always having to look over his shoulder. And how good it was to have seen Asil. He had shared a drink with him in Ibrahim's garden bar on Sunday night, this being Namik's only night off because the Turtle's Rest was closed. Not that he knew Asil would be there, but, as soon as his friend had spotted him, he came over and slapped Namik on the back with a hearty greeting.

It was soon after this that Asil 'told' of his visit to the Five Finger. How, sitting on the next table to Arif Camal, with a beer and a plate of chips, globe artichokes and melted butter, he witnessed the exchange between the two men. Asil described Camal as a regular customer, but had only seen the other man on a couple of occasions. He appeared a decent family sort, so, when Arif Camal plied him with drinks, it was wise to keep an eye on them.

As the evening had worn on at Ibrahim's, and a few beers were enjoyed, Namik had chewed all this information over. He wasn't going to be beaten to a pulp again, at least not by Arif Camal. Now he had something on the man, he'd use it to his best advantage.

This wasn't the only highlight to that evening, either. Ibrahim, seeing his friends' happy delight in each other's company, joined their little table when the few customers he'd had had made for their homes. Both he and Namik had learnt that their deaf and dumb friend had spent much of his time nursing a badly injured vulture. Asil had found the bird high in the mountain range but after a couple of weeks it had eventually died. He then 'told' them what he intended to do with the bird, and that was to have it stuffed. Along with a taxidermist, they would make it whole again.

Asil didn't say much after this, but sipped his beer and seemed to be lost in happy thoughts. Still, Ibrahim had something to say, and this pleased Namik so much that a huge smile spread across his good-looking features.

It had turned out that, since Ibrahim had last spoken to Namik in the sorting office, he'd had a word with a few of the men. Another meeting was to take place. All they wanted was for Namik to be there. Explain everything that had happened. He owed them that, surely.

When word had reached the Hamids' son that his parents had been ousted from their cottage, he drove over in his old truck straightaway. No smoke came from the chimney, and, apart from getting no answer at the door, it proved the rumour to be true.

Just under six feet tall, Eran had the same physique that his father once had: a lean frame, but with sinewy limbs that could do a hard day's work. Screening his eyes against the dazzling sun, he scanned the area around the cottage, hoping for a sighting of his parents. Seeing nothing that would indicate their presence, he looked beyond the cottage and towards the gentle slopes where a herd of goats grazed. Trees lined these slopes, and leaves fluttered from them, cascading in a flurry of autumnal colours. Apart from this, all was quiet, except for the sound of a lone buzzard as it wheeled overhead, before dipping into the thick scrub below the trees.

Screening his eyes once more, Eran peered through the living room window. The fire had burnt down to a fine ash, but a pile of logs still stood in the grate. His father's chair was placed around this, a newspaper neatly folded across the seat. On the table, a water jug, half filled, was topped with a beaded lace cover. A bowl in the middle of the table contained a few pieces of slightly wrinkled fruit.

Eran's wiry body tensed. He looked about him, then remembered the window at the rear of the house, his parent's bedroom. He darted round to this, and then peered into the metal-framed window. The bed, a small double, was covered neatly with a mustard-coloured throw. Plump pillows, pristine white, matched his mother's dressing robe, which lay neatly across the bed. Scanning the small room, which had little natural light, Eran noted his father's old robe behind the bedroom door. He straightened. Where the hell were they? And exactly how long had they left the cottage?

Why he'd come up here he didn't know, but instinct told him to keep searching. Looking down the slopes, towards the little cottage, Eran's heart went out to his parents. As for the goats, roaming on the hillsides, he pictured his ailing father among them, head protected from the blazing heat, a stick encouraging the animals to move on. He turned now, making his way onwards, and into the dense scrub. He hadn't gone far when, skirting a clump of fallen branches, he reeled back in complete horror. At first he couldn't move, unable to take in the sight of the two bodies lying in front of him. He stared down at them, his mouth agape, while every vessel in his body seemed to quiver uncontrollably. He swallowed, feeling rather giddy. They were lying close together, a thin blanket wrapped around them. From what he saw, it looked as though they were fully dressed. His father's hand, splayed outside the blanket, looked as if he'd been clutching the small bottle, which now lay empty some inches away.

Eran looked heavenwards, his hands covering his face. Is this the way they died? Two gentle people, who never harmed a soul, driven to take their own lives? And for what? Because his father was no longer able to attend those goats?

He wasn't aware of it before, but a sharp, pungent smell from the many pines thereabouts caught in his throat. That, and the two bodies lying in front of him, caused him to cup his mouth and throw up into some undergrowth.

Moments later, without looking back, Eran ran from the wooded area and into the bright sunlight. He didn't stop until he reached his old truck. Before starting up, he gave a final look towards the little cottage. Still reeling from shock, he was at a loss as to what he'd do now. But do something, he must. Those Bileklers must pay for what they'd done to his poor parents!

Ibrahim smiled to himself. It wasn't the first time he'd seen barbed wire along the walls of buildings. Even lofty walls like those of the Bileklers' residence, he'd scaled them all. He clicked his cheek, stood back, and noted the extra security lights, placed at strategic intervals. He thought so: his guess was spot on. He'd known about the additional dogs, but wasn't this all a bit excessive? Well, not if you'd become paranoid as Bilekler senior had.

Ibrahim smiled again. What he didn't know about the Bileklers wasn't worth arguing about. Yesterday evening, he'd watched quietly while two bodyguards left the premises and went to their car. How did he know of them? Because the same two men, dressed plainly, were of the same squad he'd once had the pleasure of working with. Of course, the professionals that they were, even he wouldn't get past them these days. All this was about seventeen years ago, when assisted by a couple of other underworld intelligence. In their fight against the opposition, these brawny guards were brought in to aid them. Reminders of those days were clearly etched in Ibrahim's mind, some of which he didn't care to think about!

At present, Ibrahim was hidden between two fully grown cedars, which stood a few yards from the rear of Bilekler's large house. He removed a small bottle of vodka from his coat pocket, took a hefty swig from it, and then replaced the little that was left into the same pocket. In some undergrowth, which stood about nine inches high, he checked to see if the old wooden stepladder was still there. It was, and he smiled at this, scraping his shoe against the coarse grasses to hide the ladder.

It wasn't the first time he'd seen this. On his first reconnaissance here, he was more than surprised to stumble upon such a find. Just how long it had been there, or indeed where it had come from, he wouldn't know. Still, what did that matter; it was his luck to have found it. As for anyone else coming this way, well, that was unlikely as the area surrounding Bilekler's home would normally be off limits to others. And, in any case, if the ladder were to be somehow removed, there were other means of getting into the premises. After all, experience had taught him to look into all prospects, cover himself, because nothing was hundred per cent fail-proof.

Looking around him, Ibrahim moved along the length of the rustic wall. Almost at the end, he stopped, scanned the area again, then, satisfied he was alone, bent and examined the lower brickwork. It was here that the mortar was loose, so much so that, brushing his shoe against it, a pale chalky dust dropped readily into the grass. Again, Ibrahim covered this quickly, careful to leave no trace of anything which might be seen. What he didn't want was for somebody to carry out repairs. If they did this, there could be builders all over the place.

On moving away from here, he went the way he'd come and that was from the rear. It was most doubtful anyone would ever come this way, to or from the house. Moreover, wild boar roamed the forest further ahead, and two people had already been badly mauled on previous occasions, one fatally. Ibrahim himself would have to go through that same forest, but not by any normal route. His way would take him away from those dangerous boars. He'd used it before, all those years ago when he worked for the Turkish Underground Liberation, and was leader of Ozankoy area.

Not much was known of the Turkish Liberation, and the Greeks never got to know of it until 1963. That year, all over Cyprus, Greeks tried to kill opposition. This included the slaughter of all Turkish civilians living in villages in the south.

When the Turkish underground came to rescue them, the Greek Cypriots were taken by surprise, unaware this operation existed.

In March 1964, it was in Bellapais, the east side of Ozankoy and another Greek village where Greek Cypriot fighters set up machine guns. Some Turkish families fled in fear, but these were the lucky ones. Some were not so fortunate.

Ibrahim, never having been one to shirk responsibilities, always gave a hundred per cent of himself. This included his part, when joining other Turkish fighters along St Hilarion to see off the Greek militant. Needless to say, when peace was announced in 1974, after long bloodstained years and many lives lost, everyone was more than glad to lay down their ammunition.

Now, having taken the same track as in the past, Ibrahim skirted the rest of the forest in no time at all. He'd caught the odd glimpse of a wild boar, but, apart from this, he'd managed to evade them. Before he took to the road leading him back to Ozankoy, he paused to look back. That would be the same way he'd lead the men when, hopefully, they broke into the Bileklers' property. No, he told himself. They almost certainly would. No hopes about it.

Ibrahim hadn't gone far when he heard the unmistakable baying of Bilekler's dogs, their eerie sounds reverberating through the woodland like long-lost ghosts. He smiled to himself, his thoughts on Namik. Unlike his friend, he had no fear of dogs, even Dobermanns, and, in any case, there was more than one way to deal with them!

CHAPTER
TWENTY-ONE

•

WHEN OSMAN BILEKLER came to the door, he scrutinised the man standing there with cold steely eyes. He turned quickly to Fatma, who hovered close by. 'Who the hell is this?' he asked testily.

Fatma didn't like the tone of voice directed at her, and it showed in her faltering answer. 'He said it was urgent. Important.'

'That is right, Mr Bilekler.' Eran's face looked gaunt, but there was much anger beneath the surface. 'I have come about my parents. The Hamids who lived up at that cottage.'

'I've never seen you before.' Osman leaned heavily on his stick. 'I have no knowledge of the Hamids. Now, get off my property.'

By now, Fatma had left the scene, preferring to keep out of Osman's way, but Eran's anger had no bounds. 'My parents are dead! I found them in woods beyond their cottage. My father looked after your goats, but when his health became a problem, he—'

'Your father, was it?' interrupted Osman. 'Well, he deserved to get kicked out. The man was unable to work. Now go, before I have you thrown off my land.' The door shut in Eran's face.

The words that had sprung to Eran's throat were left unsaid. With fists clenched tight, he had no other choice but to walk away. Halfway down the long drive, he stopped to glance back at the house. Although normally a meek man, his features were set grimly. He wasn't about to let this go. Somebody had to deal with people like that.

At first it sounded like a clap of thunder, the noise so loud it felt as if a wall had caved in. Jolted out of his chores, Rauf's eyes widened as he looked at his employer. No words were said, but he hastened from the drawing room to investigate further. He hadn't got far when he pulled up short, a look of disbelief on his dark features.

Hasan had hurried down the stairs, for he too had heard the noise. 'My goodness!' he boomed. He was looking at the front door of the villa, where it had been cleaved through from top to bottom, the splintered edges sticking out like sharp daggers. 'Who was the cause of all this?'

As the two men stood there, their mouths gaping in dismay, the sound of shattering glass disturbed that brief silence, jolting them both from their stupor, and it was now that the dogs joined in, their raucous barking adding to the mayhem.

Hasan dashed into the nearest room, looked at these windows, found them intact, then hurried into the drawing room. His father was still in here, sitting in an armchair where

Rauf had left him. His pallor worried Hasan, and, seeing the way he'd slumped sideways, he saw now what had caused it. 'This too!' he snapped, alarmed at the broken windowpanes, which had littered the room with shards of glass.

Osman Bilekler, gripping the sides of his chair, put all his strength into pulling himself up straight. 'What the hell is happening?' he queried, after finding his own voice.

His son, having no answer to this, rushed outside, though not from the front as it was no easy task getting the door to open easy. Once there, he spotted the culprit right away. 'You!' he yelled, taking just a few steps before grabbing hold of Eran's jacket sleeve. 'Who are you? And what right have you to enter my property?'

'Every right, Mr Bilekler!' Eran's words came out harshly. 'I came before but your father refused to listen. It was you who caused my parents such anguish. They are dead because of you.'

Nonsense!' His grip was firm on Eran's arm. 'You cannot hold me to account. Anyway, you'll pay for this damage. I'll see to it personally.'

Eran screwed up his face. 'You haven't asked who they were, have you? You do not care. People like you never do.'

'Whoever they were, it isn't my worry. My concern is for my father, who has been greatly shocked by your actions. You'll certainly suffer for what you have done.'

Shaking himself free from Hasan's grip, Eran spat on the ground. 'That is what I think of your kind. You think that people like us are dirt. Still, we will see. Now my folk are dead, having been turned from their cottage, there is nothing to be lost.' He glared hard at Hasan, his steely gaze hinting of things to come.

He was about to walk away when Hasan lurched, bringing Eran to the ground. While there, a fist came into contact with Eran's face, leaving him with blood spurting from his bottom lip. 'I'll stand for no threats.' Hasan told him. 'Who the hell do you think you are? You'll pay for that damage.' He inclined his head towards the house. 'And mark my words: now I know who you are, I'll hound you and your family until you beg for mercy. And, yes, I did turn your father from his cottage – my property, in fact: he was not doing the job he was paid for.'

Leaving Eran on the ground, Hasan straightened his clothing, then walked back to the house. The dogs were still barking, and it didn't appear that they would stop.

'But, if they work at night, what are the chances of breaking in?' This query came from Namik when meeting up with the others in Ibrahim's sorting office.

His friend smiled. 'They deemed it best for those security guards to be present then. Isn't that when most break-ins occur? No, we will strike during daytime hours.'

Kazim stepped forwards. 'And this time we'll be a hundred per cent behind you.' He turned to the rest of the men. 'Is that not true?'

A few cheers came from the back, with Doctor Yusuf's son, Ramsay, adding his voice. 'And has anyone heard about that elderly couple that were found dead? Turned from their home because the herdsman's health had failed.' Ramsay still worked in the local abattoir, and, if anything, his powerfully built body appeared even more muscular in his short-sleeved T-shirt.

'What is this?' enquired Namik, all ears when anything like this was mentioned.

'Does anyone know Eran Hamid?' asked Ramsay, looking at one then the other. 'I got it from him. It was his poor parents. He discovered both in woodland beyond their homestead. His father worked hard, even when crippled with pain, but, well, that Bilekler's son turned them from his land when he'd missed a few days' work.' He didn't add that Eran felt great remorse because he was unable to help in the rescue.

'I have met him, once maybe twice. Nice man,' recalled Namik. 'Well, speaking on behalf of everyone, this makes us even more determined, doesn't it?'

A murmur of voices was heard loud and clear around Ibrahim's sorting office, all in favour of this. And while the men chatted among themselves, Ibrahim took a small bottle from beneath the bench in front of him, turned his back, then gulped down a good measure of the colourless stuff.

The weather seemed to be holding good, with only a moderate breeze, and that only at intervals. Boats at the harbour side bobbed gently as men made ready to take their craft out to sea. It was Sunday, and that morning Namik had rode his scooter into Kyrenia to take advantage of the fine sea air.

Along the harbour wall, stood another man looking out to sea. His eye seemed to be focused on the boat that looked to be heading for Adana over in Turkey. Shortly before, it had picked up passengers from the customs office. There were a few locals, but most were Turkish citizens returning home having visited relatives, and were laden with goods. These were either personal items, all bundled into an old bedcover, or some boxed goods. The amber-coloured Pyrex ware in these cartons proved to be very popular with these passengers.

The man along the harbour wall looked faintly familiar. Namik glanced over, looked away, then glanced again. Yes, he knew him now. He recognised Richard Hampton by his irregular gait, as the man moved a short distance towards him.

Catching Richard's eye, Namik gave a little smile, unsure if it would be precipitated. He was glad when it was, because, having never spoken to him, it could now be a starting point. After all, he'd been married to Melanie and perhaps he'd throw some light on a few facts about her death.

'Richard Hampton, isn't it?' enquired Namik.

'Yes.' Richard smiled again, but this time a glint of pleasure showing in his bright blue eyes. 'Still, I don't think we've met, or have we?' He stepped nearer as he spoke.

'We have not – well, not personally. But my name is Namik. I've seen you before, at my restaurant, in fact.'

Richard turned towards the many eateries which looked on to the harbour. 'One of these, you mean?'

'At the end there. The Turtle's Rest.' Namik pointed to the left.

'I've only been there once, I'm afraid,' answered Richard. 'We bought a nice picture before we left.' He paused for a moment. 'Ah, yes, I remember you now. You showed us a few prints.'

Namik noticed how a dark cloud seemed to spread across Richard's features, and he said jokingly, 'I remember it being brought back, too. Not to your taste, perhaps?'

Now Richard laughed. 'Not guilty. No, my wife was at fault on that one. Admittedly, we didn't need more paintings, but, well, let's just say it's a woman's prerogative.'

'What is this?' Namik had never come across such a word.

'Changing their minds.' Richard smiled. 'Your English is very good, but you can't know everything.'

Namik would have liked to say how sorry he was to hear of Melanie's death, but, since she'd told him of her involvement concerning his brother, he couldn't bring himself to be hypocritical. Still, it didn't much matter because Richard brought up the subject. 'You heard about my wife, I suppose?'

'Yes,' Namik hesitated before he spoke again. 'Did she tell you that we met up a couple of times?'

'No, but then she never told me everything.' Richard shrugged. 'She led her life, and I... well, it doesn't matter.'

Namik took out a packet of cigarettes, offered one to Richard, which he declined, then lit up his own. 'It wasn't what you might think. Let us say I wanted some information, about the Bileklers, you understand. Nothing more.'

'Go on, I'm intrigued.'

'Do you really want to know?' asked Namik, raising an eyebrow.

'If it concerns my wife, I'm ready to listen.'

'I don't know; maybe I am speaking out of turn,' Namik spoke warily. 'Your wife is dead, and you'll not want to listen to my problems. After all, apart from my family and friends, who would go against those Bileklers?'

'I have some idea about the sort of things they're involved with. I've been here too long, met many good and decent people, but I must say not everyone is honourable.'

'Did you know they are capable of murder?' asked Namik. 'I am referring to the Bileklers.'

Richard shook his head. 'No, I had no reason to suspect anything of that nature. But what makes you say that?'

'It was Melanie. She told me. Oh yes, I'd always believed it, but I wanted proof. Someone who knew them intimately. You see, it was personal. It was eating me inside.'

Richard was frowning. 'But what could she tell you? Surely, if they had killed someone, they wouldn't take her into their confidence.'

'I am sorry, but you said you wanted to know. Well, she was there when this terrible thing happened.'

'I don't quite understand. Who was this who'd been murdered?' Again, Richard looked puzzled.

Namik had been watching the boats but turned to face him. 'My brother. They killed my young brother. Melanie was with them. Presumably using her as bait.'

'She told you all this?' Richard was stunned by these revelations, and he reached out to steady himself on one of the chairs at a nearby table.

'Of course, but I had to prompt her. It wasn't easy, but there you are. Anyway, what bothered me, after I'd had time to think about it, was that someone must have had a hand in your wife's death. It makes sense.'

'I suppose it does,' answered Richard. 'You must have heard that they'd questioned me over this. Many times, I can tell you. But I didn't harm her. I could never do such a thing.'

'No, of course not! Something like that would be difficult to believe,' said Namik. He liked this man, liked his whole demeanour, sincerity gleaming in the bright blue eyes which met his own. 'I wondered, though, that, if someone wished to silence her, that road incident would have suited them.'

Richard sighed. 'You'd be right. The authorities maintain she was murdered, and, being her husband, I was their man. Had no proof, but I'm sure I'll see them again!'

They stared at each other for some moments before Namik spoke again. 'It does not take much working out, does it?'

'No,' replied Richard, 'perhaps not. I must say the Bileklers have been distant of late, and we were great friends. Something to hide, do you think?'

'Yes, just as they covered up my brother's death. And I am hopeful of proving it,' stated Namik, his features hardening.

'What exactly happened to your brother?' enquired Richard.

Namik looked out to sea, a painful look in his hazel eyes. 'He was killed in Bogaz, where we once lived. Melanie told me it was inside an old olive press.'

Richard frowned. 'The olive press? But that was where I stumbled across Daisy. Yes, she'd mentioned you. I'd been visiting an old army friend, and saw her go inside. I recognised her, as we first met at the Bileklers' dinner party.' He shook his head. 'I can't get over my wife, though, having been part of this. I'm at a loss what to say.'

'We are not responsible for others.' Namik gave a little smile. 'It is still painful, though. I will never forget my poor brother. Anyway' – he gave Richard a knowing look – 'don't worry too much about the police. One day, the real killers will have them knocking on their door!'

The two men stood silently, watching as a local fisherman brought his boat ashore, its engine chugging away in the almost-still waters.

Having met and spoken to Richard Hampton, Namik had done a lot of thinking, one such thought concerning his dead brother. He positively seethed inside at how the young lad had died: not for his country, like so many others had, but by one of his own kind. Namik's mouth formed an ugly line. The Bileklers were not one of his kind. They were killers. Cold-blooded killers!

Since that meeting, it had taken him but a few hours to finally make up his mind. He wanted to see where Aygun was killed. Not the hillside where the shepherd had found him but where he'd actually died.

Namik had arrived in Bogaz about half an hour ago, and at the moment was seated, unbeknown to him, beneath the same cedar tree as Daisy had when she had come here. His scooter was close by, and the cigarette he'd been smoking was now being squashed hard into the ground, the action showing only too clearly his intense feelings of being here.

Rising slowly from the seat, Namik looked over to the old defunct olive press. It had to be that, for what else could it be – and, anyway, an elderly man here in Bogaz had directed him to this spot. He glanced behind him at the cedar tree, first brought over from Lebanon, their holy tree. The conifer was a fine specimen, with its tiered, arching branches standing glorious at a height of around twenty-five metres, with fifteen metres' spread. Stooping, Namik picked up a long, greyish-pink cone. He gazed at it, hardly believing that something so beautiful could live and survive beside something so horrible as wanton murder! He wanted to go over, open that decrepit wooden door and enter, but, each time he made to move, his feet seemed nailed to the ground. He guessed it to be no more than forty paces, just forty paces from where he stood, but why then did his reluctant feet fail him?

Glancing at his wristwatch, he realised that it would not be too long before darkness fell, having already noted a band of orange on the horizon looking westerly. Well, if he didn't go into that old olive press now, he never would. Steeling himself, Namik walked over to it slowly, in his head, counting those forty paces as he'd estimated earlier. He'd reached the large door, splintered and broken in places, its once-green paint now hardly visible, and felt as though a hand had brushed him lightly on the shoulder. He shivered at this, and automatically made a movement with his fingers, as if to flick off whatever it was. Hesitating a little longer, he glanced over at the tree, his brow furrowed. But how could this be? How on earth could he have guessed right, that just forty paces were all it took to reach this antiquated door? Again he felt as if someone had touched his shoulder, but strangely, this time, he imagined he felt his brother's presence.

He turned to the door, pushed it but it wouldn't budge. He tried again, and felt the vibration as it scraped the concrete floor. He was aware of an acrid, musty smell, and, walking slowly to the big press, Namik noticed that underfoot there were darkish marks, which he guessed to be oil pressed from the olives so long ago.

Slowly, he reached out, brushing a finger across a double-spoke wheel, in which an iron pole bore through, helped by concrete supports. There were traces of rancid oil on his fingers, and he wiped these on a handkerchief.

Having never been in an olive press, let alone one of the older ones, Namik was more than surprised at how crude some of the workings were, especially the wooden rafters, which were supported by a large tree trunk. He was also struck by the huge stone grinding wheels. These were set across a ninety-by-two-hundred-centimetre iron drum.

Taking this all in, Namik hated to think his brother died here, at night, probably in darkness. He gazed over to a small window with iron bars, before looking again at the crude machinery. His eyes narrowed. Something caught his attention in one of the lower cogs. Bending down he frowned, as pulling out the item he saw that it had a slight glint to it. Namik started, his eyes widening in disbelief. Lying in his palms was the gold St Christopher, the one he had lent Aygun on the night he'd died! A sudden gasp escaped his lips. So it was true. Aygun had been killed here!

Grasping hold of the gold chain, Namik rushed from the olive press, not wanting to think of the circumstances in which his brother had died. As for this village, he wanted to be away as fast as he could.

With his mind weighed down with all manner of things, and tears stinging his eyes, he rode the scooter back to Kyrenia at breakneck speed.

CHAPTER
TWENTY-TWO

•

THEY WERE TWO men short: the lithe young man who worked out at the gym and another, whose wife had just given birth to a premature boy, which had caused much worry. Ibrahim had only learnt of this recently. His place, he'd said, was with his wife and child at this time as there wasn't another close family member to lend a hand.

Today, with the weather looking fine, two tables were set out beneath the Turtle's Rest, where a passing customer could sit with a coffee, or anything else they cared to drink. Ibrahim was sipping his coffee when Namik came down the steps to join him. 'Why the glum face?' he asked, as he pulled out a chair.

Putting down his cup, Ibrahim looked up at him. 'We seem to have a problem. Two men short, I'm afraid. One, as you know, has just become a new father, and, well, his wife needs extra help.'

Namik frowned. 'There is nobody else she can ask?'

His friend shook his head. 'Still, we will just have to manage.' Ibrahim paused before speaking again. 'Wait! Did we not hear about that other man, the one whose parents were thrown from their home? He may be of help.'

'But' – Namik shrugged – 'we do not want to beg for favours. The others appeared most willing.'

'Yes, but this man, though I do not know him personally, has good cause to get involved. Look what the Bileklers did to his parents! He found those two poor souls dead in the woods.

'Well, if we can speak with him, and he agrees, it is OK with me,' answered Namik, shading his eyes against the bright sunshine.

'Look out for that man who told us about him,' said Ibrahim, about to take his leave. 'He lives in our village. It should not be difficult.'

Watching Ibrahim walk away, Namik pondered on this. It seemed straight forward, but he hoped nobody else would pull out. They couldn't afford to let this happen, as they needed all the help they could get.

As he let himself back into the restaurant, he felt thankful for one thing. At least he could rely on Ibrahim. He was a good man, but, more than this, someone who knew his way around, and how to work around a sticky situation. He'd done all this throughout their battles with the Greek Cypriot terrorists. But, most of all, Namik trusted his judgement. The man was no fool. Whoever helped on the chosen day, Ibrahim was sure to keep everyone safe. All the same, this was all right in theory. What mattered now was that Ibrahim abstained from any alcohol when that time came, as, good judgement or not, drinking alcohol when serious work was carried out dulled a man's senses.

Having tried but failed miserably to make his presence felt, Eran Hamid chanced his luck again at the Bileklers' residence. He knew he would not beat them – they were far too powerful – but he wasn't about to ignore their ill-treatment of his beloved parents. However, Eran had never been a violent man; on the contrary, he elected for a quiet life, but he wasn't a coward, either.

Last time he had turned up at the Bileklers', it was during daytime hours, but on this occasion he decided to pay them a call after dark. His aim was to unnerve whoever was at home, though hopefully both father and son would be there. It was still early, so perhaps Hasan was still at home.

Eran looked down at the gun he was holding. He sneered. That would frighten them. That is exactly what he wanted: just to scare them, nothing else. Did he feel bad about this? He had asked himself the same question earlier, but, no, he was adamant. Nothing compared to what they had done.

Moving stealthily, Eran inched towards the front of the premises. A plaintive bark of a dog could be heard from the rear, though was it coming from the back, or was the animal closer? Pausing for a moment, he inclined his head to the right, listening for other noises. None came so he moved on, the gun gripped tightly. A light showed in two lower windows, but these were muted on account of heavy curtains. Raising his arm, Eran smashed the gun into the nearest window, shattering both inside and out with shards of glass. This was met by a loud gasp, then someone shouting to stay clear. More dogs were heard then, and soon it sounded as though others had also joined in.

Then suddenly, Eran was taken off guard by a vice-like grip. He half turned to find a thick-set man, his arms wound around him pulling him towards the ground. Lights from the house flooded the area, and then another, taller man joined the first, his even broader frame outdoing the other. 'Who are you?' The first man at the scene tightened his hold. 'You are trespassing!'

Having heard the security guard's booming voice, Hasan appeared at the door. His eyes widened on seeing Eran. 'So, it is you again!' he bellowed. It was then that Hasan saw the gun. He drew back, his face draining of colour.

'Yes, Bilekler, and I would have shot you if it hadn't been for these men.' Eran's words were full of malice.

It was then that the second security guard noticed the weapon. He retrieved it from Eran's tight fist, checked it and was glad to find it wasn't loaded.

'Get him out of here!' Hasan ordered. 'He deserves what he gets, and not just for the damage he's caused.'

The dogs hadn't stopped barking while this was going on, and, as Eran was taken off, held securely by the guard, he called a warning. 'You'll rot in hell, Bilekler, believe me!'

Ignoring this, although still badly shaken, Hasan went back inside. There was a lot of damage, but nothing that couldn't be fixed. His father, well, that was a different matter. That sudden blast through the window could have caused the elderly man to suffer another heart attack.

Up in her room, Daisy too had heard the crash of glass. Then, looking from the window, she had seen the cause of it. She didn't know Eran, but it hadn't taken her long to guess the cause of all this. There would be plenty of enemies out for Bilekler's blood, and one day justice would prevail. How soon that would be, she wouldn't know, but she had always hoped that Namik would work out a way of having them both locked up.

Daisy bit hard on her lip. Was Namik doing anything to secure her release? She had been here for what seemed a lifetime. Surely something would happen. If it didn't, heaven knew what would become of her.

Eran was held on charges of gross criminal damage. While in custody, he seethed with anger at the unfair injustice of it all. His explanation at doing what he did held no sway with the small court where he appeared. And the police themselves appeared oblivious to any wrongdoing concerning the Bileklers. Eran guessed this could be because they were clever enough to cover their tracks, something that someone like himself would never be lucky enough to achieve. However, his sentence wasn't to be a long confinement, though long enough to make him understand that what he'd done wasn't to be tolerated. The law was there to protect society.

Shaking his head at the way things had turned out, Eran looked around at his cell. There were another three men in here, two of whom were somewhere in their late sixties, and a much younger man whom Eran placed to be no more than twenty. The two older inmates were lying on the top bunks, one looking to be sleeping, while the young lad sat reading on the edge of his narrow bed.

What these men were in here for he didn't know, as nobody had volunteered any information as yet. All three bore the trademarks of gloom and despondency, perhaps waiting to be transferred to a much harsher prison, but this could only be guessed at. Still, it wasn't too cosy in here. Inside these musty cells, with just a thin blanket, meagre helpings of bland food and not a shred of privacy, he supposed all prisons were the same.

Earlier, Eran had seen a few others brought into the prison. They looked like a right bunch of miscreants, as jailers shoved and dragged them into line, with one bedraggled prisoner threatening one of the younger officers.

A lot of noise was coming from this particular cell, with loud shouting and coarse language, and soon, no doubt, someone would be sent to deal with the troublemakers.

Falling heavily onto his own bunk, Eran had much to think about. Had he got off lightly? He'd presumed that the damage he'd done would have brought a harsher sentence. He then wondered if the authorities had ever suspected the Bileklers of any unlawful act, hence his soft treatment. It may make things awkward if they looked on the Bileklers as a bad lot, as most hereabouts were aware they put good money into many causes.

Eran sat up with a start, admonishing himself. The local police certainly wouldn't be implicated in any criminal activity involving the Bileklers, or anyone else for that matter. They had always been known for their hard-line views on any lawbreaking.

But, like a few others, Eran wondered how Osman and his son seemed to escape the law. Anyone else would never have got away with anything they were rumoured to have done. He suspected that they were so cunning that they covered their tracks well.

Rising from his bunk, Eran gripped the cold steel bars of the prison cell. He missed his family, his children, but most of all he missed his beloved parents. After all, it was the latter he'd never see again. As he stood there, his thoughts jangled and frustrated with the whole system, he was no longer aware of the din coming from the new inmate's cell, or the clanging of steel doors as prison staff went about their duties. He was unaware, too, that one of the older men in his cell had not long been taken out by one of the officers.

Word had soon got out about Eran's arrest. Namik had even paid a visit to the Bileklers' residence, seeing for himself the damage he'd caused. As he pulled up on his scooter, keeping a safe distance from the house, he saw a couple of men replacing one of the windows, while a young lad was kept busy with a yard broom. Namik hadn't been there long when Hasan made an appearance. At first he thought he'd been spotted, but Hasan was casting his eye around carefully, as if making sure no other damage had been done.

While there, Namik glanced to the upper floor of the property in the hope of seeing Daisy. He'd done this before, but wasn't always lucky. From where he was now, sitting astride the scooter, he couldn't see that clearly but thought he'd give it a few minutes. Then, as these minutes ticked by, Namik's heart sank, and carefully he manoeuvred the bike away without turning on the engine. He hadn't got far when, glancing to the upper windows once more, he saw a movement. Stopping in his tracks, his heart raced. Daisy! It was Daisy; she was at one of the windows, her face just how he'd remembered. He didn't acknowledge her at first; he couldn't, and felt as though he'd been rooted to the spot.

She was still there, looking down on him, and it seemed as if she too was finding it hard to believe he was so close to her. Then suddenly, slowly, she lifted her arm and waved, her smile growing wider in her pleasure at seeing him.

He smiled back, not daring to wave in case his actions were caught by anyone in the house. Nonetheless, he managed to make clear his feelings, and that they hadn't changed. At least, he hoped this explained how he felt, as he tried to mouth his sentiments.

Namik could do nothing else after this, but he hadn't felt this good for many months. He hoped Daisy felt the same, that seeing him, if only briefly, had helped her too.

Just before leaving, he gave a slight nod of his head, followed by a cheering smile.

As for Daisy, she came away from the window with her spirits soaring high. Nobody was sure of any possible outcome, but what happened a few moments ago would stand both in good stead for the time being.

A few days later when Namik entered the house, having left Ibrahim at the local café, he found nobody home. He surmised that his father, Ahmet, might possibly be out working, as he often helped to deliver logs around the neighbourhood. However, from the moment he'd walked through the door, the house seemed somehow different. He couldn't quite detect what, if anything, but it certainly didn't feel the same.

Namik glanced around the kitchen. Everything was in its place; even the copper pot used for brewing coffee sat atop the stove. The table, covered with its lace-edged cloth, and the vase of red and white silk roses which stood centre-place: that too was normal.

Nothing seemed amiss in the bedrooms, and, going back into the kitchen, Namik looked around once more. His mother, of course, could have gone to visit one of his sisters, but something made him doubt it. He couldn't account for this, but that was his feeling, albeit an uneasy one.

Namik suddenly shivered. The room felt cold, unusually so, but outside the sun shone bright, streaming through the kitchen window, spilling golden light across most of the room. Namik's eye travelled to his mother's daybed. Something here was different, too. Normally, when not in use, it was always covered neatly with a crocheted quilt. It wasn't the case now. The quilt was hanging to the floor, and the pillow squashed against the wall, as if the bed had been left in rather a hurry.

In that moment, Namik knew his mother wasn't visiting one of his sisters. Nor had she popped into a neighbour's house. Something had happened, he was sure of it. Pulling out a chair from the kitchen table, he sat heavily. It was only about two hours ago that he'd left the house, then everything was just as it ever was. His mother was sitting right here, listening contentedly to the radio, while his father was grumbling about something he'd read in the newspaper.

After some moments, still troubled, Namik went over to the window. Nobody was in sight, no vehicles, nothing. He swallowed nervously; something definitely was amiss. Namik hadn't removed his jacket, and just about to leave the house, on what mission he never knew; he saw his father turn into the front path. His head was bowed, his footsteps slow, and he seemed to have aged a great deal in these last few hours.

When at last the door opened, Ahmet just stood there, his eyes red-rimmed and rather puffy.

At first, Namik was unable to move, then, reaching out, he drew his father to him. 'You do not have to say; I already know,' he told him. 'My mother is no longer with us.'

Ahmet would not allow himself to speak, but the look on his face answered for him.

It was a week later, and Namik was in Ibrahim's sorting office to check if any mail had arrived. 'A pity about your mother,' the older man said. 'She was a good woman, liked by all.'

'Well, the good die too soon, so they say,' replied Namik, his face disclosing nothing of his feelings.'

'Still, it is a great loss.' Ibrahim handed over a letter. 'Only one today for your household.'

Looking at the handwriting, which was addressed to him, Namik frowned. He turned away, tore open the envelope, then slipped out a sheet of paper. 'Oh.' He left the rest unfinished.

'Bad news?' asked Ibrahim, using a hand to scrape back his thick mane of steel-grey hair.

'Not really, I thought it was from someone else, that's all.' The letter was from his uncle, who owned the Turtle's Rest. He was still in England and wanted to know how things were running.

Ibrahim looked up from the letters he was sorting. 'You seemed disappointed; that is why I asked.'

'I... I am, really. The handwriting is very similar to someone else I know.'

A deep, throaty chuckle came from the other side of the rough bench on which the sorting took place. 'Your face reminds me of when you were a young boy. You cannot have what you cannot have.' Ibrahim chuckled again.

'I thought I'd be hearing some better news, that is all,' said Namik. 'A young woman – you know her too, actually. She appears to have disappeared.'

'How? In what way? And who are we talking about?'

'Some time ago, I met up with Aisha, Bilekler's daughter. She promised to keep in touch, but I have not heard anything since then.'

'Of course I know of her. She and your brother...'

'Yes, and I will always hold that in my heart. It makes me feel…' Namik searched for the right word. 'Closer. Yes, it makes me feel like Aygun is here.' He touched his chest.

'What do you think has happened?'

'That I do not know, but Aisha is a good woman, nothing like her family. In fact, when she last spoke she was afraid for her life. Someone was out to harm her. Her own family, possibly.'

'Do you believe that? Why? What reason would they have?'

'Because she was seen with me,' replied Namik. 'We lowly sort are scum, just as my brother was.'

Ibrahim looked up from the bench, a look of concern on his face. 'Then I fear for her, my friend.'

Namik said nothing but slipped his uncle's letter into his pocket.

Then, picking up a sack from the floor, Ibrahim shook it out in case he'd missed any stray letter. This wasn't the case so he reached to a shelf and pulled down a small bottle of white rum. He peered at its contents and grimaced. 'There isn't much left, but we can share,' he told Namik.

'No, I'll not bother. I was thinking, though. Suppose they have killed Aisha.'

Ibrahim drank from the bottle, but only took a few gulps of the rum. 'Who knows what their limits are. We know they'll stop at nothing – but their own flesh and blood?'

'I think they are capable of anything. And look,' Namik handed over the gold necklace which he'd found.

'Whose is this?'

'Aygun wore it on the night he was killed. He borrowed it from me, and I found it among the machinery in the old olive press in Bogaz.'

There was a chair close by, and Ibrahim sank onto this, the bottle still in his hand. 'I was very fond of your brother. I would have loved one like him of my own. I can see too well how you hate those Bileklers.'

'I do not think that word covers what I feel for those murderers. What they have done, and got away with, I wish nothing good for them. Still, you'll see, they will get what is coming. It has to, one way or another.'

Namik took his leave after this, but, when he left the restaurant the following night, he saw a dark shadow hovering outside one of the gift shops. It would have closed some hours ago, but a strip light was always left on for security. The dim lighting, placed to the rear of the shop, didn't quite show who lurked there, but Namik was pretty sure it was a man. Then another movement, although swift, showed this to be true, as the man hastened into the door's recess.

It was just after eleven-thirty; all other staff had gone home, but Namik had stayed behind to catch up on some unpaid bills which had to be met. As usual, his scooter was nearby, but, before heading for this, he glanced again towards the gift shop. There was no sign of anybody now, so, making for his scooter, he dismissed the uneasy feeling he'd had earlier, telling himself he was fast becoming paranoid.

A young couple strolled past him, followed shortly by an aged man with a stick. Namik nodded to the latter in recognition. The man muttered something, to which Namik smiled, and then, about to turn on the scooter's ignition, a hand grabbed him roughly from behind. Turning swiftly, he saw his aggressor, then, before he could say anything, a sharp implement came down on his back. Cursing, Namik sputtered, caught his breath, and then lashed out, disarming his opponent of the weapon. This bounced on the ground, the open blade of the knife landing a short distance from the front wheel of the scooter. He couldn't tell how badly the knife had pierced his flesh, but could feel a stinging sensation where he'd been jabbed.

It was extremely dark at this end of the harbour, as Namik had turned off all the lighting in the restaurant which was directly behind him. However, he recognised the man who still held him. 'Get your hands off, Bilekler!' he yelled.

Hasan wasn't about to let Namik go. His loathing and animosity for someone who'd done him no personable harm poured out of every sinew. 'You think I did not see you?' he hissed. 'My house. You were at my house. What for? That is what I'd like to know.'

Namik winced. This wasn't because of Hasan's rough hold on him but the lower regions of his back were beginning to sting quite painfully. On touching this area, his hand felt sticky with blood. 'Why ask?' He winced again, as a sharp pain tore at his insides.

Ignoring the question, Hasan inclined his head, and then seconds later a second man pounced on Namik, dragging him away from the scooter.

'Is the car nearby?' Hasan addressed his helper in muttered tones.

With his arms pinioned behind him, Namik could just make out who the other man was. He couldn't mistake Arif Camal's profile, or the stale odour that always came from his breath.

Caught between the two men, although Namik struggled, he was pushed and pulled towards the car. He'd tried to yell out, but, before he could be heard, a clammy hand was clamped over his mouth as he was shoved into the car.

It was Arif Camal who sat beside him in the back, leaving Hasan in the driving seat. Where they were heading he wouldn't know, but the vehicle shot forwards and moved at an alarming rate, swerving often at several bends as it made for the open road.

The drive was certainly a long one, and, owing to a starless sky which blanked the countryside in darkness, it appeared to be never-ending.

'If it was Daisy you were looking for, you may as well forget it.' Hasan had turned his head slightly. 'She is no longer interested, so there you are.'

Although the knife hadn't cut that deep, blood still trickled in a steady stream through Namik's clothing. He wanted to answer, bite back with some sharp reply, but he felt quite faint. He was sure he'd pass out at any moment.

The car must have hit a pothole or something, because Namik awoke with a start. He didn't know if he'd actually been asleep or if he had lost consciousness. In any case, they were still travelling, and he had no idea just how much mileage they had done. Looking out of the rear window, he could now see a little of the landscape, made visible by a waning moon. A farm building came into view, backed by a line of tall trees, their trunks showing silvery-white as the moon made a full appearance.

Namik clutched at his wound, hoping the car would soon reach its destination. Where that was he shuddered to think, but he hoped the odious man next to him wouldn't always be in attendance. The stench from his sweating body was more than he could bear.

'Phew.' Namik puffed out his cheeks. The pain in his back was absolute hell.

CHAPTER
TWENTY-THREE

•

AHMET WAS SLOWLY becoming a mere shadow of the man he'd once been. First his youngest son, killed before he'd had chance to taste what life may have to offer, then a beloved wife whose poor health had failed her, having put everyone's welfare before her own, and now this. As could be expected, Namik had taken his mother's death badly. Nothing much was said, but Ahmet knew how it had hit him. It was all too much. And, what with his concern over Daisy, and not knowing if he'd ever see her again and continue the relationship they had once enjoyed, it had all added to the strain.

For three days now there had been no sign of Namik. It wasn't his nature to stay away, leave without a word while his father was in the early stages of grieving. So where was he? Ahmet's fears were growing daily. After all, there was only so much his son could take.

Now, pushing open the door of Ibrahim's sorting office, Ahmet stepped slowly inside, to be met by four other men. One by one they turned to look at him, each expression conveying their sympathies. It was Ibrahim who spoke first. 'No word yet?' Although he knew the answer, he felt he had to ask.

Ahmet shook his head. 'I thought you might have heard something.'

'I'm afraid we have not. As I said yesterday, I would let you know at once if any news should come this way.'

Unhurried, Ahmet looked to see if any post had come for him. When none was found, he looked around at the men's solemn faces. 'You understand my concern, don't you? What kind of man would I be if I did not worry about my son?'

Kazim was among these men and he stepped forward. 'Of course we understand. Like you, we too are concerned. In fact, we had hoped to meet up quite soon. We have a meeting. It is…' He glanced at the others. 'It is a friendly gathering, a few men putting the world to rights.'

A heavy silence hung in the air, followed by the shuffling of feet, which to Ahmet spoke volumes. The men here were all friends of his son, and even a fool could see they weren't at ease with the situation. 'I'll go home,' he said flatly. 'He may be there now. Namik wanted time to think, eh?'

Watching Ahmet leave the hut, his shoulders slumped, the men all had the same question in mind. Exactly what had happened to Namik? They were so near to finalising their plans that his disappearance just didn't make sense.

The days were becoming cooler, and, as Eran Hamid walked out of the prison gates, he shivered, while taking in his surroundings. The men he'd been sharing his cell with were still there, but, apart from one who was supposedly to be released soon, the two remaining were awaiting a retrial. It wasn't clear what they had done, though most certainly it was far greater a crime than his own.

Nobody had come to meet Eran, and this was to be expected. His wife, though a quiet individual, keeping herself to herself, had stern views on lawbreaking. Moreover, she'd never been an affectionate woman, so this would have been against her nature to have been waiting outside the prison for him. Nonetheless, home was home; like it or not, she was the mother of his children and, above all, Eran was, in essence, a family man.

Was he sorry for what he'd done? He didn't think so. Still, if faced with a chance to do something similar again, would he want to? Eran shook his head. Being locked up, no matter how short the period, wasn't an easy ride. True, it was nowhere near as bad as it once was. He remembered how they used to treat prisoners in mainland Turkey, and other such places.

Going in search of a bus, Eran stopped briefly to look back at the building he'd not long left behind. It looked grim, the high walls screening out what lay behind. In his mind he could still hear the shrill sounds of one inmate echoing throughout the corridors. He'd had to be taken off to a psychiatric unit.

How many times he'd drifted in and out of sleep he had no idea, but in his wakeful moments Namik's inability to move his limbs seemed almost impossible. His mouth was dry, too. Each time he swallowed, in the hope of creating some kind of moisture, it felt as if his throat was filled with sawdust. The small slash, just inches from his spine, had stopped bleeding, or so he imagined, but the area was painfully stiff, and his shirt clung uncomfortably. He tried pulling this away from his body, but without success.

Though, worse than all this, his senses reeled, as if in a stupor, and with each movement of his head he felt the room turn giddily around him.

The room! Where was he? He might have found out if only the place would stop turning. Even so, no sooner had he tried to get his bearings than sleep dragged him into another world, a world where the most alien of dreams made no sense at all.

During one such wakeful moment, Namik thought he would die of thirst, and peering through half-opened eyes he could have sworn he'd seen stacks of wooden crates. Close to these an array of bottles covered a long table, some having seemingly rolled onto a dry earth floor. How long had he been here? A few days? A week? It couldn't have been longer: he'd have died of hunger, surely.

Namik blinked hard, shaking his head. He stopped this soon enough as the room swam before him. How had he come to be here? Had he been forcibly brought to this place? He was still struggling to make sense of all this, but his brain was so jumbled he came up with nothing. There was one thing, though. Apart from the injury to his back, caused by that sharp blade, the only thing that would have had this effect on him must be drugs. That was it: someone had drugged him. As he came to terms with this, and who the culprit might be, it wasn't to last for long, as Namik's head began to feel like cotton wool. Much worse than it had been, with all reasoning lost, as he sank into a deep sort of coma.

Elsewhere, Hasan curled his lips at the now-empty bottle of Scotch, then picked up a full one and brought this to his chair.

He was sitting in the spacious lounge, the blinds opened at one of the windows, showing a crescent moon. Only one table lamp was switched on as he couldn't be bothered with the rest, having drunk his fair share of the whisky.

Unscrewing the second bottle, he poured a good measure into his glass. Half of this was gulped back within seconds, while the rest sat idly in his hands. During the time spent sitting in here, his thoughts were centred on Namik.

What he had wanted was to kill him there and then, but something had stopped him. Another killing: could he chance that? Would another person, put out of his way because it suited his purpose, cause suspicion? The body, of course, would be concealed, hidden until decomposed, but would he be called to answer some questions? Besides, Hasan was well aware that there were some who knew his animosity towards the Guven menfolk. No, perhaps there was a better way.

There was no woman in Hasan's life at the moment. There was nobody he was particularly fond of, either. Daisy had been the one, and then, having got used to her presence in the house, his feelings had turned rather sour. This wasn't supposed to have happened, but it had and there was nothing he could do to turn back the clock. As with everything that was new – a relationship or something materialistic – he quickly tired of the thing, although letting her go was out of the question. She knew too much, would go straight to the police, and he wasn't about to let that happen. No, he would just have to let things settle, and in the meantime, who knew, his feelings for Daisy may well return.

Hasan poured the rest of the Scotch down his throat, left his chair and walked over to the window. From here, he could see one of the security guards moving among the shrubbery. The extra lighting that had been installed had automatically switched itself on and was illuminating a vast stretch of the garden, the man included.

The guards weren't really needed, but according to Osman he'd maintained that their safety was paramount, and that he personally would feel much safer in his bed.

All this expense was totally unnecessary. He'd said as much to his father, but Osman was adamant. They had the money, of course, but their wealth wasn't what it once was, owing to the failure of one or two business adventures going bust.

Osman was kept in the dark regarding these, and, not wanting to cause him any distress, Hasan let him think all was well.

Irritated by all that glaring light, he pulled down the shutters. Another drink was poured, then, taking the bottle, he went upstairs. Alone in his room, with just the radio for company, he might be able to think more clearly. See what he could come up with regarding Namik.

As the ill-fitting door was pushed open, it scraped along the concrete floor and almost lost one of its hinges, but Arif Camal grabbed at this, and fixed it as best he could.

Although Namik had been awake for some time, his eyes were closed. He opened them now and peered at the man who had entered. 'I thought you would show yourself eventually,' he sneered. During his time here, his memory of events had slowly come back to him. He was aware of leaving his restaurant, and spotting a lone figure in a shop doorway, but, apart from being grabbed by Hasan and this man, as well as being bundled into a car, all else was lost to him.

Namik hadn't noticed the dog at first, but now it came from behind, sniffing at him from all directions. It was a big dog, rough-haired and with rather a long, sharp face. Its jaw opened and it edged closer, its pointed fangs looking ominous.

Arif Camal stood some distance away, amusement glinting in his eyes. 'You are not fond of dogs?'

Namik wasn't tied up; in fact, he had moved a little, but couldn't have got far on account of his heavy sedation. Even when awake, this period wouldn't last long before he was pulled into another deep coma. However, the man who had just spoken seemed to have engaged his brain into some kind of activity. 'Dogs are no problem,' he lied. 'It is people who cannot be trusted.'

The oily-faced man ignored this, and walked over to where Namik was slumped against a thick wooden post. 'We brought you here out of harm's way. Still, you will not be staying; something will have to be arranged.'

'Anyway, why choose this place?' Namik had since discovered that the stone building was once a wine distillery, as, apart from crates of bottles, large stainless-steel cylinders were in evidence.

'It should make no difference to you where it is,' Arif said mockingly. 'Here, there, it does not matter. You will not be seeing any of your friends, anyway.'

'What have you in mind? Another death?' Namik's head hurt and his tongue felt as if it had doubled in size.

The man grimaced. 'That, my friend, is out of my hands, unless of course I'm given an order. But this we will see.'

The dog had moved away, and was sniffing around some empty bottles that were lying on the earth floor. This area looked as if it had been waiting to be concreted over, but the owner had given up.

'Do you know what I think?' said the man, his face inches from Namik's and reeking of garlic. 'I think you would be better off dead. Your brother, that English girl – Daisy, is it? What is there to live for?'

Arif Camal's words were more than Namik could bear, and before he knew it he made a grab for the man's shirt collar. He grappled with him for a moment, sending the wretched man off balance. Then he was on the ground, his back wriggling in the dust as he gasped for air.

It was then that Namik's own clothing was grasped, not by another person but by the sharp teeth of the animal. This was accompanied by a series of grunts and snarls, a sound that had always terrified Namik. Nonetheless, the dog held on as though his life depended upon it, while saliva dripped from its jaws.

It was impossible to roll clear, and, coupled with this, Namik's strength seemed to have left him.

Soon after, with Arif Camal on his feet, a substance was forced down Namik's throat, and was followed swiftly by some bottled water taken from the man's pocket.

Moments later, Namik fell into a deep sleep, and wouldn't have had a clue as to what was happening.

Daisy gasped in horror after Fatma had finished speaking. At first she was unable to speak, but then finally found her tongue. 'You say you overheard them?'

'Yes, it is wrong, I know, but I did hear correctly. Mr Osman, he was angry. Very angry indeed.'

Daisy was still coming to terms with what she had been told. 'Did they say where?'

Moving quietly towards the bedroom door, Fatma listened for any footsteps. When none were heard, she joined Daisy on the opposite side of the room. 'No, this I did not catch, but it may be a barn of some sort.'

'But why would Hasan's father want him dead? Namik has done them no harm, at least none that I am aware of.'

'Who knows, though there was talk of his prying. Perhaps they found him around this property.'

The colour had drained from Daisy's face. She wondered if Namik had been waylaid after she had seen him looking up at her bedroom window.

'I did not mean to upset you,' said Fatma, reaching out for Daisy's arm.

'That family think nothing of taking someone's life.' Daisy's lips tightened. 'If I was out of here, I'd tell of everything I know.'

Fatma grunted. 'They are aware of this; it is the very reason you are kept here!'

It was Daisy who reached out now, gripping Fatma's arm firmly. 'Please, I beg of you, report the Bileklers immediately. Tell the police what you have heard.'

Getting to her feet, Fatma folded her arms, a look of despair written on her face. 'What would I say? Why would they believe me? I may be out to seek revenge. Perhaps I have not been paid for the work I do.' She shook her head, 'No, the police would not believe me, I know.'

'I have wondered many times if Namik is already dead.' Daisy, too, came to her feet. 'That was until recently, when I saw him, and I was so relieved. Now, I have that fear again. You heard them, Fatma: they want Namik out of the way for good!'

'Daisy.' Fatma spoke in hushed tones. 'There is one thing in Namik's favour. Mr Hasan does not agree. He is still to decide what is best.'

'Yes.' Daisy swallowed. 'But he is a big problem to them both. Like me, Namik knows too much.'

The housekeeper's expression became grave; she turned away, then after a few moments began to pace the room. Daisy became even more uneasy, wondering at the thoughts going through the woman's head. 'What is it?' she asked. 'What else do you know?'

'I know as much as you, Daisy,' answered Fatma, gesturing with both arms. 'I cannot make a habit of listening. Once, I was called into Mr Osman's office. Asking, no, telling me not to repeat anything I may here. He was warning me of my job and maybe my home. If I lose one, I lose both, then what would I do?'

There was no answer to this, and Daisy was left wondering what else could be done. She understood Fatma's dilemma, for where else was she to go if her home was taken away? The Bileklers owned most of those cottages, and, apart from this, one word from them and a person could be blacklisted from all sorts.

Remembering Namik's face from her bedroom window, as he looked up at her, had given Daisy renewed hope. It promised of something good about to happen. Now it seemed his life hung in the balance. Where would it all end?

In the small front garden of his run-down cottage in Catalkoy, Eran Hamid shovelled earth from one heap to another. Dark circles ringed his eyes, and the stubble on his jaw which was normally present was fast becoming a real beard.

Catalkoy almost fringed the village of Ozankoy, and, when Ibrahim reached it, he immediately recognised the bearded man.

As Ibrahim got out of his car, dust-covered owing to weeks of neglect, Eran looked up from his chore and then promptly resumed his digging, but he could not ignore the man who stood before him. 'What is it you want from me?' he asked, his eyes still averted.

Ibrahim cleared his throat. 'I heard you were out of that prison and have come to offer my sorrow at what you have endured, that and the death of your poor parents.'

Eran grunted, leant on his shovel and looked Ibrahim in the eye. 'My sentence was not as bad as some, but not good, either. Prison does no favours for any man. My parents, well, nothing will be the same again, especially the way they came to die.'

A strong gust of wind caused Ibrahim to push back the thick clump of hair which had blown across his eyes. 'I agree, totally. I think also that these animals that were responsible should pay for what they did.'

'Have you ever been locked up?' Eran's eyes narrowed as he asked the question.

'It matters not one way or another, but what are you really saying?'

'I'm saying that I'm through with the Bileklers,' answered Eran, defiantly. 'I did what I did, but I'll not get involved with anything else you may be planning.'

Halfway through a cigarette he was smoking, Ibrahim coughed, spat something out and then took another puff on the thin roll-up. 'Did you hear that one of our friends was missing?' he enquired.

Eran shook his head. 'Anyway, what is that to do with me?'

'You are, perhaps, unaware that the man who is missing has also lost his brother. Not through seeing off EOKA in that bloody war, but murdered.'

'Murdered?' repeated Eran. 'Who was it that did this?'

Ibrahim trod his cigarette butt into the ground. 'Take a guess!'

Having taken in what was said, Eran shrugged. 'Security guards are up at the big house. I thought you should know, if of course you thought of going up there.'

A huge grin spread across Ibrahim's face. 'Of course we are going up there. As for security guards, I'll meet that problem when and where. But…' Ibrahim paused. 'I thought you might be interested.'

Taking a few steps closer, Eran spoke rather harshly. 'Not me. No more upheaval. I have had enough.'

It was Ibrahim who had the last word, but his were spoken softly, yet decisively. 'The friend, the one who is missing, is very much in love with a young woman. The Bileklers are holding Daisy against her will. Imprisoned, just like you were but perhaps worse. Anyway, if and when we free her, she'll tell the police everything. Kept there all this time, she will know a great deal. We have enough on them already, but this girl will verify all we say.'

Ibrahim allowed time for his words to sink into the man's head before continuing. 'The police, well, most are decent, always known for fair play, but they have good reasons for thinking highly of the Bileklers. Still, we know otherwise, and this we will hope to prove.'

After Ibrahim took his leave, Eran's spade could be heard swinging at the dry earth with more gusto than was necessary.

CHAPTER
TWENTY-FOUR

•

Dawn had just broken, and this brought shafts of thin light through a filthy window set high above the long bench that held numerous empty bottles. There would have been more daylight if a huge fir tree outside the ramshackle building had not grown so close in proximity to the window.

Namik had been awake for some time, and had watched, head half drooped, as the new day had made its appearance. Although not as groggy as he had been, his mind couldn't assimilate things as quickly as was normal. Still, his mental ability was far better than yesterday, or indeed previous to this. Bit by bit, he had worked out the reason for all this: it was because the odious Arif Camal had somehow missed out on the drug he'd been administering.

Sitting with his back against a stout oak beam, Namik sniffed with disdain at his clothing. Stains showed down the front of his dark jacket, and a few buttons from his shirt were missing. Also, it was not until now that he noticed he was wearing only one shoe. He had no idea how long he'd been here, though he did not feel hungry so it couldn't have been that long. On the other hand, he might have been brought here as much as a week ago and been given some kind of nourishment, but his brain was so clouded he couldn't tell.

Although limited for natural light, the little that came from the filthy window had now gained in strength, casting long, golden beams that slightly improved the room's temperature.

He may not have felt hungry but Namik was overtaken by a terrible thirst. Flexing his shoulders, he realised he wasn't fettered, but his arms, as well as the rest of his body, felt as leaden as a ton weight. He hadn't noticed the water before, or, if he had, he'd forgotten it. Peering at it, through drooping eyes, Namik reached out in an effort to grasp the half-empty plastic bottle. He swore when his fingers failed to make contact with it, but, undeterred, he tried again and this time he succeeded.

The water was warm. It wasn't pleasant, but he let the liquid spill down his parched throat until his thirst was sated. In any case, he'd drunk the bottle dry so this would have to suffice.

As the time slipped by, Namik seemed to be able to think more clearly. He had read somewhere that putting water back into the body enabled a person to do this much better. In fact, his limbs, too, appeared to move more freely, though this could be due to whatever drugs he'd previously been given having worn off. This wasn't to say he was completely back to normal – far from it – but it was a vast improvement.

Namik noticed that his wristwatch was missing. He felt that was strange as he was never without it these days. He considered that someone must have stolen it, but couldn't think why, as it was such a cheap watch.

A sizeable gap showed from beneath the wooden door, allowing a thin pencil of light to enter, and, shifting his body, he found he was now able to shuffle towards it. At one point, he tried to stand, but his legs buckled beneath him. The room, or makeshift factory, was quite spacious, with the largest area at this end narrowing only slightly to the other end of the building. Because of this, Namik worried that he might not make it to the door without being caught. Arif or maybe Hasan might be planning a visit. Or perhaps someone might already be on the other side of the door, lying in wait.

Trying again to stand, his eyes fell on a long, thin pole with a hook at the end. He recognised it now as the same which was used in schools for reaching and opening windows. Forcing his body to obey his demands, Namik finally reached this and clasped it tightly. This proved useful as it helped with his mobility, though, by moving the pole, a mouse nest must have been disturbed, because at least half a dozen tiny creatures scampered away in various directions.

Namik didn't know why he shivered at this, because he wasn't nervous of mice, never had been, but their sudden movement had caught him off guard.

He jumped now, and almost toppled over when the low purr of a car's engine was heard. Panic-stricken, he looked for somewhere to hide. He soon found a spot and hobbled to where he'd seen the pole. As quick as was possible, he hid in the shadows, where pallets and wooden crates were housed. To say it was cramped in this space was putting it mildly, but he had to stay put. Moving just a fraction would have alerted whoever it was to where he'd hidden.

By now, the person had already taken their first few steps across the concrete floor, having noisily scraped open the ill-fitting door. Namik still hadn't seen who it was, as his body was pressed against something which obscured his vision. It felt very much like some rubber garments, but he couldn't be sure. Then his shoulder nudged something. He grabbed it quickly before it fell to the floor, and found it to be a large wicker basket. Something did fall, though, making a soft rustling sound as it landed on his shoeless foot. It was one of the rubber garments, and he guessed it to be worn in the process of wine-making.

A voice called out, and Namik knew at once who had entered the building. The voice was gruff, not someone of Hasan's breeding. 'I'll find you soon; you'll not get far!' Arif Camal called again, only this time he could be heard moving from one end of the long floor to the other, his voice echoing behind him.

At one point, Namik held his breath, perspiring freely when the sound of footsteps came within an arm's length. In normal circumstances, Arif Camal would no way beat him in a clean fight. Namik's time in the army would have seen to that. Added to this, his lifelong friend Ibrahim had taught him tactics: tactics he had learnt working for the underground, during troubled times. However, this wouldn't have been a fair fight. Unfit as he was at the moment, with his head still fuzzy, he would most probably flounder.

'You will not beat me,' Arif continued. 'I will not be Bilekler's whipping boy, oh no. You will come out now from wherever you are, and face this gun.'

At those words, Namik's body stiffened. He wasn't going to look down the barrel of a gun, or anything else that would see the end of him. He badly wanted to take a deep breath, feel some of the tension leave his body, but the man, although his back was turned against him, was still too close. Namik could just make this out from the limited space and deep shadows that concealed him.

'So, I was told not to kill you, as your fate has not yet been decided.' Arif snorted, and then laughed. 'Myself, I would have seen to that on the first day. Nothing would satisfy me better than to see you dead, my friend.'

This time, it wasn't what had been said, but Namik felt so weak he felt sure he was about to topple over. Perhaps it was because his body was still dehydrated; he didn't really know. Fumbling about him, his arm clutched at the rubber garments, and, luckily, these were hanging from good, strong hooks. With his eyes closed, while waves of nausea washed over him, Namik stood like this for some minutes. He could still hear Arif, but whatever he was doing seemed to be coming from somewhere above. But how was this? Wasn't this a one-storey building?

Namik thought for a moment. Yes, there was a top floor, or maybe a mezzanine. This had been noted in one of his more wakeful moments.

Namik knew he had to move, get away before Arif discovered him. Peering from his cover, he edged quietly out. He then moved towards the outer door, praying that, on opening it, the sound would not alert attention.

With the help of the thin pole he'd salvaged, he limped softly along. The odd, slight tap it made against the concrete floor was barely audible. Still, it wasn't this which brought Arif Camal back downstairs, but, having no luck elsewhere, he had decided to begin his search again.

At the door, Namik had already seen his enemy walking towards him, but pulled hard at the bolt which had been slid across. On his first attempt, nothing happened, and then, aware of Camal's close presence, he yanked again at the door. It did open, but not enough to get through, and as it scraped across the floor one of the hinges broke away and bounced inches from his feet.

Sweating profusely, Namik turned to find Camal only a couple of yards behind him. His eyes travelled to the man's hand, and he was surprised that there wasn't a gun, but instead a sturdy length of wood. He also noted some ferocious-looking nails poking out at one end.

It was true that Arif Camal wanted Namik dead, but Hasan said only to drug him. The table would have been well turned against Camal had Hasan known those drugs had been recently forgotten.

Still looking at the plank of wood, Namik considered making a grab for it, but changed his mind when he realised his chances were slim. And the malicious glint in the other man's eyes somehow confirmed this.

From somewhere outside, a dog could be heard, its constant barking becoming closer, and from the corner of his eye he could not only see the bright sunshine filtering through the slightly open door but heard, too, a man's gruff voice calling the dog. Rivulets of sweat trickled along Namik's back, and the prickles at the back of his neck caused him to shudder.

Just how long Namik stood there it was hard to tell, but it appeared that Arif Camal was undecided on his next move, until, eventually, he spoke. 'You know what I've decided to do, don't you?' he said, tauntingly. 'I'll take great pleasure in using this.' Arif gestured at the plank he was wielding. 'I'll say you were trying to escape; it's as simple as that.'

'But Hasan will know you had forgotten the drugs. How else could I have managed it?' Namik was playing for time, working out his next move. A glimmer of hope was on his side as his head was clearing by the minute, and, luckily for him, his body, too, was gaining strength. Glancing down at the pole he'd found, he reckoned it would be no match for the heavy one that Arif had, so he'd have to come up with something else.

'Were you always so weak?' Arif Camal looked full of himself. 'It seems you are not the big man you made out to be.' Parading himself around Namik, he shoved him with the end of the thick lump of wood.

The man was clearly enjoying himself, and Namik reckoned he wasn't used to being in charge, at least not one to one and in an honest fight. He was hoping to be nudged again, would welcome it, and so tried to provoke Camal. 'I lay a bet you never saw action. The only fighting you ever did was to lean on someone else.'

'You have no knowledge of me,' Camal said, tight-lipped. 'What is more, nobody cares for your opinion.' He moved closer, an evil look in his eyes, while his arm was raised ready to cast blows upon Namik.

Awaiting his chance, his eye keenly on the heavy chunk of wood, Namik caught the man's arm moments before his head made contact with it. Four hands grappled with the rough-edged plank, and painful splinters dug themselves into Namik's fingers. Ignoring this, he wrenched the object free from the other man's grasp, sending him crashing onto the ground with a final shove.

Camal wasn't down for long, and in seconds he had got to his feet and lunged at Namik, but was thwarted by the heavy object which was placed between them.

A sharp kick was aimed at Namik's shin, but, standing his ground, his arm shot up and curled itself around Camal's neck. By now, the wooden plank had dropped to the ground and it ended up a short distance away.

'I may not be the big man, but perhaps I am stronger than you, Camal.' Namik felt deep hatred for this man, and feared he would kill him, but common sense prevailed. Nonetheless, his grip automatically tightened, until the pressure brought prominent veins to the man's face and neck.

Namik could not afford to stay here much longer, Hasan could make an appearance at any moment. He shoved the man off roughly, holding him down with his foot. Then looking towards the spiked lump of wood, he said, 'You can forget that. I'll be taking it. Do not bother to come after me, either; you'll not stand a chance.'

This item was heaved from its resting place, then carried to the door. Because it was slightly open, Namik yanked at this with one hand, then, once outside, kicked it until the door was almost closed, then made his way to the open road.

On his way, he threw the lump of wood into a thick clump of scrub. It was much heavier than it had looked, and he couldn't help but think that, if caught by the rusty nails that stuck out, the unfortunate victim would be looking at more than a tetanus jab!

It was an elderly man who came to Namik's aid. Seeing him propped against an old, gnarled tree, and wearing only one shoe, he asked if he was lost and needed help. At first, Namik had been disoriented, having no clue to where he was, but it hadn't taken too long to find his bearings. 'Thank you for your kindness,' he gasped, 'but I seem to know this place, or at least recognise it.'

The aged man, whose goatee beard was tied with thin ribbon, had seen Namik from his window and with not much to do in his twilight years, he had made his way to the grassy bank opposite. 'If it is food that you want, my wife will have plenty over from her lamb stew. I know a man when he is hungry.'

This fact was evident, as Namik's cheeks were ashen and slightly sunken.

'There is something I need more,' he replied. 'I would like some water. Then I would like to get home.'

'We may be able to help, though this depends on the distance.' The old man smiled. 'But first you must have nourishment. Come, you see my wife? She is at the gate now, and will gladly feed you.'

Accepting the man's help, Namik walked with him to the house. He hadn't realised until now just how hungry he was.

Namik wiped his mouth on the paper napkin which had been put beside his plate. The lamb and potato stew, which had been garnished with parsley and fresh lemon, was similar to the one his mother used to make and he had thoroughly enjoyed it. Looking over at the elderly couple, who had already eaten, he thanked them for their kindness. He then drank more of the water he'd been given.

They were sitting around their fireside, and the woman threw up her arms. 'No need, my boy. It is us that are grateful.' She reached out for her husband's hand. 'You see, we had two sons. They were taken from us, killed during that terrible war.'

The old man squeezed her hand. 'And there is not a day that passes that we do not miss them. Of course, we did not always live here. No, that happened in Tokhni, a mixed village then, back in '74. They came and dragged them off: men, boys, it did not matter how old they were.'

Wanting to say something, but afraid of his emotional state, Namik kept the words to himself, but this didn't stop him from remembering.

The village to which the couple were referring was just one mentioned in all the newspapers at that time. Many families lost someone in those atrocities. These Turkish Cypriots, sixty-nine of them, and all males, were between the ages of thirteen and seventy-four. They were taken from their homes under the leadership of the evil Andriko. The following day, Andriko's men rounded up fifteen more Turkish Cypriot males. Fifty of their captives were driven by bus to a place near Limassol, and there, with a ditch already dug, the males were shot, ready for burial.

With this, and similar images brought to mind, Namik shook his head at the terrible fate these men must have suffered. He also recalled Daisy having included these facts in her notes for her novel. She could hardly believe everything his country had suffered.

'Still, we moved from that place,' the elderly man continued. 'You cannot shut out the memories, but we have family here, my wife's brother and his children.' He laughed softly. 'Not children now but big, strong lads.'

'Anyway, I will have to go.' Namik pushed back his chair and slid it beneath the table. 'I have been away too long, and my father will be concerned.'

Eager to be of help, the man tried to move too quickly, and, in doing so, tottered unsteadily. 'You cannot make your journey alone. Where do you live? Perhaps our nephew can take you back.' It was obvious to both him and his wife that their guest had been in some trouble, but it wasn't their business to ask questions.

Nevertheless, Namik was not a fool; the man's demeanour alone told him what their thoughts were. In any case, he felt he owed them some explanation for his appearance. 'I do not always look this way,' he laughed. 'Something happened, something bad, though this had no bearing on me – I mean, nothing that I had done wrong.' He waited but they said nothing, and, looking them in the eye, Namik continued. 'Believe me, the people who did this are scum, but I have nothing to approach myself for.'

Enough was said; no other explanation was needed, and this was evident in the elderly man's next words. 'Our nephew does not work on Saturdays. I'll ask him now as it is only two doors along. I am afraid he only has an old van, though.'

Namik felt a lump in his throat at their concern for him. He watched while the man made his way to the door. 'I cannot live more than forty kilometres away,' he said. 'Ozankoy, it is a little village near Kyrenia, but I would not really expect that of your nephew.'

The man appeared not to have heard this as he left the room without looking back, though his wife answered Namik instead. 'You can tell my nephew this when he arrives.' She smiled, then, picking up a piece of tapestry she'd been working on, sat down heavily onto a chair. 'Yes,' she continued, 'we have all had sons, and we mothers must help each other.'

Smiling in recognition of her words, Namik could most certainly understand that. He peered down at his feet. He wondered if the gentle old couple had even noticed he was wearing only one shoe!

CHAPTER
TWENTY-FIVE

•

With his mouth agape, Ahmet looked at his son as if he'd seen a ghost. He had just finished his meal, and, still at the table, he was about to catch up on an article he'd been reading in yesterday's newspaper. 'Where have you been?' he managed at last.

Namik, who had just stepped into the kitchen, was all too aware of his dishevelled appearance. 'I am sorry, Papa, for causing you to worry, but I had no choice in the matter.'

'But... look at you. It has driven me crazy. I have counted the days, and then forgotten. And your shoe: what has happened?'

Not wanting to sit any more, on account of his long days of inactivity, Namik moved to the sink and poured out a glass of water. He gulped this down while thinking of how he would explain his absence.

'You talk about crazy.' He spoke light-heartedly, not wishing to upset his father any more than was necessary. 'I thought I was going crazy, too.' He chuckled. 'These men, they mistook me for someone else!'

Standing up from the table, Ahmet scrutinised his son for some moments, his eyes becoming mere slits. 'You expect me to believe this? Where do you think I have been all my life? I have raised seven children, and known when somebody is lying. I am no fool, Namik. You owe me the truth.' He stamped his fist on the table, sending some cutlery onto the floor.

It was hard knowing where to start. To tell his father that he'd been bundled into a car, driven off to some remote spot, then heavily drugged was like repeating something only seen on television. The whole thing was bizarre, and it would be difficult to swallow.

Ahmet had not moved, and the look on his unshaven face held a variety of mixed emotions. 'I am still here,' he said softly.

Namik took a deep breath. 'I think that you should sit down again.' Crossing the room, he helped his father onto his chair.

Explaining his absence was easier than he'd expected, although the end result was unsettling. Ahmet, having heard everything, sat white-faced and with his hands clenched.

'Anyway, I am home now and things will soon return to normal,' Namik added.

'Normal! How can that be? Those sadists are getting away with murder. Yes, I know how many lives they have taken. And they have had others to help them do this. It is the same, though, no matter whose hands are on that trigger!' By now, Ahmet's face had turned a bright red.

'Nothing can be done at this moment,' stated Namik. 'But it will soon, though. You mark my words.'

'You think that, do you?' answered Ahmet angrily. 'And what about that other time when you were set upon? I hope and pray there'll not be any more of this. I'll not let it rest, even if it kills me!'

Before Namik could grasp the implication behind this, his father had left the house and was walking up the garden path much quicker than was his normal pace.

However, after all that had happened, Namik's responses were not as swift as they had been, so it was a little time after this that he went in search of his father. He had no idea what direction he had taken, but peering from left to right, he saw no sign of him. He only hoped he wasn't about to do something silly.

A man such as Ahmet, who over the recent months had become increasingly frail, would stand no chance against someone like Hasan, or his father!

At the sight of Ahmet's bent posture, as he laboured up the hill, Namik's heart went out to him. Mixed with these feelings were anger and frustration at pouring out his troubles in the first place. Had he not told his father of his plight, getting him all wound up, he wouldn't now be chasing after him in the direction of the Bileklers' residence. What his father intended to do he was not sure, but, whatever it was, the outcome was certain to take its toll on his health.

In truth, Namik was overcome with rage, furious at everything the Bileklers had thrown at them. Apart from his brother, he blamed them for his mother's death, for the years of heartache leading up to this. And he blamed them for his father's poor health. As for Daisy, the distress they were causing was unforgivable. Both for her and for himself.

Now wearing another pair of shoes, Namik called out to his father. 'Wait! Please wait, Papa. You will gain nothing by this except make yourself ill.'

Turning round, Ahmet looked back along the winding road, hesitated for no more than a few seconds, then continued on as before. He muttered something, and, although Namik was only a short distance away, whatever was said was lost to the wind which had recently blown up.

He soon caught up with Ahmet, and, reaching out, Namik caught at his arm roughly, almost spinning him off balance. 'I told you once that all those who have done these things will pay for their crimes. We have had many setbacks, and things have gone on long enough, but we have to do it right.'

Trying to regain his breath, Ahmet's watery gaze fell in the direction of the Bileklers' house. He tried to speak but could not find the words.

'We are going home.' Namik managed a weak smile. 'I am back now; everything will be better. I promise.'

Taking it slowly as they walked back to their village, and with one arm linked through his father's, Namik wished that this was true. In fact, he often wondered if things would ever get better. He had been praying, too. Every single night.

The Turtle's Rest had not suffered any loss of custom during Namik's absence; in fact, word had slowly grown as to how good the food was. Expats would often bring their friends and family here, too, when they flew over to Cyprus. However, Namik had now returned to work and he'd soon slipped back into his normal routine.

Nothing much had been said, except that he'd had business to attend to, and that he knew his workers could be relied on.

It was early evening, and, having put in a full week's work, including all the necessary paperwork, Namik felt the need to take a stroll around the harbour. He'd stopped at one table along the curved waterfront to have a brief conversation with a couple of young men, one of whom was thinking of moving to London. Then, moving along, he paused to watch the small fishing boats as their owners checked they were ready for putting to sea.

He was enjoying the fresh, clean air that blew in from across the seascape, and the cries from gulls dipping in and out of the water brought back fond memories of his first ever sighting of them.

As he carried on walking, Namik's relaxed features took on a puzzled look. He paused, watching as two figures left their vehicle and hurried over to the car rental office. Only two minutes passed before he decided to do likewise.

From where he stood, Namik could clearly recognise one of the men who'd entered the shop. It was Hasan. He appeared much leaner than he was, and at first he could have been anyone.

Through the glazed door, Namik took only darting peeks at the men, who also included Arif Camal. There was much gesturing, with Hasan more animated than the other two. Then, extremely red-faced, he strode around the desk, grabbing Arif Camal by the collar. Hasan raised his fist, looking as if he was ready to strike the man, but after a few moments he let go of Camal.

Namik came away from the door, crossed the road and walked quickly back to the restaurant. He had a shrewd idea of what that was about. Hasan was giving Arif Camal a right tongue-lashing, on account of his negligence in allowing Namik to escape.

Later that evening, after Namik had returned home, it came to him, not for the first time, what Hasan had intended for him if he hadn't fled from that building!

It was the first sign of winter, with some of the island's strongest winds in memory. Branches snapped from trees, and olive groves, left open to the wilds, looked as if the strengthening gusts would strip away their silvery foliage, leaving the ancient trunks bare. With this came news of heavy snowfalls across the mainland, which often happened at this time of the year. This inclement weather, now in its fifth day, concerned mostly those who farmed the citrus groves. The driving force of these winds could wreak havoc with the delicate blossom, and huge hectares of fruit could be lost.

'And it isn't just the citrus groves causing problems,' announced Hasan to his father. 'What about our vineyards? When the grapes were harvested in October, much had to be scrapped. We had the rain, and that was good, but those vines had not dug in their roots well enough.'

Osman, sitting comfortably in his leather recliner, was looking at his son, and had been doing so for the last ten minutes, but he hadn't heard a thing. His mind was on something different, something of a more worrying nature.

For three nights in a row, he'd had a recurring dream, the same one that he'd had a few months previously. They didn't follow the same pattern. But, nonetheless, they were as disturbing and as vivid as before. There was an armed stranger, hovering by his bed during nightfall, with intent to kill.

These dreams were so frightening, he felt that, if he told someone, related everything that had happened, he would be thought of as someone who was losing their mind. Of course, this wasn't true, but the nightmares were so unsettling they infringed on his day-to-day activities to the point where he could no longer think clearly.

'Not only that.' Hasan continued his rant. 'The drainage does not seem as good. It should; there is a decent stone bed beneath those foothills.'

'Enough!' Osman eyed his son angrily. 'Why do you go on so? I have no interest in your problems. You should not be having them, anyway.'

Hasan's lips tightened, and, moving towards his father, he looked ready to strike him. 'If you showed more interest, perhaps some of our business ventures would not flounder. I have all the worry.'

'So, you think I have none? Perhaps you would care to change places. You would learn what real worry is.'

With no idea of what was meant by this, Hasan, fired up, left the room and made for the stairs. Daisy might be in a reasonable mood. She understood him; at least she appeared to.

It was Fatma who first heard the scuffle. Having just left the linen room, with a pile of bedsheets, she wondered what all the shouting was about in Daisy's room. For a moment she listened at her door. Daisy's voice was raised, a nervous tremor running through it. Then, before she had finished speaking, another voice broke in and there was no mistaking who this voice belonged to. Hasan was on the edge of hysteria, his angry tirade sounding as though he'd been drinking.

Fatma feared for Daisy and feared for her sanity, wondering how much more she could take. This wasn't the first time the two had argued, but Hasan was getting the upper hand. In fact, on no other occasion had Fatma heard such a commotion as this. An inner door was being punched – that or someone had pushed the other against it.

As this continued, Fatma dropped the linen onto a nearby chair, moved swiftly back to Daisy's door and then opened it wide. One look was all it took, and her sallow skin drained to a deathly white on seeing the young woman's swollen eye.

'How dare you?' Hasan stormed, as his housekeeper entered the room.

'I... Mr Hasan, I wondered what was happening.' Fatma swallowed, while snatching a quick glance in Daisy's direction. 'I thought I might be able to help.'

Hasan made to straighten his collar, but not before Fatma had seen two white streaks across his neck. 'Help?' he growled. 'And in what way would that be? The only thing you can do is to stay out of things that do not concern you.'

At first, he hadn't noticed Daisy's movement behind him, but now she was at the door, and seconds later she could be heard running down the stairs.

Fatma, still shaken, tried to make her escape from the room, but Hasan pushed her roughly aside and then dashed in pursuit of Daisy. His father had been right all along: there was no way she was leaving the house. She had tried it before, and he'd shown her who was master.

In any case, although he never cared in the way that he once had, nobody else was ever going to have her. Least of all Namik Guven.

From the first day of meeting Fatma, Daisy had never known her as anything other than a very proud woman. Nor was her heart worn on her sleeve, instead preferring to keep a stiff upper lip, no matter how she felt. Today, though, something seemed to have broken that mould.

A few moments ago, she had quietly tapped on Daisy's bedroom door, puffy-eyed and with shoulders drooped. At first, the housekeeper couldn't speak, and when she tried she became tearful.

'Something bad must have happened,' said Daisy. 'This is so unlike you.' She was still reeling from the previous day, when Hasan had burst into her room. 'What have they done now?'

Fatma had been led to one of the chairs; she looked at Daisy now, her eyes red-rimmed. 'I have to go. My job here is over, as I'll no longer be welcome in this house.'

'But who will take your place?' A look of profound pity registered on Daisy's face. 'You have always been here. Nobody could fill your shoes. The Bileklers wouldn't find anyone as loyal as you.'

'That is not all,' continued Fatma. 'My cottage, too, that will be taken from me.'

It didn't take much to work out why this had come about. Fatma's intrusion on yesterday's incident would have been enough to incense Hasan. Still, after all Fatma had given to the Bileklers, all her years of loyalty, what they had done was sheer cruelty.

'Where will you go?' Daisy's sudden question startled the housekeeper.

'Oh,' Fatma waved her hand dismissively. 'My sister. I will go to my sister. It will be hard, believe me. I have never been used to...' She paused for the right word. 'To charity.'

'But your sister will not see it as such. None of this is your fault.' A thought struck Daisy, and it didn't sit well at all.

'There have been threats, too,' sniffed Fatma. 'If anything that has happened here gets out, it will not only be me that will suffer. My family too will be taken care of. Not in a good way, I may add.'

Daisy had always been aware of her own safety, should the same happen to her. 'It might not come to that,' she told Fatma. 'As long as you keep quiet, say nothing to anyone, you and your family should stay safe.'

The housekeeper gave her a grave look. 'I do hope that is true.'

But, when Fatma left her room, Daisy was left with plenty to think about. Most disturbing was that a very proud and independent woman was about to be ousted from her property, let alone fear for her life, if just one word should leak out. But, this apart, who would take Fatma's place in this house? Could that person be an ally of the Bileklers'? If that were the case, her life would become even more miserable.

Daisy's fears over what might lie ahead were justified when one morning she opened her bedroom door to a stranger. 'Who are you?' she enquired, noting the woman's stern expression.

The woman, looking to be in her late thirties, was holding a pile of freshly laundered white towels. 'I have come to tidy your room,' she said. 'And I have been given other instructions.' She stepped inside after this, looking at Daisy with dark brooding eyes.

'Instructions? What sort are they?' Daisy tried not to let the woman intimidate her, but she was ignored.

The woman was of average height, with dark shoulder-length hair which was held back with an Alice band. A pair of large looped earrings swung in her ears as she went about her tasks.

If this was the new housekeeper, Daisy didn't like the look of her. She touched her sore eye, feeling self-conscious of the small cut beneath her brow, caused by Hasan's ring, but the woman made no comment about this. 'I wasn't told anything about you,' she said now. 'Are you local?'

'It should not concern you,' snapped the woman, her dark eyes glinting maliciously. 'I do my job, and that is all you should care about.'

Daisy shrugged, but a tremor of fear tingled in her veins. It was obvious this was the new housekeeper, but where had they found her? Who was she, and what changes could she expect?

A little later, as the woman made to leave, she stopped suddenly at the half-opened door. 'My job is to serve Mr Bilekler, nothing else,' she said plainly. After this the door closed behind her.

During the last twenty minutes, the atmosphere in Daisy's room had been as dark and foreboding as anything could. It had left a distinct chill in the room, and the feeling felt likely to remain, so what, if anything could be done about it? The housekeeper had seemed quite full of herself too, which was unusual for someone who'd just been taken on.

From her window, Daisy could see the woman on the curved driveway. She was talking to Hasan, her arms gesturing dramatically. She hadn't been working here long, no more than a day, so what could the woman be telling him? There was nothing that she herself had done. Daisy had had been careful not to speak out of turn, as she didn't trust the woman one bit.

Unknown to Daisy, the new housekeeper lived a stone's throw from the Bileklers'. Her name was Alina, and she was the mother of two married daughters, both living here in

Bellapais. On hearing of Fatma's dismissal, she had lost no time in approaching Hasan, and after a short interview he had taken her on under his employment. Osman had something to say on the matter, though, when his son explained, the older man seemed happy with the arrangement.

'Nonetheless, you will have to be watchful,' lectured Osman, from his comfortable leather chair. They were sitting in the conservatory a few days later, and the scent of lilies pervaded the air.

'This should cause no problem at all,' answered Hasan, a smile lighting up his face. 'Did I not explain that this woman is just what is needed? The whole idea is that she would not blab. I happen to know the family, and Alina is the very thing, completely trustworthy.'

'How is she fitting in?'

Deep in thought, Hasan hadn't quite heard his father. 'You were saying?'

'The woman. Is she fitting in?' said Osman irritably.

'Of course, and she will not let us down. Only a few days, and she has proved her worth.' Hasan grinned again, then, just as he was about to leave, Rauf appeared with his father's medication. Unlike the new housekeeper, who had lost no time in becoming friendly with Hasan, Rauf remained unfathomable. The male nurse was neither liked nor disliked. He did his job and seemed to keep well into himself.

The new housekeeper smiled cunningly, peering at her employers as they ate their breakfast. She was collecting the leftover food from the sideboard, her back half turned towards the two men. She couldn't help but grin again, knowing what she knew. Still, she would hold this back, keep her thoughts to herself, as well as the dark secret she carried around.

Her eldest daughter, Rosa, only partly resembled her, and even that only in mannerisms, but there was more of her father in her. This was not the man Alina had married, but when the child was born he truly believed she was his. All this time both he and the girl had been kept in the dark.

Of course, her biological father wouldn't have had a clue that he'd got Alina pregnant. Their brief spell together, lasting less than a week, would have soon been erased from his mind, seeing that it was he who had called it short.

When Alina had approached Hasan, asking about the job as housekeeper, he had no idea she was the same woman he'd taken out a few times, as he hadn't known her family then.

In those early days, all those years ago, Alina's appearance had been quite different. Gone were the long, silky black locks, and also the slim, shapely body which she had flaunted.

Alina's marriage hadn't been a bad one, but over the years nothing much had changed: the same tired furnishings, mostly given by her mother-in-law, no holidays and not enough for new clothes, which, once fashionable, she had long since been unable to afford. Even her social life was lacking, as her husband, content to stay home, drove away any friends they'd had.

Well, all this was about to change. Hasan would be reminded of the relationship they once had. He would also be told he had a daughter.

During her quieter moments, when Alina had time to ponder on these matters, she realised that, by working here, much could be gained. Apart from her daughter, Rosa, something else had come to light, something she had overheard. In itself, this information may not have meant much, but on the other hand it could prove invaluable to the Bileklers.

Alina, filled with hope for a better future, had already started to put her plans into action, though, right now, she would look in on Miss Collins, the British girl.

As she started up the stairs to Daisy's room, the housekeeper's mouth tightened. Unlike most Cypriots, she disliked the British. Since her first glimpse of Daisy, that animosity was strengthened.

Each time there was a tap at Daisy's door, her heartbeat quickened. Just in one day alone, the housekeeper would pay her at least three or four visits. It was hoped that these would lessen as most weren't essential, but, after four days, it seemed unlikely.

Daisy wondered what all this was about, because it was clear the woman disliked her. In fact, she was so spiteful that it was impossible to even try to be on decent terms with her. As well as this, the woman seemed to be chipping around for information. These questions regarded all staff, even that of Fatma, the previous housekeeper.

Daisy was adamant, not wanting to be drawn into this. If the new housekeeper wished to know anything, including the staff's personal business, she would have to go elsewhere.

There was still much to add to Daisy's manuscript, and, with nothing else to do, she sat down and picked up her pen. Now and then, she looked towards the door, convinced she had heard someone there. It was an eerie feeling. Something else she was finding hard to cope with.

Hasan was getting worried. The household bills were spiralling out of all proportion. What on earth was his father thinking about, talking of hiring more staff? And this wasn't inside the house but surrounding it! When questioned on this, his father had been reticent about his reasons, though it was clear something was bothering him.

Hasan was beginning to fear that some sort of dementia was at the heart of all this. Still, the elderly man, although somewhat doddery, appeared quite normal in most things, including everyday happenings in the running of the house. There was something amiss, though, but his father was not giving anything away.

Because of all this, Hasan had much to think about, so on this particular morning he was in no mood for common gossip with the housekeeper.

'What is this?' he snapped. 'What is this nonsense?'

Alina was putting some crystal wine goblets onto a small silver tray that she'd just washed. 'It is as I said: they were talking in that bar in Ozankoy. We had gone there on Saturday, my husband's birthday. At first, I didn't think they meant here, at this place. Oh yes, it definitely sounded like some sort of plan.'

'Nobody would even think of doing something like that.' Hasan's irritability was reaching new heights, as a glimmer of doubt crossed his mind on the chances of a break-in at the villa.

'Mind you, I may have been mistaken,' said Alina, while continuing with the glass arrangement. 'Perhaps, like you say, this conversation I heard was about something else. Maybe they were speaking of another property. Perhaps I had not got the whole picture.' She eyed him slyly.

'Who were these people, anyway?' Hasan really didn't want this conversation, but, what with one thing and another, he felt rather disturbed at what Alina had overheard.

She shrugged. 'I hadn't seen them before, but my husband thinks that one of these men has a small business: vegetables, bread. He delivers to the locals in Ozankoy and thereabouts.'

Hasan had been on his way out when Alina had waylaid him; he was already late for an appointment, but the woman now had his full attention. 'This man, what did he look like?' 'Well.' She searched her mind. 'Big, yes, that was it: he was a big man. I could not catch everything, though, because his friend had a terrible cough. It held back the conversation.'

It wasn't difficult to guess who the first man was, because Hasan had seen a small truck in Ozankoy serving the local housewives. And, if he weren't mistaken, the other man was Ibrahim, the local muhtak.

This knowledge left Hasan even more troubled. Ibrahim was a clever man. During the troubles the man had worked alongside the British, against EOKO. Before 1963, not much was known of the Turkish underground, but he had played a dominant part in this and was feted by all who knew of him.

Leaving Alina to get on with her work, Hasan thought of his father. What was he afraid of? He may have to question him. Moreover, was something being planned? Or was it simply that the new housekeeper was hoping to keep on his right side?

Either way, Hasan felt he must stay alert. He couldn't gamble with his father's health. And as for someone about to break into the villa, or considering such a thing, it filled him with absolute horror. Still, he reminded himself, they had enough protection. His father had seen to that!

CHAPTER
TWENTY-SIX

•

WHEN THE LITTLE shopkeeper had finished serving the woman, Namik walked up to the counter. He was about to buy some cigarettes and a daily newspaper, but turned instead to see the woman leave the shop. Yes, it definitely was Fatma. Hurrying after her, he stopped her with a polite 'hello'.

'Oh, it is you,' she said, as though she'd been in deep thought. 'Is everything all right with you?'

Namik said that it was. 'But what are you doing in Kyrenia?'

Fatma did her best to smile at him. 'My sister, she lives nearby.'

'And how is Daisy?' Although Namik ached to know of her welfare, his heart lurched at any bad news that may come his way.

The ex-housekeeper's head was bowed, and he guessed at once that something was wrong. 'Perhaps you would rather not know,' she answered at last.

'Fatma, what is it? What has happened?'

'I no longer work there. Mr Hasan was very angry. It was something I did, and I was told to leave.'

'It must have been serious.' Namik frowned. 'You have been with them a long time.'

'Well, I would not say I did wrong. Raised voices were coming from Daisy's room, and I was afraid for her.' Fatma avoided Namik's penetrating stare. 'So, I went inside.'

Afraid to ask what this was, Namik stood mute. All sorts of images flashed through his mind, things he didn't wish to think about, until at last, he could bear it no longer. 'Fatma, what has happened to Daisy?'

'On that day, I saw her eye was cut, just here,' she touched her brow. 'It was swollen, too, very badly.'

Namik took a slow intake of breath, his face set hard. 'That man, he'll pay for this!'

'Please, do not distress yourself.' Fatma tried to console him. 'Daisy is strong. She manages to take care of herself.'

Namik's hands were balled into tight fists. 'But for how long? That man needs to be taught a lesson, the sooner the better!'

Reaching out to him, Fatma clutched at his sleeve. 'It is easy to talk, but you must be careful. They have guards outside. More dogs too, I have heard them.'

As before when those dogs were mentioned, Namik's insides gave a sudden jolt. The fact that more had been added to the fold had made him extra wary. Anyway, Ibrahim had already mentioned this on his last check of the property.

The ex-housekeeper had gone quiet, while she chewed on her lip.

'Is there something else?' asked Namik, anxiously.

'Perhaps not, but you never know, not now this Alina has taken my place.'

'I know nothing of this lady, but what is she like? You seem concerned.'

'I am concerned, Mr Guven. 'You see, I do not like her. She is a terrible woman, and someone who should not be working there, indeed not with Daisy, anyway.'

'Do you know the woman personally?'

Fatma shook her head. 'Not myself, but I have heard so much about her. An elderly woman in Bellapais says she stole her purse. You think this is nothing, but when she questioned her this Alina went very mad. She hit the old lady, breaking her teeth!'

Namik had turned deathly pale. His heart raced at such a speed he could feel the vibration in his ears.

'Well, I have to get to my sister's now,' said Fatma, bursting into Namik's thoughts. 'I have her shopping here.'

Watching Fatma walk away, Namik's fury knew no bounds. If this Alina had such a wicked temper, what might she do if Daisy displeased her? Working for Hasan, too, could cause problems. The two together, both of the same mind, could prove disastrous for Daisy!

Hasan had driven to a quiet spot just outside Bellapais. The sun shone bright, but a cooling breeze kept the temperatures moderately comfortable for this otherwise warm island. As he sat in his car on a rough, narrow track, birds chirped above from a canopy of trees, but he was oblivious to their sounds, as he tried to come to terms with what he'd been told.

He frowned, shaking his head at the ludicrous statement Alina had made. She said there was a daughter, and that he was the father. But how ridiculous! How on earth had that come about in the first place? Yes, after some thought, he did recall someone, a village girl, but their meetings would have been few. Had his father found out, all hell would have broken loose.

When Alina had approached him concerning the vacancy, he would never have guessed it was the same girl he'd once known. There was no resemblance whatsoever.

Apparently, his daughter was called Rosa; she was now eighteen and had not long been married. None of this meant anything to him. What was more, he didn't wish to see her, ever. Not only would this cause unnecessary trouble; the whole sorry thing would be a constant reminder of his sister's affair with a village boy.

Hasan removed his dark glasses, and then scraped his fingers through his dark hair. He still couldn't believe what the woman had told him, but somehow he had to. Money was involved, and that was the point of this meeting. She had not mentioned a figure, but first Hasan wanted some evidence of all this.

He sat up when he saw two women walking along the track. One of these was Alina, but the younger woman was slightly built and much taller. As they got closer, he wondered where all this would end. And, if this Rosa was his daughter, what then? Exactly how much would Alina likely to ask for? Still, one thing was certain. If this proved to be true, his father, Osman, must never find out!

'Well, here she is, your daughter,' said Alina, gently pushing the young woman towards him.

Rosa looked nothing like Alina; in fact, she could have been anyone's child. Her skin was darker, a deep olive-tone, while her willowy figure bore no resemblance to that of her mother.

'Why do you expect me to believe this nonsense?' snapped Hasan.

'You still cannot remember me, can you?' replied Alina. 'It was a long time ago, perhaps, but you could not possibly forget. You said you could not see me again, but you knew nothing of my condition, and if you did I suppose you wouldn't have cared. You heard nothing from me after we split up. You once told me that your father would disown you if he found out about us. A disgrace to the family, you said.'

Rosa remained silent, and her manner gave nothing away, no clue to her feelings, although her eyes hadn't strayed from Hasan all the time she'd stood there.

'If you think you'll get money from me, I'm afraid you are mistaken,' Hasan tried, hardly able to take his eyes off Rosa. 'There is no proof of this, and, furthermore, perhaps we'll reconsider your position as housekeeper.'

'Oh, no!' Alina came closer. 'We will not reconsider. Besides, did I not say I have heard some talk in Ozankoy, in that garden bar? This was of a serious nature, and something you should not ignore.' Her dark eyes narrowed. 'Of course, I will keep my ears alert. Who knows, your home and your lives could be at risk.'

Remembering his father's fears, and the declining state of his health, Hasan's flesh began to perspire. 'It is money that you are after, isn't it? Tell me how much, and that will be the end of it!' He'd had a change of mind about this as he wanted the matter over and done with.

Alina smiled sweetly. 'Later, when I am at work in your home, be sure to have a decent cheque waiting for me. Maybe we can go from there.'

Before Hasan had time to reply to this, Alina and Rosa turned back in the direction in which they'd come.

A couple of days earlier, there had been a discussion between the two women. All had come out, including the admission of not really knowing who Rosa's true father was. It was a fair chance that it could be Hasan, but perhaps not.

Rosa, although shocked at this, having believed that the man who'd brought her up was her biological father, was quick to see the advantage of all this. Like most young women looking for work, she had found that any jobs that were going were poorly paid. And, having seen Hasan, how well dressed he was and with that certain air about him, it was obvious he was worth something. His car alone spoke volumes.

Hasan didn't drive straight home. Instead he found himself on a remote stretch not far from Guzelyurt. He had left the car and was now staring out to the wild craggy landscape, which was a familiar sight in these parts.

As he stood there, with the wind tearing at his jacket, he tried vainly to rid the image of Rosa's face, which constantly popped into his thoughts. He would have liked to have thought she wasn't his daughter, but it was those eyes, dark green and luminous: they reminded him of his own. Hasan's thoughts turned to his father. There was no knowing what he would do if Alina felt it her duty to inform him about the girl. Osman had no liking for the housekeeper as it was.

Neither knew the whole truth about the woman, such as Alina never having been too popular among those around her. In fact, some hereabouts would keep a safe distance, finding her attitude surly and most unpleasant. However, this would not have bothered Hasan. Apart from this latest revelation concerning Rosa, he needed to keep abreast of what was happening in the next village. It greatly disturbed him on hearing talk of a break-in. Had the woman heard correctly? What made her think it was this property those men were discussing?

Hasan thought of the other homes up here in Bellapais. Most were cottages, modest ones at that, and the local café wasn't even a shop as such but a small private dwelling with only a few tables outside. There was of course a decent restaurant, much frequented by himself, but, although a good eating establishment, nothing would have been of great interest to anybody should they force an entry. He knew the owner well enough. Nothing of any value was ever kept on the premises.

This led him to think of his own home. The rambling villa and gardens were just ripe for undesirables whose dream it was to break in. Still, that was all it could be with all the security set up. Furthermore, nobody had ever tried their luck before.

Hasan pulled himself up. This wasn't exactly true. Didn't Eran Hamid inflict damage to the property only recently? True, his motive was purely revenge, but he'd had the audacity to do that much.

Returning to his car, Hasan drove home to speak to his father. He wasn't sure what he would say, though a warning concerning a possible burglary would be worth mentioning.

When he reached home, Hasan found the housekeeper waiting for him. She seemed to have moved fast, and was even wearing the black dress which was expected of her. Hasan could only assume that her prompt return was because someone had driven her back.

'Well, what did you think of her?' asked Alina. She had pulled her hair into a ponytail, and this served to highlight a small scar above her brow. Today her only make-up was a pink lipstick.

'Rosa? Is that who you mean?' Hasan growled. 'Somehow I think you are lying.'

'You only have to look in her eyes; it is you all over.'

'This means nothing! Not to me, anyway. Still, what is important is that you keep your ears alert. This is what you are paid for. It is now part and parcel of your job.' He eyed her carefully. 'When will you be at that bar, the one in Ozankoy?'

Alina gave a brittle laugh. 'So this is more important? More important than your child?'

Her words were lost on Hasan, because for the last few moments his eyes had been on that facial scar. Until now, he hadn't been aware that it existed, but his memory had just kicked in. He panicked. The girl he'd once known had a scar. It was just above the brow like Alina's. Still, the fact that she'd had a child after he'd stopped seeing her didn't prove she was his.

'If you want money, you would do well to heed what I say.' He wanted to avoid the subject about him being a father, but now and then an image of Rosa's face flashed before him, especially those large green eyes.

'I'll do what I can,' Alina answered, aware that at least she had his attention and that some money would come her way. If she could convince him about Rosa, it would be better still.

'So, you will keep to our bargain?' Hasan was studying her intently, still wondering what to make of her.

'Oh, you mean about keeping my ear to the ground? Yes, I will do this, but you cannot take my word for one thing and not another.'

'Just be at that bar, or anywhere else these men are likely to gather. I promise you will be treated fair, that is all I ask. If someone is planning to target us, we need to be ready.'

There was a smile on Alina's face, but it was difficult to know what her thoughts were. Hasan, for his part, would have dearly loved to have known. He hoped she would stick to their bargain. He hoped, too, that she'd keep her mouth shut concerning their relationship all those years ago! He left her alone a few moments later, with the intention of seeking out his father.

Daisy's heart gave a jolt. She had been in the process of leaving her bedroom when Alina pushed her back inside, her short stature belying her strength. After her conversation with Hasan, the housekeeper had come up here for no other reason but to intimidate the younger woman. Even in the short time she'd been working at the house, Alina had discovered quite a bit, though nothing of Daisy.

'I must say, you take a lot on yourself,' stated Daisy, her heart still thumping. 'What is this about, anyway?'

Alina's back was pressed to the door and her face held an ugly expression. 'Why are you here? Is it for him?' She inclined her head towards the door.

'My being here is nothing to do with you! You are employed as a housekeeper, and that is all you are.'

'So, I am right. You are in love with him. If not, you would not be here. Alina's mouth curled maliciously. 'Hasan is not in love with you, you know. He told me.'

'Not that I'm interested either way,' replied Daisy, her initial fear wearing off. 'He would not confide in you; it wouldn't be appropriate.'

Shifting her stance, Alina came face to face with Daisy. 'But he would with you, is that it?'

Pushing the woman gently from her, Daisy made to move away, but she was grabbed roughly by the shoulders. 'What is it, then? I ask again, why are you here?'

Daisy struggled, but she was pushed against the wall, the woman's face inches from her own. For a split moment, she wanted to hit out at Alina, but instead broke free from her.

Before applying for this job, Alina hadn't known there would be another woman in the house, one whom Hasan might well be fond of. And, if this were the case, then things could prove awkward.

'I will tell him what you did,' she said. 'I will tell him you attacked me!' Alina was white with rage. 'Do you think he would allow you to stay then? I knew him well before you. Did you know that? Oh yes, and we have a child, a girl. Rosa has always been a pretty thing, and is very much like her father.'

A father, Hasan! It was the first Daisy had heard. No, the woman was lying, the same as she was about everything. Mind, if only that would happen, then Hasan would set her free. Still, the question she'd been asking herself was why this woman hated her so much? It made no sense, unless she was jealous. But why, because she thought something was going on between Hasan and herself? The woman had just insinuated that, and obviously believed it to be so.

'Now you have said your piece, you can go,' said Daisy. She nudged the housekeeper towards the door. 'I will not be intimidated by you, or anyone, and you would do well to understand this.'

Left alone, Daisy's legs felt ready to buckle beneath her. What was Alina up to? She didn't believe she'd come here just looking for work. And, as for the child she and Hasan were supposed to have had, it would make no difference to her, either way.

Sitting quietly, it took a while for Daisy to get herself together, by when she'd had time to think. That new housekeeper wouldn't get the better of her; she'd tried a few times but would never again. If she did try those bullying tactics, then Daisy would be ready for her.

However, there was something she found disquieting. It was the look in Alina's eyes as she left the room. Something evil lurked there. It was alarming to say the least.

CHAPTER
TWENTY-SEVEN

•

'IT IS ALL ready; our plans have been put into place.' Ibrahim was addressing the men who'd gathered in the sorting office. Eran was present, having since changed his mind about not wanting to be involved, as he felt he owed something to his dead parents for what the Bileklers had done to them.

Besides Eran, there was Kazim, who'd finished his rounds earlier and had left his grocery truck outside his house in the village. This left Ramsay, who worked in the local abattoir, Namik, and of course Ibrahim.

Eran's wife wasn't at all pleased about her husband's part in all this, but he'd been adamant, and stood now with a look of defiance on his face, proving if only to himself that this was the right thing to do. Namik stood next to him and was getting to quite like the man.

'There are two security guards, both working at nightfall,' continued Ibrahim. 'As previously discussed, our mission will take place during the day. The old man attends a clinic one day a week, on Tuesdays. This has always been mornings, and there isn't any reason to think otherwise. This new housekeeper, well, something can be arranged. A message saying one of her daughters are in trouble, perhaps? Anyway, the idea is that she'll have no option but to leave the house.'

'You seem to have forgotten something,' said Kazim, speaking for the first time since he'd arrived. 'What about his son, Hasan? Where will he be?'

Ibrahim held up his hands. 'Do not worry about him. He has been having troubles. Some of his business ventures are in grave decline, and, watching the house, I see he has been leaving the premises every morning. He is usually gone some hours, at least when I've watched him.'

'Don't they employ a nurse to look after Osman?' Namik spoke now, concerned that most of the household, especially those that mattered, had been considered but not this man.

'That Rauf, you mean?' Ibrahim laughed softly. 'He hardly leaves the old man alone. He must be a thorn in Osman's side! No, every Tuesday morning he accompanies his patient. Takes him and brings him back.'

This brought a chuckle from everyone, with Ramsay adding his piece. 'I bet the old man says something about that. I expect he feels he's being treated like a two-year-old!'

'I think you must be right,' laughed Namik, his thoughts turning to the idea of hopefully being reunited with Daisy. He missed her so much, he couldn't wait for the day they would finally be together.

'And don't forget something else that is important,' Ibrahim reminded the men. 'Getting Daisy out of that property will mean the police will be involved; she'll see to that. They can't ignore the fact she'd been abducted. The

Bileklers may have been on good terms with them, but the law is there to keep us safe.'

It seemed they were in agreement with this, as the five men made favourable noises. 'And this has been a long time coming,' added Namik, a tremor of anger in his tone. 'Let us hope they get what they deserve, not just for this but other such crimes.'

Bright golden sunshine flooded the spacious conservatory, but it was saved from overheating by blinds which were drawn half-mast. However outside, the temperatures were steadily climbing, as it had been for the last couple of days. Rauf had given his patient his medication and had just left the room.

'I would like a word with you, father.' Hasan had been waiting patiently for the nurse to leave. 'We may have a problem, or perhaps not, but it is better we err on the safe side.'

'Problem? What kind of problem is this?' queried Osman, reclined on his sunbed. At his side was an earthenware pitcher filled with iced water.

Hasan hesitated. He thought his father looked even older of late. The dark circles beneath his eyes were more pronounced, his jowls were flabbier and he had started to dribble.

'There has been talk of a break-in.' Hasan held up his hands. 'It may not concern us, but we have to be vigilant.'

As soon as the words were out, Osman's hand crept to his chest. He couldn't speak for a moment, but eventually found his tongue. 'Are you suggesting it could be in this village? And who's been saying this?'

'This was overheard in Ozankoy. It does not take much working out. Bellapais was mentioned, though they may not have been talking about us. Still, what other property is worth the effort around here?'

Osman had taken a large handkerchief from his cotton robe and was mopping sweat from his brow. He was filled with panic but tried in vain not to show it.

'You are ill; I should not have mentioned this,' said Hasan, hurriedly.

'You know what this means, don't you?' replied Osman. 'It tells us we need even more security.'

'I knew how you would react. I was hesitant to tell you, but in the end I felt you should be aware of the situation. However, we have enough security already. Many of our businesses are losing money. The accountant has showed me the figures.'

Osman grunted. 'Typical. Years of effort, all our hard work, and it comes to this!'

There was nothing more to say; he had said what he had to, but Hasan was in a hurry to get moving. He had to see the new goat herder over at the Hamids' old cottage. He wasn't pulling his weight either. The man was no different from Eran Hamid's father. This meant that the herd were suffering, and it was having a marked effect on the produce. Plenty of other farms were doing well, their cheese and yoghurt bringing them a good price in the retail business.

Recently, Hasan had got to thinking that his businesses were being targeted. Someone was spreading the word, blackening their name. Was it that Eran who was making mischief, with his grudge about what had happened to his parents?

As he drove over there, he was determined to find out if this was true. And if it was, and the new man had been listening to gossip, then he too would be without a home.

But left alone, and with time to think, Osman began to feel unwell. The odd pain darted across his chest, and a peculiar sensation ran along his jaw. He was sweating even more now, and he made a mental note to tell his doctor about this. He was loath to, of course, not wanting to hear more bad news. Still, it may be nothing. He'd just sit here, see if things improved. No need getting steamed up about a small twinge or two.

There was something different about Namik. He had a bounce in his step, he smiled more, and at odd moments Ahmet saw a twinkle in his son's eyes that hadn't been there for some while now.

They were eating breakfast, and, looking out at a cloudy sky, Ahmet grimaced. 'Winter's approaching, but we will not suffer the cold, not now I have chopped all those logs.'

Namik noticed that a large stack of them was piled neatly by the hearth. 'We always have plenty, Papa, so do not overtire yourself.' He laughed. 'I was talking to this man; he is from England and taking a winter break. He was surprised we have a winter, I mean cold spells and that.'

'It lasts no longer than two months, sometimes not even that. But did you tell him that sometimes it can bring hailstones? I bet he has never seen anything like it on these Mediterranean isles, eh?'

'I told him, Papa, and he said he cannot believe it. Just wait until he sees for himself, even if it is only rarely.'

They both laughed at this, until Ahmet said, 'I haven't seen you happy, son for a long time, but this makes me happy, too. What has changed?'

Namik put down his coffee cup, reached over, then poured out another cup of the strong, hot brew. 'Nothing has changed; life is always as it was, but at last our plans have finally been put together.'

Ahmet rubbed a calloused hand over his unshaven chin. 'You mean up at Bellapais, the Bileklers' residence?'

'I have told you, Pa, we have to help Daisy, get her out.'

'Yes, yes, I know, but how many of you would be doing this?'

'Counting myself, it will be five of us; Eran, Ramsay, Kazim and Ibrahim. Anyway, it is Ibrahim who has done all the hard work. From the start, he wanted it this way.'

'I only pray it goes to plan.' Ahmet's expression was serious. 'A nice girl, yes, but I hope it is all worth it.'

'Yes, I agree about Daisy, she is nice, more than nice, and she is worth it. But it isn't all about Daisy, oh no. Most of these men have all had dealings with the Bileklers in one way or another, not forgetting what they did to us! And what about Eran, and how his elderly parents were treated? Yes, they died alone, in the woods among wild animals. These monsters, the Bileklers, will get all they deserve. They'll be locked up for the crimes they have committed. Or something worse may happen to them, who knows!'

'But what proof do you have?' Ahmet looked puzzled. 'Without proof, you have nothing.'

From his pocket, Namik retrieved the gold St Christopher. 'I have this. I found it in Bogaz, in an old olive press.' Namik did not care to go into detail, wanting to spare his father from needless pain. 'I lent it to Aygun. He wore it the night he was killed.' For a brief moment a shadow past over his face. 'It did not bring him any luck, though.'

Laying a hand on his son's arm, Ahmet's face softened. 'I told you once to be careful, son. I'll tell you once more.'

'I will, and I'll never forget my mother. She will always be in here.' Namik laid a hand against his chest. 'I have to be careful for her sake, don't I?'

As Namik made ready for work, his father's chair scraped across the floor. 'You are the only son I have now. Be watchful, that is all I ask.'

Namik gave his father a knowing smile as he left the house.

'Have you thought about the money?' Alina had crept up behind Hasan as he was sorting out some papers.

Knowing full well what she was on about, he rounded on her. 'I'm afraid I need proof that Rosa really is my daughter.' As usual, he was irritated by the woman, regretting the day he took her into his employment.

'You know I cannot do that, but you only have to look at her. She's yours all right!'

His nostrils flared. How much was all this likely to cost him? Earlier that day, he'd discovered yet another business venture had hit the rocks. 'If I give you money, it will have to be a one-off payment,' he declared. 'I will not be blackmailed. Is this understood?'

'We will see how it works out,' announced Alina.

Hasan scribbled out a cheque and pushed it into Alina's hand. 'This is for any new information you may hear. It has nothing to do with your daughter, and it is about time you understood this,' he snapped.

Alina's eyes opened wide when she looked at the amount written on the cheque, then shoved it into the pocket of her black dress. She stared at her employer. She'd never seen so much money, but hoped for more of the same.

Hasan was thinking the opposite. The woman was greedy, out to get as much as possible out of him. But he wasn't allowing this to go on. She wouldn't get another lira out of him. All the same, he wished he could erase Rosa's face from his mind. Looking into her eyes was like looking into a mirror.

Soon after this, Hasan went upstairs, hoping he could talk to Daisy, as he needed someone to hear him out. He hesitated outside her room, then gave a gentle tap at the door. 'Daisy, may I speak with you?' Hasan had found it locked. 'It is important, at least to me.' His voice came soft, but it had an urgent ring to it.

Sitting at a small but elaborate table, Daisy had been in the middle of a rewrite. She had been satisfied with her work, but with much time on her hands she used it to add a little more detail and alter any errors. She moved from the table now, and looked towards the door. Usually she ignored Hasan. He would tap at her door, wanting to talk, but she had refused. Still, he had ceased giving her unwanted advances of late, and she was certain he'd given up on all that. Listening to his pleas once more, she had to admit that there was something different in his tone. She hoped he'd had a change of heart about keeping her here.

Unlocking the door, she looked into a pair of dark green eyes. Not the ones she once remembered, though that seemed a lifetime ago now, but ones that were filled with deep concern. On the one hand, Daisy couldn't have cared less, but wondered now if anything was amiss regarding Namik. She was aware that her breathing had become shallow. 'Well,' she said, after a few moments. 'What is it?'

Hasan looked at her. Now he was here, he was unsure what to say.

'Well,' she repeated. 'What was so urgent that you thought I might be interested?'

'I did not think that you would, but that maybe you would listen.' Now that he had started, the words came swiftly. 'It is Alina; she tells me I have a daughter, but I do not believe this. How is it so?'

Daisy felt a surge of relief that Namik hadn't been mentioned. She took a deep breath, trying to steady her heartbeat. 'But why do you come to me?' She frowned at him. 'As for how it happened, I don't think I want to know.'

'Oh, you know what I mean,' replied Hasan spreading his hands uppermost. 'And I am speaking to you because I do not believe everything the woman says.'

Daisy, remembering all that had gone before, suddenly felt spiteful towards this man. 'Have you told your father about this? I mean, don't you think he'd like to know?'

'Tell my father?' Hasan's long fingers raked through his hair. 'He must not know! If this were true, he would disown me.'

'The same as he did with his daughter, your sister? And there wasn't even a child involved.'

'That was different,' he countered hotly. Visions of Aisha in that forest flashed before him. He shook his head and continued. 'It was not the same. Aygun was a common village boy. They would have brought shame on my family.'

'You come to me with this, expecting some kind of sympathy, yet it is a similar story, don't you think?'

'It is not,' Hasan answered defensively. 'I only saw Alina a few times. I thought it best.'

Daisy was curious. 'How long ago was this?'

Hasan shrugged. 'I cannot remember. Perhaps twenty or so years ago, I do not know.'

'Have you met Alina's daughter?' Daisy enquired out of interest.

Pacing the floor, Hasan was even more agitated. 'Yes, she set up a meeting place. Both were there.'

'Then what were your thoughts when you saw her?'

'I… I do not know. All this had come as a complete surprise.'

'I expect she has asked for money. Alina is spiteful, a wretched woman.' Daisy was aware of how much this was affecting Hasan, but was unmoved by any of it.

'She has asked for money, yes, but she is not getting any more than I have given her.'

'Yes, she will. If you don't pay her, she'll go straight to your father,' said Daisy, pointedly. 'And then what will happen?'

Hasan's troubled eyes bore into her. He didn't answer for some time, and then said, 'Rosa is not my daughter! That woman will not bleed me dry, I swear.'

'Then why not get rid of her? Tell her to leave.'

'That would not work. How could it? But whatever happens, my father must not hear of this.'

Moving closer to Daisy, Hasan made to reach out to her, but changed his mind. 'Perhaps you could speak to her. Enquire after her family, get to know her, that sort of thing.'

There was venom in Daisy's eyes as she spoke. 'No, I detest the woman. I hate her near me, and everything about her.'

'Then I'll have to deal with her, won't I, Daisy?' replied Hasan.

Daisy looked at him in horror. 'Deal with her? In what way?'

Hasan made no comment, but instead turned sharply and moved to the door. Before leaving, he looked back at Daisy, and, swinging the door wide, he strode from the room.

Osman Bilekler wasn't the only one having bad dreams, for Namik, too, was also experiencing troubled nights. However, unlike the older man, who feared someone was out to get him in the dead of night, Namik's nightmares were of dogs. For most things in life, whatever fate threw at him, Namik had coped. He'd never been afraid to stand up for himself; he had grown up fast and had to, on account of the troubles concerning his country. Those beasts, though, were of a much different nature.

His kinfolk had tried, in the past to allay his fears. Dogs were, they had told him, man's best friend, but Namik wasn't swayed. He'd reminded them how he'd been badly bitten as a small boy when a stray dog had set upon him.

Namik, having just woken from another bad dream, which had seemed to have been never-ending, sat wearily on the edge of his bed. His head bent forward, elbows on his knees, he tried to erase the images still sketched in his mind.

These images were vivid. As if what he'd dreamt were real, so real, that since waking up he could have sworn that he'd been sharing his bedroom with a pack of snarling beasts!

Glancing down at his right leg, Namik grimaced. If he had tried to forget what had happened all those years ago, it would not have been possible. The scar, a fair-sized indentation, was a few inches above his ankle. The dog who had attacked him had ran into his road, having escaped from its kennel. Namik had never seen it before, had never previously feared dogs, but, trying to befriend the wolf-like animal, it had plunged its teeth into his leg. Namik's high-pitched screams had brought his parents out. It only let go when his father, Ahmet, threw a pail of water at the beast; the bite had caused much blood flow.

Thinking of the recent events relating to the Bileklers, Namik wasn't at all surprised at these bad dreams, which had resurfaced of late. The dogs, which were kept behind their gates, always looked as if ready to pounce. Their numbers had increased, too, and a few of the Dobermanns were free to roam the Bileklers' yard!

Namik had tried not to think about this, but every time he had closed his eyes, especially when cut off from everyday activities, he saw those fierce-looking Dobermanns staring him in the face. Still, if he were to help Daisy, support the rest of the men, he would have to find the courage to break into the Bileklers' property, wouldn't he?

He'd often asked himself this question but knew there wasn't an option. For how could he leave the others to fight his personal cause? He would also lose face, and that, perhaps, was the one thing he felt he could never do.

He stood now, pulled back his shoulders, then moved towards the bedroom mirror. Namik looked into this, his expression tortured. 'Oh, Daisy,' he muttered. 'How could I ever think of not helping you?'

'Rosa!' The young woman turned on hearing her name being called. She had been sweeping the path of her employer's small garden. It was a stone-built house, average in size, well maintained and with a variety of vegetables surrounding a young lemon tree. The house was on the outer reaches of Bellapais, a small distance from Ozankoy.

When Rosa looked up, she saw Hasan. He had stopped his car as soon as he'd spotted her. 'What is it you want?' she asked, still clutching the yard broom.

'I wish to have a word.' Hasan edged closer, eyeing her keenly. 'Can we talk?'

'What is there to say? My mama has told you everything.'

Hasan's eyes glinted. 'Not everything. Not what your father thinks about these accusations. Has anyone even told him? From what I remember of him, he is a decent sort.'

Rosa had stopped doing her chores, but now began brushing at the garden path with even more vigour. 'I would not know. I leave that to my mama.' She did not look up as she spoke.

When Hasan had made threatening sounds about dealing with this matter, he had not thought it through. In truth, he had felt that not much could be done. Not without his father finding out.

Ever since Alina had told him that he was Rosa's father, he kept thinking of his young sister. Aisha's affair with a common village boy all those years ago had caused much anger. Not only to his father, Osman, but also to himself. Now, wasn't history repeating itself?

Rosa turned to walk back into the house but Hasan wasn't giving up. 'I used to know your father; he was a proud man. Suppose he found out, believing all this to be true. It isn't, of course, though, once something like this is planted in his mind, he'd be a broken man. It simply wouldn't be fair on him.'

Not having seen Rosa's father for so long, Hasan couldn't be certain of anything. Still, he had to use every ploy he could.

Hurrying down the path and standing close to the low wooden gate, Rosa's cheeks had flushed a bright pink. 'Please keep your voice down,' she urged. 'The people here.' She crooked her thumb towards the house. 'Any scandal and they would spread it around the village.'

'But I am not looking for scandal; this I am trying to avoid,' said Hasan, steadily. 'I have paid your mother well, not that I needed to, but, if need be, your father will learn what is going on. And then what will happen?'

'Look, I will have a word with my mama, ask her to change her mind.' She was clearly flustered, and now and then looked back at her employer's house.

As for Hasan, he hoped that this chance meeting might put an end to Alina's blackmailing, but, if this failed, then what?

He took a few moments to think this through. There was only one answer to his dilemma. Like it or not, if all this failed, he would then have a word with Camal. The man was always ready to do him a favour.

'Anyway,' he added, 'think carefully about what I have said. I would hate to see any harm come your way. Or your mother either, for that matter.'

CHAPTER
TWENTY-EIGHT

•

Across Osman's lap lay a heavy book. He was studying this with great interest, while sipping iced water from a crystal glass. Now and then, Hasan stole furtive glances towards him, trying, without success to loosen his shirt collar, which was bothering him. Earlier, his eye had begun to twitch, it was doing so now while beads of sweat glistened on his brow.

'It is very warm in here,' remarked Osman, his eyes not straying from his book.

They were sitting in the conservatory. A window was open, but Hasan hastened over, closed it, then pulled at the cord on an overhead fan. 'It is no good having the window open,' he grumbled. 'We will be plagued with flies. The fan is better.'

'Why are you so jumpy?' Osman looked up now, his tone demanding an answer.

Hasan got up from his chair. 'It is nothing. Like you, I am feeling the heat. Perhaps I'll walk in the garden, get some air.' He would have invited his father to accompany him, but remembered then that he never enjoyed this activity. Anyway, this suited him as Hasan really preferred to be alone right now.

Osman looked up from the heavy tome, having admired some rare and beautiful pictures of butterflies. 'Do you think I'm a fool, not knowing when my son is troubled?'

'Troubled? Of course I'm not,' lied Hasan. He took a glass tumbler from a small tray, then poured himself a glass of iced water. After this, he set out for some fresh air, hoping to mull over a few matters.

It was beginning to dawn on Hasan that, left to Rosa, nothing would have been heard of this nonsense concerning her birth. Alina: she was the real problem. But why, after all these years? The cheque, made out to Alina and shoved into her grasping hand, had been a generous offer, but she wanted more. Just how much, he shuddered to think, but whatever it was, he couldn't keep that going. He was still unsure if he was Rosa's father, but, either way, his life wasn't going to be blighted by that greedy woman!

Recently, Hasan had been thinking a great deal about that family. Even if Rosa were his daughter, did he really care? Well, he knew the answer to that. When his father was no longer here, the estate, and all its worth, would be handed down to him. If a hint of any of this reached his father's ears, Hasan would be cut off, severed completely from his father's will.

Of course, his father was everything to him, but his health was poor. The frail figure Hasan had seen at the breakfast table this morning had very much concerned him. Even in the last few weeks Osman's pallor gave cause for alarm. He had lost weight, too, especially noticeable in his face.

It was only a few days ago that Alina had demanded more money. Another cheque was given, but this time for a lesser amount. The look on the woman's face when she had taken it had been ugly, as if saying, 'this will not be the last'. Well, it would be; she wasn't getting another lira out of him. This had come to Hasan during the early hours of the following morning. No more money, no more threats. The new housekeeper would no longer be a problem. And, as for his little talk with Rosa, it would appear that she hadn't heeded his warnings.

It had taken a couple of days to track down Camal, though, having found him, the man had become difficult. Not content with Hasan's offer of money, Camal had also pushed for more.

As much as he detested this man, it took no more than a couple of minutes to weigh all this up. The way Hasan saw it, as things were going, Alina was by far the more destructive!

Rauf was halfway down the stairs when he heard the front doorbell. He had just given his employer his medication and had left Osman to rest in his room. Hasan had been out all morning visiting the dairy in Catalkoy, but was now home, delighted that their new yoghurt-making equipment was now up and running. However, his face soured when Rauf called him to the door.

'Ah, Mr Bilekler. May we have a word?' Two police officers faced Hasan, one of whom eyed him from head to foot. 'Perhaps we could come inside.'

The one who spoke appeared to be the friendlier of the two, but Hasan's face remained sullen. 'But who do you wish to speak to?' he demanded. 'It cannot be me, surely.'

The same officer gave a hint of a smile. 'If we can just come inside. It should not take long.' He removed his cap as he spoke.

By now, Rauf had taken his leave, and Hasan could do no more than allow the officers to enter his home. He was angry at this invasion of his privacy so took them into the study, instead of the comfort of the lounge. When they were inside, he shut the door rather noisily. 'Well, please say your piece. I am rather busy.'

'We have not met, Mr Bilekler, I am new here. Until recently, I worked in Turkey, my homeland, you understand.' He allowed himself a slightly broader smile this time, showing a good set of teeth. 'My name, well, you may not have heard of me, but it is Yakub Huseyin.'

'You still haven't said what you want.' Hasan's mouth had gone dry, and he looked towards his desk, hoping to find a jug of water. He cursed inwardly, furious at his man for having neglected his duties.

'It is about Alina, the woman you employ. Nobody has seen her, though perhaps you yourself have.'

Hasan was taken aback. 'Yes, I mean, she did work here. I think perhaps that she was here up to a few days ago.' He glanced quickly at the officers. 'Of course, I might be wrong. I am not always here myself, you see.'

'What about your father? Would he know?' said Yakub Huseyin, his smile tightening.

'My father?' Hasan was alert. 'He must not be disturbed. He has just been given his medication, and is resting.'

'It was her husband, you see. He came to report her disappearance.'

Giving Hasan time to digest this, Yakub Huseyin looked swiftly at the other officer, for both were aware that Alina's husband was loath to visit this house, let alone question the Bileklers. 'Anyway,' he continued, 'it is most odd. Nobody, not even her daughters, has seen her, so you can understand why we are here.'

Hasan cleared his throat. 'Of course, but, like I said, I am not always here, and the rest of the staff have their own homes. They do not work the whole of the day, not all of them anyway.'

'The nurse, the one who opened the door, what about him?'

'He does live in, yes,' answered Hasan. 'But he has his free time. We are not his keepers.'

Yakub Huseyin sighed. 'It is best we try to find her, Mr Bilekler, satisfy the family. Do you think we may borrow that nurse? Take him to the station, so as not to cause you any more disturbance. Especially your father,' he added.

'Do this now?' It was the first time the other officer had spoken.

The leading officer glanced at him. 'What do you mean, now?' he snapped. 'Of course I do. I am trying to find answers. This woman appears to have gone missing!'

Within ten minutes Rauf was accompanying the officers to the station.

From the window, Hasan watched as the trio walked down the path. He swallowed, drew in a deep breath, then went to sate his thirst.

It was late afternoon when Daisy took a stroll around the garden. She was about to do this earlier, but, nearing the bottom stair, she'd turned back on seeing Rauf leave the house with two uniformed officers. As in similar situations, she'd been tempted to ask for their help, telling whoever it was that she was being held against her will, though who would believe her? She could end up worse off. Hasan was never far away, and when he had left the house there were others about.

Even after all this time, Daisy would not know who to trust. There had been Fatma, of course, but the poor woman was too nervous, afraid of losing not just her job but her home. Still, in the end it had come to that, and where was she now? At her sister's home, presumably.

This had also come from Hasan himself. He could no longer trust her, he said, and therefore had no alternative but to dismiss her.

Then what of Rauf? As Osman's nurse, and trusted ally, could he be relied upon?

Somebody would only have to step forward, deny everything, then what? Who to believe, her or the Bileklers? Daisy knew what the consequences would be if she spoke out against them. Apart from herself, Namik would be in real danger. That, she knew, without doubt.

As she strolled among the shrubs, kept immaculate by the new gardener, Daisy had a lot to think about. Most of these thoughts were of Namik. It was ages now since she'd had word that he'd try to get her out of here. Well, when was that likely to be? Since she'd last seen him at the window, albeit at a fair distance, she'd had no contact with him. Although she had waved, smiled and made little gestures towards Namik, he was unable to do likewise. She understood this, as any show of acknowledgement, no matter what, could have put him in jeopardy. However, she knew he'd felt the same, because why else had he taken the risk to come near this house?

But it was since that day that Daisy had felt increasingly disturbed. Was Namik still interested in helping her? And what about his friends? Were they still willing to give their support? She couldn't help but think that they might have given up. Perhaps they had tired of the whole thing; after all, they had their own families to worry about.

There was a small, cast-iron seat beneath a large jacaranda, its pretty blue flowers moving gently in a mild breeze, and here Daisy sat, mulling over her life spent almost in confinement.

She wondered if she would ever see beyond this environment again. She mused, too, on the fact that, most likely, Namik had lost all interest in her, and all his promises had been a lot of hot air.

Daisy cast her gaze towards the house. She frowned. Where was the new housekeeper? There had been no sign of her recently. That was just how she wanted it, but how come? A niggling thought struck her. She could never have liked Alina, but she wouldn't wish her any harm. Daisy's brow creased in alarm. Something had happened to her, it must have. Hasan had said he would deal with her, put an end to her threats. He would not allow the woman to blackmail him any longer.

Daisy, recalling that angry look in Hasan's eyes, and his set jaw, when he left her room the other day, now answered that very question. Like the others, Alina must have come to a bad end!

Rauf returned within a few hours. He was unable to tell the police much, except that he hadn't seen Alina recently. He was employed by Mr Bilekler senior, and his sole job was to look after him to the best of his ability. All else he left to other staff, including the general running of the household. What he did not say was that he found his employer most difficult. Nor did he add that the man's son was equally so, at times losing his patience with everyone around him. Rauf, himself, had often been at the mercy of Hasan, as well as his father, feeling the sharp end of his tongue for no particular reason.

It was only a few days ago that he'd been accused of taking a book from the library and not replacing it. He had stayed quiet, not bothering to explain that Osman had it in his room. The way Rauf saw it, to keep denying all these accusations was a waste of time. Hasan would hear none of it.

At the moment, Rauf was helping Osman into a chair. They were in the lounge and he'd just put on some soft music. The nurse wondered when the police would question the rest of the staff about the housekeeper's disappearance.

But, elsewhere, rumours were circulating that the Bileklers' new housekeeper had gone missing. Rosa must have been putting this around, or perhaps her father, but, whoever it was, the news had reached Namik's village. Only one person here knew of Alina, but it hadn't taken long for the local gossips to have another subject to talk about.

Rosa and her father had been given strict orders from the police to stay away from the Bileklers. All enquiries concerning Alina would be dealt with by them, they warned. Rosa refrained from saying that she didn't need to be warned. Nor did she tell them that Hasan Bilekler had recently spoken with her, and on doing so had made veiled threats.

Of course, Rosa was concerned about her mother, as was the rest of the family, but in truth she wanted to keep as much distance from the Bileklers as possible. Her mother, though, had never gone missing before. So where, she asked herself, was she now, as it seemed an age since she last saw her?

'Still, it does seem strange, doesn't it?' Kazim was drinking coffee with his friend in the local café in Ozankoy.

'Well, anyone working for those Bileklers is asking for trouble,' answered Namik, replacing his empty cup on the rickety table which was set outside.

'Everyone?' Kazim raised a bushy brow.

'Look at poor Fatma,' Namik pointed out. 'That poor woman even lost her home.'

'I suppose you have something there, my friend. But their new housekeeper, what possible trouble did she bring them?'

Namik lit up a cigarette. 'Who knows? But maybe she upset them, something they wouldn't tolerate. Anyway, it wouldn't take much!'

Soon after, the two men took their leave; however, Namik was feeling even more hopeful now. Ibrahim had informed everyone that everything was up and running!

At the car hire office, Arif Camal's assistant had been left completely in charge. He'd told the girl that he would not be around for a little while, and that he needed a much-earned rest. She never quite understood this as he was often away from the office, but then she thought he might have other business interests. Whatever, he never once spoke of any of this, and, furthermore, she would not dare to ask. Jobs were in short supply around Kyrenia. And Bellapais was no better, either, while travelling further afield was out of the question for many.

The girl looked up when the doorbell jangled. Hasan came across to the desk, his jaw set angrily. 'Where is he? Where is Camal?' he stormed.

The girl knew Hasan and had often seen him in here. She shrugged. 'He did not say. I have not seen him of late.'

'You mean he hasn't been to the office? What about his business here?'

'I have a key.' She gestured towards the door where she'd left it in the lock. 'Anyway,' she continued. 'I can deal with most things.'

Turning on his heel, his eyes blazing, Hasan left the small office, leaving the glazed door wide open.

Driving home, he seethed. Where was the bloody man? He'd disappeared without a word to anyone. It looked bad. In fact, it looked very bad, considering the circumstances! Had he not told Camal to carry on as usual? Be seen in all his usual haunts?

Recalling that conversation with the new police chief, Hasan began to feel quite warm. He loosened his shirt collar. What was his name? Yes, that was it: Yakub Huseyin. Well, he hoped that he wouldn't see too much of him. Facing him like he did made him quite unsettled, and he wasn't used to that one bit. It was as if Yakub Huseyin could read his thoughts. No, he didn't like that at all. The air condition was on, but, reaching out, Hasan wound down his window. He had broken out in a right sweat.

It was difficult to avoid Hasan, and today, while reading in the garden, Daisy saw him coming towards her. 'Oh, there you are,' he said. 'I think you have found quite a pleasant spot here.' He seemed to have cast his problems aside since leaving the car hire firm. Or, if he hadn't, his demeanour gave nothing away.

'Well, I was just leaving,' remarked Daisy, refusing to meet his gaze.

'Leaving? But why? After all, who do you have to speak to, if not me?'

In truth, Hasan had nobody else whom he wished to talk to. His father was sleeping; Rauf, well, he never conversed with that man; and now that Alina… in any case, the woman had been a thorn in his side.

'I do not wish to talk to you, Hasan,' answered Daisy. 'Once.' She shook her head. 'But that was a long time ago, and too much has happened.'

'Maybe you think I have changed.' His voice had softened, almost to a whisper. 'But perhaps I have, though only because we have had a few problems. I mean, my father, and…'

'Any problems you have, you bring on yourselves,' Daisy pointed out.

'Yes, and we have to answer for them. Not all, but some.' He took a step towards her, but she moved away.

'By the way,' she added, 'what happened to Alina? I haven't seen her for days.' She was looking at him intently now.

Hasan swallowed hard. 'Alina? Why, I would not know. We are worried about her.'

'But the conversation we had, when you were up in my room. You spoke of dealing with her.'

'Oh, did I, Daisy? He gave a small chuckle. I say a lot of things. You must not pay too much heed to what I say. Not when I get angry. Like I once said, we Turks, well, we are hot-headed.'

Daisy didn't answer but picked up her book and left Hasan staring after her.

The mule tethered alongside Namik's house brayed in anticipation. Glancing out of his window, Namik smiled as his father took some carrots from a wooden tray, then fed these to the friendly creature. A sack of small logs was then taken from a pannier which the mule had carried from a neighbouring village.

Turning away, Namik sat down at the kitchen table and finished off his coffee. He felt a mixture of emotions while sitting there. Earlier that morning, he'd been leafing through an old family album. He'd felt true joy as he'd looked at his parents' wedding photos, which were now even more sepia in colour than he once remembered. There were pictures, too, of his sisters; some also of their own weddings. Thumbing through the album, with some loose snaps falling onto his lap, Namik smiled affectionately as he picked up one particular snap. It was taken in Bogaz, and Aygun was standing between his parents. He had a mop of unruly hair and he was happy then as he was smiling. Namik wondered if his brother was already seeing Aisha, or would be soon after. Still, the photo was a good one, clearly defined, and with the golden sun highlighting his boyish features.

Namik wanted to put that photo into his wallet, carry it with him, but thought it best to leave it in the album. His father, Ahmet, would also want to look at it from time to time.

Nonetheless, it wasn't only his brother that Namik had fond memories of. His mother was never far away from his thoughts. It was only a week or so that Namik had removed his beloved mother's piece of crochet from the daybed. He hadn't wanted to, but everyday reminders were not always a good thing.

Ahmet came into the kitchen now, removed his cap, then beamed at his son. 'Look,' he said, 'do you see that lovely weather! Even that mule out there enjoys it.'

Namik smiled too; in fact, his grin lit up his hazel eyes. 'Yes,' he agreed, 'it is very good. Good enough for a nice cold beer tonight.'

Apart from the maudlin thoughts he'd had, Namik felt that a great weight had been lifted from his shoulders. He had good reason to feel like this. In a week's time, on Tuesday morning, the men, and he, would be getting Daisy out of the Bileklers' clutches. As for those dogs, he'd deal with that problem when the time came. At least he hoped so.

'Damn!' Hasan gulped down the rest of his coffee. Word had already reached him that Camal's photo had been displayed in a shop window, and now this. It appeared that the police were now questioning the man! Hasan had not yet seen today's newspaper, but hurriedly snatched it off the hall table now, after overhearing one of the groundsmen talking outside Bellapais Abbey.

He scanned the front page. There was nothing here of much interest, except matters of a political nature, and a long column concerning Northern Cyprus's president, the much-respected Rauf Denktas. But it was an article on the next page that caught his attention.

Far too jittery to take a seat, Hasan's eyes scanned the piece without bothering to even finish a single line in the article. He saw, all too soon, that things looked bleak. He cursed, the words hardly leaving his lips. What was the man thinking of, getting himself caught like that?

There were sounds coming from the floor above, and voices were heard. He listened at the bottom of the stairs, the newspaper still in his hand. The voices were coming from his father's room. He could have sworn Alina's name had been mentioned. Looking around quickly, he made for the lounge and stuffed the newspaper behind one of the armchair's fat cushions. He started at the shrill sound of the doorbell.

'Yes?' He'd turned to find the young girl who helped in the kitchen.

'It is for you, Mr Bilekler,' she said, quietly. 'The police want to talk to you. Chief Inspector Yakub Huseyin.'

'Me? But why?' Hasan's face had lost some of its colour. 'Shall I send him in?'

'Yes, but allow me some privacy. I do not want my father to be disturbed.'

Yakub Huseyin was of medium height, moderately slim, but the uniform he wore showed off a lithe body. He declined the seat that was offered, but removed his peaked hat. 'Well,' he said, his dark eyes looking directly into Hasan's. 'We now know what happened to your housekeeper.' He stroked the dark bushy moustache, which slightly overlapped his upper lip. 'I do not know if you already have had news of this.' He paused. 'Or maybe you haven't.'

'I... well, I have only just read the news. Not all of the article, as the girl who you have just seen interrupted me.' Hasan's eyes kept darting towards the door in case his father's curiosity had been aroused.

The chief inspector brushed this aside. 'No matter. It was my duty to let you know. Anyway, I suppose this has come as a shock.'

Hasan shrugged. 'Well, she was a strange woman, as I got to know. She would speak to anyone who would listen to her tales. I once overheard her—'

'We have already looked into her background,' interrupted Yakub Huseyin. 'Of course, we have more enquiries to make. 'And we have someone at the moment. He has been taken in for questioning.'

'Is it her husband?' asked Hasan, lamely.

'No,' Yakub Huseyin shook his head. 'Not him, but a man by the name of Camal. Arif Camal. It was a shepherd who saw him. He was tending his flock of sheep in Guzelyurt when he stumbled across the woman's body, but, soon after, the elderly shepherd saw the man run from some scrubland.'

He grimaced. 'At the moment, it is not clear if she died there or elsewhere.'

'But how do you know it is this Camal? It could have been anyone.'

'Who else, Mr Bilekler? His wife first reported him missing; that is how we got hold of a picture of him. He matched the shepherd's description. Still, at the moment, he refuses to talk.'

'Well, I hope this is all sorted out now,' said Hasan, showing Yakub Huseyin to the door. 'A terrible business, I know, but at last we know what happened to the unfortunate woman.'

When the chief inspector left the house, Hasan hurried to the lounge and grabbed the newspaper. He then tore it in half, screwed it into a ball, then tossed it into the kitchen bin.

He chewed on his lip, worried in case Arif Camal's tongue started to loosen.

CHAPTER
TWENTY-NINE

•

IT HAD BEEN three days since Arif Camal's arrest. He had
been no help at all down at the station over the discovery
of Alina's body. He was being questioned again, while
another officer looked as if he'd taken root in a corner of
the room. While the interview was taking place, Chief
Inspector Yakub Huseyin either sat at his desk or moved
freely about the room. At that moment, he had chosen to
sit.

'So,' he said, his arms splayed wide on the desk. 'You tell
me that it was not you in those hills in Guzelyurt.'

Camal curled his mouth, shaking his head. 'It could not
have been. My brother, he will tell you.'

The room was silent for some moments before Yakub
Huseyin spoke. 'But you were seen. I will not say at this
stage by who, but we have this information on good
authority.'

Camal was doing his best to stay calm. 'This person, he could say anything. It could be him who did this. Have you thought of that?'

The chief inspector gave a tight smile. 'He recognised you by your photo. The one we had displayed in shop windows, Mr Camal.'

'I…' Camal spread his hands. 'The reason you had my photo was because my wife gave it to you. We had rowed and I had gone to my brother's. We did not tell her, and she was worried for my safety. It was natural that she would do that.'

Reaching out for a glass of water, Camal's trembling hand had not gone unnoticed by Yakub Huseyin. His years in the force had taught him a great deal about a person's demeanour, and he didn't much like the way this man acted.

While Camal quenched his thirst, gulping the water down as though his life depended on it, Yakub Huseyin had time to think. He had not been sent over here for nothing. In Turkey, he had been one of their top men. Since he'd been here, he had been helping British police to look out for a few criminals. These British men had left England and had moved here, to north Cyprus. They thought it was a safe haven, going openly about their business, not hiding away, though, as yet, nothing had been proven; no large sums of money had changed hands. Nonetheless, Yakub Huseyin had kept a very close watch on these men.

Yakub Huseyin continued. 'Yes, Mr Camal, you were seen not too far from that poor woman's wretched body. You were running from some scrubland. So—'

'This scrubland,' interrupted Camal, 'where in Guzelyurt is this?'

'You would know that, surely. You were there!'

How many times had Yakub Huseyin interviewed suspects? He had dealt with so many, he had lost count. He could tell when a man was lying. They could not hold eye contact, at least for no more than a few seconds. They were also short on explanations, floundering at answers, and sometimes, like this man, a nervous twitch played at their temple.

As for Hasan Bilekler, he had not given too much away, but, there again, he was hiding something. True, he was more sophisticated, knew how to handle himself, but nevertheless he, too, would be watched.

When the interview with Arif Camal was finished, Yakub Huseyin stood by the window. He gazed out, his thoughts going over everything he had gleaned concerning the dead woman. As well as this, much more had been dug up about this suspect's past. Still, there was one thing he would not waste his time on, and that was Camal's brother. Families stuck together. He would support Camal's story, stick to the same alibi.

Around ten-thirty on the following Tuesday morning, Ibrahim turned his head to find that his men had kept up a similar pace to himself. A short distance ahead, bright sunlight filtered onto small patches of open ground, showing that their trek through the dense forest was nearing its end.

The journey had not been without problems. For Ibrahim, although carefully mapping their route, keeping as far away from the wild boars as was possible had not ruled out the odd sighting of one. In fact, two huge ones, complete with tusks, were seen. One of these was close by, stumbled upon when one of his men stopped to relieve himself. It was common knowledge that, if attacked, an injury could prove fatal, and this particular beast looked awesome, looking to weigh well over a hundred kilograms.

Ibrahim had had to think fast. Club the animal to death, because it looked ready to attack, or throw it some food. Thinking quickly, he chose the latter, pulling a handful of acorns from his pocket and aiming them as far as his swing allowed. The man in question, who had been standing close to a golden oak tree, which was prominent in this forest, had not noticed the wild boar until it grunted, it being just a metre away. Together with Ibrahim, they breathed a huge sigh of relief when it bounded for the food that was thrown.

'Ah, daylight!' said Namik, as he came into the clearing. 'It is amazing how gloomy it was in that forest on such a fine day.'

'How are you feeling?' Ibrahim put the question to Namik, knowing his fear of dogs.

'Sometimes it is people who are the more frightening,' laughed Namik, doing his best to hide his nerves on account of the dog issue.

'No need to worry about that,' answered Ibrahim. Shielding his eyes against the bright light, he peered across a small area of grazing land. There were no sheep or goats here at the moment, but, seen clearly, the Bileklers' property stood out proudly on the graduating hillock at the edge of the field.

'Anyway, we had better get on with this,' continued Ibrahim. 'Bilekler senior left for the clinic at ten-fifteen.' Taking a small bottle of vodka from his back pocket, he gulped back a few generous mouthfuls.

With Ibrahim were Eran, Kazim, Ramsay and Namik. As they walked, Eran glanced back over his shoulder. 'Did you see that? There was another boar. It gave chase, but I stamped at the ground, then threw those acorns you gave us.'

'It can happen,' warned Ibrahim. 'These forests are just the thing for wild boar. They like nothing better than those old oaks. We took the best route to avoid their usual eating ground. More of those oaks there, you see. Still, there are the strays. You can never tell.'

Shortly after this, having reached the rear of the Bileklers' property, Ibrahim, looking about him and seeing nothing untoward, reached out and removed the first loose brick. It was fortunate that the crumbling mortar at this lower part of the high wall had not yet been rectified.

Following Ibrahim's orders, as close to the arranged plan as was possible, the other four men were lying low until the signal from Ibrahim beckoned their advance. During daylight hours, only one security guard would be on duty, and this Ibrahim had found out only recently.

About an hour or so previous to this, Ibrahim had visited this same spot, just like he had a while back, when he had first sought out the best place to break into the property. Before he had even met up with the men, he had brought with him some pet food. This was loved by dogs, and mixed with this was a good measure of a particular drug. Since then, Ibrahim had hoped that the dogs, those that roamed freely, would sniff out the treats. He had deemed it best to replace the bricks, if only for a short while. There was always a chance somebody could pass this way, and therefore become suspicious.

Standing there now, he listened. No sounds came from the dogs, not even the caged ones. This told him that the latter had been fed and were now sleeping. This left those that ran loose and were hopefully in a deep stupor owing to the drugged food.

Of course, the others, the caged ones, could wake when he and his men crept into the grounds, but that could not be helped.

Ibrahim could not see the security guard at the moment, but moments later heard someone close by. He waited, then spotted him. It was now that he beckoned to his men.

One by one, they moved stealthily, each keeping an eye on the surrounding area. In the stillness of the morning, only the constant but familiar sounds of the cicadas could be heard in a patch of scrub.

Kazim's son had had to pull out, but Ramsay, who for the last few years had worked in the abattoir with him, in nearby Ozankoy, was chosen to tackle the guard. Apart from his height, his muscular frame lent itself to taking care of himself, some even referring to him as the giant! He followed Ibrahim now as he crawled through the sizeable gap. Once inside, Ramsay threw a small stone, keeping himself well hidden. With bated breath, they watched as the security guard's ears picked up the soft thud it made as it hit the ground, and, curiosity roused, the man went to investigate the source of the noise.

Bracing himself, Ramsay lunged at the unsuspecting guard's turned back, pulled him to the ground, then quickly bound him with strong tape, while keeping him face down on the parched earth.

Losing no time, the rest of the men hastened towards the house, knowing that Hasan, like his father, would be away for at least another hour.

There were four dogs that were not caged, and each one sprawled a short distance apart. All were sleeping deeply, having evidently ingested the drugged food, but this would have meant nothing to the guard, as the weather alone would have made them drowsy.

As Namik crept gingerly past one of these, the dog let out a small whimper, its limbs jerking involuntarily, before drifting back into a deep sleep.

Unable to take his eyes from the Dobermann, and his body leaden, Namik knew he must continue, and eventually steeled himself to move. As he did so, his own body jerked when the caged dogs started to yap, each setting the other off.

The noise became strident and it was now that one of the staff, a young female, made her presence felt. However, she froze on finding the men coming towards her, her face draining of all colour, while her mouth gaped.

'In here,' said Namik, ignoring the girl and careful not to use any names while addressing the men.

They moved faster now, Kazim's eyes darting around each room he passed.

Eran, following Ibrahim, also made sure nobody else was about. But, hearing a scuffle, the two men turned to see another, slightly older woman, shut herself inside the kitchen. They heard the sound of a chair or some other object scraped across the floor to hold it secure.

None of these men had ever been inside this house, and only Eran and Namik had come as far as the front porch. Because of this, nobody knew the layout of the property.

Namik did, however, have a fair idea of where Daisy's room was situated. When he had seen her at the window that day, he had never let that image of her slip from his thoughts. With this in mind, he took the stairs two at a time, his heart beating rapidly.

'Daisy!' he called. 'It is me; I am here, outside your room.'

Moving swiftly along the corridor, Namik looked at all the doors to his right, knowing that these rooms faced the front of the house. None of the doors opened, and no movement was heard within. It was now that he worried that Daisy might not even be in the house. Or, worse still, had since been taken somewhere and... No! He refused to think along this line of thought.

He could still hear those dogs. Their incessant barking seemed to monopolise all else, and he wondered if the rest had awakened, adding to the din.

Namik thought he heard a man's voice coming from one of the rooms. He paused and listened, but decided it must be coming from a radio. Moving quietly, his ear against the closed doors, he halted, his eyes widening in hope. Yes, this must be Daisy's room, for in clear tones he heard the voice of a British male newscaster reading out the BBC world news.

'Daisy,' he called again, 'please open the door. We have to be quick! The others are waiting.' As he spoke, he heard Ibrahim's hushed tones talking to someone downstairs. Then he heard Kazim: a coughing fit had got the better of him. It stopped now, but the caged dogs were still making a racket.

Then, to Namik's surprise, the door where he was standing edged open slowly and Daisy peered out. She gasped at seeing him. 'It is you! I thought I imagined it.'

'Daisy, there is no time,' Namik's words were rushed. 'We must hurry!'

With just a few strides across the room, Daisy grabbed the thick folder on her desk and snatched up her purse. Then, losing no more time, they hurried down the staircase, to be met by Ibrahim. He had taken another few swigs of the vodka, which was beginning to concern Namik.

'Is it here yet?' enquired Namik. 'Is the car waiting?'

'Hush!' Ibrahim strode to the window. 'No, but the old man is back; his nurse is helping him from the taxi.'

Following on Ibrahim's heels, Namik and Daisy hurried to join the rest of the men, though, had Osman not returned so early, they would have used the front door.

Outside, at the rear of the house, they moved swiftly past the still sleeping dogs, although it looked as if they were about to stir. Then, one by one, the men made their way through the large gap where Ibrahim had removed the loose bricks.

'The car should have been here by now,' explained Ibrahim. 'It is probably waiting somewhere close by, because the taxi was spotted.'

'I cannot thank you enough,' said Daisy. 'All of you.' She had guessed that the rest of the men, who were now sighted nearing the outskirts of woodland, had also lent a hand in her rescue.

Namik looked after them, just in time to see the last man disappear from view. 'But we cannot stay here. We have to move, now!'

As he spoke, a small, grubby-looking dark car pulled out from a clump of trees. The driver, unknown to Namik, jumped out, signalled to Ibrahim, then hurried to catch up with the rest of the men.

'That was someone who worked with me in the underground movement,' explained Ibrahim. 'Now, get Daisy into that car—' His words were cut short when a loud cry rang out from somewhere close by, and, turning their heads, all three were met by the most horrific scene.

'Oh, no!' Daisy averted her eyes while Rauf tried desperately to scare off the wild boar, which was attacking Osman.

Helplessly pinned to the ground, while the hefty beast trampled all over him, Osman's feeble attempts to free himself proved useless. As he lay there, one hand still clutching his cane, a trickle of blood ran from his ear, staining the collar of his shirt.

While this had been happening, Namik, Ibrahim and Daisy had took refuge among the clump of scented scrub which was close by. They watched now as the boar turned, sniffed at a patch of wild thyme on the opposite side of the road, then broke into a fast run towards the forest, its ferocious tusks smeared with Osman's blood.

Ibrahim clamped a hand on his friend's shoulder. 'I'll see you later, Namik. Keys are in the car. I'll catch up with the others. But go straight home; anything else we'll deal with tomorrow.'

Soon after, Daisy and Namik drove away from Bellapais and down into the village of Ozankoy.

On the short journey, neither Daisy nor Namik seemed able to find the right words they wanted to say. So much had happened, but both knew it could wait. The important thing was that they were together.

CHAPTER
THIRTY

•

AT FIRST, DAISY found it strange, somewhat unreal, that she was no longer kept confined, unable to see the outside world. She had spent the rest of that day and a whole night with Namik since escaping the Bileklers' clutches, but it would take time to put all that behind her. She gazed over at him, thinking how lucky they all were to have got safely away from Bellapais. Not that she hadn't already told Namik this, and how sorry she was that he'd lost his mother. She also told him how very relieved she was to find that the Bileklers hadn't found some way to harm him.

'But look, Daisy,' said Namik. 'We now have a car. We can go anywhere! It did not cost much, either. Ibrahim's friend, who had owned the car, wanted a bigger one for his family.' He had not stopped smiling since he'd seen Daisy. 'You have your things, too,' he added. 'I collected them months ago. That lady was very nice where you stayed. She had them all packed up.'

Daisy smiled back at him. 'I still can't believe it. It feels as though I'm dreaming.' They were sitting round his dining table, Namik drinking a cup of coffee, while Daisy sipped some tea. It had been purchased especially for her, and she felt gratified by that. He wasn't going to tell her about the times he'd been beaten up. It might upset her, and would serve no purpose.

'Well, it is real enough.' Namik squeezed her hand. 'And I am taking you for a nice ride, somewhere you have not been before.'

'I suppose I'll get used to it. The freedom, I mean,' answered Daisy. 'Still,' she gave a wide smile, 'where is this divine place?'

'It is good to see you smiling.' Namik pulled her up from the table, then kissed her. 'You ask where? Well, it is very nice. More than nice: lovely. I have been there only the once. But you will love it. It is the Karpas. The Karpas Peninsula. I told you once about some Greeks who have made their home there. They must not come here, of course, but they do no harm to us, and just get on with their own lives. We may also see the Caretta turtles. They breed there, and maybe we will watch them hatching. I must warn you, though, that some of the roads are quite narrow. You will enjoy it, though, the plants – what is it called?'

'Flora? Do you mean flora?'

Namik laughed. 'I suppose so. Anyway, what do you think?'

'I think yes. Sounds like heaven!'

Ahmet, Namik's father, had left earlier to meet up with a few friends in the local café. With a clear blue sky looking set to last, and not a leaf stirring in the garden, the men would most likely sit outside, with the big wooden doors thrown wide open. Apart from politics, which was the men's usual line of conversation, they, like most people in the village, would go over the unfortunate business relating to the demise of Osman Bilekler, killed by a wild boar.

Hasan had blamed Rauf for his father's death. What was the man thinking, allowing this to happen? He refused to listen to any excuses, and, when the two female staff tried to defend Rauf, Hasan became even more irate, telling the male nurse to leave the house immediately. As for those men, breaking into his home and taking Daisy, he could hardly believe it! And it puzzled him how fearful his father had become, stepping up security around the property. It was as if he'd seen into the future, knowing their home was at risk from undesirables! As soon as Hasan had learnt that Daisy had been taken, he'd known who was behind that.

Gazing out onto the garden, his brow creased and face drawn in sorrow, he tried to come to terms with his father's death. No wild boar had ever come as far as this before, not to his knowledge, anyway. So why had this happened? Unless those men had traipsed through the forest, perhaps disturbing their hunting ground.

Osman's body had now been taken away, but Hasan would never forget finding him battered, bloodied and lifeless.

Although he'd blamed Rauf for his father's death, his ears closed to any explanations, he felt he had to lay the blame somewhere, as it was easier that way.

Crossing the room, his face dark with loathing, Hasan snatched up the keys to his car, and went in search of Namik Guven.

While this was happening, a grim-faced Chief Inspector Huseyin, and another officer, had come to make an arrest at the Bileklers' residence. It had not taken too long to wear Arif Camal down. His whole demeanour showed how weak he was, and the man could not look at you for more than a few seconds. He also changed his story, not once but several times, until, in the end, Yakub Huseyin had him in the palm of his hand. Word had not yet reached him of Osman's death, so he expected everything to be much the same, with all the occupants carrying on as before, and none expecting a visit from the police.

It took three pushes of the doorbell and a hard rapping at the door before it opened. 'Yes?' It was the same young woman who had stumbled on Ibrahim and his men.

'Is Mr Bilekler at home?' enquired Yakub Huseyin. 'That would be the son, the younger man.'

'You have not heard?'

Yakub glanced at the other officer before turning his attention back to the maid. 'What is this?'

'Mr Osman has met with an accident. He died. But, no, Mr Hasan is not at home. He left earlier. I do not know where.' She paused, wondering if she should continue. 'Yesterday, some men broke into the property. Perhaps I shouldn't say, but...'

Yakub Huseyin shuffled his feet impatiently, feeling he may hear of this later, but at the moment his only interest was making an arrest. 'Well, I am sorry to learn of the man's death,' he said. 'My regards to his family.'

Wasting no more time, Yakub Huseyin and the other officer moved swiftly down the long drive. Before getting into his car he peered back at the house, his mouth curling thoughtfully. 'You can guess where he went, can't you?' he remarked to the young officer sitting beside him. 'I would not mind betting it is something to do with that break-in. Odd that nothing had got back to us. Makes you wonder!'

As they sped along, Yakub Huseyin was in an even more thoughtful mood. He had guessed from the start that it was Hasan who had been behind the killing of his housekeeper, Alina. He hoped to find him. Not just for Alina but other unresolved cases, and whatever happened, one way or another, he would suffer. For a long time now, Yakub and one or two of his officers had kept a close watch on the Bileklers. Nothing at first had been proved, but little by little every shred of evidence had been garnered and set against them.

The good work that the Bileklers had done, putting money into various charities and causes, stood for nothing. Not when absolute evil had been committed.

From Kyrenia, Namik had followed the road to Nicosia, and made for Famagusta. From here, he and Daisy would travel to Karpas, their journey taking between three and five hours, depending where they decided to stop.

The Karpas Peninsula, a long, finger-like shape, was situated near the tip of north Cyprus, and this easternmost part of the island stretched towards Turkey. Known as the pan handle of Cyprus, the breathtaking scenery was, without doubt, never to be forgotten.

'Of course, I do not know how far we will get; it depends,' Namik was saying. 'But if we reach Golden Sands Beach, you will love it. It is one of the finest in the world, over six kilometres long. And it even cleans itself because of the never-ending breeze.' His enthusiasm was infectious. 'Oh, it is paradise, I tell you.'

'Then there's the donkeys,' added Daisy. 'Don't forget them!' She stifled a grin.

'Of course not. And in the Karpas you will see that flora and fauna, as you call it. It is a part of Iskele district, and they are the richest in Cyprus.'

Daisy let out a huge sigh. 'I never thought this day would come. I mean, you and me together.' She turned to Namik. 'Your friends are good people. I'll never forget what they did.'

He gave a low chuckle. 'Nor me. I tell you, Daisy, those dogs were the most frightening. Still, Ibrahim sorted those out!' A thought struck him. 'Anyway, how did you manage it? You must have been outside sometimes.'

'Hasan was present at times. The dogs must have sensed I wasn't a threat. And, anyway, it is a large garden, well over a hectare, and part of this is a small private area.'

Namik changed the subject, not wanting to dwell on the last few days. 'Well, you had better get used to your freedom, Daisy. Like I said, it is real enough.'

Their journey took them past many fishermen's wharfs and open-air fish restaurants, whose boards advertised kebabs and mezes. There were also wild donkeys nibbling on patches of grass at the roadsides.

Daisy had picked up a booklet, and it explained that, in the past, there had been something like a thousand donkeys roaming these parts, but now their numbers were around four to five hundred. Known as idle donkeys, most of these were now protected and living in a fenced-off reserve on the eastern side of Dipkarpaz.

There were no large hotels on the Karpas Peninsula, though basic wooden bungalows were plenty. These were common along the beaches, where stretches of secluded golden sands gave way to green rolling countryside. The population here was small in comparison to other areas of north Cyprus. Heavy industry, too, was kept to a minimum.

It could only be classed as paradise, especially in springtime, when wild flowers abounded.

'Here!' Namik's tone startled Daisy. 'Who is that behind us? They have been following us for miles. I did not pay much attention at first.'

Looking round, Daisy saw a silver car. It seemed to be travelling at a steady pace, though no other vehicle was in sight. 'Are you sure?' she asked. 'The driver may be taking in the scenery, like us.'

'No, definitely not. They seem to be going at the same speed as us. I'm certain they are following!'

'For what reason?' queried Daisy. 'Who knows us around here? Anyway, we have done nothing wrong.'

'Maybe – and you are right: nobody knows us here – but it is clear someone is after us.'

Daisy's face paled. 'If they are following, what do we do?'

'I do not know, Daisy. Just keep going. They might lose interest.'

Even as Namik spoke he did not believe this to be true. Peering through the mirror, and seeing the silver car edging closer, his heart lurched and his own face paled. He would have liked to keep his fears to himself, but it was evident that whoever was driving the vehicle was pursuing them with sinister intentions.

'I will have to put my foot down, Daisy,' Namik warned her. 'Perhaps we will lose them.'

After another two kilometres, past unspoilt countryside, Daisy very much doubted this, as the car behind seemed determined to keep apace with their own speed. Whenever Namik put his foot down, so did the other driver. Alternatively, if Namik slowed, then the car behind did likewise. Many times it edged dangerously close, the nose of the bumper alternating from side to side, almost hitting theirs. It was on one of these occasions that both Daisy and Namik looked aghast when they saw who the driver was.

'No, I cannot believe it! It is him, Bilekler!' This came from a shocked and shaken Namik.

'I don't understand,' gasped Daisy. 'How did he know where we were?'

'He must have seen us from the start,' answered Namik. 'But why after all this time? We have been travelling for a few hours!'

They were not to know that, when they had pulled up at one of the cafés for a spot of lunch, Hasan had kept well clear. What he wanted was to run them off the road, and for most of the time Namik had kept to a minimum speed so as to take in the scenery. Hasan, eager to carry out his plan, was patient enough to bide his time, and that, sometime soon, the roads could become quite narrow.

Apart from the shock he had had when realising they had been followed, Namik was also filled with anger. He could still not believe their bad luck, and, while he kept a close check on both mirrors, his anger was at bursting point.

'Do you know, Daisy, I am afraid I will have to sort that man out!' Namik's face had fused a bright pink. 'I will punch his lights out if I do, so be warned!'

They had been travelling well over the limit for the last few kilometres, and it was obvious to Daisy that Namik was about to carry out his threat, as the car slowed and appeared to head for the roadside.

'No! Please, Namik,' she gasped. 'It's dangerous. He may have a weapon!'

Daisy's stress caused him to take heed. He nosed the car back onto the road, put his foot down, then sped onwards, not knowing where this journey would take them.

Namik was still full of anger, but could see that Daisy made sense, so kept his eye firmly on the road ahead.

The road was narrow, so much so that Namik's attention was now fully focused. It was a cloudless day and Namik had to screw up his eyes, dazzled by the brightness of the sun.

The camping site, dotted neatly along an area of grassland, was lost to them as their small car gathered speed. They were also oblivious to the long stretch of coastline, its turquoise sea glistening beside a wide expanse of golden sands.

Hasan was not far behind, and, apart from a small open-backed truck, piled high with crates of fish, the road was otherwise clear.

The truck driver pulled over, giving Hasan a clear run, and it was not long before he made up for lost time, with just a short distance between vehicles, but Namik, spotting this, drove even faster.

The road was not only narrow but often winding, and it was on one of these bends that Namik felt he would lose control as the car seemed to spin on two wheels. Luckily, he managed to keep the car upright, but was conscious of the sweat dripping from his face. His shirt stuck uncomfortably to his body, and he wished he could remove his jacket.

Hasan made another appearance now, having seemingly rounded the bend with no trouble. He was fast gaining speed when, taken by surprise, the road twisted sharply and the car lost control, swerving from one side of the narrow road to the other. It hit a small pothole, lurched forward, left the road, then rolled down a steep bank before landing on its roof.

Daisy and Namik saw all this through the car mirrors. It was clear what had happened. It would be a lucky man who survived that. Pulling over, they stood by the roadside, watching in disbelief at Hasan's overturned car with him still inside.

Shaking violently, Daisy reached out, clutching Namik's arm. 'Are you going to check, see if there's anything you can do?' she stammered.

'Yes, I will take a look.' Namik was already easing himself down the steep bank, and towards the upturned car. 'But I doubt if there is anything we can do,' he called out.

As far back as he could remember, he had always hated the Bileklers, but, if by chance there was hope for the man, he would try to get help.

'I would have rather seen justice done in the usual way, not this,' remarked Namik.

He and Daisy had returned from Karpas a few days ago, and today had taken a picnic and driven to St Hilarion. The area was well known to Namik, and he hoped to show Daisy the wildlife in this mountainous region.

'I think the same as you,' she agreed. 'Still, Hasan knew what he was doing when he came after us like that.' She was silent for a moment, then continued. 'There was nothing you could have done. He must have died instantly.'

The day was comfortably warm, the sky a clear blue, except for the bank of dark clouds which obliterated the top peaks of the mountain range.

'Do you know,' said Daisy, as they walked towards St Hilarion's ruined castle. 'I will have to get my work typed up. Perhaps it needs a trip into Nicosia.'

'No need for that.' Namik slid his arm around Daisy's waist. 'My eldest sister will do it. You may have to pay her something, but her work is very neat. She lives with her family just outside Kyrenia.' He turned to Daisy. 'You mean you have finished it?'

She laughed. 'I've had plenty of time! There was not much else to do.'

'Mind you, she does not speak much English,' he warned.

'No matter. She'll just copy type. But if she doesn't mind?'

Namik shook his head. 'I think not. The rest of my family would like to meet you, anyway.'

Two flags, fluttering in the slight breeze, seemed to signal their arrival as they neared the castle. Below this chimney-shaped turret from where the flags were placed, they could see both the middle and upper ward of the castle, and, amid these ruins, large coarse tufts of grasses and other wild foliage had sprung up everywhere.

Walking on a little further, Namik put the bag of food onto a low, flat rock. 'We may as well sit here,' he suggested. 'Look, what more could you want?' He threw his arms wide.

Daisy had helped him make up the picnic, and among the food was some local cheese, flatbread, cold chicken and some fruit. They sat quietly while eating, and afterwards Namik washed his food down with a small bottle of local beer, while Daisy enjoyed a glass of pomegranate juice.

'Oh, look at that!' she gasped. A griffon vulture, riding the winds on a two-metre wingspan, had snatched up a smaller bird which had flown into its path.

'You have probably never seen that before,' Namik told her. 'Snakes can also fall prey to some large birds. Speaking of snakes, I saw one here. I was with my friend Mehmet. He told me it was a whip snake, and, I tell you, it was quite large. I think this one was about three metres, but not to worry, they are not...'

'Venomous?' put in Daisy. 'Is that what you are saying?'

'Yes, I think that is what it is. But they slither up trees for birds' eggs, or the young.'

They did not see one of those while they sat there, but they did, however, discuss their future. It was not quite decided yet if that future lay in England or here in Cyprus.

Not wanting to rush things, it was a few days later before Namik returned to work. But, before he did this, he walked the short distance from his home to Ibrahim's sorting office. He was about to speak when his eye was drawn to the letters which were laid out neatly on the rustic bench. 'Oh, something for me?' he said, picking up the envelope which was addressed to him.

Ibrahim had just taken a bottle from the shelf. It contained a small amount of vodka and, nodding to his friend, he swigged back the remains.

Namik frowned at the handwriting and, uncertain of who had written it, he tore open the envelope and read:

'My dear Namik, today I saw the news on television concerning my brother's death. Not too much detail, but only that his car had overturned on a sharp bend. I will not pretend I am sorry, as some time ago he left me for dead!

'If it had not been for the kind actions of a man, walking his dogs, I would have died. As it was, my stay in hospital was a long one. When the doctors questioned me on this, I told them nothing, and anyway, at the time, everything was vague to me. I know why my family wanted me out of the way. It was because I was seen with you, but never, ever blame yourself, because I certainly do not.

'Still, all that is now behind me, and I am getting on with my life. I will never return to Cyprus, but I am happy here, in Turkey. Thank you for your friendship. I'll never forget you.

'Love, Aisha.

'P.S. I know also about my father.'

This news stunned Namik. He had wondered what had happened to Aisha but was not that surprised at what the Bileklers were capable of. He said nothing to his friend but was heartened that Aisha had found contentment.

Leaving Ibrahim's sorting office, having thanked him once again for his help up in Bellapais, Namik stuffed Aisha's letter into his trouser pocket, but he could not help but think of his brother. Once, there were happy times, when all the family were together. Namik would still treasure these memories, but now his future was with Daisy. Since arriving in his country, she had been through so much. Still, she was safe now. Even thinking about her filled him with a warm glow, and, if that was called love, well, he would certainly hold on to that.

Walking with a bounce in his step, Namik began to whistle. It was one of the latest songs, one of Daisy's favourites. He was met by her smile as he walked through his front door later that day.